A.D. 62: POMPEII

A.D. 62: POMPEII

a novel by Rebecca East

iUniverse, Inc.
New York Lincoln Shanghai

A.D. 62: Pompeii

iUniverse, Inc.

For information address:
iUniverse, Inc.
2021 Pine Lake Road, Suite 100
Lincoln, NE 68512
www.iuniverse.com

ISBN: 0-595-26882-X (pbk)
ISBN: 0-595-65633-1 (cloth)

Printed in the United States of America

Acknowledgements

The heroine of this novel tells paraphrased versions of stories and quotes excerpts from poems; the material she draws upon for inspiration (e.g., Hans Christian Andersen, John Donne, Propertius, William Shakespeare, and Walt Whitman) was published prior to 1922 and thus is in the public domain. The one exception is a modern fairy tale. I owe special thanks to Jeanne Desy, who graciously gave permission for the inclusion of a paraphrased version of her wonderful story, *The Princess Who Stood on Her Own Two Feet*. The full text of her story appears in A. Lurie (Ed.), (1993), *The Oxford Book of Modern Fairy Tales*, New York: Oxford University Press.

The translations of lines from ancient Latin sources, such as the Roman poet Propertius, are my own. The cover art is my own design; it incorporates a photograph taken at Pompeii by my husband.

Thanks also to Dr. Barbara Burrell, Archeologist, Associate Research Professor in the Department of Classics at the University of Cincinnati, who critiqued an earlier draft of this novel. Of course, I bear full responsibility for all remaining historical inaccuracies.

Finally, heartfelt thanks to my greatest source of advice, inspiration, and moral support: my husband Ed, *sine qua non*.

CHAPTER 1

My Shakespeare-loving parents named me Miranda; and like my namesake, I longed for distant worlds. I searched for refuge from the sound and fury of modern times; I lived through books and dreams. I was a beige country mouse of a person, small and shy. A poetically inclined friend said I had faraway eyes and pre-Raphaelite hair, so perhaps I looked less drab to other people than I believed in my darker moments. My classmates called me "the walking encyclopedia"; the nickname was a compliment of sorts, but it reminded me that I was a misfit.

In spite of my meek temperament and ordinary appearance, I cherished secret hopes that I might someday become a heroine in a life of great adventure, and find a place where I could belong. Because of my fascination with the massive picture books in the dustier regions of the library, and the drawings and photographs of once-proud cities they contained, I fixed my interest upon one particular distant world: ancient Rome. I studied classical archaeology at Harvard and made plans for a quiet life as a teacher and scholar. I was just one among the many who trudge to and from work every day through the winter-gray streets of Boston, comforted only by an imagined world of warmth and color that might exist only in my mind. And then one day, fate intervened to offer me a different path.

A group of researchers discovered the means to transport people into the past; they kept their discovery secret while they ran experiments to assess the limitations of their methods. They encountered a problem early in their work: The energy required for time travel was related to the person's weight. This meant that they needed to find unusually small people to serve as time travelers; most adult males were far too heavy. They wanted to test the limits of their methods by sending someone as far back in time as they could manage, about two thousand years. They needed someone who could understand people in the ancient world.

Through this marvelous coincidence of circumstances, I perfectly suited the researcher's requirements. I had studied Latin, Greek, and classical archaeology, so I could be a knowledgeable observer in the ancient Mediterranean world. My unremarkable appearance and short stature would make it possible for me to pass through the ancient world without attracting much attention; and I weighed less than a hundred pounds. I had keen senses and a retentive memory; these would enable me to bring back a detailed account of whatever I might encounter. I was discreet enough to keep their project secret, as they required. The only important qualification I lacked was the reckless courage of an adventurer.

But I had something else: Imagination. An astrologer told me that I was born with Neptune conjunct my natal sun, and a palm reader said I had the trident mark of Neptune in the palm of my hand. These were signs of exceptional sensitivity and attunement to other realities, they said. Perhaps they just sensed my spiritual discontent and told me what they thought I wanted to hear. I was skeptical; but the connection with ancient myths appealed to me, and I liked to think of myself as a person with hidden gifts.

I do not know how they found me; but when the researchers approached me, interviewed and tested me at great length, and eventually made me an offer, I was tempted by the offer of adventure and terrified by it. At the time I was just completing my doctorate and I had no job prospects or close personal ties, so I was free to consider the possibility they suggested. They offered me a substantial sum of money to participate in their project, but the experience itself was the most powerful inducement: it was a chance to visit a world that had always fascinated me. When I was just a little girl, I heard the call of other worlds. Now I could go, if I could summon up the courage.

The researchers soothed my fears. They would implant a signal device in my arm; I could return to my own time at any moment. As for the paralyzing terror I felt, they would give me drugs to counter it. My yearning for other worlds conquered my fear of the unknown, and after a period of anxious indecision, I allowed myself to be persuaded.

We agreed on a plan. They would send me to the first century Roman world, far enough in the past to test their technology to its limits; and yet, a relatively civilized and peaceful time, a time for which I had the necessary knowledge. I would bring food and provisions for a visit of several days. I would find a city or town to explore and observe. I would interact with people as little as possible. At night I would seek a hidden place to sleep, perhaps a vineyard or grove outside the city walls; or I would use the coins I brought to pay for a room at an inn, if this did not seem too great a risk. When I had seen enough, or if danger threatened, I would signal for instant return. They would debrief me, pay me, and the adventure would be over. Nothing could go wrong, they assured me, although they admitted that their methods did not allow them to be precise about the year or the location where I would go.

And so it was that I found myself falling, plummeting through a vast darkness toward the rippled surface of the sea. The shock of cold water in my nostrils stunned me; I struggled to regain the surface. For a moment I was terrified that the impact had driven me so deep I wouldn't be able to reach the surface before my lungs filled with water. After an indeterminate time that seemed like an eternity, my head broke through the surface. I choked the seawater out of my nose and mouth and breathed sweet fresh air. I had survived the transition.

I paddled to keep myself afloat as I looked around. The shore was distant; a scattering of stone dwellings clung to the cliff like a rookery. There was no sign of the twenty-first century world I had left behind. The science team planned to send me to the Italian peninsula in the first century A.D.; but they had warned me that neither the time nor the place would be exact. Was I where I was supposed to be, and where I wanted to be?

Now that I had arrived in this brave new world, its beauty overwhelmed me. The sky was as heavenly blue as the trumpet of a morning glory. The sea was cobalt blue; a net of golden light danced and sparkled on its surface. The yellow sun gleamed like a ripe lemon. Rocky cliffs towered above the sea, and atop the cliffs, umbrella pines crowned with emerald needles towered against the sky. In contrast to the cold gray streets of Cambridge, the warm colors were invigorating.

I took a few measured breaths. I reminded myself that I could go back to my own time whenever I wanted—or so they had promised me. As I became accustomed to these new surroundings, my fears diminished. I attempted to make my way toward the shore. I struggled to swim against the currents, but they pushed me away from land. Soon my arms and legs felt rubbery from cold and fatigue. I knew I wouldn't be able to make it to the rocky shore.

I looked out toward sea; in the distance there was a small fishing boat. It seemed that the current was bearing me toward it. All right, I thought. I'll see whether I can get as far as the boat. Perhaps the fishermen will help me.

As I approached I could see two men drawing in the coarsely knotted net hand over hand; their backs were toward me. With the help of the current I came within a few yards of the boat. I tried to make my way around to the far side where they would be able to see me.

I felt something brush against my leg, and I tried to pull away. But it was too late: I was entangled in their net along with a number of slimy sea creatures. The net dragged me under the surface; I struggled to free myself. I breathed water instead of air, the pain an unwelcome surprise. As my head broke through the surface again, I heard the men shout.

They labored to drag in the net. They must have thought they had captured a tuna or dolphin, at least. With a great effort they heaved the net with its contents into their boat and dumped it in a tangled mass. I wheezed and coughed up salt water. Muddy water ran from my hair, which had come loose from the knot at the base of my neck and fell in a tangle around my shoulders. Ribbons of iodine colored grasses clung to my body. The fishermen were quite still for the first few moments; they looked down at me in silent amazement. I struggled to clear my lungs and regain my composure, retching and gasping.

I don't know how ancient the mermaid legends are; but perhaps they thought they had caught a creature from some other world. The taller man fingered an amulet that hung from a cord around his neck, perhaps for protection and reassurance. They were apparently as wary of me as I was of them. I was still entangled in the net, and now that I could breathe normally, I attempted to free myself. They moved to help me, but they were practical enough to sort out the fish that had accompanied me and toss them into a barrel of water.

Curiosity began to replace panic. They made no immediate move toward me, and I began to fear them less. The men looked enough alike to be brothers. They wore the simple tunics that were common throughout much of the Mediterranean in ancient times: the rough cloth was worn and grubby as if the garments had been worn for years without laundering. Their faces were creased and darkened by the sun. I sat motionless in the bottom of the boat; they sat as far away from me as possible, never removing their eyes from me. They began to discuss me, their voices low. I caught the gist of it although the accent and vocabulary were unfamiliar. Perhaps it was a local dialect; it wasn't the kind of Latin I had learned at Harvard. They stared at me fixedly, but with obvious uncertainty.

If I had more chutzpah, I thought, I might pretend that I am the goddess Aphrodite herself, rising from the sea foam. However, I knew that I looked like a bedraggled waif, not a goddess. They commented on the strangeness of my clothing. Somewhat hesitantly, one of them offered me a drink; I accepted it, saying nothing for the moment. I checked that I still had my bag of carefully chosen travel supplies. Everything was wet, but nothing had been lost. I combed my hair with my fingers and straightened my disheveled clothing.

The taller man said: "Mother will know what to do with her". The other grunted in assent. The slanting sunlight indicated it was late afternoon, and apparently their work was done; so they set off for shore. They beached their boat on the rocky coast a little way from town, and helped me step onto the shore, and indicated by gestures that I should follow. We climbed a stony path that traced a zigzag course up the cliff. We passed clusters of stone houses, simple one room shelters, more like animal sheds than human dwellings; they were windowless and completely dark inside.

I tried to process and remember what I saw; but the shock of novelty was so intense that it was difficult to sort out and store the flood of impressions. So far it appeared I was in no immediate danger, but the situation did not appear promising. As long as there was no immediate threat, I decided to wait to see how events would unfold. I wanted to learn at least what year I had visited before I returned to modern times. I hoped to obtain some small pieces of physical evidence as proof I had really been in the past, and to leave a written trace of my visit; perhaps I would still have a chance to do those things, even in this bleak little village.

The men called out as we approached one of the meanest hovels and a woman turned from a cook fire, wiping her hands on the front of her tunic. At first they all spoke at once, so rapidly that I could not make sense of it. Like modern day Italians, I was amused to note, they used their hands to punctuate their speech. She seemed older, so I assumed she must be their mother. I looked at her warily. She studied me with shrewd bright eyes. Her face reminded me of the dolls that crafts people make from withered apples; it was brown and lined. Poverty ages people rapidly, so I realized that she might not be as old as I initially guessed. She approached me and took my hands in hers and studied them. It must have been obvious that I had never done any hard work, for the palms of my hands were soft and my nails were neatly trimmed. She looked at my face quizzically. She fingered the sleeve of my tunic, assessing the quality of the unfamiliar fabric. She gestured for me to sit on the stone bench outside; she sat opposite.

"Where do you come from? Do you understand me?" These were the first words that anyone had addressed directly to me. She spoke slowly, rather loudly, as people often do when they think that they are talking to someone who may not understand them; but her words were recognizable to me as Latin.

"I was on a ship. It sank in a storm." I decided that this would be my best cover story, under the circumstances. If I claimed to be from their land, my ignorance of local customs and geography would give me away immediately. Or worse: they might think that I was a runaway slave, which would create problems for them. There were severe penalties under Roman law for harboring or assisting runaway slaves.

"Where did this ship come from?"

"Far away." It seemed prudent not to volunteer more information than was absolutely required by their questions. So far this contact was going reasonably well. Their uncertainty about who I was and where I came from might prevent them from harming me. But I felt uneasy; would they let me go?

"What happened to the others?"

"I don't know; I think they all drowned."

"Where were you going?"

"We were lost, in a storm...what place is this?"

"Campania." Ah, I thought, I am approximately where I wanted to be, somewhere to the west and south of the city of Rome. I asked: "Who is the emperor?" She looked astonished at this ignorance. "Nero."

"What were you?" she wanted to know. "You don't have the hands of a slave."

The lecherous looks the men gave me made me extremely uneasy. I thought perhaps I needed a more protective cover story to deter unwanted advances.

"I wasn't a slave. I was...a priestess." I was making this up as I went along, but I thought this might be a workable identity and perhaps one that would provide some protection.

Next she turned to my sack of possessions. I didn't dare to protest when she dumped the contents on the ground and pawed through them with acquisitive hands. Predictably, she took all the things she could use: the knife, cheese, bread, coins, and my wooden hair comb. She uncorked the small pot that contained antibiotic salve; I had brought this to apply to the blisters I expected to develop in several days of non-stop walking. She dipped her finger in it, stuck it in her mouth, grimaced at the taste, and tossed it aside. Fortunately she didn't seize upon my one object of value: a silver pendant, an image of Neptune hidden in a pouch on a cord around my neck. I had brought it as a good luck token.

Why Neptune? I had a hunger for myth as a way of making sense of my identity and my place in the world. The ancients thought of Neptune as the god of the sea, earthquakes, volcanoes, horses, and other wild forces of nature; in modern mythology, Neptune is associated with imagination, the urge to escape from reality, and spiritual yearning—my own inclinations, for better or for worse. Ever since the astrologer and palm reader told me I was a Neptunian type, I had adopted this as my talisman.

If she noticed the pouch at all, she probably thought it contained some sort of amulet or sacred artifact. She let it alone. People in the ancient world generally thought it prudent not to annoy unknown gods.

Next she held up my wooden recorder and handed it to me with a questioning look, making gestures to indicate that she wanted to know whether I could play it. I had brought this instrument to provide myself with a cover story; if I were picked up for questioning—something I hoped to avoid—I could claim to be an itinerant street musician. My recorder didn't look or sound like the flutes of ancient times; in fact, modern scholars weren't sure how their instruments were played, although they knew what they looked like. After some thought about this problem, I had decided to bring an instrument I knew how to play, even though its sound and construction would be unfamiliar to them, rather than an instrument I had no idea how to play. I gave a brief demonstration that I could make music with this flute-like instrument. She allowed me to keep it; I suppose it had no value to her.

That was not the end of her thefts, however. She returned her attention to my tunic: "Give me that." She started to untie my sash. I began to balk; her sons looked at me with hungry eyes, and I didn't want to undress in front of them. She laughed at my discomfiture and pushed me into her hovel, and handed me a bundle of rags. I emerged wearing the clothing she gave me: a dirty, tattered tunic tied at the waist with a piece of rope. I felt increasingly vulnerable. While she admired the rest of her loot, I palmed the jar of antibiotic that she had tossed aside and slipped it into the bosom of my tunic; that felt like a small triumph. Still, I had lost almost all the resources I had counted on. I began to wonder whether it was time to give up on my adventure and signal for return.

The mother turned to her sons. The one who appeared older tentatively said, as if seeking her agreement: "We found her. If no one claims her, then she belongs to us."

I protested. "No. My people will come to look for me." They paid no attention to this.

"The sea has given her to us," the old woman said.

"Perhaps I'll keep her as my woman." The older son's claim sounded hesitant; clearly he was accustomed to defer to his mother's decisions.

"No, son. You need a woman who can work hard. This one looks useless to me. She's probably lying. She may be a runaway slave, or who knows what. If someone comes to claim her, we'll lose her. We could get into trouble. But consider the possibilities. We can sell her to the slave dealers outside Neapolis." (In modern Italy, this city would be known as Naples.) "Then no matter what happens, we'll have the money."

Things were not going according to plan. I'd hoped to find a road and be on my way, free to explore the world of the past; but within my first hour of life in the ancient world, I had been claimed as a slave, a possession. I'd heard enough; I stood up and attempted to make a run for it. I didn't get far; the brothers tackled me and dragged me back to the hut. They tied my feet together to hobble me, and the old woman warned me in no uncertain terms not to attempt escape again.

By that time the sun was poised on the horizon, half in and half out of the sea, a coral glow against a darkening sky. They ate their evening meal—a stew of fish heads and a loaf of coarse bread. They offered me a small piece of bread. I was reluctant to accept it; I'd planned to eat only the food I brought with me, but I was so hungry I decided to try it. It was dense and coarse; I was hardly able to chew it. I seemed to have no saliva, and could swallow only with difficulty. The bread formed an indigestible lump in the pit of my stomach.

As the sky darkened, they prepared for sleep; they had an oil lamp, but they didn't light it—I suppose oil was too costly for everyday use. They shoved me inside the dark stone hovel with its packed dirt floor. The space was just enough for three or four people to lie down; a variety of things, pots and so forth, hung from pegs or sat on shelves above our heads. They spread out pallets stuffed with straw; I looked at these with distaste. Populated with fleas, doubtless.

I think the sons still had some ideas about entertaining themselves with their catch, but the mother thought this unwise. She tied my wrists as well as my ankles, and placed me between herself and the wall. She slept beside me, clasping me in an unwelcome but protective embrace, snoring. Clearly she wanted her sons to have nothing to do with me. Perhaps she thought it was possible that someone would show up to claim me, and that she would be in a lot of trouble if I had been abused.

I didn't sleep well; insect bites and bits of straw that poked through the coarse fabric tortured my sensitive skin, and I felt irresistible urges to scratch that only seemed to make this minor torment worse. I couldn't scratch with my hands tied; I gave up trying to loosen the bonds, as my squirming only annoyed her and chafed my wrists. Don't be a *Princess and the Pea*, I scolded myself. Don't let this incident upset you so much that you give up on this adventure. I would not be among the fishermen for long; perhaps the next stop on my journey would provide a better vantage point on the ancient world.

I was afraid, of course; and yet, the experience didn't seem quite real. It seemed more like a play or an extraordinarily vivid dream. I knew I could opt out—at least, I would be able to do that as soon as my hands were untied, and I could reach the signal device—and I clung to that knowledge for reassurance. Small and meek I might be, but I was not entirely defenseless. I had the power of escape, or so I believed.

CHAPTER 2

The next morning they gave me a small piece of coarse bread washed down with thin watered wine that tasted like vinegar. The old woman cleaned my face with a wet rag and brushed me off to make me look presentable; she used the stolen comb to subdue my tangled hair and then took it away again. We set off on foot: the mother and older son each held me by an elbow; they kept my hands tied together. They walked purposefully, rapidly, at a pace that left me too breathless for questions—which they did not seem to welcome, in any case. A rocky path led us away from the sea; the path joined a road paved with massive flat blocks of stone. This appeared to be a major highway, one of the many that were built so well that some were still usable in the twenty-first century. There were deep ruts from the wheels of carts. Traffic was brisk; we mingled with oxen drawn farm wagons and pedestrians as we walked north. A curtained litter passed, borne by eight slaves who walked at a brisk pace. The mother and son didn't speak to me as we walked. Apparently, now that they had decided what to do with me, they didn't want to learn anything further that might upset their plans.

We passed olive groves; the trees were twisted into unique shapes and crowned with silver-gray leaves that quaked in the light breeze. Beside the road, there were clumps of coarse green grasses, each stalk tipped with a tiny orchid-shaped flower of canary yellow. This was wild broom, a plant whose flax-like fiber was used in weaving cloth. This world was strange to me, but I had enough knowledge of its ways to understand much of what I saw, and that knowledge gave me pleasure and reassurance. It was a world where things had meaning for me.

We passed fields of beige grasses scattered with scarlet poppies; and roadside hedges of wild oleander, abundantly frosted with pink, rose and wine colored blossoms. Judging from the flowers in bloom, and the warmth of the breeze, it must be about mid June. The land was well groomed and the sweet soil seemed fertile; the vineyards were staked out into neat rows, with green grapes just formed on the vines. Plump and prosperous looking sheep grazed in lush fields of grass. Bees visited roadside clumps of wild flowers. The air was ripe with the scent of adventure.

In the distance, I saw the pointed cone of a volcano. Could that be Vesuvius? That sight gave me a momentary sense of unease; I counted the years in my head and did a few calculations. If Nero was still emperor, the cataclysmic eruption of Vesuvius must still be several years away. There was no need for me to worry, I told myself, for I would be gone long before that. The apprehension I still felt heightened my senses and spiced my perceptions with delicious intensity.

Most of us live much of our lives in a state of half-consciousness. We stop noticing what is familiar and ordinary; our attention is seized only by the unusual, the changeable. We don't pause to notice the blossoms of spring splashed across the hillsides like impressionist pastels. We don't taste the metallic cold of spring water, or feel the sun's gentle fingers touch our faces. But in this brave new world, everything was novel, and my senses were fully engaged; I experienced everything with stunning immediacy. I felt like Dorothy in the *Wizard of Oz*: I'd left behind my monochrome everyday life in wintry Boston and arrived in a magical world of vibrant color. Everything seemed more intense, and in a strange way, more real, than the world

I had left behind. I felt that surely the luminous beauty of this day must be an omen that my adventure would go better from now on.

We walked nearly half the day and I began to drag my feet. My composure was seriously upset when we stopped briefly just outside the city walls. The old woman said to me, in a tone that seemed suddenly menacing:

"We are going to sell you. If you behave yourself well, you'll be sold to a good household where you may have enough to eat. If you're obedient, they won't have to beat you. Say nothing unless I tell you to speak. I will do the talking. If you say anything that makes the dealer unwilling to buy you from us, make no mistake, we will beat you. Do you understand me? Not one word."

I indicated that I understood, but now the fear returned in its more unpleasant form; my soul was possessed by dread. For the moment there was nothing I could do to help myself. I reassured myself that the signal device was embedded safely on the inner part of my upper arm, available whenever I might call upon it; but with my hands still tied, I couldn't run my fingers over the scar to reassure myself.

We entered a walled compound; I guessed that this was a marketplace where slaves were bought and sold. We passed through a massive gate with heavy wooden double doors held ajar by hooks; we passed through a short dark hallway into a large open courtyard. Along one side of the courtyard there were outdoor cages, with walls of coarse woven reeds, of the sort one might use for livestock; many of these pens were crowded with people, most of them squatting or sitting on the ground. They looked even more miserable than I felt after a long day on the road with nothing to eat since morning. The old fishwife took hold of my arm and walked me in to the office.

The walls were crudely decorated; diagonal black stripes on a white background gave the cubicle the look of a prison cell. This was, I supposed, an attempt at decoration. The only furniture in the room was a massive, scarred wooden table with a stool behind it. Behind it sat a bored looking clerk, the very picture of a petty bureaucrat, scratching himself on the neck, slow to notice these obviously unimportant customers. We stood before him in polite silence for a few minutes; my fear rose, I felt a bitter bile in the back of my throat, but I reminded myself…this is only a role I am playing. I can escape when I choose.

For several minutes the clerk pretended elaborate busy-ness with his writing materials. He rattled the brass beads on a small abacus, no larger than a hand held calculator; I was amused to see it had Roman numerals as labels. He totaled columns of figures and scratched the results onto a wax tablet with a stylus. Finally he looked up and acknowledged our presence, in a manner that communicated that he found us utterly insignificant.

The mother was deferential, but she refused to be intimidated. She presented me and announced:

"I want to sell this slave. She's healthy and plays the flute; she ought to be worth a good price. What will you give me for her?"

"Where does she come from? She doesn't look native born."

"Gaul", the woman said, with a sidelong glance that warned me not to contradict this lie. I looked down at the floor and tried to control my face. In spite of my anxiety, I began to find this interview amusing.

He looked at me as if he didn't believe this. "She looks more German to me."

I was aware, from my study of Roman history, that a distant country of origin was considered an undesirable thing in a slave. People from various countries were thought to differ in intelligence and temperament, and therefore in their suitability for various types of slavery. Germans were thought to be strong and brave, but stupid, while Greeks were thought to be clever and sophisticated, but dishonest. When a slave was sold, the country of origin had to be specified so the buyer could have some idea what he was getting. This of course translated into market value: a highly skilled Greek could easily be worth ten times as much as a northern barbarian. She was trying to pass me as a Gaul. Apparently she thought this would result in a better price. The transaction reminded me somewhat of a used car deal. In spite of my fear, I began to see comic elements in the situation; or perhaps the inane desire to laugh was an expression of my fear. I stifled the urge to snicker and tried to appear impassive, as required.

"She speaks Latin. She's a good girl, she works hard", the mother said, apparently trying to create the impression that I had been in her possession for years. I kept my face expressionless.

"Let her speak, so I can judge for myself." He began what seemed to be a fairly standard interview, and noted my replies in a kind of shorthand. He didn't ask for my name; this apparently wasn't important. He felt the muscles in my arm, poked my neck, and prodded my abdomen with a bony finger.

"Open your mouth."

I showed him my perfectly straight teeth, a miracle of modern dentistry; he registered momentary astonishment, but quickly reassumed a look of studied boredom.

The game evidently was that he would try to run down my value in every way possible by finding faults, while she would try to inflate my value.

"Any sickness?"

"No."

I began to fear that he might ask me to take off my clothing; the old woman would probably agree to anything to make a sale. Fortunately he didn't seem to think such a thorough inspection was necessary. I also wondered what I would do if he asked me to speak whatever language a native Gaul should know.

The mother took the wooden recorder out of my sack and placed it in my hands; I played a brief tune; this ability was duly noted. I was happy to find that my recorder had not warped as it dried, so it was still in tune.

He asked me a few questions, more to assess my fluency in Latin than because he cared about the answers. "Strange accent. Must be some rural part of Gaul," he commented.

"Do you have a bill of sale, proof of ownership?" The mother looked flustered; this was a question she apparently had not anticipated. "No papers. We had her a long time, you see, my sister gave her to me...". She started to develop a story, but he cut her off.

"Without papers, some people wouldn't buy her at all. You're lucky you came to us; we can do business. But not so good a price, without papers. One hundred sesterces."

The mother's face reddened, and her jaw set.

"You must think I am a stupid old woman, to offer such a miserable sum. Those rich people in Capua, they would pay a thousand sesterces for a good girl like this, nice and clean, speaks Latin, knows music. I will not take less than that. If you don't pay I'll go somewhere else."

He laughed scornfully. He tipped a little wine into his clay cup and drank it, without offering her any refreshment.

"Some places they would ask questions about this, questions you might not want to answer. She could be a runaway; you could be arrested, sold into slavery yourself, perhaps. You aren't in a position to dictate terms, old lady. One hundred sesterces...take it, leave it—I don't care. We have lots of slaves here; one skinny little woman more or less is no concern to me. One hundred sesterces, and you don't have to tell me your name or where you came from."

The woman and her son turned aside and argued in low voices.

"Not enough, but I'll take it", she said, in a sullen tone. I tried to remember what I knew about the purchasing power of sesterces; this sum didn't seem like much—not much more than the price of a choice piece of meat. Certainly this low price meant that I had little value, even compared to the least skilled slaves. He counted a stack of coins into her hand; she watched keenly as if afraid he would cheat her. She seemed satisfied with the amount, and the transaction was concluded. She and her son departed in haste, as if afraid that there would be further questions.

A guard was summoned.

"Put her in with those prisoners from Germania." He cut the bonds that bound my wrists—I suppose there was no need for that now that I would be caged—and tied a written tag to my wrist; this described my qualifications. The guard took me out into the court-yard; he opened the gate to the largest holding pen and pushed me inside. I found myself facing a crowd of about twenty dirty, tired, and worn looking people—men, women, and children. Most were blonder than I was, and taller than our Roman captors.

The tallest one, a bear of a man with an unkempt beard and snarled long hair, approached and spoke to me: the rising intonation led me to think it was a question, but I didn't understand him. He repeated that same question twice, and then tried other words; I responded, in Latin, "I don't understand." He shrugged; he didn't understand me, either.

It was clear to them that I wasn't one of them, in spite of my northern European appearance; and so they shunned me. I was grateful that they chose to ignore me, and didn't molest me. I found a place in the corner next to the wicker woven fence that separated this pen from a neighboring empty enclosure, and knelt on the ground. They kept a wary distance from me. Perhaps that's just as well, I thought; they appear to be crawling with fleas. By that time it was late afternoon. The guard returned with a bucket—of slop, I thought at first, but it was dinner. We were given coarse wheat por-ridge, a gray substance about the consistency of wallpaper paste, but lumpier. It was bland but warm and filling. I picked sand and peb-bles out of my food as I chewed, trying to spare my teeth from damage.

Things weren't going according to plan. As the evening sky dark-ened, I wrapped my arms around my knees and tried to keep myself warm. I fingered the scar on the inside of my left upper arm and con-sidered whether to activate the signal device that was implanted there and return to my own world. Perhaps if I waited just a little longer my luck would improve. If I were sold as a field slave, I knew I would have no choice but to judge this time-trip a failure and return to my own time. I couldn't survive menial labor, and such a miserable existence wouldn't give me a chance to see any of the things I longed to see. Given the turn of circumstances, it seemed that the best I could hope for was to be sold as a house servant. That might be better than the walking around I had planned to do in public places; if I got into a wealthy household I would have a much more intimate look at their world.

I was, I understood later, too naïve to be properly terrified by the prospect of slavery.

CHAPTER 3

Two days later a new group of slaves arrived; many appeared to be Greek. They were more adequately dressed and better treated than the group I had been placed with; clearly, they were more valuable. They were placed in the neighboring pen after a systematic interview, inspection, and tagging process, which took place in the open courtyard. I watched the proceedings with interest. At this point, discomfort and boredom were my chief complaints. The prospect of being sold was potentially quite frightening, but I continually reassured myself that I could escape if things didn't go well. I really wanted to see something of this world before I returned to my own time, and so far, I had hardly seen anything except slave pens, a far cry from the magnificent villas and bustling towns I had imagined from my books.

Many of these new prisoners had special skills—they demonstrated that they could read, write, sing, or dance. These people would be far more valuable as slaves than someone like me. I was the lowest among the low. That was not a pleasant or reassuring thought.

From my corner of the pen, I was in a good position to observe the new arrivals as they were herded into the neighboring holding pen. Early on the first evening there was a vicious fight about a dice game. The young man who won most of the tosses got into a quarrel with a much larger man. Apparently a close inspection of the young man's dice made the loser suspicious that he had been cheated. He cursed the young man, accused him of playing with loaded dice, knocked him down, and kicked him several times. The angry loser gathered up all the coins that had been staked on the game.

The injured Greek crawled away from his attacker and took shelter in the rear corner of the enclosure. He was only a few feet away from me, on the other side of the fence; he nursed his injuries and mumbled profanities. He seemed worried about the bleeding wound on his shin. I beckoned and got his attention; he came closer and peered at me through the gaps in the woven reed fence.

I spoke to him in Latin, hoping he would understand:

"Your leg should be treated. Do you have any cloth for a bandage?"

Although he seemed to welcome my concern, there was a touch of disdain in his expression—a reaction to my strange accent, I supposed. I added:

"If you get wine and water, I can clean it. This is medicine." I showed him the jar of antibiotic salve.

He went over to the fence and engaged the attention of a guard, who brought a jug of relatively clean water and some cheap wine in return for a small bribe. It was, at least, cleaner than the slop jars provided for general use. I waited for him to return with the water. I reached through the gaps in the woven twig fence and he moved closer so that I could attend to his leg. I washed his wound with wine, wiped it carefully with the cleanest part of his tunic, and applied antibiotic salve to the wound. Then I bound his leg with a piece of cloth that we tore from the hem of his tunic, which was considerably cleaner than mine.

He thanked me, although I suspect he doubted that my medicine would be efficacious. He settled himself on the other side of the fence and we talked. I said: "Please excuse me, there are many things I want to know; can you tell me?" He grinned in response. As I would soon learn, he liked to be in a position of authority. His Latin was more fluent than mine; my accent was based on twenty-first century educated guesses about what ancient Latin might have sounded like that were clearly wrong, in many cases. So at first I think he did have some difficulty understanding me.

His name was Demetrius; he had been a scribe in a household in Capua. He boasted that he knew philosophy and poetry, and several languages in addition to Greek and Latin. He hoped to be purchased by a wealthy household as a tutor, scribe or secretary.

"I have never heard an accent like yours", he said, and asked where I came from. I evaded this question, saying only that I came from an island far to the west; he didn't press for details. He commented that he could tell I didn't belong to the group that I was imprisoned with. With my fair hair and light skin, I somewhat resembled the German prisoners; but it was clear that I didn't speak their language or share their customs, and I was not as tall or robustly built.

I told him my name was Miranda; his right eyebrow rose in surprise, as if to say that did not seem a very likely name for a dirty barbarian slave girl.

He had a wonderful, lively face: arched eyebrows that he used expressively to convey surprise, contempt, or amusement; a fine, if rather prominent, nose; and penetrating dark eyes. He had a well-groomed beard; he stroked it when he paused to think. He was talkative and charming and his eyes were bright with mischief, although his mouth assumed a sardonic expression in repose.

Already I had violated rule number one: minimize personal contact with the people of the past. But I was, I confess, rather taken with him; I wanted desperately to be able to find out what year it was, and where I had landed; and he seemed well informed and willing to talk. He would be an ideal informant. Already I felt so isolated in this world that I desperately wanted someone to talk to me. He enjoyed having an audience, and so we fell into long conversation.

After he answered my questions about recent historical events, I was able to work out that it must be the seventh year of the reign of Nero, that is, A.D. 61 by the modern calendar. I was not really happy to hear that. I had hoped to visit Rome during the rule of Vespasian (or one of the other relatively sensible emperors). Nero was so pathetically weak during the early years of his reign that he seemed almost comic; as he grew more and more mad, his cruelty became evident. Perhaps I could obtain a few coins with Nero's bull-necked portrait on them, I thought; I could bring these back with me as evidence that I had really reached the past. How I was going to get hold of any money was not clear to me at that moment.

The next day Demetrius showed me his leg: it had begun to heal. That cheered him up considerably. He began to take an interest in my welfare, and to coach me about what one had to do to get a good master. I didn't know whether he really knew what he was talking about, or whether he was just making things up so that he could sound authoritative. (Later I would come to know that he always gave an air of knowing what he was talking about, even when he didn't.) He told me that if a buyer appeared who looked like a bad master, he planned to stay out of view, or if that was impossible, to look ignorant and unpleasant.

Demetrius intended to find himself a good master, preferably a wealthy man who lived in a city. He wanted a master who would allow him to accumulate savings and perhaps allow him to purchase his freedom after a reasonable length of time; then, with his former master's patronage, he could set up a business. On the other hand, he said, he might be willing to remain a slave if he could find a situation in a really good household, perhaps as a steward.

It amused me to learn that Demetrius was a great believer in facial physiognomy as a clue to character. He believed that the shape of the mouth, the wrinkles in the brow, the height of the forehead, and the size and formation of the skull would tell him how kind, how cruel, or how intelligent the potential buyer was. It was clear that Demetrius intended to choose his owner, if possible. He seemed to have no doubts about the matter.

He began to become concerned about me. I was touched and reassured by his solicitude. Perhaps, after all, he had become a friend. I didn't look healthy. Since my arrival in the past I hadn't eaten or slept very well. The hard ground and the company of lice made for an uncomfortable bed. My hair was dirty; my face was sunburned. He said he felt that he owed me a great favor because I helped him heal his leg. So he said he would help me to find a good master, too. He instructed me that when undesirable potential buyers came, I should try to move toward the back of the pen where I would not be so easy to see. If a man with a cruel face looked at me, he said, I should stick out my chin a little; that would make me look obstinate. I should narrow my eyes. I should try to look stupid and unattractive; I should hunch over a little. He advised me to tie the cloth band that served as a sort of brassiere more tightly around my breasts to flatten my chest. He coached me on how to stand, and critiqued my performance.

"Hunch over slightly. No, don't stick your chin out that far, that does not look natural..." He said that if he attracted a good buyer, he would try to convince his new master to buy me as well. I tried to remain hopeful; it seemed that there was still a chance that I might end up in a good household situation. But I did not think I could endure very many more nights sleeping on the ground. The temptation to end this experiment by sending the signal that would return to my own time was growing stronger; I missed my soft bed with its cozy flannel covers, and all the other comforts of home.

He heard the guards speak of a slave auction would be held at the next market day. This was not a good time to go on the market, Demetrius said. On market day the slaves would be put on the auction block, naked, in front a large group of prospective owners, and this would not give us the opportunity to appeal selectively to just the right potential owner. However, he learned from quizzing the guards that a few preferred customers would come to look at us before the auction. He thought this preview sale presented the best opportunity, and he advised me to be prepared.

I fingered the signal device embedded in my arm and thought about using it to escape. However, now that I had a friend, I was not so eager to leave. His confidence about future prospects was contagious. It occurred to me that if I were purchased as a house slave, and went to live in a wealthy household for a few days, I would get a much more intimate look at Roman life than I ever could have gotten from walking around in the streets. It seemed to me a chance worth taking. If my new owner proved to be cruel or abusive, I would have the ability to escape—so I believed. I wanted to see something more of their world; so I remained and waited to see what would happen.

Several potential buyers came through early in the morning; apparently they didn't suit Demetrius. With a few subtle alterations in his face and posture, he managed to look stupid and ill tempered, and he was passed by. I followed his instructions about deportment; I was also passed over.

Then a prospective buyer appeared who seemed to be up to Demetrius's standards. This man was lean and tall; the fabric of his clothing suggested a household that was prosperous but not ostentatiously wealthy. He had a neatly trimmed beard that gave him the look of a philosopher. The vertical crease between his eyebrows created a permanently worried look; this, and the stiffness of his body movements, gave him an air of self-conscious seriousness and dignity. The shadow of a smile came and went on his face as he conversed with Demetrius. Would his household be a good place? Demetrius seemed to think so. Demetrius stood erect and made direct eye contact. They conversed in Greek and Latin; Demetrius demonstrated his writing skills in both languages. There was a lengthy haggle between this man and the dealer about price. Paperwork was completed, and his new owner began to lead Demetrius away. I watched this from my pen.

I felt a sudden terror of abandonment as the only person who had showed any concern or kindness toward me in this strange new world departed.

At the gateway to the courtyard, Demetrius took the man aside for a talk. Demetrius pointed in my direction and began a persuasive appeal. They returned to the courtyard and approached my pen. Demetrius's new owner looked me over; he did not seem impressed. Demetrius's voice was honeyed as he made his plea. Surreptitiously, out of sight of the Roman clerks, he broke off the part of the tag on my wrist that indicated I could play a musical instrument. Aha, I thought; if I don't have any distinguishing abilities, they can buy me much more cheaply.

The sales pitch that Demetrius made to his new owner was in Greek. I had studied Greek and could read it fairly well; but the pronunciation I had learned bore little resemblance to the way he spoke the language, so I had trouble understanding what he said. He gestured in my direction from time to time, and he seemed to be arguing my merits. I gathered later that my chief selling point was my low price. How humiliating! His arguments were effective, for within a short time more papers were signed and I was turned over to them.

I learned that the man who had bought us, Alexander, was the steward for a household just outside a small city. He and Demetrius had much to talk about; I just looked around and listened. We walked out of the compound and climbed into an ox-drawn wagon; this would take us to our new home. The wagon was loaded with sacks, barrels, and amphorae; apparently Alexander had also purchased supplies on this trip.

As we rumbled along the road, jerking and tossing in the cart, we headed south along the same major road that I had traveled earlier. Another slave drove the wagon; Alexander and Demetrius perched on sacks near the front, engaged in lively discussion. I was in back with the supplies, free to look about and study the landscape. The dominant feature was the same mountain I had noticed earlier. I recognized its shape from a famous mural that had been found in Pompeii: it was the classic pointed shape of a volcano. At the moment it looked deceptively peaceful, with orchards and vineyards rooted in the rich volcanic soil on its flanks, and villas as tiny as dollhouses on the lower slopes.

I was certain I knew what it was, but I asked Alexander the name of the mountain to make sure, and he told me:

"Vesuvius". He informed me that our destination was a villa was just outside the city of Pompeii. I couldn't have been more pleased! Pompeii…

I had walked the excavated streets of Pompeii in my other life. Archaeologists had found jewelry, dishes, tools, surgeon's instruments, furniture, statuary, stashes of coins, and countless other personal possessions. Even the remains of eggs, cakes and chicken set out on tables for lunch on that fatal day had been excavated. The murals of gods and goddesses and garden landscapes still retained some of their vivid colors; the floors were still paved with black and white stone mosaics of detailed nature scenes or elaborate geometric patterns.

The words of ancient Romans had also remained—accounting records, lawsuits, letters, military discharge diplomas, love poems, and curses. The walls of buildings were covered with neatly lettered advertisements and political slogans, and with sloppy graffiti of all sorts, ranging from the poetic to the scatological. Quotations from the Aeneid: "Arms and the man I sing…" Rueful apologies: "I wouldn't have wet the bed", one guest at a local inn wrote on the wall, "but they didn't provide a chamber pot!" Scrawled words on the walls recorded the gossip, loves, hates, and rivalries of people who lived almost two thousand years ago. Their words fascinated me.

The outlines of their bodies made a chilling impression on me. The bodies of victims who were buried in the eruption left cavities in the hardened mud and lava; archaeologists made casts of these bodies by filling the cavities with plaster. So much detail was preserved that even facial expressions and the folds of clothing could sometimes be recognized. A father sheltered his child in his arms; a dog lay twisted in agony as it struggled to break loose from its chain. A fully armored soldier stood guard at the gate of Herculaneum and died standing at his post. A wealthy woman, draped in expensive jeweled necklaces, was found in a cubicle at the gladiator training school—had she merely taken refuge there as she tried to escape from the town, or had she gone there for a tryst with a lover? Some people suffocated; others were blown to bits by flying debris that had been flung with deadly force.

I was more interested in their lives than in their tragic deaths. The surviving writing provided tantalizing clues about the nature of those lives. Only a small portion of the writings of ancient Romans still existed, repeatedly copied and handed down across the centuries. Surviving documents included a letter home from a soldier, complaining about hardships and begging his parents to send him money and warm clothing; a love poem in which a man idealized the beauty of his mistress and complained about her fickleness; and a lawsuit in which a freedwoman fought to retain her freedom and recover ownership of her property from her greedy former mistress.

I had fallen in love with that lost world, and so, in spite of the poor job prospects, I had studied Classical Archaeology. That knowledge was the main reason the science team had chosen me for their time travel project. And now, to my great delight, I was going to see the city that had inspired my fascination with the past.

The eruption that would bury Pompeii was still eighteen years away; and I didn't expect to stay in the past for very long, perhaps only a few days. And yet the sight of the volcano chilled me. This was a city whose death I could foresee, and that was distressing knowledge.

CHAPTER 4

We arrived at our new master's estate. Demetrius and I got out of the wagon and walked along the hard packed dirt road that led up to the rear gate of a sprawling country villa surrounded by olive groves, vineyards, and vegetable gardens. Tall pointed poplars bordered the road that led up to the front gate, like rows of silent sentries; a more modest kitchen garden lay outside the rear gate. The house was a great walled compound with two enormous doorways; the red and white painted walls were topped with sloping roofs of terra cotta tiles. We approached the rear entrance where massive wooden double doors studded with nail heads stood propped open. I caught myself fingering the scar inside my left arm again, and I scolded myself to stop—I mustn't bring attention to the smooth metal disk that had been implanted in my arm. I needed to reassure myself that the signal device was still there. I needed to feel certain that once I went through that gate into the walled compound, I would have a way out again.

An old doorman sat just inside. He slept in the peaceful afternoon warmth of the sun with his dog's head in his lap; our presence startled him into attention. This was the watchman, I supposed, although he didn't seem to take this responsibility too seriously. The elderly dog that had been asleep on his lap also came to life, and ambled up to me awkwardly as if his bones hurt. I offered him my hand to smell, as my father had taught me to do; for smell is what interests dogs most. Apparently I was the source of an absolutely fascinating olfactory blend, for the dog gave me an extremely thorough going over, and I could swear that he appeared puzzled, as if these were odors he could not identify. No doubt I still had the residues of many modern foods and drugs in my system. I hoped that I didn't smell so obviously different that other people would notice this peculiarity.

Alexander led us into the slave quarters at the rear of the house. We entered a plain courtyard with a shallow rectangular stone lined pool in the center; he pointed to a stone bench; I sat. I looked around at my new home. The walls were rough and pitted, painted in some places, bare stone showing through in others. The courtyard wasn't paved, but the earth was packed so hard from the ceaseless wear of feet that it might almost have been solid rock. Around the edges a few spots had been dug out to create garden patches, and the plants looked edible and medicinal, rather than ornamental. Dark doorways lined the perimeter of the courtyard; judging from the smoke that issued from the largest doorway, this was the kitchen. The walls here were stark and plain; the corridors in the service quarters were whitewashed, or had relatively simple designs painted on them, except for one quite elaborate painting of two young men set above a shelf and framed by a sort of pediment, that I guessed represented the household Lares, the guardians of the house. One doorway provided a glimpse of a wall painted a mellow wine red and decorated with delicately rendered architectural motifs. This must lead to the formal area of the house, which I was eager to see.

Two women came out of the kitchen to look me over. Alexander introduced them: "Damaris is the housekeeper; you will help her with cleaning. Iris is the mistress's maid and hairdresser."

Damaris was clearly the older of the two. The pale softness of her rounded face and neck reminded me of bread dough: wholesome, plain, nourishing. Her hands showed years of menial work; the skin was coarse and her fingernails were ragged. She moved as if she had arthritis, and her joints seemed swollen. She wore a shapeless tunic belted at the waist. She gave me a welcoming smile, and said to Alexander: "Good; she can do the lamps, the bedchambers, the floors." The welcome had little to do with friendliness; she was merely pleased to have another set of hands to do the work.

If Damaris had the maternal softness of bread dough, Iris had the brittle beauty of porcelain. Her fine complexion was ivory with tones of olive, and her face was delicately modeled, and so perfect that it hardly seemed possible it could be real. The simple tunic that seemed shapeless on Damaris was draped about her slender figure in a manner that was artful yet artless. Luminous brown eyes dominated her face; dark brows dramatized their beauty. Praxiteles himself could not have improved upon her profile. With an elegant finger, she adjusted a strand of the curling dark hair that formed a cloud about her face. Even without a smile, her face was endearing; something in the tilt of her nose and the line of her brows suggested gentleness and at the same time a hint of sadness. The way she held herself, shoulders back, chin high, made it clear that she knew she was beautiful.

"She looks German!" Iris said, in a tone that made it clear this was no compliment.

They seemed in no hurry. As we talked, I learned that the master was on business travel for a few days, and the mistress was out paying calls, so they had little work to do that day. My arrival was welcome diversion. They asked me where I had come from and what I had been.

I had been thinking about my cover story. I wanted my story to impart some dignity without raising too many questions. If I planned to stay for more than a day or two, I needed to avoid any background story for which my knowledge was inadequate. If I said I was from Britannia, for instance, my lack of detailed and current knowledge of language and geography could be discovered quickly by anyone familiar with that part of the empire. I needed to be from a place beyond their known world.

In answer to their questions, I told them that my people lived in a land called America, very far to the west, beyond the Pillars of Hercules (Gibraltar). It seemed harmless to use the real name of my country of origin; I couldn't name any country known to them as my homeland—I wouldn't know the details necessary to make such a claim stick. And a liar needs a good memory. I was afraid that if I made up too elaborate a story, I would forget or confuse the details. Since America was beyond the edges of their known world, that name was as good as any other, and it was easier for me to remember.

They asked what I had been before I became a slave. I told them I had been a priestess. This seemed like a reasonable approximation to the truth. They would not have believed me if I had claimed to be a scholar or a teacher. Women were rarely scholars in the ancient world, and teachers had even lower pay and less prestige in Roman times than they do in modern times. I thought it possible that I might be left unmolested if I could lay claim to the protection of some strange god; they took the gods of other cultures rather seriously, and were afraid of offending them.

They seemed willing to believe I had been a priestess, but that information certainly didn't impress them. Don't give yourself airs, their looks seemed to say. Forget your past. You are just a slave now.

By now my mind was blurry with fatigue. I told them that my people had fled on a ship when our country was destroyed by earthquakes and floods; and that our ship was driven off course by storms, far to the east of where we intended to go. I needed to explain how I turned up in the Mediterranean, so I said that pirates had captured us. (Piracy was a problem in the Mediterranean, off and on, in ancient times, so this account wasn't quite as ludicrous as it might seem.) I said that the pirate ship sailed near to their coast and sank; I clung to a piece of wreckage overnight, and was picked up by fishermen. I said I didn't think anyone else had survived. I am afraid the story became rather more colorful than I intended as I went along (rather like some of the Greek novels that people of that period read for entertainment, that tended to be full of pirate abductions, ill starred love affairs, cases of mistaken identity, and other unlikely adventures). The story I ended up with sounded fairly unbelievable to me, but they seemed to accept it.

"What was the name of your country, again?"

"America..."

Demetrius frowned a little. "America? I haven't heard of this place."

"It's very far away."

It seemed to puzzle him that I spoke Latin (with a deplorable accent, it's true); and yet I claimed to come from a place beyond the known limits of their world. Fortunately, he didn't raise further questions. In fact, I would discover, Demetrius didn't care to talk about any topic on which he was not the expert.

As they studied me, I studied them. I was reassured that my appearance wasn't too conspicuously different. I could pass for just one more barbarian from the outer fringes of their known world. They seemed willing to give me a chance to fit in.

Rather timidly, I asked them about their own backgrounds. They seemed surprised that I should presume to ask. Iris was "verna", that is, a slave born in the household of her mistress. It was clear from her tone that she thought this was a great distinction.

"What kind of household is this?", I wanted to know. "A very fine family", Alexander informed me in a lofty manner that reminded me for all the world of a pompous British butler. "This is one of the wealthiest families in Pompeii. The master is descended from a branch of the family of Marcus Tullius Cicero, who was consul of Rome. The mistress is daughter of the Holconii. He is a kind master; he permits us to save money, to have a peculium. Some slaves in this family have been permitted to buy their freedom. You will be most fortunate if he decides to keep you here." So, I was on probation, it seemed. Alexander spoke of the master reverently, as if he were a walking paragon of all the drearier traditional Roman Republican virtues: Clementia, dignitas, frugalitas, industria, prudentia, humanitas, severitas—all of these terms meant about what one would guess from their English language equivalents. He made the master sound dreadfully stuffy.

I decided that I would stay for a while and see what developed. This was even better than I had hoped: I would see much more than the public life in streets and markets; I would get an intimate, "*Upstairs, Downstairs*" peek at life inside Roman household. I could hardly wait for the drama—or the comedy—to begin.

CHAPTER 5

By now it was early evening; they lit a few olive oil lamps that cast puddles of liquid yellow light on the floor and walls. I was hungry after the long journey; Demetrius and I were shown to the kitchen doorway to be fed.

"Unfortunately, I have learned that this household has a Roman cook," he informed me. He raised his right eyebrow. I understood his comment. In spite of being conquered by the Romans, many Greeks still felt themselves superior to Romans in matters of taste and intellect. A Roman cook, by implication, was a poor cook. Of course, because I appeared to be German, both the Greek and Roman slaves looked down on me as an ignorant northern barbarian.

Cnaeus (the cook) heard what Demetrius had said. Without a word, and with considerable slamming of pots, he dished out bowls of bean soup and gave one to each of us, with pieces of coarse bread. His face softened a little when he handed me the bowl; I must have appeared waif-like in my torn dirty clothing. "Hunger sweetens beans", he said. The momentary softness of his expression seemed incongruent with the harshly scarred appearance of his face and arms; he must have been severely burned at one time.

I sat on the stone bench just outside the kitchen door to eat this meal. Cnaeus and Demetrius followed me outside to continue bickering. Cnaeus offered me a cup of watered wine.

"Enjoy the wine; it is like nectar of the gods", Demetrius said. The wine was terrible, but at least it refreshed my thirst. I remembered reading a recipe for slave wine given by Cato the elder, who was notorious for his strictness and stinginess. They used the first pressing of grapes to make good quality wine; a second pressing for lesser quality wine, and the remaining mashed grape residue was used to make slave wine. The author commented helpfully that any slave wine left over at the end of the season could be used as vinegar.

"Greekling, do not annoy me further," Cnaeus said. This seemed to be the beginning of a feud. Demetrius was deliberately needling Cnaeus; perhaps he enjoyed having a fresh target, and an appreciative audience, for his wit.

I chewed the bread carefully. It was made from better quality grain than the bread I had been given by the fishermen or the slave dealer; there did not seem to be any pebbles in it. Nevertheless, I suspected that the coarse bread and the beans would cause severe digestive problems until I got used to them.

Demetrius's next sally was: "Pay no attention to him…he has not even thumbed through Aesop." (This was a manner of saying that he was so ignorant he hadn't even read the book used as a first reader.) Cnaeus spat, growled, and retreated to his kitchen. Demetrius grinned and raised both eyebrows, apparently satisfied that he had won this round. The Greek slaves looked down upon the Romans, but the Romans also looked down upon the Greeks, it seemed; the one matter on which they might agree was that they were both superior to northern barbarians, like me. I ate self consciously, aware that Iris and Damaris were looking me over with critical eyes.

When I had finished eating, Damaris spoke to me: "You need a bath; come this way." She and Iris discussed how to manage this. They decided to give me a preliminary wash near the pool in the slave courtyard. Unlike the pools in the formal gardens, which were purely decorative, this one was functional. They helped me remove my dirty clothing. Of course I was not used to being bathed by other people, but they seemed to assume that as a barbarian I would not know how to take a proper bath by myself. And of course, bathing was a social activity in their world. I tried not to be too obviously embarrassed by my nakedness. They took away my soiled clothes and sat me on the edge of the pool in the courtyard, and they talked while they helped me wash.

I was becoming too tired to make the effort needed to follow the unfamiliar cadence of their speech, so I let their gentle words and laughter envelop me. They used olive oil to loosen the dirt; they scraped my skin clean with a strigil and wet rags, and poured buckets of water over me to rinse my body and hair. The water was cool, but it felt wonderful to be clean. At least my enthusiasm for washing met with their approval; they behaved as if they had expected some resistance from me.

"You are so thin, like a boy", Iris said. This was true; I had been anxious about my future and had not eaten or slept well before my departure. I had lost weight and appeared somewhat gaunt. They asked nothing more about my background; their lack of curiosity was a relief, as I was already getting tired of making up stories and trying to keep track of my lies to avoid tripping myself up with inconsistencies. Their only interest in me was to make me over into an acceptable house servant. Apparently, to judge from the looks they exchanged and their suppressed giggles, they thought this was going to take a lot of work.

They washed and combed out my hair—they were impressed with my hair. It was my only real beauty, I thought; it was ash blond, with a mixture of silver and golden strands. I once received a memorable compliment on it: "You have pre-Raphaelite hair", a friend told me. As my hair dried, they gathered it into a loose knot at the base of my neck. They dressed me in a worn but clean tunic, gathered the loose fabric around my waist with a belt, and put soft indoor sandals on my feet. Although my Latin accent made it difficult for me to converse with them, I found that I could follow their words when they spoke slowly. Iris looked at me in curiosity. I thought that perhaps we might become friends. So far she was the only woman I had met who seemed close to my age. There was clearly a hierarchy even among slaves. I started at the bottom of the ladder, while skilled slaves like Iris and Demetrius were far more valued.

I was given an iron ring engraved with the family name to wear on my finger; this was apparently customary as identification for slaves in this household. I had worn a ring only once before in my life—a silver-plated ring give to me by a man I thought was in love with me. When he broke his promises, I threw that ring into the Atlantic in a melodramatic and angry gesture of grief. The weight of the plain iron band on my finger seemed strange to me, a tangible sign of my new bondage. I reminded myself again that this was a temporary bondage. When I had seen enough, I would leave. And yet, I found it oppressive.

The next day Damaris gave me a tour of the house and explained my duties. This country villa was substantially larger than the town houses I had seen on my tourist walks within the city walls of Pompeii. Its floor plan consisted of four hollow rectangles, with the rooms all on one level. I got a slave's tour, starting at the rear of the house.

Each of the four major parts of the house was an open rectangle with a courtyard in the center. The first of these rectangles, at the rear of the house, was the slave quarters; a kitchen, toilet cubicle, storerooms, and small sleeping cubicles surrounded a plain open courtyard with a pool in the center. The kitchen was larger than the ones I had seen in the excavated ruins of Roman town houses. The metal and pottery cooking pots, the ladles and strainers and knives, were well made. Many of the serving dishes and goblets were silver, another clue to the family's status: not as ostentatious as gold, but more costly than the crockery that a poorer family would use.

Some of the goblets used for everyday reminded me of museum pieces. The silver chalices had fabulous raised designs of olive leaves and mythical figures twined around the bowls. Other pieces were amusing, such as a clear drinking glass painted with garish designs of gladiators and animals. Did they have "free glass day" at the amphitheater, I wondered, or were these tawdry souvenirs sold at nearby shops?

The second and largest rectangular courtyard was located adjacent to the slave quarters. The elegant peristyle garden was open to the sky. A colonnade and covered walkway and the family's private rooms surrounded it. The master and mistress had separate rooms, which was apparently common enough here to be unremarkable.

A summer triclinium (dining room) and several reception rooms overlooked the peristyle garden. This garden was the loveliest part of the house; the early summer roses were in bloom, simple wild roses like the ones I knew and loved from New England beach towns, their blossoms cherry and white and pink. Green shrubs and small plants spiced the air with fragrance: Mint, rosemary, sage, basil, and lavender perfumed the air. Ivy, boxwood, and oleander all grew luxuriantly. A series of fountains and pools provided the refreshing sound of running water and attracted birds that came to drink and bathe.

The third rectangle was the atrium at the front of the house; this was where important visitors entered. This atrium had a tiled rectangular pool called an impluvium, with a fountain in the center. Above this pool an opening in the roof allowed sunlight to stream into the courtyard. The roof sloped downward and inward on all sides around the pool, and rainwater fell into the pool in the center of the atrium through elaborately carved and painted drain spouts.

The formal reception areas near the front of the house were all gorgeously decorated with frescoes and patterned mosaic floors. Several cubicles surrounded the atrium, some used for storage, some as offices, and some as sleeping quarters for guests; there was also a formal indoor triclinium, that is, a dining room with three couches. At the rear of the atrium there was a tablinum, the office and reception room. Damaris told me that this was where the master received his clients most mornings. When a visitor entered through the front doorway, he would see the master of the house framed by columns and ornately decorated partitions with the peristyle garden and its colonnade in the background: a most impressive setting.

The floors were mosaics with patterns of tiny black and white stone tiles. Some were simple geometric designs; others had more realistic images. Their front entry had a "cave canem" (beware of the dog) mosaic on the floor. The floor in the indoor triclinium had a playful mosaic of table scraps, such as bits of fruit and nuts and fragments of crab shells, which looked as lifelike as if they had just fallen from the table; and even a mosaic mouse that foraged among the table leavings.

The floors and walls of each room were entirely different in color and design. The colors and designs were so intricate, so bold, that to my eye they were overwhelming, even garish. Everything—ceilings, walls, and doors—was elaborately carved and richly painted, with lavish expanses of classic Pompeiian red. Most walls were divided into panels, which were often separated by cleverly painted false columns; some panels were mostly solid color, with small images centered in the open space, like paintings. Other walls were filled with murals, scenes from myth and nature, with an unusual prevalence of muted (and expensive) blues and yellows and browns. They were restful and stimulating to the eye. I admired the graceful painting of a pale reclining Venus on one wall of the peristyle, mostly white and aquamarine. On the opposite wall was a darker rendering of her lover Mars, standing with a spear in his hand. These sacred lovers embodied a Mediterranean ideal: the dark man, the pale woman.

The painting I admired most was the image of a brown nightingale surrounded by lifelike red roses on a dark green leafy background; it was in the master's private study. When I went there to clean I took my time, for that room was my favorite. A broad doorway offered more light than in most rooms, and a view of the peristyle garden. There were shelves and buckets full of scrolls in this room; I would have loved to examine these, but scrolls were valuable, and I knew a housemaid would not be permitted to handle them. Among them were many that had not been preserved into modern times; he had, for example, an extensive collection of Livy's histories. I longed to read them, but I only looked at the dangling labels on the outside that identified their contents. I did not dare to touch them.

Few of the rooms had windows on the outside of the house, except for an occasional narrow slit; the only light admitted into most rooms came from the doorways that faced the atrium or peristyle; or from the soft liquid glow of olive oil lamps. Most rooms were dim, and it was only when they were filled with daylight or lamplight that the details of the paintings were brought fully to life. I missed having an abundance of windows to welcome in the light, but I knew that this walled in compound was fairly typical; it made the house less vulnerable to robbery, and kept the rooms cool on hot summer days.

There was little furniture or personal clutter. A typical sleeping cubicle had a sleeping couch, a small table, perhaps a chest for storage of personal items. Chairs were few, and mostly reserved for the use of the master, ladies, and elderly or eminent guests. The few pieces of furniture were themselves works of art: beautifully carved rare woods with elaborate inlays; three legged tables with fantastically wrought legs that resembled lion's claws or satyrs; chairs that had fixtures of gold. We slaves did not sit in the presence of our masters. When we were in the privacy of the slave quarters, we squatted on the floor or sat on stone benches. Our quarters were of course much plainer in decoration and sparser in furnishing. Only crude stripes relieved the severe plainness of walls in the slave quarters, although Cnaeus had some amusingly obscene representational art in his quarters.

A fourth hollow rectangle, off to the side of the atrium, was a disused older portion of the house, in disrepair, with undecorated rooms used primarily for storage.

Altogether, it was typical of the more affluent homes of that time, as far as I could tell; and from the decorations of the house, I guessed that this family was somewhat old fashioned and conservative, even before I saw the master or any members of his family.

It was a most impressive house. But from my point of view as a new house slave, the most notable feature was the extensive acreage of floors that needed to be swept and washed. Because the atrium and entry hall were often filled with clients and visitors, the floors there needed to be washed more often than the floors in more private areas of the house. This was to be my most important job, Damaris said: washing floors. All right, I thought: I can do that for a few days.

I wasn't permitted to go outside at that time; as a new slave, and one from a relatively unknown background, I was on probation. Damaris told me a little about the surroundings: there were outbuildings to house the field slaves; presses for production of wine and olive oil; store houses for tools, supplies, and produce from the farm; stables; and many other small structures. This was a fairly large working farm, although not as large as the latifundia (or industrial scale farms) in Sicily and North Africa. The master owned numerous vineyards, olive groves, herds of sheep, and farms spread around the neighboring countryside.

My provisional routine was soon established. At first my work was limited to house cleaning; I was not deemed worthy to wait upon members of the family, as I had not been trained properly, and my Latin accent still left much to be desired. And so I did not see the family; I only cleaned up the messes that they and their visitors left behind. This was a disappointment, for it meant that the only part of the household I really knew anything about was the slave quarters; I hoped that before I left I would have a chance to see the family.

In the meantime, in the morning after the family members had risen, I emptied any used chamber pots and rinsed them. Demetrius began to call me "the princess" because of my obvious distaste for this chore; I held them at arm's length and washed my hands and arms thoroughly after finishing my rounds. Next I cleaned and refilled the olive oil lamps, shook and aired the bed linens, and if necessary, swept floors. I also scrubbed floors in the public parts of the house such as the triclinium or dining room. The abominable Roman custom of throwing food scraps on the floor while dining meant that this floor was usually quite messy. I helped with the household laundry (except for certain items, such as togas, that were taken to the fullery in town for professional cleaning). As the new girl I had been given many of the most menial tasks in the house. How strange, I thought: I have made this great journey into the past, and I may return to my own time with little to show for it but dishpan hands and housemaid's knees. I felt like Cinderella.

I thought that I should try to fade into the background. However, I found it extremely irksome to be a non-person, a housemaid assumed to be stupid. I scrubbed floors, while others were valued for their abilities: Iris for her skill in arranging hair, for example. Demetrius lorded it over me because he could read and write, for God's sake. I wished that I could tell him that I too was an educated person; but my Harvard Ph.D. would mean nothing to him. I was not a person of value here. That was bothersome. At first I thought I could treat this life in the past as a role-play or a game, but I quickly found that I could not feel so detached.

I pumped Demetrius for information, eager to fill in the details about my new world. He was an excellent informant. He loved to gossip, and he had many sources of information both inside and outside the household. But of course, I had a secret source of knowledge that was unavailable to him: I knew their future. At that time it was summer in the year A D. 61. I remembered that in early A.D. 62, a massive earthquake leveled many of the buildings in Pompeii. There was some rebuilding, but the damage was so extensive that the city had still not been completely restored by the time it was buried by Vesuvius in A.D. 79. This knowledge about their future was troubling. Even though I didn't know these people well, I began to feel that I would want to warn them before I left, for I hated to think of the harm that would befall them if they didn't know what was going to happen.

Of course there were no secrets in such a crowded household. As he learned about the family, Demetrius told me about relationships within the household. The master and mistress were not happily married, according to Demetrius. They had not shared a bed in years, not since she had produced the desired three children; a daughter and one son had survived. The son was the focus of mistress Holconia's relentless ambitions; the daughter was a quiet little thing. Iris was the master's frequent bed companion, and thus off limits to the male slaves in the household who would otherwise have pestered her.

The mistress Holconia sent Iris to take her place in her husband's bed after the birth of her last child, and of course she was aware that they continued to sleep together. Even though she had sent Iris to him, she was jealous of any attention the master showed to Iris, and envious of her youthful beauty. The mistress found innumerable small ways to torment Iris.

At first, I was disappointed that I would not have much contact with family members, but upon reflection, I thought, this was probably safer. I didn't look attractive because I felt unwell, but I knew that if my master or any man in the family demanded it, female slaves were assumed to be available for sex. For the moment I was safe from this kind of unwanted attention; I wasn't attractive enough, yet, for this to be a problem. Other slaves made a few half-hearted advances at first, but I brushed them off rather easily, and no one forced me. The attitude of the male slaves seemed to be that—if I weren't willing, all right then, someone else would be. Disorderly behavior was not permitted in this household, and attempted rape was viewed as destructive to domestic tranquility. For the moment, it seemed I was safe.

I found Demetrius attractive, but I had no interest in becoming romantically involved with him. I would only be there a short time, and the risks of a romantic fling far outweighed any pleasures, I thought. Still: as the novelty of the adventure began to wear off, I began to feel downhearted. I had assumed that because this was just a role-play it wouldn't matter what people thought about me. I was wrong about that. It still mattered very much; I wanted to be valued, as much as I ever had. However, in a strange way, it felt less lonely to be an outsider in the past—where I was after all just a tourist—than it had been to feel like an outsider in modern times, where I needed to make a place for myself. Safe but dull, I began to think, as the days in Pompeii went past one by one.

I was not as invisible, or as safe, as I hoped.

The next day I was scrubbing the mosaic floor in the atrium when the mistress passed though. It happened that the sun was coming through the opening in the roof over the center of the atrium. I was kneeling in a pool of light, and my hair was brilliantly illuminated. When it is backlit, it can look like strands of silver and gold; I know, for in rare moments of vanity about my appearance, I have admired it in front of a mirror. Holconia noticed my hair and called me to stand in front of her. This was the first time I had seen her face. Her features were well proportioned. In fact, she looked strikingly like Iris, except that she wore costly jewelry and an exceedingly haughty facial expression. She had a sharp vertical crease between her eyebrows, as if an impatient sculptor had struck her there with a chisel; on Alexander this feature seemed worried; on her, this similar mark appeared peevish. She frightened me, the way she looked at me. She yanked out the wooden hairpins that held my hair in a knot at the back of my neck, and pulled out a long strand of hair for a closer look. Involuntarily I shied away from the approach of her hand; the tapered fingernails seemed like claws. And then she issued a sharp summons.

"Tell Stronnius to come, and bring his shears." (I would learn later that he was the master's barber.) "Cut it close to the scalp; give me as much length as possible."

I was horrified, but there was nothing I could do. I knelt meekly in front of the barber while he sheared me, none too gently. I tried to take this loss lightly, but I was distressed. My hair had been my only beauty. I knew that I now looked pathetic. There were no good mirrors, of course, but I could see my reflection in the pool in the courtyard pool, well enough to judge that what was left of my hair was nothing like a stylish short cut. My skull was tufted with uneven wisps of hair. I looked as ugly as a baby bird, all eyes and beak and rumpled feathers.

Damaris smiled at me, and tried to comfort me with a sympathetic look. I couldn't help myself: I burst into tears, like a fool. She put her arms around me and spoke soothing words. It was some comfort. In a very minor way, this incident made me feel more like one of them, with a shared history of small indignities. Damaris was so angry on my behalf that she spat on the mistress's breakfast food before Iris took the dishes to her room the next morning. We had a good laugh over that, but it seemed to me that she should be more careful. I had been told that no slaves had been beaten in this household for a long time, but she could be punished if the mistress came to know of her insolence. At least it made her seem like my friend. According to the old proverb: "The enemy of my enemy is my friend", and we were now united in our dislike for Holconia. With Damaris's help I trimmed and arranged what little was left of my hair. My gaunt appearance and short hair gave me an oddly androgynous appearance.

At the end of the week the master returned from his business travel. I was sent to the atrium with a basin and towels. I had been instructed to go and wash his hands and feet, and to present myself for inspection. This was the first time I ever saw him. Alexander introduced Demetrius as the new scribe, and reviewed some business matters with our master. I held a basin in front of him, and as he talked, he rinsed his hands and I dried them. He looked at Alexander and spoke to him; I studied him covertly, curious to know something about the man who (for the moment) owned me. He had a wonderful face. Like most upper class Romans of this period, he was clean-shaven. His skin was a clear olive; his eyes were brown. His expression was one of dignity and understated melancholy. His black hair curled against his head in just the way that it does on Greek sculpture, or on the more idealized Roman portrait busts. In profile, he resembled a statue of Augustus I had admired in a museum, in my other life.

The ancients, like us, had conflicting ideas about the trustworthiness of appearances. Ovid wrote, "A good face is a good recommendation"; Juvenal said, "Do not trust in appearance". Another proverb said, "The face is the sign of the soul." I studied the face of Marcus Tullius. It seemed proud and strong, but also gentle and thoughtful. From my point of view, slavery was clearly an evil thing. This man owned us; but he did not look like an evil man. I reminded myself that for them, slavery was simply a fact of life. Some masters were cruel; but not all of them, not all of the time. I couldn't help liking his face and hoping that in this case, it was an honest advertisement of character.

After he sat down, I knelt at his feet, untied the laces of his outdoor sandals and began to wash the dirt of the road from his feet before putting on his indoor sandals. This felt like a surprisingly intimate thing to do, and it seemed very strange to do this for a man I didn't know. The men had finished their business talk. Then Marcus Tullius turned his attention to me. I was startled when he cupped my chin in his hand and turned my face up so that he could look at me, and he asked Alexander:

"And who is this little lamb who has been shorn?" (He used the word "agnella", a feminized form of "agnellus", which is the diminutive and feminized form of 'lamb'.) His gaze was direct; and I felt embarrassed at being intensely examined. They told him I was called Miranda, and explained the little they knew about my origins.

"She has eyes the color of Mare Nostrum", he said then, and he smiled at me. (The Romans often called the Mediterranean 'Mare Nostrum', Our Sea, for at that time the Empire extended all around the Mediterranean.)

Unfortunately, this new nickname (Agnella, "the little lamb") stuck. Romans liked nicknames, especially embarrassing ones. This seemed to be a term of endearment; but I suspected that the word sheep or lamb connoted docility and stupidity to Romans (as it does to speakers of English). I suppose I shouldn't have minded, but it felt like another minor indignity. I had hoped to make a good impression, but I must have looked pathetic.

Why did I care what he thought of me? I don't know. But I did care.

CHAPTER 6

After another of their eight-day weeks had passed I decided that I had experienced enough of the hardships of the past. My hands were raw and my knees bruised from scrubbing floors. The house was beautiful, but it had come to feel like a prison; I wasn't allowed to go out and see the world I was so curious about, as I was still on probation. The loss of my hair had distressed me. The rude advances of some of the men worried me.

Stronnius was my greatest problem. He had taken a fancy to me, or perhaps he just liked to bully me. One afternoon when I was on my way to the atrium with my bucket and scrub brush, passing through the long service corridor, he cornered me. "You should be nice to me; I have the master's ear." He bent over me; I shrank back against the wall, but he pressed himself against me. He began to pull the fabric of my tunic away from my shoulders. I was terrified; I didn't know the rules; what could I do to protect myself? I could feel the grease of the excess hair oil against my check, and smell the garlic on his breath, and these filled me with a sudden disgust; I thrust the scrub brush at his chest and pushed him away. He laughed, not a bit deterred by my resistance, and without taking time to think I flung the bucket at his head and fled back toward the kitchen. I ran headlong into Alexander, who had witnessed this scene.

"Stronnius, don't make a disturbance; there are willing women in the household, don't bother one who is unwilling." I felt abashed; Stronnius did not appear repentant, and in fact, began to lie brazenly to Alexander, saying that I had invited his attention and teased him and then turned away. Alexander looked at me, and I shook my head in silent but definite denial. The look on his face seemed sympathetic, I thought. I was ordered to clean up the mess, but I wasn't reprimanded for the bruised eye I had given Stronnius. Stronnius glared at me the next time he saw me; and the spite in his face increased my uneasiness. Next time, his motives would include a desire for revenge for the injury I'd caused him, and the scolding that he had received.

In spite of Alexander's intervention, I had the feeling that if Stronnius caught me alone in one of the back corridors, he would ignore my protests. I did my best to avoid him. But the conclusion was inescapable: it was becoming dangerous for me to stay; it was time for me to go. But first I wanted to see the city of Pompeii.

It wasn't clear at first how I would be able to get out of the house. By day, both the front and rear doors of the house were guarded—each one had a doorman and a guard dog. It wasn't likely I could slip out undetected in the daytime. At night, the doors were closed and barred; each doorman slept near his post and each guard dog remained on duty. It might be possible to bribe one of the dogs with a little tidbit of meat, I thought; but I was afraid of dogs, and didn't have the courage for such a risky plan. No, the doors were closed to me; I had to think of another way.

I studied the entire compound thoughtfully. There were no windows to the outside, except for a few narrow slits set very high in the walls, blocked with iron bars—such small openings that even a thin person like me would never be able to slip through them. That left only the atrium and peristyle—these were open to the sky. If I could get up onto the roof, I could escape.

As I did my housework, I looked carefully for any possible escape route. Could I climb up one of the columns that surrounded the peristyle garden? No. A more athletic person might have been able to do that, but I knew I didn't have the strength. Could I improvise a rope, and lasso one of the drainpipes above the impluvium in the atrium, and shinny up the rope? No. There was no rope in the house, I could not lay hands on enough cloth to braid myself a rope, and even if I had a rope, I doubted whether I had the strength in my arms to raise myself hand over hand.

And then I noticed the olive tree near one corner of the peristyle garden, across from the master's study. One branch extended toward the roof of the colonnade—it didn't quite reach—but that might provide me with a way. If I climbed the tree, made my way out onto that overhanging branch—supposing that it was strong enough to support my weight—and then launched myself toward the roof, I could probably make it. If I didn't dislodge any of the terra cotta roof tiles, or start to slide down off the roof, it would work. I could make my way over the roof and drop down on the outside of the wall, if all went well. I continued to dwell on possibilities, but in the end, I decided that this was my only reasonable alternative.

The science team had promised me a substantial cash bonus if I could leave behind physical evidence that would prove where I had been, and bring back some tangible proof of my visit to the past. For the first: I had scratched a few words on a pot shard in ink, stolen surreptitiously from Alexander's writing supplies; I planned to bury that in a hole, deep enough that it might not be detected by early excavators, but in a spot easy enough to identify that I could tell the scientists where to find it. For the second: I decided to bring one of the volumes of Livy's history from my master's library. Many of Livy's writings had been lost over the centuries—and I was fairly sure I remembered which volume numbers were missing from the modern set. Any one of these missing texts would be a treasure.

To steal the scroll I needed only a moment alone the next time I was cleaning in the master's study: it was almost too easy. I tied my cloth bag to my sash; this provided a place to hide the scroll. I brought my scrub brush and bucket into the master's study. I stood in silence, listening for the sounds of voices and footsteps outside the door. When it seemed safe, I selected one of the Livy scrolls—it was in the middle of a series, with all the scrolls stored in bins, and it seemed unlikely that this one scroll would be missed. I tucked it into my bag and arranged the bulky folds of my tunic to cover it. Now came the most dangerous part; I had to hide this scroll in a place where I could easily retrieve it. On the pretext of taking my bucket for a refill, I went across the peristyle garden and into the service corridor. Seeing no one there, I made my way into the empty courtyard, the one that was only used for storage. I tucked the scroll into a corner of a storeroom behind some bundles and boxes. Then I went back to housecleaning. I felt suddenly weak and shaky, but I returned to the floor scrubbing with a great show of energy and a quiet sense of triumph. My mission was accomplished.

Once I had taken the scroll, I didn't dare to delay my departure. Every hour that passed was one more hour when the absence of that scroll might possibly be detected. I decided I would leave that same night.

Damaris always slept next to me—and she was a deep sleeper; as a precaution, I urged a little more wine on her at the evening meal. When I was certain she had drifted off into unconsciousness, I rose from my pallet and slipped into my tunic. Noiselessly I made my way out of the slave courtyard and down the service corridor that led the length of the house, into the corner storeroom where I had left the scroll.

The silence was eerie. It was a night of a full moon—I wished it were not, for I would have preferred the cover of darkness, but I was unwilling to wait any longer. Now that I had decided to leave, and worked out a plan, the waiting was getting on my nerves. At best, I am not a brave person, and this plan could fail. The tree branch might break; I might fall off the roof; someone might hear me scrambling on the roof; I might meet thieves or rapists on the dark road into the city; or someone from the household might see me in Pompeii, when I was supposed to be confined to the house. Any of these mishaps could occur. Well, I supposed that if any of these catastrophes occurred, I could activate my signal device and escape. But I really wanted to see the city of Pompeii before I left, and if possible I wanted to make my exit without having anyone witness my departure.

I retrieved my sack, checked to make certain that the stolen scroll was still there, tucked the pottery shard in next to it, and tied the sack to my belt, where it hung well concealed in the folds of the tunic.

I was now in a part of the house where I had no business to be, at this time of night; and I had the stolen scroll in my possession—which I would not be able to explain, if I were caught. My breath became tight and short. I lectured myself: It's not helpful to panic. Take deep breaths. Move silently. Keep your wits about you.

I re-entered the long dark service corridor, and paused to listen. There was no indication that anyone was moving about. Good. I moved silently down the corridor and then out into the peristyle garden.

The garden was silvered with moonlight, and seemed as bright as full day. Again I looked around. Every room in the family's quarters faced onto this garden; most of the doorways were dark—except for the master's study. Damn. A lamp was lit and therefore he was certain to be awake—perhaps he was reading. For a moment I considered whether I should return the scroll to its hiding place, and go back to bed, and wait for another night.

I just couldn't. I would have to endure this agony of suspense all over again. I decided that, if I were very quiet, I could make a successful escape. The olive tree was within the line of sight from the doorway of his study, it was true, but I also knew that his couch and table were not directly in line with that doorway.

It was not difficult to climb up into the olive tree; its gnarled branches offered easy hand-and footholds. But the scrape of my hands and knees against the rough gray bark seemed loud in that silver silence and the noise of my breathing and the pounding of my heart echoed in my ears. I sat still in the tree for a few moments; and then I saw a silhouette that filled the doorway. The master stood there, his hand against the doorframe; he was looking at the disk of the moon, rising over the rooftop opposite him and behind me.

I shrank back against the trunk of the tree and gathered the folds of my tunic closer to me, trying to make certain that the pale gray fabric did not show. I dared not breathe.

He stood there for what seemed like an age; it even seemed to me that he looked in my direction. But apparently he didn't see me. He returned to his study; and shortly after that, he extinguished the lamp.

I breathed a little more easily after that; but by now, the first pink of dawn began to tint the sky. If I wanted to make my escape, I must do it soon. I crept out along the branch; it held my weight. I crouched as far out along the branch as I dared and measured the distance to the rooftop with my eyes. I tensed, and I leaped—awkwardly—and I hit the roof at an angle; I slid a few feet downward back toward the courtyard, grappling at the tiles with my hands; and somehow, I managed to cling to the roof, although a tile that was dislodged slipped loose beneath my foot and fell into the garden.

The noise that it made when it hit the ground seemed to me loud enough to wake the dead. I froze. In the distance, I heard one of the guard dogs barking, a loud hoarse bark; I hoped he was securely chained to the doorway, for if he came charging into the courtyard now, he would certainly betray my presence.

A few tense moments passed; I heard the voice of the gateman, talking to the dog; and I thought I heard footsteps headed in my direction. It was difficult, for I had no secure handhold; but the tiles were rough, and I was able to snake my way up to the roof ridge on my belly, to sling myself over, and to make my way down the other side. The last thing I saw as my head slipped below the ridge of the roof was the watchman entering the courtyard with a lamp in his hand, peering about. But I don't think he saw me; I ducked out of his sight, gripping the ridge of the roof with my hands, and remained quite still. After a few minutes he apparently decided that the dog had only imagined an intruder, and he returned to his cubicle.

I slid myself carefully down the outer edge of the roof, trying not to loosen any more tiles, and dropped as quietly as I could onto the ground outside. I followed the road south in the direction of the city. It was an hour or so before daylight, and I would wait until morning to enter the town. My plan was to explore the town, then find a secluded spot, activate the signal device, and go home. I had casually asked about the town, and noticed which direction people took when they were sent out on errands. This would be the last phase of my adventure.

I was afraid of the night. After living inside a walled compound for a couple of weeks, where the gates were barred against possible intruders every night, I shared their fear that the night must be full of robbers and marauders; but I saw no one, no one at all on that dark road.

I walked toward town, a distance of about two miles. The road was lined with tombs and monuments; I paused to read some of the inscriptions in the brightening light. Many of these were statements of the person's virtues and accomplishments in life, addressed to passers-by in touchingly direct language: "Stranger, stop and read my words. This is the tomb of a beautiful woman; her parents named her Claudia. She loved her husband whole-heartedly. She bore two sons: one still walks the earth, the other lies below it. She was charming in speech but pleasant and dignified in her manners. She managed her household well; she spun wool. I have spoken. Go on your way, stranger." One tomb had a courtyard with stone seats. This was a place where the relatives of the deceased would come on holidays to share a feast with the departed; I noticed a pipe embedded in the stone lid of the crypt, which I knew was a place to pour an offering of wine to the dead. At dawn I walked the last few hundred yards toward the city gate.

Just outside the gates I passed several magnificent villas. I recognized one of them as the "Villa of the Mysteries", so named by modern archaeologists for its splendid murals that some scholars thought depicted initiation rituals for the Dionysus cult. Ah, what I would give to go inside! But there was no way I could do that; I would have to content myself with a tour of the public buildings in town.

I entered the town through one of the small side arches in the Herculaneum gate. The guard who loitered there didn't seem to have much to do; he hardly glanced at me as I passed. Just inside the gate I passed the two-storied house of a surgeon, identifiable from the carved wooden replicas of medical instruments that hung outside. I continued along the street that I recognized as the Via Consolare, one of the oldest and busiest streets in town, paved with massive stone blocks. (There were no street signs, back in that time; the names that I associated with the streets were the Italian names posted at the excavation in modern times.) Carts and wagons rumbled through the streets, and I was careful to stay on the raised stone sidewalk out of the way of traffic. I was excited to see the row of shops; I had never seen a Roman town alive before—only dead towns in excavations—and I was desperately eager to see everything.

Along the street front, most of the ground level rooms were open to the street and set up as shops or food stalls. The storefronts were open now, during daytime business hours. Many of them were sheltered from the sun by colorful cloth awnings; tables facing the sidewalk were piled with goods. Each shop had heavy wooden sliding or folding doors that could be used to close up the store during the midday siesta and at night, very much like the shops in modern Italian towns, it seemed to me.

Many of the merchants on this street sold pottery, glassware, and cloth. People chatted with shopkeepers and negotiated purchases. In this first block of shops there were two thermopolia, or food counters. Each had a wide marble and stone countertop with deep basins set into the counter. The basins contained wine, hot soups, and stews. Most people in towns lived in small apartments or lofts above shops that had no kitchen facilities, and so all their hot food came from these food counters. The thermopolia seemed as numerous as fast food places in modern cities.

The mixed odors of garlic, cabbage, frying sausages, spiced meat pies, pastries, wine, and warm bread began to prick my appetite. A baker was putting out heavy round loaves of brown bread, cut into pie shaped segments, and hot rolls drizzled with honey, and flat breads topped with cheeses and onions. These smelled tantalizing even though it was too early to be hungry. Unfortunately these food aromas competed with the sour smells of urine and waste matter. Even though there were public latrines and baths, and relatively abundant running water available from fountains at many of the major intersections, the city smelled fetid in the heat of summer. Some Roman cities had good sewer systems, but Pompeii was a relatively old city and most of its streets lacked sewers; or perhaps I should say, in some parts of town, the streets were the sewers.

As the sun rose higher, the tufa walls and stone streets retained the heat, so that the city felt substantially hotter than our country home. The side streets were narrow and shaded by awnings or second-floor balconies that kept them somewhat cooler. Still, the heat, the smells, and the noise of the crowded town made me appreciate how fortunate I had been to find a home in a country villa where the air was relatively fresh and clean and there was more open space.

I peeked into the large open doorways between the stores; some of these, I knew, must be entries into homes. In the city most householders rented out the rooms that faced the street as shops; this was a good source of income, and the shops insulated the private living quarters behind them (to some extent) from the heat, noise, and smells in the street. A few times I caught a glimpse through an open doorway of a gorgeously decorated atrium. Each villa was a hidden garden oasis in the crowded city.

I turned left onto the street that modern visitors know as the Via della Fortuna; there I saw the Temple of Fortuna Augusta at a major crossroads. I knew that an ancestor of Marcus Tullius had built this temple to honor the first emperor because of the inscription, which consisted of the usual formula, ending with the proud statement: "Marcus Tullius built this temple, on his own land, and with his own money."

I stopped to admire this. It was the most impressive building I had seen so far. The temple was relatively small but exquisitely proportioned. The rectangular white marble building rose high above the street; a long set of stone stairs led up to the entrance. The front portico was lined with ornate Corinthian pillars, and surmounted by a peaked roof. The marble had a snowy purity that was blindingly white in the sun. Raised imperial laurels were carved in stone and gilded, brilliant against a blue painted background within the triangular area just under the roof. The pair of heavy bronzed doors was closed. In front of the stairs there was a low iron fence, and that gate was also closed. The top angles of the roof were ornamented with scallop shells sculpted from stone.

Wealthy families participated in politics; they were expected to contribute to the town by funding public works, such as roads, gates, amphitheaters, or baths, or by constructing temples, or by sponsoring games and festivals. These projects were costly, but they were expected. Unlike modern politicians, Roman politicians had to deliver at least some of the goods before they were elected, and not just make promises that they forgot after the elections. No wonder they put prominent inscriptions on each building to inform the public who had sponsored its construction. A family gained dignity and importance and prestige from these contributions. And of course, votes. The public voted most enthusiastically for candidates who sponsored great gladiatorial contests and games, or who provided public baths or built great public buildings.

I passed a house that I knew to be a brothel in the next block; how amused they might have been to know that in two thousand years this drab little building would be one of the most famous attractions for tourists. There were no signs of activity at this hour of the morning, but the graffiti on the walls outside commented on specialties of the girls and made crude commentaries about sexual rivalries. Inside, I knew, there were cubicles with stone beds and thin straw pallets; life as a prostitute must have been a hard one, indeed. At the Via Stabiana I turned right; I tried to keep a clear sense of direction, re-orienting myself when I could see a glimpse of Vesuvius between buildings at major intersections. As in other older Roman cities, this town had streets that were not a perfect rectilinear grid.

At the Stabian baths, I turned left onto the Via dell'Abbondanza; it sloped gently uphill away from the center of town. There was no vehicle traffic here; it was a much quieter part of town. I turned and looked downhill, toward the center of town. This street was lined with fashionable and expensive looking shops, most of which had awnings stretched out to provide shade. These shops had jewelry, perfume, flowers, red Samian pottery, exquisitely worked silver drinking vessels, and other fine goods on display.

There were stone paved sidewalks built well above the street level, so that pedestrians would not have to dirty their feet with the debris in the road. At each intersection, enormous stepping stones provided pedestrians with a way to cross the street; between these, deeply carved ruts showed a hundred or more years of wear from wagon traffic. At many intersections, jets of water continually refreshed water troughs; women came to fill jugs.

The lower halves of the exterior walls of the buildings were painted brilliant red, and the upper halves were whitewashed; the roofs above were terra cotta tiles. Many of the nicer shops had beautifully detailed murals above the outside doorways or on inside walls; mythological devices and images of household gods or Lares seemed to be the most popular.

Each block or insula was packed solid with buildings. Some buildings were two stories high, with timbered balconies overhanging the sidewalk. Pots of green plants and laundry decorated the railings with splashes of color. The street was full of people. It was busy, yet no one seemed to be in a hurry; people conversed in small groups and bantered with shopkeepers while they negotiated their purchases. Dogs roamed about, sniffing for pickings and apparently not finding very much. Most walls were used as billboards. It seemed a mix of political advertisement, price notices, and promotion for entertainment events, gossip, character assassination, and insults. Outside a wine shop the white had a simple painting of four jugs with the numbers 1, 2, 3 and 4 painted beside them; these were the prices for four qualities of wine.

Beyond the city, along the horizon, Vesuvius dominated the skyline: it was more sharply pointed in shape and much higher than the mountain I had seen in modern times. It slept, its slopes still showing a little green even in the heat of summer. I knew there was fire in the bowels of the mountain. No one else apparently gave the mountain any thought.

I passed a fullery. I could have located it by smell, rather than sight. Just outside the door, there were basins to collect urine from passing men. The urine, I knew, was one of the chemicals used to clean the greasy woolens that would be brought by customers; Vespasian would actually levy a tax on these collection vessels, later on, leading people to call them "Vespasiani". To the right of the entrance was a counter where people handed over baskets of clothing, mostly togas which could not be cleaned properly at home, and received tags that could be used later to retrieve them. Across from the counter there was an apparatus with weighted bars that appeared to be a clothing press. Through the doorway there was a pool that was used as a washing tank, with three men treading steadily on the linens to agitate them. Urine was one of the alkaline substances used as detergent in the first stage of laundering; clothing was rinsed, sometimes bleached using sulfur, dried, and pressed. Slaves did the work of treading on the clothes to clean them. I was eager to leave the stink of that place behind.

I had been in Pompeii before, when it was an excavated ruin, so I had some idea of the layout of the town. If my memory was accurate, then the amphitheater should be just a few more blocks up the road and around the corner. And, as I walked around the corner, there it was. Just two years earlier, according to Demetrius, this arena had been the site of a riot, a huge fight between people from Pompeii and from the nearby town of Nuceria. Nero had created a new colony of veterans at the town of Nuceria just a few years earlier, and some of the territory that previously belonged to Pompeii had been given to Nuceria to accommodate these new residents. This, and the usual rivalry over the strength and skill of favorite athletes, fueled antagonism between the two towns. In A.D. 59, games were organized by a wealthy Pompeiian who was already out of favor with Nero; he had been expelled from the Senate in Rome. He was trying to buy popularity with the crowds so that he could regain some political standing in the town. (Pompeii's local politics were notoriously contentious; the great orator Cicero once said that it was more difficult to be elected to office in Pompeii than to become a Roman senator.)

At any rate, these games were ill fated; residents of the two towns hurled insults at each other, followed by stones. Then they drew weapons and there was serious bloodletting. In the riot that followed, several Nucerians were killed and many wounded. The Nucerians complained to Nero, who was the patron of the new colony in their town. Nero was so annoyed that he and the senate ordered the closing of the amphitheater at Pompeii for ten years, and the exile of the organizer of the ill-fated games.

And so during the past two years there had been no games in Pompeii, a lack that was the subject of great complaint. There was still a gladiator training school in the town, Demetrius said, but now the fighters went to arenas in other towns. So, as I passed outside the amphitheater, it was empty, silent. It looked like a modern football stadium, except that it was built entirely of stone, and the niches were furnished with statuary.

Across the tree lined, quiet road from the amphitheater was the Palaestra: a broad, grassy field for athletic training, surrounded by ancient plane trees and porticoes. There was no vehicular traffic at all in this part of town, so compared to the areas I had walked through earlier; it had the atmosphere of a park. The outdoor swimming pool was in use, and men were wrestling, boxing, throwing javelins and doing other kinds of athletic training on the field, scantily clad, but not entirely nude in the Greek style.

I attracted unwelcome stares from a pair of men. I realized that it was not really usual for women to walk alone. They were trying to decide who or what I was. There was not much to distinguish my clothing from that of a free person, except that my tunic was a little shorter and made of coarser material. My chopped off hair might have been that of a recent fever victim, so I hid the sorry state of my hair by draping a palla over my head like a hood; but this did not entirely disguise the oddness of my appearance.

At one time senators in Rome had discussed the possibility of requiring slaves to wear special, easily identifiable clothing. They had decided against this, because it would make slaves aware how numerous they were, and possibly encourage rebellion. And so the clothing of slaves differed from that of other people only in the quality of the fabric, and not in the basic design.

Clearly I could not be a lady: my garments were poor quality and I had no servants accompanying me. They probably thought I was a freedwoman. I understood enough about their world to know that, ironic as it might seem, I would be safer if they knew I was a slave, and thus protected by a powerful household, than if they thought I was a freedwoman who had no protector. I still had the iron ring around my finger, with the name Marcus Tullius engraved on it. I could show them that if they bothered me, and the reputation of my master and their fear of his retribution would deter them. But I didn't want to identify myself as his slave when word might already be out that there was a runaway slave from that house. I did not linger, therefore, but walked rapidly and purposefully away from them. They didn't follow, but their stares unnerved me.

By now, I would have been missed back at the Tullius household, and I wondered what they would do about my absence; I hesitated at each intersection and looked about carefully to see if there was an emissary from my master's house, searching for me. But I encountered no familiar faces. Perhaps they hadn't had time to launch a systematic search yet, or perhaps they assumed that a runaway would not be so foolish as to head for the nearest town. While the possibility of pursuit made me anxious, I wasn't overly concerned. As long as I was not taken by surprise from behind, I would have enough time to send my rescue signal if I thought capture was imminent. I would prefer to do this in a private place, in a time of my own choice, but if I had to I could make a public exit.

I returned to the Via dell'Abbondanza; I remembered that the other end of the street ended at the public forum. Once the two men were well behind me, I walked more slowly, pausing to look at the merchandise for sale in the shops. Sensible linens and wools, but also silks imported from far to the east, perhaps even China, by way of the traders in the Middle East. Spices such as cinnamon and pepper, also from far to the east. Jewelry of intricate design. I was taken with a pair of earrings that were made of clusters of pearls, but those cost far more than a slave could ever hope to have; much more than my value as a slave, in fact. The breads were available in many varieties—round loaves, but also rolls and braids, and clever or obscene shapes. The air was savory with the smell of sausages frying: I wished that I had a few coins to buy something to eat, but I had no money with me. Green herbs for cooking and medicines. Glass vials and cups of various designs and colors—clear glass with crudely painted design; fine glass, ornamented with threads of colored glass. Finely worked silver goblets with raised designs. As I neared the forum, there was a sound like a great human beehive. People swarmed around the storefront stalls buzzing.

The large rectangular forum was filled with the commerce of market day. On all four sides it was surrounded by a two-story colonnaded walkway, and buildings that housed offices, temples, and shops. In an open area near the middle, tables and wagons were arranged in lines; most had tents or awnings to provide some shade. Here was a profusion of fruits and vegetables, fresh and pickled and dried foods. Cabbages with green and purple ruffled leaves, parsnips, scarlet beets, leeks, and beans. The fish market was a marvel of engineering: An octagonal stone platform had multiple levels for the display of fresh fish; cold water spouted from the top of this fountain and ran down over the fish to keep it cool and fresh. The whole fish gleamed, silver, red, green, and brown, with whiskers and glossy dead eyes. Shellfish were abundant, oysters and mussels. A nearby butcher shop offered hams and sausages, raw and cooked. Another shop had cheeses of every size and description. Apples, figs, and dried plums were available. Nuts formed neat pyramids on another table. Olives, black and green, wrinkled and smooth. Breads and cakes.

I knew the law courts and government offices were in buildings surrounding the forum, but a mere slave such as myself could have no business there. I turned away from the forum in search of the Temple of Isis, a popular religion in this city. Like any reasonable sized Roman city, Pompeii had numerous temples dedicated to Apollo, Jupiter, Venus, and numerous other gods and goddesses. The

Isis cult had become extremely popular among Romans, particularly among women, and I was curious about it. Most of the temples did not hold regular services: instead, they had celebrations on holidays, and were open at various times for people to offer sacrifices. Most Romans seemed to offer sacrifices only when they wanted something specific; I suppose they thought it sensible to bribe Mars into a better mood, for instance, before setting off to war, or to placate Neptune before a sea voyage. Unlike many of the earlier Roman gods, who were based on a mixture of mostly Etruscan and Greek deities, Isis was an Egyptian goddess. She offered the promise of eternal life; her cult offered hope to the hopeless.

The Roman view of the gods seemed remarkably broadminded. Generally when they came in contact with other people, they allowed them to keep their own gods, and in a few cases, such as this Isis cult, they brought these foreign gods back to Rome and built temples. It seemed they always had room for another god, or a new version of a familiar god or goddess. For the most part they only suppressed religious practices they saw as excessive. For instance, when devotees of Cybele conducted wild rituals that included self-castration, laws were passed to restrict that kind of excess. As long as the new "god" did not threaten order, however, the Romans seemed to be open-minded about adding new deities to their pantheon. Some even offered respect to "the unknown god", just in case some important god had unintentionally been omitted.

I entered the courtyard of the Isis temple in time to witness a ceremony in which the officiating priest sprinkled holy water from the Nile on the altar, with delicate eastern sounding music from a flute and sistrum in the background. The burning incense perfumed the air with cinnamon and clove. The fragrance of lilies drifted through the air.

It was still a small surprise to see painted statues; I tended to think of ancient sculpture as bare white stone. When new, however, many statues had gemstones for eyes and most were brilliantly painted.

The statue of Isis resembled a stately Roman matron; the sculptor had made her tunic seem almost transparent. This version of Isis lacked the magnificent horned crown and golden wings of the Egyptian images of Isis with which I was more familiar. She had a kind face. I could see how this radiant image of gentleness and love would appeal most particularly to women and to slaves, indeed, to anyone who wanted the blessings of kindness and mercy. She reminded me of the Virgin Mary.

I had nothing to offer at the altar; others placed cakes or flowers there. Along with about a dozen other worshippers, mostly women, I knelt and lowered my head, and breathed in the fragrant, peaceful atmosphere. The statue of Isis was exquisitely carved and painted in lifelike colors. The small scale of this temple gave it a more intimate atmosphere than the monumental temples near the Forum. Isis promised her followers eternal life: a promise that people through the ages have always wanted to believe.

I enjoyed the mythological beauty of the god and goddess stories, although I shared the preference of more educated Romans for the more refined Greek versions rather than their somewhat earthier Roman counterparts. I preferred to think of Aphrodite rather than Venus, Athena rather than Minerva. The gods and goddesses represented archetypal human qualities: love, anger, jealousy, wisdom, and so many other positive and negative aspects of human nature. I didn't believe in their goddesses literally; but I valued them as symbols of distinctively feminine strengths.

It seemed as if most educated Romans did not have a literal belief in these deities, although they did invoke them sometimes in speaking. Some of them believed in "the gods" in general, without taking the stories about any one individual god too seriously. Many of them seemed to share the cynical attitude expressed by Ovid, when he wrote, "It is convenient that there should be gods, and, as it is convenient, let us pretend that there are…"

Apart from the well-known gods, they had a myriad of minor deities associated with virtually every place and every human activity; for instance, there were at least three gods associated with the doorway (one for the threshold, one for the door itself, one for the hinges). No one seemed to know all the gods; but most of them seemed willing to make room for additional gods when they heard about them.

How fortunate I was, to see the city at its best, before the earthquake that damaged it so badly, long before the eruption that buried it forever. This made the entire adventure, with all its anxieties and discomforts, seem worthwhile. I felt triumphant. Small and meek though I was, I had had a great adventure and accomplished my aims.

The shadows lengthened. I explored the town until dusk, but I didn't plan to stay after dark. In darkness, the streets would become menacing. Respectable people didn't roam the streets after dark: they stayed at home, eating long ceremonial meals by lamplight, talking with guests, laughing, and drinking. After dark only seamen and cutthroats would be out, and the vigiles could not prevent the robberies and rapes that might occur in the darker corners of the town. It was time for me to depart.

I had some misgivings about my return to modern times. I wondered whether they would keep me in quarantine in their windowless laboratory, or release me as they had promised. It had occurred to me that the promises they had made to me might be lies; and that in their concern for secrecy, they might hold me a prisoner. But I certainly couldn't stay in the past as a housemaid. It seemed to me that I had no choice but to hope that they had told me the truth.

I wanted a space that was open, but private. Knowing that the amphitheater was probably empty, I returned there; I made my way up a the stone stairway on the outside and emerged near the top of the stadiums, looking down upon a slope of row upon row of stone seats; from that vantage point, I was able to get a good view. I looked around carefully to make certain I was alone. There was no one in sight.

I used a sharp fragment of pottery to dig a hole near an entrance on the northern side of the open arena. It was a difficult task, using such a poor tool, and my fingernails were pretty much ruined by the time I had a deep enough hole. I planned to leave behind some physical evidence that would prove I had been in the past; I had scratched a few words in ink on a pottery shard: "Miranda came to A.D. 61 from A.D. 2004". I buried this about a foot below the surface, and hoped that it would remain buried even when the arena would first be excavated almost two thousand years later. I patted the earth into place carefully, spreading the excess reddish soil around, and mixing it with sand; finally I was satisfied that the burial place was undetectable. I would tell the time travel team to come here and dig it up as soon as I was back in my own time.

I looked around for the last time, and stood facing the empty oval space. I was ready. I had a few misgivings about the reception that I would have back in my own time. I didn't altogether trust these people. I wondered how long they would keep me captive out of concern for the secrecy about their project. Perhaps a few months; that would be tolerable, if inconvenient. When they sent me back to my own life with two year's pay, that would buy me some fresh options. And who knows, perhaps someday I would be able to tell my story to the world, when their work became public? I had much to look forward to. I had done well, better than I expected, and better than they had expected, I think. I had the scroll with one of Livy's missing volumes in the bag tied to my belt; that would be another piece of evidence that I had really been back in the first century. I was curious to read it myself, when time permitted.

I was ready. I palpated the signal device in my arm. In a moment the ground before me would dissolve into a blur of light, and as I walked into it, I would be caught up by the forces that would hurl me forward in time…

But nothing happened. I tried again, pushing harder, the way a person repeatedly jabs an elevator button that doesn't work. Still nothing happened.

CHAPTER 7

I became alarmed at the discovery that the signal device had failed. What could possibly be wrong? Why didn't the damned thing work? I made repeated attempts, so many that I lost count.

After half an hour of failure, I had to face the fact that the signal device did not work.

I sat on the ground and trembled. I wrapped my arms around my knees and rocked myself, as a mother would try to soothe a terrified child. I was unable to think. Nothing can convey the sense of terror and desolation I felt. My world was out of reach, perhaps forever. My identity in that other life—the work I hoped to have as a teacher, a scholar—was gone. I was stranded in a time where I didn't belong. It may seem strange, but what I longed for most intensely at that moment was my home, the studio apartment I had made cozy with flannel sheets on the bed, potted herbs on the windowsill, books arranged on the shelves, and scraps of poetry pasted on the walls. It had been my refuge from the modern world; and I had always planned to return to it.

I remembered long runs around the track at Fresh Pond, and the feel of the wind in my hair and the sun on my face. I had had the freedom to plan my day, to go where I wanted, and to work on my own projects—and now it was all gone, gone beyond reach. At that moment I wished desperately that I could be back in my own bed with the covers pulled up over my head. If only this had been a dream that I could escape by awakening. But it was not so.

And then fear swept in like a dark tide. I was a runaway slave and a thief. The scroll I had taken was valuable, and its theft would be considered a serious offense. Certainly I would be punished for these misdeeds. I would be beaten, perhaps even sold. Sometimes runaway slaves were put to death.

But I knew, even in that first moment of terror, that I had to go back to the house of Marcus Tullius. Where else could I go? If I really ran away, I would certainly be caught. My unusually pale face and shorn hair would be easy to spot; I couldn't hide. Penalties for runaway slaves were severe. I couldn't last long on the streets; I would be picked up for vagrancy or for stealing food from market stalls. If I were sold to another owner, life in a different household could easily be worse. As a thief, I could even be sold as a prostitute. No: I must go back, turn myself in, and face whatever punishment they judged appropriate. I had to hope that they would decide to keep me. I had nowhere else to go.

I made my way back to the Tullius house in the dark; I was terrified that I might be accosted, but no one bothered me. From the olive grove, I peered toward the gate; for once the gatekeeper was awake. I swore under my breath; I couldn't risk having them find the scroll in my possession. I wrapped it in my cloth sack to keep it safe from the weather; I stuffed the wrapped scroll into a crook between the branches of an olive tree, hoping that I would be able to retrieve it and replace the scroll in the master's study before its absence was noticed. The gateman was angry when I presented myself. Although he was not involved in my escape, he had already been severely scolded once the mistress had realized that I was missing. I was brought before Holconia.

"Miserable girl! Runaway! Barbarian! We have no use for someone like you. You will be sold. But first you must learn obedience. Stronnius...whip her." The vertical line between her brows was as sharp as an exclamation point, as threatening as the acid in her voice. I cowered.

They tied my hands to a pillar in the corner of the slave courtyard, and pulled the tunic down around my waist. Slaves gathered to witness this spectacle; this type of punishment was rare in this quiet household, they told me later. Stronnius lay on the blows with enthusiasm; I had spurned his attentions, and now I would pay for it. The pain was something new to me; no one had ever struck me before, and I was terrified. I screamed: there seemed to be no point in trying to stifle the cries. Holconia wanted me to suffer, and it seemed better that I should let her know that she had succeeded: perhaps she would demand more pain if I didn't cry out.

Marcus Tullius heard my cries. "Enough", he said, when he entered the courtyard. "The punishment is sufficient."

Marcus Tullius and Holconia quarreled. Holconia said: "Sell her. She's worthless—clumsy and unskilled. I don't like barbarian servants; they are so—uncouth. She has proved herself untrustworthy by running away." Why did she dislike me so? Perhaps because of the wrong she had already done me.

"No, we won't sell her. She cost very little. Alexander says she works hard. She just needs proper training. She only went out for one day."

"I don't like her. That is reason enough to sell her."

"I said no…and I am paterfamilias."

There were more harsh words between them. I became weak and dizzy, standing there with the blood trickling down my back, tears streaking my cheeks, and the cords cutting into my wrist. I fainted.

When I regained consciousness I was lying face down on my pallet in the slave quarters. Marcus Tullius himself was there, washing the wounds with vinegar. This was almost more painful than the blows from the whip, but I understood that it was necessary. He applied a poultice to the lacerations and welts on my back and wrapped me in bandages soaked with wine. His touch was gentle, but the pain was nevertheless excruciating.

"Drink this", he commanded, and I obeyed. The warm wine had a bitter flavor. "The drug will dull the pain."

"Thank you...master." I knew then that I was a slave, and would remain one; and that from now on I must please them better, or I wouldn't survive.

CHAPTER 8

I had yearned for a sense of belonging; and now I was a slave, owned by these people. The irony of my situation was not lost on me. Be careful what you wish for, because you just might get it, as they say.

Now that escape seemed impossible, my problems were far more serious. My hands looked like raw meat from scrubbing floors, and there was no chance for them to heal. The unwelcome attention from Stronnius was no longer something I could ignore. And the mistress's harsh words still rang in my ears.

"The mistress doesn't like me. She didn't like me, even before I went out without permission. I won't run away again, ever. Is there something else I've done that offends her, do you think?" I went to Demetrius in search of advice. He gave me a blend of sarcasm and sympathy.

"Clever of you to figure that out. There is a reason. The master brought back a girl from Britannia, years ago, with hair the color of wheat, like yours. The master married Holconia, as his father commanded, but they say that he had no love for her even then. And she was jealous of that little girl from the north. With reason, perhaps."

"What happened to the girl?"

"She died...of a fever, some say. Perhaps she was homesick."

"The mistress wants the master to sell me."

"It's not a good thing to be in a household where you are out of favor. Perhaps you would be better off somewhere else."

I never spoke about the scroll to anyone, not even Demetrius, who seemed to be a friend. Its absence had not yet been mentioned. I hoped it was still safe and dry outside in the olive tree. There was no rain at this time of year. I was not permitted to go outside the gate, even into the grove, so it wasn't clear to me how I would smuggle it back into the house. It worried me terribly. The bag it was wrapped in was, unfortunately, the strange cloth bag I had brought with me, and therefore easily identifiable as mine. I haunted the back gate, hoping to catch the gatekeeper sleeping, but he had apparently been warned I might try escape again; he regarded me with particular suspicion.

I was terrified of being sold. It's true that my life in the Tullius household was not ideal. Scrubbing floors was hard work. But at least here, I knew a few people, and except for the punishment I had been given for running away, the treatment was not usually cruel. I was afraid that if I were sold, I might find myself in a far worse situation.

"Demetrius, what should I do?"

"Stay out of her way. Ask Alexander to give you work in parts of the house where she never goes during the day."

"And Stronnius, he keeps trying to corner me and paw me. How can I get rid of him?"

"A woman needs a protector. If you make a liaison with someone more important in the household, you won't have a problem with Stronnius."

I looked dejected.

"Little one, I'll help you. I have an idea; let me see what I can do."

It seemed unlikely to me that he could solve my problem, but I appreciated his friendly interest. Demetrius flirted with me in a casual way from time to time, but I suspected that his real interests lay elsewhere. I think he flirted with me sometimes to keep up the appearance of a healthy interest in the opposite sex, and perhaps to cheer me up. If he had a lover, I suspected it was a man outside the household. Demetrius was discreet about his sex life.

Two days later, over the afternoon meal, Demetrius was talking to Alexander.

"Ah, yes, our poets speak eloquently of the worthlessness of women. One type is like a horse: she is beautiful, and thinks of nothing but her own appearance; she doesn't work; she preens herself." Demetrius had a talent for mimicry, and as he said this, he walked back and forth in front of Alexander, tossing his head, swinging his hips, in a way that was unmistakably Iris.

"Another is like a pig; she eats, she snorts, and she wallows." Here he did an impression of one of the laundry women, who was indeed somewhat porcine in her mannerisms. The snorting and rooting were hilarious, I must say. "And then there is the fox…vicious, untrustworthy." He creased his forehead and flexed his claws in a recognizable caricature of Holconia.

He had reduced the usually staid Alexander to helpless laughter.

I knew he was baiting me, but I couldn't resist. I knew which Greek misogynist poet he was quoting. "But there is also the bee, Demetrius."

He looked surprised at this reference. "Of course…the bee…like our Miranda here. She is modest and quiet and neat. She works hard, and is a comfort and a joy to be with. The bee makes an excellent wife, if the gods favor a man." I would have been curious to see which of my mannerisms he might caricature, but he didn't imitate me. I shook my head and left.

Later that evening I returned to the kitchen to help Cnaeus clear up the dishes.

"That Demetrius…he can talk a dog off a meat wagon," Cnaeus said.

"What has he talked you into now?" (I knew that Demetrius had convinced Cnaeus to loan him some money to bankroll his gambling exploits in town, for example.)

"Not me this time. It's Alexander. He thinks Alexander should get married."

"Can a slave marry?"

"Not a legal marriage; but someone like Alexander can take a concubine as a permanent partner, with the master's permission, of course."

That would suit Damaris very well, I thought; she seems genuinely fond of the old man, and they would be a comfort to each other. But Demetrius had something else in mind.

Three days later, Alexander told me that the master had summoned me; I must go and speak with him when he finished receiving his clients in the early morning. I waited in the hallway until the last client departed. Demetrius signaled for me to enter. I stood before the master, who was seated in the tablinum, framed by the columns and a view of the peristyle garden behind him; an impressive sight, and a handsome one. Demetrius remained nearby. I stood waiting to hear what was wanted of me. He said: "I have an offer for you to consider."

What sort of offer? I wondered, and waited for him to continue. I inclined my head to indicate that I was listening.

"Alexander thinks that you would make him a very suitable concubine for him, if we could fatten you up a little bit." This announcement stunned me, not least because I found the word 'concubine' and his jocular tone offensive. He paused as if he realized that I needed a little time to adjust to this news.

My mouth went dry and I felt a bit faint. It seemed as if the stone walls had suddenly drawn closer to me on all sides, and as if the house itself was suffocating me. I felt trapped.

The old goat! I thought. He must be at least sixty!

So that was what Demetrius had been up to.

"Concubine?"—my voice sounded faint. I knew that in their world this term was not necessarily demeaning. A relationship with a concubine was socially respectable, and it was expected to be monogamous. In spite of this knowledge, I was horrified. Not that old man! I thought. I don't want any man imposed on me, and certainly not him. I would be the slave of a slave.

I saw the corner of his mouth twitch slightly. Was he amused at my reaction, or annoyed? I wondered. Perhaps both.

It might be funny to him, but I had no choice but to take this situation quite seriously. I realized I was wringing my hands, and stopped. "I...do not wish to be a concubine", I told him. Truly I did not know whether to laugh or cry. I felt myself trembling, and wished that this might be merely a joke.

"He has been a faithful servant to my family all his life. As our steward, he is too important to us to be given his freedom, but he has a special and respected situation in this house. He has never asked for a concubine before now. If you accept, the two of you will have a room for yourselves. You should consider the advantages of this quite seriously." (He sounds like a lawyer! I thought. Of course, arguing cases in the local courts was one of the services he provided for his many clients.)

"He has saved a considerable sum of money. He would be able to leave this to you, and it would be enough for you to purchase your freedom. If you have children" (God forbid! I thought to myself) "...you might also be able to buy their freedom. He is a kind and honest man who would treat you well. As his concubine, you would have lighter work to do. Mostly you would look after him."

Was this an offer, or a command?

"Must I accept him?" My voice was shaky.

He looked at me intently. "I would not force you to accept his offer; it is best for a household if servants are content with their situations. But you should consider this seriously; perhaps you do not understand what a difference this would make in your situation."

I tried to look as if I was seriously considering this proposition. In fact, momentarily, I did consider it. I thought: He is just wants a body to keep him warm at night…as the nights grow longer. I imagine that the winters here can be cold. He would be kind, if a bit of a stiff.

And then there was the missing scroll, outside in the tree, wrapped in my bag. When it's discovered, I thought, I'm going to be in a great deal of trouble. Perhaps if I were Alexander's…concubine…they wouldn't sell me. But a slave who steals is likely to be sold, and probably as a field worker, not as a house slave. Things could get much worse for me.

But no, I thought. I can't. This is absurd.

I tried to think how to phrase my refusal. "I am thankful for the honor that Alexander shows me by making me this offer. But I do not wish to become his concubine, or anyone's". That was the best I could come up with.

"You do not wish to have time to consider this matter?"

"No, thank you."

"Is there some other man in my household that you favor?"

"No, master." I longed to escape; I was sure that if this interview went on much longer I was going to laugh, or cry, hysterically. It was simply not possible that I should face this kind of future.

"I understand. I will inform Alexander that you are not willing. You may go, then".

I bumped into Demetrius in the doorway. Eavesdropper!

As soon as we were out of the master's hearing he began to upbraid me.

"Little fool! What can you be thinking of, to turn this down! Believe me, it was hard work to convince him to ask for you. I did it because I knew you needed protection, and he was the best prospect."

I apologized; I thanked him for his interest; but, I explained, I didn't want a man.

There was no chance that this would be kept secret now. I hoped that this would not be humiliating to Alexander. He was so reserved that if he did have some special feelings for me, he would never show them. I didn't think this offer had been motivated by romantic feelings. He probably thought that I was diligent worker, quiet, and easy to get along with. But I didn't really know what he might have felt. I knew better than to assume that age makes people incapable of strong feelings.

Of course, by the same afternoon, Iris began to tease me dreadfully about my "lover". She even made some ribald and very specific observations on Alexander's possible qualifications as a bed partner. I still hoped that as the only other woman in the house near me in age, she might be my friend, but it seemed to me that she often found ways to make fun of me or talk about my relative unattractiveness, and I was beginning to find that tiresome.

Damaris never forgave me; and the cool Alexander became positively frigid. I had so few friends in this household, and now I had even fewer. I had made a mistake; I had alienated people. But what else could I have done?

*   *   *

Cnaeus sometimes had dark moods; at those times, I avoided him. Most of the time he seemed quiet and withdrawn. There were scars that looked like the result of serious burns on his arms and face. I suspected there was some tragedy in his past. I would have liked to ask, but I was still too new here, and his manner did not invite questions. I thought that perhaps when I had become more accepted as a member of the household I might find out something about his past.

Cnaeus was lord of the kitchen. On days when he prepared simple meals for the family, the kitchen was comparatively quiet. It was entirely different when he prepared elaborate meals for guests. He became a maniac; confusion and disorder reigned. At those times he reminded me of an excitable French chef. Pots boiled over, and people ran to and fro getting into each other's way as he shouted conflicting orders. Somehow organization emerged from the chaos. At the appointed time for each course, a slave left the kitchen with an artfully arranged platter. One dish he produced that looked especially nice was a circle of roasted stuffed game birds arranged in a circle on a round platter, with fresh vegetables in the middle, garnished with wedges of citron. After surviving the preparation of a special dinner like that, we were all worn out—not so much from the work as from the emotional frenzy. It was remarkable to see what elaborate dishes could be produced using such minimal equipment. Most of the cooking was done on a large brick platform in one corner of the kitchen; on top of this platform there were small charcoal fires with tripods to hold cooking pots.

I missed having hot tea, and I thought perhaps there was a way to have some. I approached Cnaeus one afternoon when he seemed to be in a better mood than usual and asked: "May I put a pot of water on the fire?"

"What for?", he growled.

"In my country we had a custom of purifying water by heating it and adding leaves to give it flavor; it is a pleasant drink." I showed him a handful of green herbs I had gathered from the garden, mostly mint.

"Why should I build up the fire now?"

"Please…if you do this, I will play you a song", I said, showing him my recorder. He looked interested.

"All right then." He added fuel to the fire and set a small pot of water on the tripod. "How hot do you want it?"

I wanted the water to boil long enough to purify it, but I could not think of the word meaning "boil", so I said: "As long as it takes for the song."

He grunted assent and settled himself on a bench. Many of the songs I knew were in the older traditional scales characteristic of folk and early music, such as Ionian and Mixolydian. I thought these older melodies might sound musical to Romans. I knew only a little about ancient music, but I was aware that their instruments did not produce the full 12 note tonic scale used in modern music. I decided to begin with songs that might sound more natural to them, and so I played him several Appalachian folk ballads. He listened, rapt with attention. I played until the water reached a rolling boil. Then I made myself some tea by steeping herbs in the hot water. This process interested him. He asked whether this was medicinal, and I said no; it was just a custom in my homeland. He said he would like to taste it, so I made a cup for him. For the first time, as we shared the tea, we sat in a silence that felt companionable instead of sullen. It began to seem possible that I might make friends with him. The tea soothed my stomach; I was still having some problems digesting the unfamiliar coarse foods.

Over the next few days, I came to understand that he thought that this tea ritual had some kind of religious significance for me. He was willing to continue the bargain: he would boil my water if I would make music.

Other slaves began to listen when I played, and soon my songs became part of the life in the slave's quarters. Alexander judged my music good enough to be of possible interest to the master, and he told me that when the master returned at the end of the week, I should play for him. Now it seemed more likely that I would be kept here; I had something worthwhile to offer.

And then one afternoon, when I came to the kitchen to make tea, Cnaeus took me aside; and without comment, he opened a wooden bin so I could see inside. There was my bag! He must have noticed it when he was outside.

"Cnaeus. Thank you, how can I ever thank you enough?"

"Say nothing, and put it back. Make sure you don't get caught."

I took his advice. Late that moonless night, I slipped into the kitchen to retrieve it and crept out into the courtyard. No lamps burned anywhere; I breathed easier when I saw that. I made my way into the study and slipped the scroll back onto the shelf approximately where it had been, and left, taking my bag with me. At least this time I was not caught.

❋   ❋   ❋

It surprised me to find how keenly I missed privacy: the very sort of disconnection I thought I had had too much of in my other life. These sociable people didn't seem to value solitude, but I found at times that I really needed it.

One afternoon I slipped away to the disused courtyard for a few private moments. I sat on the ground, and as I brooded about my situation, I scratched a few words into the dirt with a sharp stick. I had always kept a journal as an outlet for my feelings, but in this world writing materials were prohibitively expensive; still, the habit of putting feelings into words was strong, and even these temporary traces of written words gave me some comfort.

I was so absorbed in this activity that I wasn't aware at first that I was being watched. The little daughter Tullia came up so quietly that I did not hear her, and asked: "What are you writing?" I was startled. Hastily I rubbed out the few words in the dirt, and I put the stick aside, and tried to think of an explanation. The best explanation I could think of at the moment was:

"I'm writing a story". This was not well thought out, but at the moment it seemed like a reasonable thing to say. She then wanted to know:

"What's the story about?"

I thought, perhaps I can beg off and make the excuse that I speak Latin too poorly. But I pitied her. She was no one's favorite child. According to household gossip, the mistress spoiled and nagged her son and made him the focus of all her hopes and ambitions. The nurse kept Tullia neat, but didn't give her much to do. She had a fey, otherworldly quality, as if she spent much of her time lost in dreams.

I decided to tell her a story, but I kept my story simple and brief. The story I chose to tell was based on my recollection of an old folk tale known as *Stone Soup* or *Nail Broth*.

"An old soldier was traveling along a road, and it was cold. Night approached, and he wanted to be in a warm house and eat good food. What could he do? He knocked on the door of a house near the road, and an old woman answered. 'What do you want here?' she said, in an unfriendly tone. 'I want a place to sleep for the night, and some food.' 'Go away', she said. 'I don't have anything to eat here.'

'Oh', he said, 'I have something good. I have a magic stone that makes soup out of water.'

'A magic stone! That would be something. Why don't you just use your stone to make a meal?'

'I need a fire to cook the soup', said the soldier.

'Well, come in then, and let me see this stone', she said.

She put a kettle on the tripod and added a few sticks to the fire. The soldier got an ordinary looking stone out of his pocket and dropped it into the kettle. 'Now you'll see something!' he told her.

They watched the kettle boil for a few minutes. Then he said, almost as if talking to himself: 'It's too bad that we don't have any cabbage. The soup is much better if you add a little cabbage to it.'

The old woman thought, and then she went and rummaged in her storage room, and she came back with a small cabbage. They added this to the pot.

'Oh, the soup still looks watery. Some barley would make it nice and thick.'

Well, she didn't know if she had any barley. But she went and scraped in the bottom of a storage container and found one handful of barley, and they put it into the pot.

'The soup would have so much more flavor if we just had an onion to put in the pot.'

She found one onion out back in her garden and they washed it off and cut it up and put the onion into the stew.

Now the soup was beginning to smell savory and good.

'You know, if we only had a little meat, this would really be a feast fit for rich folk' was the next thing the soldier said.

Well, she remembered now that she did have a little bit of salted meat she had been saving. They added that to the pot."

I started prompting her for suggestions. "What else would be good in this soup?"

"Garlic!" She said, laughing. So we added that to the story. We continued, adding to the recipe together.

By the end of the story, the soldier and the woman sat down to a hot stew and a glass of wine, and they shared a feast. And when he left the next morning, he made her a gift of the magic stone that could make soup out of water.

Tullia loved it. "I'd like to learn how to make soup, just like that", she said. I didn't know whether I should encourage this. The old Roman tradition glorified women who kept a good house and who could spin and weave and do practical things like the women glorified in verses from Proverbs. Now Roman matrons didn't seem to do any of those domestic things. But perhaps it wouldn't do any harm to encourage this interest. So I dared to make a suggestion:

"Cnaeus might let you visit in the kitchen one day when he isn't too busy, and perhaps he'll let you stir the soup pot."

"Can we do it tomorrow?" she wanted to know.

"I'll ask him", I promised.

The poor child; she had so little to do. She had been taught basic reading and writing, but they didn't see any need for her to share in the more advanced lessons that her brother received, in rhetoric, language, history, and so on. Her personal attendant kept her clean and neatly dressed, but she seemed bored and lonely. Perhaps I could spend a little time with her. I was lonely too, and I had enjoyed this visit with her. My heart went out to her.

Tullia reminded me of a darling little mouse: bright eyed and timid. She seemed like an intelligent child, with a sweet little face, about 13 years old. In modern times, she would be an adolescent; but adolescence is a modern invention. In Roman times, she would be a child until her first menstruation, and then, overnight, she would become a young woman, considered old enough for marriage.

Cnaeus was more cooperative than I expected about the kitchen visit. I brought Tullia in, and he was touchingly gentle with her. He didn't let her handle any of the knives, but he let her concoct a soup. He cut up all the ingredients she named and let her drop them into the pot. He let her stir it too, holding her up so that she could reach it, and keeping her well out of the reach of the hot coals under the pot. He made a few adjustments to the seasonings when she wasn't watching, and the result was a quite decent stew, which was served to the family at dinner that night.

I wasn't waiting on the table that evening, but I was present, standing in the background, watching what other servants did. This observation was a preliminary step in my training. I was told that, sometime in the future, I might be permitted to act as a stand-in for one of the more experienced servants, if one was sick. Meanwhile I was pleased to be able to see the family at dinner. This was my first real chance to observe them. I stayed back in the shadows, in a corner; but I could see how excited she was.

She told her father proudly: "I made the soup, all by myself! Cnaeus helped me." This in itself was extremely unusual. She adored her father, but when he asked what she had done during the day, she rarely had anything to tell him. This time she initiated a conversation with him. He was surprised and obviously very pleased. He beckoned, and had her sit next to him on the couch, and gave her a hug.

"Did you? Tell me about it. What gave you this idea?"

Holconia was clearly displeased. "You should not be in the kitchen, Tullia. That is slave's work. You ought to be thinking about becoming a young lady; you need to pay more attention to your clothes, and not spend so much time playing childish games."

This dampened Tullia's enthusiasm. "We'll talk about it later", her father said quietly, sending her off to her own place at the dinner table with a pat on the back.

Holconia went on, speaking now to her son: "Marcus...your tutor tells me you are inattentive. You neglect your Greek and rhetoric. You have possibilities, but you need to show that you are worthy. I know you prefer athletics, but you ought to be equally concerned with your studies. We will have enough money to get you a good position; but you have to earn your place."

Marcus was about fourteen, and within the past year he had been elevated to the status of formal manhood. His tone was unpleasant. "My tutor is an idiot. He gives us exercises that have nothing to do with current politics, ridiculous hypothetical cases from a hundred years ago. It's a waste of time; we just copy the same sentences over and over. He doesn't even read what we write. He drinks too much; sometimes he even falls asleep when we recite. He beats me."

"You wouldn't have to keep copying if you would pay attention and get your lessons correct the first time. My brothers will help you advance your career, but you have to prove to them that you have the ability."

"I want to be a soldier, mother, not an administrator. Fighting is more manly than studying; I can beat cousin Rufus already, even though he's older than I am."

"Your instructor says you thrash around in anger, instead of learning to fight with skill and discipline."

Mother and son glared at each other. During this exchange, the rest of the family had remained silent. The father looked angry, but said nothing. From what I had heard in the slave quarters, this was a typical family dinner conversation. Holconia had great ambitions for her son; and she was relentless.

After the children were sent off to bed, the parents continued to talk. They behaved as if we servants were part of the furniture. Either it didn't occur to them that we listened, or they didn't care. "Marcus, you must make him do better. He is stubborn, like you, but you can make him obey. He has to work harder."

"Holconia, it may not be possible to make a politician of the boy. He doesn't have the inclination, and he may not have the ability. The person who wants this career in politics is you." Something in his face made me wonder if this was an argument that they had had many times before; he seemed weary of it.

"We need enough money to get Marcus a good position; with my family connections, even the senate is possible. We should offer a good dowry for Tullia so we can obtain a husband who will be a strong political ally for him; at least two hundred thousand sesterces might be required, as the girl has so little charm to offer. You are too conservative; you need to invest in more speculative enterprises. I can see that we will never live in Rome; but if I can't do that, I want to make sure that my son does."

The master looked tired. He spoke quietly, but with suppressed anger. "I am paterfamilias. These matters are for me to decide. I've heard what you have to say; I know what you think. I will do as I think best. Now leave the matter alone."

They said no more. After a brief period of silence, he went to his room and she to hers.

*   *   *

After the first story, Tullia began to seek me out, asking for more stories, asking me what I was doing. It was good practice for me. I would hear a more cultured accent from family members than from the slaves. I asked her to correct me when I made mistakes in pro- nunciation—I still made many mistakes. It seemed to make her feel useful to do that.

In the evenings my flute songs became a regular routine in the slave quarters. I gave my songs Latin names so that they could request their favorite ones over and over. I knew that by making music and telling stories, I called attention to myself, and I wasn't certain that was safe. But I couldn't continue to be as passive as I was the first few days, or I would never do anything here except scrub floors. I wouldn't last long if I had to do such hard work all the time. I was tired of being a person of no value, and of doing the most menial work in the house. Perhaps becoming a storyteller would provide me with a more comfortable identity. Being able to amuse and educate would increase my value as a member of the household. I enjoyed having an appreciative audience. Like many apprentice teachers, I had discovered that the lure of a captive audience was one of the things that made me love to teach. If I was going to survive here, I needed to become a part of their world.

I tried not to do anything they would consider misbehavior. However, once in a while, when I couldn't sleep, I walked in the peristyle garden. On nights when the moon was full and the sky was flecked with stars, everything in the garden was touched with silver light, and it was unearthly beautiful. The columns reflected the light and the white flowers glowed in the dark, and they seemed to give off a more potent perfume in the night air. Often I saw a lamp burning in the master's private study. I wondered why he was up so late. Perhaps he was a reader, I thought. Was he also a lover of stories, of poetry?

CHAPTER 9

There were no secrets in that household. There was sexual activity among the slaves, although not of the flagrant public sort that historians and novelists like to dwell on in their accounts of orgies at the Imperial Court. Our master was an old fashioned Roman who preferred the more wholesome values that were supposed to have been dominant during the Republican period (although, honestly, I don't think there ever was a time when people were that virtuous). Accordingly, members of his household were expected to behave themselves decorously, particularly in public. Relationships among slaves were not forbidden, but we were expected to be discreet. Iris spurned the male servants; she was the master's favorite. Otherwise, there were many liaisons. Damaris sometimes went off to Alexander's quarters—although I confess I found it impossible to imagine the plump and arthritic Damaris, and the dignified and chilly Alexander, in passionate embrace.

Cnaeus sometimes lured one of the housemaids into his quarters with the promise of choice food tidbits, but he accepted my refusals in a good-natured way. Once he offered me a revolting bit of boiled eel; I'm sure he thought it a rare delicacy, but it was no temptation for me. If he had discovered my fondness for roasted chicken, I might have been more seriously tempted. I tried to learn to like unfamiliar foods, but I had always been a fussy eater; and my parents spoiled me. I think I was twelve years old before I knew there was anything but white meat on a chicken. My sister used to call us "the Presbyterian Princesses". Well, I was no princess now; I had better learn to adapt.

Only Demetrius and I remained outside this pairing off. I think Demetrius preferred men—perhaps even one particular man—but old fashioned conservative Romans disapproved of homosexuality, so he was careful to provide no clues about his love life, except for an occasional show of flirtation with me or another housemaid; and I think these were red herrings. One evening a week, he went into the town to drink and gamble in the wine shops—he always cleared a nice profit on these evenings. Apparently he had become more skillful at concealing his cheating. Cnaeus often warned him that he would get into trouble, but Demetrius only laughed, and said: "I only shear them; I don't skin them"; and continued to rack up winnings that he banked with Alexander.

He soaked up the local gossip on these outings, and kept our household well informed; this was not only entertaining to us, but also sometimes quite useful to the master in his business dealings, and so (unlike me, confined to the house in disgrace), he was allowed the freedom to come and go as he wished. Demetrius needed little sleep, and was fresh and alert early in the morning even after a late night in the taverns. I suspect he was as popular an entertainer in town as he was in our own kitchen, for he had a genius for mimicry, and recitation of epic poems, ribald songs, and comical bits of plays.

After a while, I noticed that there were only two people in the household whose behaviors he did not mock—or at least, I never saw it. I was one. Just as well: I was easily hurt, and probably would have been distressed to see a broad caricature of some foolish mannerism I wasn't aware I had; and my accent, I guess, was too easy a target for ridicule to interest such an inventive performer. The other person he never imitated was Marcus Tullius.

Demetrius had his role in the household: joker, gossip, and general authority on Greek and Roman culture. I had no clear role, at first, and no clear idea how to defend myself from unwanted attention. At first there was some pestering, in spite of my gaunt appearance and short hair. Demetrius seemed to think my androgynous appearance attractive. At dinner one evening he sat very close to me, and pressed his thigh against mine; I moved away. He moved close again, and snaked his hand around me; I jerked myself out of his grasp. I was still quite annoyed at his interference in my affairs.

"Find yourself a nice boy!" I said.

Cnaeus found this hilarious; he roared with laughter. Demetrius glowered. And later, privately, he said to me:

"Keep your virtue, but use your head, you little ox. If it appears to others that we are partners, it may discourage some of these men you have a problem with."

After that, we flirted with each other in public and sometimes went off alone together—just to talk. Most people in the household assumed that we were lovers. But we were friends, and that friendship was the one thing that kept me sane in those early months; when I fell into despair over the loss of my past life, Demetrius joked and teased, or gave me new tidbits of household gossip to think about, and these distracted me from my pain. I came to understand that he felt some private pain as well, although I had no idea what it was.

In spite of my pretense of sexual involvement with Demetrius, Stronnius continued to make obnoxious advances from time to time, but I was careful never to be alone with him. There were other willing women, and I hoped that it was not worth his while to risk trouble. Slaves who made trouble in the household were sometimes sold, or sent away, I knew. These slaves regarded banishment from such a good household as a great threat. And I feared being sold. My position in this household wasn't good: I was the least skilled and least valued among the house servants. For now at least, all the dirtiest, hardest work fell to me. But I knew that I could find myself in a far worse situation somewhere else.

Demetrius began to suspect that I might be rather intelligent, and he teased me about it. He liked to say, perhaps anticipating the cynical views of Juvenal and Martial: "A learned woman with opinions is a great curse to mankind". He salted his speech liberally with lines from Homer and Aristotle and other great writers of antiquity. His usual way of winning an argument was to produce a relevant quote (or sometimes an irrelevant one!) from an indisputable authority. "I have never met a woman who was half as intelligent as I am", he liked to boast, matter of factly. This made me fume; I tried to think of some way to show him up. I had a large arsenal of quotations to draw upon myself, but mine weren't associated with authorities known to him, so they didn't have the same weight.

And so, in addition to ransacking my memory for stories and songs for Tullia, I also lay awake at night trying to think of witty put-downs for Demetrius. Perhaps I wouldn't win this war of words, but I was determined to put up a good fight.

Because it seemed likely that I was stuck in this household for the rest of my life, I tried to make friends with everyone. I was particularly curious about Iris; she was the woman nearest to my age, and I hoped we could be friends. I wondered how she felt about being the master's bed partner. And so I started a conversation with her one evening.

"Iris, when you leave the slave quarters in the evening, where do you go?" (I already knew the answer to this from household gossip, but it seemed to be a tactful way of opening up the subject without presuming that I knew her private business.)

"To the master's bed; I thought everyone knew that."

I wanted to know how she felt about this arrangement, but I wasn't sure how to frame the question. "Is it something that you like to do?"

"It's all right. He's kind, and I get extra money."

"Is there some other man you like?"

She looked flustered at that question, and denied it, but the way in which she denied it made me wonder whether I had hit upon a secret.

"Have you been his bed partner for a long time?"

"Ever since Tullia was born. The mistress made it clear that she didn't want any more children; she hasn't bedded with the master since then. I was almost fourteen, and she sent me to him; he was my first man."

"Do you love him?"

"Who?"

"The master, I mean."

"Oh! No. I had foolish ideas that something might happen to the mistress and that he might take me as his concubine. That sometimes happens. Not often. After a while I realized it was foolish to think of such things. He enjoys me, that's all. I don't have any choice, so I might as well do what is expected. He gives me money. Someday perhaps I'll have enough money to buy my freedom, and maybe then I can think about love. But I'll be so old…" her voice drifted off. We were sitting on the edge of the rectangular courtyard pool, and she was combing out her hair. She looked sideways at her beautiful reflection, and smiled in pleasure at the sight of her own prettiness.

I was always ordinary looking, and so I decided early in life that my face would not be my fortune. I knew I had to cultivate other qualities: and so I read, I studied, I wrote. In spite of that, I couldn't help feeling a stab of envy and a sense of inferiority when I saw a really lovely woman. I wished that I too could be beautiful.

I envied Iris her beauty, and yet I pitied her. In this situation, beauty was a danger to a slave. It made a slave the object of lust, often unwanted. I was relatively safe from that during my first few weeks. I looked forlorn with my ragged fringe of short hair and my skinny body. Even when I looked my best, I knew, I would never draw the kind of admiring looks that Iris always attracted.

Was I jealous of the attention the master paid to her? Yes, in a way. I found him attractive, although I resisted that feeling. I would have liked to have him notice me. However, I didn't want to be summoned for a casual sexual encounter, with no choice in the matter and no consideration for my feelings. That was the only connection possible between us. And so I told myself that I had better suppress these feelings. In any case, he wasn't likely to want me when he had Iris's beauty and the pick of the woman in the household.

❧   ❧   ❧

One evening when he was not occupied with entertaining visitors, the master summoned me for an interview. Now that I had been under observation for a while, and had not made any further attempts at escape, they had decided that I was sufficiently responsible to be trained as a house servant. Evidently he had spoken with Tullia about the stories, and with other servants about my music. Now he wanted to assess my abilities himself. I went to his private study; he was seated behind a table. I stood quietly waiting to be noticed.

"Tullia says she saw you writing. Is that so?" the master asked, lawyer-like in his manner.

"Yes, master."

"Show me." He presented me with a wax tablet and stylus. I wasn't accustomed to these, but I was able to scratch a few words in Latin that were recognizable as writing even though my script was not in the same style as theirs.

The master began a more systematic interrogation.

"Where do you come from? How did you learn to write?"

"I learned to write in my father's house when I was young."

"Tell me more."

I repeated the rest of the story I had told previously about my background. I came from a very distant land far across the sea, I told him. I said that among my people, storytelling was greatly valued, and that I learned many stories from books, and from storytellers in my father's household. I had also learned some music. I repeated the lie that had become so familiar to me that by now it almost seemed true: that I had become a priestess. It seemed to me that this had been true, metaphorically, if one thought of Harvard as a temple of knowledge. Perhaps this metaphor was as close to the truth about my situation in my own world as I could get without attempting impossible explanations.

"You have some education. What things have you learned? How do you know Latin, if your country is so far from Rome that we haven't ever heard of it?"

I told him that occasionally, people and even scrolls had come to us through trade or shipwrecks, and that the prevailing winds and tides often sent ships from the Roman empire to our shores, but that we rarely sent ships out to sea ourselves. I told him that we had treasured and preserved this information and that my work had involved learning Latin. This apparently seemed plausible to him.

He wanted to know where my country was. I tried to convince him that when I had left, all had been destroyed; and that I had no way of knowing how to return, and only the vaguest idea of the route we had taken across the sea. I certainly didn't want him to launch any trading expeditions in search of my homeland. Fortunately he didn't pursue this issue.

"Do you know many stories? Many songs?"

I have always been a voracious reader, and I have a retentive memory. I had two thousand years of literature that was yet to come to draw upon, I thought. I could spin stories out of that material, enough to last a lifetime here, if need be. And songs too.

He asked me to tell him a story. I suppose he wanted to have some idea what kinds of ideas his daughter was being exposed to in these stories. Plato thought that the stories children heard had a great effect on their moral development; modern psychologists speak of the healing power of stories. I believe that the stories we hear, and the stories we tell to ourselves, are important in shaping the people we become. I thought for a moment: what would be most appropriate? I decided to tell him a traditional British story called *Dick Whittington's Cat*.

In this story, a small boy called Dick (or "Decius" in this rendition), left his home in the rural provinces and made his way to the city. He became a servant in the household of a wealthy man. (My intent, of course, was to flatter my master by speaking of a benevolent master in the story; later it occurred to me that this story was rife with achievement imagery.) He worked very hard. He fell in love with the master's daughter, but it was impossible for him to approach her because he was only a servant. He earned his freedom, but continued to work as a servant.

The master was a merchant, and he planned to send a ship to Africa. He offered each servant in his household a chance to send some trade goods on the ship. The boy had nothing to send except for the cat that he had adopted to kill the mice in his sleeping cubicle. He sent his cat on the ship. All the other people in the household thought this a very silly thing to send, naturally.

But it turned out that this was a great piece of luck, for the ship went to an African country where cats were entirely unknown—and this country was overrun with mice and rats. The ship's captain visited the palace of the king and queen, and saw that the banquet hall was infested with these mice. He fetched the cat, and it quickly cleared the banquet hall of mice. The king and queen were delighted, and paid more for the cat than for all the rest of the ship's cargo.

When the ship's captain returned, then, Decius became a rich man. He set up his own household and became a wealthy merchant. He was then able to marry his former master's daughter and they lived "happily ever after".

For a second time, I saw this serious and dignified man smile, just as he had when his daughter had been so excited to share her news about her accomplishments in the kitchen. The smile illuminated his face and softened it. He seemed amused and pleased.

Next he asked about my music. Demetrius had told him that I played songs on my unusual flute. I had been told to bring my recorder; and so I played a French folk tune from the Middle Ages. Early music might please them with its elegance and simplicity, I thought. "It's nothing like any music I've ever heard, but it's very pleasant", he responded.

The master was pleased. A slave who could tell stories and make music would ordinarily have been costly, but he had discovered this talent in a housemaid. He decided that I should continue to tell his daughter stories, but in the evenings, so that he could also listen. It may have occurred to him that, even though the first few stories seemed morally sound to him, some of my other stories might be inappropriate for his daughter to hear, or even subversive of wholesome Roman values. Or perhaps he was simply curious.

By now I understood that having the master's ear was the key to my future survival in this household. If the men thought I was important to the master, they wouldn't bother me. I had better become important to him, I decided.

CHAPTER 10

Gradually I spent more time performing songs and stories, and less time doing menial cleaning chores. This was a welcome change. It increased my status in the slave quarters, for now even the Greeks treated me with more respect.

In the evenings I went to the master's private study to tell stories. He and Tullia reclined together on a couch, I seated myself on the floor, and I wove tales from memory, tailoring them to make sense to my audience. One evening after Tullia left, he indicated that I should stay, as he wanted to ask me some questions. He wanted to know more about my country, he said. He added, as a sort of after thought, that I looked very much like the women he had seen in Germania and Britannia. Well, I know I have a German looking face; many of my ancestors were German, in fact. But I knew that the Romans regarded the people of upper Germania as savages, and I had become impatient with this prejudice. My response to this made him laugh.

"I am not a Roman. But I am not a barbarian."

He controlled his amusement and put on a straight face. "I did not say that you were a barbarian. Tell me more about your country."

"What do you want to know, master?" I parried. If I spoke too freely, I feared I would begin to reveal more than I wanted.

"How far to the west was it?"

"I don't know; I was on a ship for many days."

He sat back and looked thoughtful for a moment. Then he selected a scroll from one of the shelves beside him and unrolled it on the table. He beckoned for me to step closer and look. "Do you understand what a map is?"

I looked at his map with interest. The outlines of most of Europe, although not identical to those on a modern map, were recognizable to me. It was less detailed than the maps that would later be drawn by Ptolemy, but the outlines were recognizable. The boot shaped Italian peninsula was in the center (each civilization constructs its world map so that it is located in the middle, it seems.) The outer edges more or less corresponded to the extent of the Roman Empire at that time. Of course, beyond the extent of the Roman Empire, there were few details. Possibly that peninsula on the eastern end of the map was meant to represent India, I thought. He interrupted my thoughts:

"Do you understand? What is this?" he said, pointing to the Mediterranean.

I hesitated a moment. I thought: should I play the fool? Or should I impress him with what I know? It might be safer to pretend ignorance. The more extensive my knowledge, the more difficult it will be to explain my background, the more questions it might raise in his mind. A non-Roman would not be expected to know much about geography. On the other hand, I thought, I really am tired of being dismissed as stupid because I am a slave, a woman, and a barbarian. I'm tired of scrubbing floors. If I impress him as intelligent, perhaps he will give me better work to do. And so I gave in to the temptation to show off.

"This is the sea that you call Mare Nostrum", I replied. He quizzed me further, and although the names I gave for the countries were not always perfectly consistent with first century Roman usage, it became clear to him that I understood his map. He pointed to Gibraltar. "The Pillars of Hercules", I said.

"What is this sea?" He asked.

"My people called it the Atlantic."

"Show me where your country is."

"It is not on this map."

"In what direction, then."

I pointed to a place on the table, several inches beyond the western edge of his map, which ended in the eastern Atlantic. That startled him.

"And what was the name of your homeland?"

"America." I had decided early on to use the real name of my country; one name was as good as another, and the truth was easier to remember.

He looked thoughtful. This was far beyond the edges of the world that his people knew.

"Tell me about your country and your life before you came here."

"What kinds of things do you want to know?"

He smiled a little. "Everything."

I did not want to lead him to think that I came from some wonderful place that their merchants would want to seek out. I couldn't tell him that my country would not exist for many hundreds of years. In fact I wanted to convince him that there was nothing there now. I tried to stick to my cover story.

"My home was destroyed by earthquakes and fire. A few of us escaped on a ship." However, this did not end the questions; he still wanted to know about my country, my background, and my education. He wanted to know all kinds of things about this country with the strange name. I wanted to end this line of questioning somehow, perhaps by indicating that there was really nothing to talk about.

He continued questioning. It felt like a cross-examination, although not a hostile one. He sent for wine. I feared he might be settling in for a long evening of questions. He indicated that I could sit on the cushion on the floor. To my surprise, when he poured out a goblet of wine for himself, he poured one for me as well. He handed it to me. I was surprised, and thanked him with appropriate humility. I thought of a Roman proverb: "In vino veritas" ("In words spoken under the influence of wine, there is truth").

Aha, I thought. He thinks he can loosen my tongue with wine. Well, that won't work. I thought I had a steady head and enough sense to resist this temptation.

I was surprised at the taste of this wine: it was nothing like the vinegar we had been given in the kitchen. He noticed my reaction, and laughed pleasantly, explaining that this was one of the better wines produced in Falernia. It tasted of fruit, flowers, and sunshine. It was, in fact, irresistible; and he had added less water to it than usual, so it was also strong. I thought I could enjoy this without losing my head. Whether it was a bribe, or a drug, it was too good to pass up.

That was a mistake. I hadn't had anything this strong to drink in a long time, and it went directly to my head. He kept my goblet refilled, so that I quickly lost track of how much wine I had consumed. I'm quite sure this was intentional. He questioned me about inconsequential things to put me at ease. Under the influence of his wine, I began to relax. This seemed harmless enough, but I was aware (in an increasingly fuzzy way) that he was luring me into a trap. I admired his cleverness, but tried to remain wary.

He continued questioning me persistently, returning to questions about my cultural background. I tried to plead fatigue, hoping he would let me go, but he said: "I want clear answers to my questions. I am prepared to keep questioning you all through the night, if necessary, to get them." At this point, I was not thinking very clearly. I thought that if I could get him to believe that my country no longer existed, he might lose interest. At the same time I wanted him to think that I had come from a civilized place. I needed to explain how I knew so many songs and stories, and so a civilization that spent its last days telling stories about past glories seemed like a plausible background.

And so I said: "My country is so far that no ship could reach it. Even if it were possible to return to the place, there would be nothing there, nothing of the civilization that I remember. The stories and songs I know are all that remains." This, again, was literally correct, although admittedly deceptive. He asked me again: "What happened to your country?"

I repeated my earlier story: "Destruction by earthquakes, fires, and floods."

At this point, he drew an interesting conclusion. He reflected on the location of my country, far beyond the Pillars of Hercules, in an ocean that I called the Atlantic, and the few things I had told him about its great culture and its destruction. He said a single word, aloud, but softly, as if speaking to himself, in a questioning tone.

"Atlantis…" He got down another scroll, written in Greek, and spread it out on the table and searched for the reference he wanted. And he found it, and read. Then he started questioning me along these lines. It became apparent that he thought my lost civilization was, perhaps, connected with Atlantis, in spite of the fact that Plato had described Atlantis as having been destroyed thousands of years in the past. From his questions I deduced that he was looking at Plato's account.

It became clear to me that he had an idea that my 'America' might be a colony of people who had fled westward from Atlantis when it sank into the Atlantic Ocean. I wasn't sure whether to deny this. It seemed to me, as I gradually became fuzzier under the influence of that excellent wine, that I should not dispute this association too strongly. He was starting to think I might be a descendant of a highly developed civilization that was connected with Atlantis. That idea was not too far from the truth I could not explain in any plausible way: that I had come from a highly advanced technological society that shared some of his cultural heritage. So I admitted that I, too, had heard stories of Atlantis.

After a little more prompting, I told him what I remembered of Plato's version of the myth of a great island called Atlantis many generations before. "Many generations in the past, Atlantis was a great civilization of wealth, knowledge, and wisdom. It flourished for centuries. There were great centers of learning, wonderful buildings and palaces, extensive trade routes. Poseidon was the father and protector of the Atlanteans. However, people lost their reverence for the gods, and greed and evil became widespread. The gods were displeased. Prophets warned that destruction was coming. Many people fled, taking with them the memories and legends of this past greatness. Some fled to the east, others to the west. This was many generations ago; we do not have any idea how many years in the past this great migration took place."

I was pleased with myself. Any one sentence in this story was not, in the literal sense, a false claim about my own origins. I had simply mixed together the Atlantis myth with the name of my own country, in order to give him the kind of exotic background that might make me valuable and interesting to him.

It worked. Too well, in fact.

He was, in fact, quite excited about this story, and he cross-examined me on details. I had read translations of Plato's *Timaeus* and the *Crito*, and I knew the version of the Atlantis myth that he was probably familiar with, and kept my answers to his questions more or less consistent with these accounts by Plato. Yes, I said, in answer to his open ended questions: Atlantis had temples of gold and silver and red; and it was ringed with great circular canals. There was supposed to have been diverse plant and animal life, not seen elsewhere; the greatest king was named "Atlas". I was impressed, actually, that he knew enough about the danger of leading questions to ask me about these things without letting me know what answers he expected. Of course, like many upper class Roman men, he acted as an advocate in the courts quite often, so he knew something about the problems of obtaining evidence from a witness.

He showed me the scroll. "Can you read this?"

"Yes." The ability to read and speak Greek was one of the main accomplishments that distinguished more educated and aristocratic Romans from their less educated peers; upper class Romans usually learned Greek, just as the educated Europeans of a later age knew French.

He returned to another aspect of my cover story.

"You said you were a priestess…of knowledge. What kinds of knowledge?" I sighed, thinking, he is giving me more than enough rope to hang myself. I explained that I had been given languages to study, using texts that had been obtained third or fourth hand from traders, and also stories and songs. Nothing else in my modern education would be of much use here, as far as I could think. This story seemed to make sense to him.

"Did you take a vow of virginity?".

"I was chaste", I replied. Well, that happened to be more or less the truth. During my last years of graduate school I had been celibate—partly because work consumed all my time, but mostly because I hadn't found anyone to love and trust. This background just might be useful, I thought. The Romans were fairly open-minded about new gods. If they had any respect for my 'gods', particularly for the great and powerful Poseidon who was supposed to have created and destroyed Atlantis, and whom I would claim as my god, if questioned, then perhaps I would not be molested.

At first I didn't dispute the theory he seemed to have developed—that my people were descendants of Atlantis. This cultural background would account for my extensive knowledge of stories and myths that sometimes overlapped with theirs and sometimes did not, for this story implied a shared cultural background between our civilizations many generations in the past. Perhaps both my country and theirs had both been populated or visited by refugees from lost Atlantis.

It had occurred to me by now that I should warn him about the major earthquake that I knew would happen during the upcoming winter. The Atlantis story and my fortuitous choice of "priestess" as my former occupation might give credibility to my claims that I could foretell the future, particularly for Poseidon-ruled events such as earthquakes. I congratulated myself on my cleverness.

However, as he developed enthusiasm for this story, I began to worry that I had been foolish to associate myself with this legend. If he told other people about this, it would attract more attention and questions. I could end up being dangerously conspicuous. At this point I began to deny the association. I tried to clear up his misconception, saying that Atlantis was only a remembered legend and that most people in my country did not really believe that we had any connection with Atlantis. This delayed denial only seemed to strengthen his belief that he had hit upon a truth that I was unwilling to reveal. Now he attributed my unwillingness to talk about my background to a fear of being conspicuous as a particularly exotic species of foreigner.

Fortunately, after some thought, he decided that he did not want to make this matter public. He suggested that it would be better to say I was from Germania. That background would account for my fair hair and complexion, at least. It seemed to me that he looked at me now with greater interest than before.

"You have eyes the color of the sea. Perhaps you really are a daughter of Poseidon!" he said. He seemed to enjoy this mystery about my past. If he were more pragmatic, less romantic, he might have sold me to the highest bidder as an exotic specimen. It seemed strange to me that he could believe this myth about my past. Like many Romans, he could be so cynical, and yet so gullible; so practical and sensible about managing things, yet so superstitious. He believed this partly because it pleased him to believe it, and because it seemed to explain the mystery.

I felt badly about my lies, although I rationalized that the circumstances required me to tell him something, and I could not tell him the truth. Even if I had been able to explain that I was a time traveler in a manner that he could understand, and even if I could have persuaded him to believe this incredible story, this explanation would have raised more problems and questions than I could ever deal with. This Atlantis story was an account of my past that seemed to make sense to him, and could be incorporated into what he already thought he knew about the world. I couldn't possibly explain that I came from two thousand years in the future.

The following morning, when the warm intoxication of the wine was gone, I winced to remember the magnitude of the lies I had somehow led him to believe. However, now I was stuck with this story. For the moment, he did not press for more information.

Now that my work responsibilities had been established, and my work took me all around the house, I was able to get a reasonably clear idea of the household routine. We all rose at dawn to take advantage of the daylight hours. Personal attendants helped family members wash and dress and eat a light breakfast, usually in their sleeping cubicles. The master's barber shaved him; Alexander briefed him on household matters. During the early morning the master received clients in the atrium, and Demetrius accompanied him, taking notes and keeping records.

The mistress did not have much to do except amuse herself, it seemed. She seemed to delight in tormenting Iris about her hair and makeup. Holconia's coloring was handsome, dark hair and olive complexion; but she was determined to have fashionably pale skin. Iris spent hours every morning applying pasty cosmetics (almost certainly containing lead, I noted, with malice) to whiten her skin, and other unguents to redden her lips and outline her eyes. The effect was starkly artificial, something like a geisha. Her hair was usually elaborately arranged in high rolls of curls that required an hour or more with the curling iron. The mistress was most particular about her choice of clothing and jewelry. Heavy perfumes completed the effect. It often required two hours or more for her to finish her morning toilette.

One day Iris accidentally tore the fragile golden beaded hairnet while she was dressing the mistress's hair. Holconia struck her with a heated curling iron, branding her cheek with a scarlet mark. We tried to comfort her, and to treat the burn with cool water and ointments, but Iris was distraught. I was thankful I didn't have to wait on 'her majesty': I feared her temper and her violent jealousy.

I was struck again by the similarity in appearance between Iris and the mistress. I found myself wondering whether perhaps Iris might be the mistress's half sister. She had been born in the same household; it was quite possible that they had the same father.

During midday, the master went out to do business and to socialize at the public baths. The mistress often went out to visit friends, to socialize at the public baths, or to shop. She liked to play knucklebones for small stakes and to gossip.

In late morning after the master had left, Demetrius escorted Marcus junior to the house of his tutor in town. Some days the son accompanied his father on business rounds, as a sort of apprenticeship.

As soon as the family members had gone out, we did routine house cleaning. Like all slaves, I learned to look busier than I really was. The work was not that time consuming. I could sometimes find an hour to be alone, to think, even to write a little; now that my writing was known, I was able to beg some scraps of old correspondence from Demetrius that were usable. Because I had run away, I was still not permitted to go outside the house by myself. My world was limited to the space contained within the walls, and I began to find this life quite confining.

Around midday in the hot summer season, most upper class Romans had a bath (either at home or at the public baths), a massage, and a siesta. During their nap we usually had time off too. We were expected to keep ourselves clean; we used the family bath facilities at times when they were not in use by the family.

If the family was entertaining guests, or if it were a holiday or festival day, the main mean or "cena" became a major event in the household. Much of our work consisted of preparations for this meal. When there was a company dinner, I was sometimes recruited by the cook to help with preparations. If it was just a family meal, he did the preparations himself, as they did not have elaborate food at ordinary meals. For the dinner parties, though, Cnaeus made a much greater production of the cooking. Perhaps it was just because I didn't share their liking for garlic and garum, but I thought he was an abominable cook. Even his fancier dishes didn't smell appetizing, although they were artfully presented. The Romans seemed to favor strong smells; plates were sometimes rubbed with a smelly herb called asafetida; its acrid odor was reminiscent of stale gym socks and Limburger cheese. Many dishes had odd combinations of flavor, sweet and sour, honey and vinegar; this served to mask the odors of meats that were, sometimes, not quite fresh.

There were many aspects of Roman culture that I found admirable: their genius for law and organization, their cleverness in engineering, the peace that they brought to the world for a time. But their food was something I never learned to like.

Late afternoon or early evening was when we served the main meal or cena—some days just to the family, other days to company. I loved to be able to eavesdrop on conversations at these meals. Really, that's why I had come: to get an inside view.

The cena was presented one course at a time, somewhat like a Chinese banquet. The diners reclined on three couches arranged in a U shape around one small table, with up to three diners on each couch (for this reason, a dining room was called a triclinium). Our family had two dining rooms: an enclosed indoor triclinium with three wood framed couches, for winter or inclement weather; and an outdoor triclinium that was open to the peristyle garden. It had stone platforms in place of dining couches; these were padded with cushions and draped with linens to make them comfortable.

Each dish was presented as a separate course; all of the diners used their fingers to take tidbits from this shared platter. Spoons were used for foods that couldn't be eaten with the fingers. The diners wiped their hands on cloth napkins. (They brought their own napkins, and sometimes used these to wrap up choice bits of leftover food to take home.) We slaves stood nearby with basins of water to wash and dry the diners' hands repeatedly between courses. Unwanted or inedible bits of food, fruit pits or fish bones, were let fall on the floor. It would have been poor manners to put such things back on the shared platter.

Sometimes there was entertainment: a slave might read or recite poetry, or play music. Sometimes they just talked. They talked at great length about people's health. Wealthy Romans tended to be great hypochondriacs, I concluded, and easy prey for quacks with incredible remedies. They gossiped about people in the town, and events in the city of Rome. They told stories and jokes; they argued. In a world without television, conversational skill was highly valued.

After cena, the family and guests sometimes continued to talk and drink for hours; the passage of time was leisurely. There were no clocks; there was no urgency to get on to the next activity. In the law courts, water clocks were sometimes used to limit the amount of time someone might speak, but for the most part, time telling was approximate. Morning was for work or errands, but afternoon and evening were for leisure.

The morning after a family dinner party we cleaned up. Because they threw scraps of uneaten food on the floor, there was always a greasy mess to clean up. We usually had some free time after the cleaning was done, and often a break during the hottest hours of midday.

Of course, we slaves didn't get to eat the meat dishes that were prepared for company. I was told that we would get special things to eat on some festival days or holidays, but usually we ate bean soup, wheat gruel, coarse bread, cheese, simple vegetable dishes, olives, and our daily measure of watered sour wine (actually more like vinegar than wine). There was always garum to add some flavor to these bland dishes. I wouldn't have wanted most of the exotic things that appeared on the table at more formal banquets, such as dormice, brains, or eels. The mostly vegetarian victuals in the slave quarter didn't whet my appetite with appealing flavors and aromas, but at least they weren't disgusting, only dull.

Garum was a popular cooking ingredient and table condiment made by adding salt and spices to fish entrails and allowing the mixture to ferment—or rot. Nearly every dish contained garum, as basic to the Roman kitchen as ketchup to modern American fast food, or soy sauce to Asian cooking (a little like Worcestershire sauce). Like the wine, it came in better and worse grades. It had a strong taste and gamy smell I was never able to learn to like. I had seen a Roman recipe for "correcting" garum that had "gone bad". Gone bad? I wasn't sure how they could tell...Garum was one of Pompeii's major exports, and our master had a financial interest in production of garum, and so of course we used the garum his own workshops had produced.

Life settled into a comfortable pattern. I became more accustomed to the coarse food, and my hands began to toughen up from the housework. I reviewed my memories of stories and songs, ransacking the storehouses of memory in search of things that would be suitable my small audience. Some stories, mostly fairy tales, were easy to translate. Others simply could not be made to make sense. I began to earn respect for my storytelling, and it was good practice for me, as my Latin gradually improved with practice. After a few months, my speech sounded almost civilized, according to Demetrius.

From time to time I palpated the place on my arm where I could feel the hardness of the embedded signal device. It never worked. As time went by I thought less about my previous life, which seemed lost to me forever.

CHAPTER 11

Iris had a pink flush in her cheeks and an exalted expression on her face. I ventured a guess. "Iris, you look like a woman in love," I said.

She was in an unusually forthcoming mood. "It's true, I am. Promise you won't tell?"

"Have you been with some man you love, Iris?"

"Yes. You must not tell. No one in the house knows. The master told me not to go with other men, but as long as he doesn't know, well, no matter."

"Who is he, will you tell me?"

"I won't say his name…he's a freedman, he has a shop. He says when we have saved enough money we'll buy my freedom, and we'll marry then. I won't have to comb that bitch's hair ever again!"

I envied Iris this secret love, and felt sorry for her at the same time. It occurred to me to wonder whether her lover might be stringing her along with false promises. I hoped not. I also hoped that if, or when, this secret became known, she would not be harshly punished. She had a childlike selfishness that charmed me, and at times she was pleasant company. We had little in common except for dislike of Holconia; but I liked her, and wished her well, and feared that she was going to get herself into trouble with her small deceptions.

❀   ❀   ❀

Cnaeus became accustomed to my visits to the kitchen. It seemed to me that his outwardly forbidding manner was a shell he had put on to shield some inner hurt. He and Demetrius had an ongoing war of words, but he became friendlier toward me, even though I didn't share his dislike for Demetrius. My odd little ceremony of boiling water and adding leaves of herbs had amused him at first, as a barbarian oddity. However, he judged this beverage to be pleasantly refreshing. One morning we were sharing a cup of tea in the kitchen, and I finally asked a question that had been in the back of my mind ever since I had arrived.

"Cnaeus, how did you come to be a slave in this house? People say that you were free born."

He blew on his tea to cool it. The lines on his face did not change; they seemed permanently set into a pattern of sorrow. The tone of his voice dropped, and his eyes were outwardly directed at the floor, but seemed to be focused inward into his own memories. "I rented a thermopolium in a good location, at the corner across from the Stabian baths. It was a good business. I had a wife and daughter, and we lived in the loft over the shop. I had a license, too, from the aedile, to sell food at the amphitheater during the games; things were going well for us. My grandfather had been a slave in the Tullius household and we still had the patronage of this family."

"I had a clumsy assistant, may his soul be cursed by the gods forever. I was away one day selling sausages at the amphitheater and he was tending the cook fires. Somehow, I don't know how, he managed to let the fire spread. The stairs and loft were made of wood and they caught fire quickly. My wife and daughter were upstairs. He fled without seeing to them."

"My neighbors tried to put out the flames, and the vigiles came. Someone came running to summon me and I ran back to my shop, faster than I have ever run in my life. I went in although already the loft had fallen down, I tried to reach them." He extended his arms mutely. This was when he had been burned, I understood.

"It was too late."

"Cnaeus, I am so sorry."

He shrugged, as if trying to let the pain drop from his shoulders, but it seemed that he still carried this grief with him, and that it had not diminished over time. For a moment, I almost thought he would weep, but he did not.

"What happened after that?"

"My funeral society paid for a decent funeral for them. Everything I owned was in that shop; now everything was gone. I couldn't make a living. And so I came to Marcus Tullius. I knew his cook was getting old. I hoped that he would allow me to work in his household and to train as a more skilled cook. And he did so. The old cook taught me how to prepare dishes for fine people. I owe a great debt of gratitude to our master. If he had not taken me in, I don't know what I would have done."

He added, after a moment of silence, "She would have been about the same age as Tullia, my little daughter."

"Do you hope to be free again one day, Cnaeus?"

"It hardly matters. I have much less work to do here than in my shop. If I wanted another wife, perhaps I would work to save enough to buy my freedom. But I loved that one, and I don't want another. This is my life now. It is enough."

"You have had a life of great sorrows, Cnaeus."

"Like many others, I suppose", he replied, with a dismissive gesture.

This story brought tears to my eyes; I put my hand on his shoulder. I couldn't think of anything to say, but I think my tears somehow comforted him. Now I thought I understood his affection for Tullia.

"I am honored that you have told me your story".

This made him laugh. "Phagh! It is nothing." He busied himself then, with vegetables to wash and chop for the dinner. It was clear that his confiding mood had passed.

I still thought he was a terrible cook, but now I understood that he was a more sensitive man than I initially thought. His face was somewhat disfigured by his scars, but his soul was intact. He was still dealing with a grief that he had never been able to express. He began to seem less bitter, and I began to feel that I had a friend.

❦   ❦   ❦

As Tullia approached marriageable age, I began to think of stories that had some message for her (and her father) about her situation. One night I told the story of Atalanta and the three golden apples, which went like this. Atalanta was the beautiful daughter of a Greek king; she was famous for being very beautiful and also exceptionally fleet of foot. She won all the foot races, even at the Olympic games. Her father wanted her to be married, but she wanted to remain free to run, to explore the woods and mountains.

At this point, Marcus Tullius frowned a little; I think he felt this particular story, which was certainly one he knew, was subversive of parental authority; but he permitted me to continue.

Atalanta said that she would only marry a man who could outrun her in a foot race, and that any man who attempted to outrun her, and lost the race, must die. She thought that this would discourage all her suitors, but it did not. She was so beautiful that many men risked their lives to race against her—and they all lost.

One man, prince Melanion, wanted to win her for his bride. He prayed to Aphrodite for her help; and Aphrodite gave him three golden apples, and told him want to do.

The day of the race came, and the two of them set off. Atalanta was certain that she would win, so she allowed Melanion to have a head start. Just as she was catching up with him, he threw the first golden apple at her feet. She saw how beautiful it was, and she just had to have it, so she stopped for a moment to pick it up. Soon she was gaining on him for a second time, and this time he threw the second golden apple, just a little away from the path. She left the path to retrieve the second golden apple and returned to the race. Now they were approaching the finish line, and she began to pass him. He threw the third, and last, golden apple, far into the woods. By the time she had found it, he had crossed the finish line! In this way he won her for his bride, and he also won her love. She cherished her intelligent husband dearly and they lived long and happily together.

Tullia asked: "Why would Atalanta stop for the golden apples?" So we talked about what the apples stood for. I said I thought he had offered her a choice, and a chance to have a man whose qualities she would admire. But I had gone too far, and her father said at that point that it was her bedtime—and that he wanted to speak with me.

"Be careful about the stories that you choose. She can't choose her own husband; and reminding her of myths about women who can choose isn't appropriate just now." He was not seriously annoyed, I judged from his face. I said with pretended meekness:

"I will do as you command, master."

I thought at that point he would dismiss me, but he did not. He told me that, as Plato had said, stories can shape children's values; and warned me that I must not tell any more stories of a sort that would lead Tullia to be discontented with her life. I bowed my head in submission, thinking, "Well, not while you're around, I won't". He dismissed me. I think he suspected what I was thinking.

The shift in time had given me a fresh perspective on both the past and the future. Both times now seemed to me so strange, so marvelous, that I couldn't take anything in them for granted. Everyday small events now had an impact and immediacy greater than anything I had ever experienced before. It was exhausting and exhilarating, at the same time, to live life fully in the moment, aware of every small detail. How strange that I had to go far into the past in order to learn how to experience the present.

The center of my world was Tullia, and Marcus Tullius. When my stories made him smile, I felt an unreasonable sense of joy. I tried to tell myself that I only felt drawn to him because he represented all the things that intrigued me about the ancient world, contained in one human soul. But I knew that what I felt was far more personal than that. I wanted to know him, body and mind and soul; but that was impossible. I was only a slave, and not a particularly attractive one at that. I didn't want to be a slave mistress, casually used, and casually discarded.

I was no longer an objective observer—if, indeed, I ever had been. I was starting to tinker deliberately with events in a way that I had promised myself I would not. I had thought myself only a small pebble, dropped into this little pond in time, a source of a few small ripples that would quickly disappear. I hoped that the small things I changed would not have unforeseen negative consequences. But I understood, suddenly, that the moral dilemma of changing the future through the unintended consequences of our actions was one that everyone has to face everyday. The possible future consequences of my actions were a concern to me—whether I returned somehow to the place and time where I was born, or remained in this other place and time.

CHAPTER 12

I wanted to have a more interesting life than just housework, and a wider view of the world than I could see within these walls. I recalled Juvenal's words: "If you would study the ways of the human race, one household is enough". If I wanted to understand the Roman way of life, perhaps this one family would be enough, I thought. However, I became restless because of my confinement to the house.

Tullia was my shadow. She followed me about as I did my tasks, asking questions, pestering sweetly for stories. I was pleased to talk with her. It was excellent practice for me, because my accent was still less than perfect. It seemed likely to me that I might acquire a more aristocratic manner of speech by imitating members of the family rather than the kitchen servants. As I talked with her I gradually learned more words and improved my accent. I began to pick up the rhythm and music of their speech.

As I saw more of the family, it became clearer to me how they spent their time. Marcus junior often accompanied his father as he received clients or went about his business rounds, learning about the family's social connections and obligations and affairs by watching how the father handled them. He had teachers for wrestling and the javelin, and for other athletic and military skills. Sometimes Marcus wrestled with his son or sparred with him, partly playfully, but partly to teach him the skills he would need in military service.

Marcus junior lost his patience easily, throwing things to the ground in a sulk when he did poorly, or complaining when he lost at wrestling that his opponent had done something unfair. Their father noticed this, and he frequently admonished his son for his impatience, saying things such as: "Remember that you are a man"; or, "Let your desires be governed by reason."

It was not considered necessary for a daughter to have as much education as a son. Still, Tullia received some instruction in poetry and the classics at home. Sometimes when I washed the floor in the atrium I was able to eavesdrop while Demetrius tutored her. At first, Demetrius seemed to think that it was a waste of his time to teach a young woman. In fact, he had a heavier workload in this household than he deemed appropriate, for he acted as tutor, scribe, and reader, which kept him busy at nearly all hours of the day. In the early morning he kept records of any business matters that arose during the master's meetings with his many clients. Later in the morning, he taught lessons to Tullia. In the evening, he sometimes read to the master or the entire family. Everyone in the family was literate, but reading from handwritten manuscripts could be tedious, and the evening lamplight did not provide really adequate illumination. Thus, it was common for the family to listen to Demetrius read out loud. Demetrius's services were often on call.

Demetrius did not have a very positive attitude about his teaching responsibilities. Tullia was dutiful and she tried to be attentive to his lectures on mythology and history, but she had little real interest. However, Demetrius soon noticed that whenever it was possible, I lingered nearby, and eavesdropped on their conversations. In spite of his attitude that education was wasted on women, and his initial belief that I was an ignorant barbarian, I could tell that Demetrius was flattered by the interest that I showed in his teaching. Teachers are, after all, only human. We enjoy an attentive and appreciate audience, as much as an entertainer does. He began to test me by asking questions, later, to see whether I had actually understood what he had said. I had the answers correct often enough to impress him. As time went on, he seemed to put more heart into his teaching, and he seemed to be tailoring his presentations more to my level of understanding than Tullia's.

Apart from this, I used Demetrius as my calendar, my dictionary, and my history book. I pestered him with questions about vocabulary and grammar. At first he tolerated this in a relatively good-natured way, but as the months passed, he began to see this as yet one more unpaid job added to his excessive workload. He complained that he was tired of being my "lexicon", and began to ignore my questions when he was not in the mood to be bothered.

One afternoon when I came to him with yet another question ("how do you say...?"), he let loose his annoyance.

"Why should I spend my time answering your questions? I get nothing from you!"

He paused, stoked his beard, put his finger alongside his nose in a gesture that I knew was a characteristic sign that he was thinking, and then held his finger up in front of my face in a gesture that said, "Aha! I have it."

There was a wicked gleam in his eye. All right, I thought, let's hear it.

"If you will come and sleep with me when I want, then I will teach you."

By now, I knew him well enough to suspect that this was a joke rather than a serious offer. I thought to myself: Demetrius, you are at that awkward age: not yet old enough to be the ancient bearded philosopher who attracts the adoration of young disciples, but far too old and hairy to be attractive as one of those young boys. But then again, perhaps he was bisexual. Whatever his inclinations were, I was not going to play games with him.

"No, I won't. But I will pay you money."

That was apparently a satisfactory answer, although perhaps not the one he would have preferred. He said: "Two 'as' (the smallest denomination of coin) per day deducted from your peculium and added to mine, and you may ask questions only during the evening." This was an exorbitant amount, equivalent to my entire allowance as a slave.

We bickered and bargained. Finally we agreed on an arrangement. I would obtain a few coins from Alexander each week, instead of allowing cash to accumulate in a peculium as I had been doing. I would give him one as each evening, after he had answered my questions. This represented half my income as a slave, still an exorbitant fee. However, by handing him the money myself I would be able to remind him that I could terminate the bargain at any time if I did not get good value for my money.

This was a good deal for both of us. I could not imagine any life for myself as a freedwoman; and I still hoped that, somehow, I would be able to return to my own time; so it hardly mattered whether I could accumulate a large enough peculium to purchase my freedom.

There was much commerce among the slaves, in fact. Hair trimming and letter writing, massage and sexual favors, bits of food and money, and every other imaginable small commodity went from person to person. It seemed strange to them that I would not barter with my body, but I was too proud for this. There was so much more touching in this world than in modern times, both wanted and unwanted. When we bathed, we slaves would take turns massaging each other; I learned how to do this from Iris. On cooler nights, I often slept close enough to Damaris or Iris or other women to feel the warmth from their bodies. Sexual flirtation and sexual coupling occurred often, usually in private places, but I avoided this kind of contact. I didn't want to risk pregnancy or sexually contracted disease, and I did not want to be used in a casual way by someone who didn't care about me.

Gradually I began to have more contact with family members. I still remembered the way Marcus Tullius had taken my chin in his hand the first time he saw me. It had left me feeling confused and somehow sad. Had that touch been meant as a sign of affection, or was touch merely one of the privileges of power? The kind of affection a master might feel for a slave, I suspected, might be rather similar to the sort of feelings people have for pet animals.

Touch can have two meanings: it can be an intimate gesture between equals, a way of saying: I care for you. But between people who are unequal, there's an asymmetry: the powerful may touch the weak—a pat on the back, for example; but the weak may not lay hands on the powerful. His touch probably meant nothing. Any touch I might receive from a family member would be difficult to interpret. It could be a gesture of affection, a bit of condescension, or worst of all, a sexual overture. Or perhaps it might be a confusing mixture of all of these.

A sexual overture from the master or his son would be a command, not an invitation. Some accounts I had read suggested that sometimes a master would decide it was worth cultivating Stoic virtue by resisting the temptation to force himself on an unwilling slave; Marcus Tullius might be such a man, so perhaps a tactful refusal might be accepted; but this was a theory I hoped I would not have to put to the test. Masters had the legal right to do whatever they wanted to slaves, almost without limit, except that in the later days of the empire there were legal restrictions against selling slaves into prostitution or putting them to death when they had committed no offense. I hoped that I was simply not pretty enough to attract unwanted attention; but I felt uneasy. I wanted for him to notice me, and yet I knew that there was danger for me in that kind of attention.

The storytelling continued. Marcus Tullius and Tullia often asked for my stories in the evening. After cena, on evenings when there were no guests to entertain, the father reclined on the couch in his private study. Tullia curled up close to him. I sat on the floor nearby, telling and sometimes retelling my stories. Shared enjoyment of these stories, and conversations about them, began to bring him closer to his daughter, and I was very pleased to see this. I spent a lot of my floor scrubbing time daydreaming and remembering, thinking of stories that I might be able to revise in ways that would make them appropriate for my audience.

Sometimes wall paintings in the formal areas of the house provided inspiration. There was a fabulous painting of a nightingale on the wall in the master's study; in it, a beautiful brown bird perched on a bamboo cane against a background of dark green foliage and red roses. That image inspired me to retell Hans Christian Andersen's story *The Nightingale*.

In choosing my stories, of course, I usually had a message in mind. *The Nightingale* was one of my favorites. My retelling of the story went like this.

"In a country far away, and long ago, there lived a great emperor...he lived in the most beautiful palace in the world, and he had a garden in which fragrant flowers bloomed. A forest of graceful trees surrounded it. The woods extended all the way from the garden to the sea, and in the densest part of the forest, there lived a nightingale. He was a plain brown bird, small and unimpressive looking. But he had the most delightful song in the world. The woodsmen and the fisher folk stopped to listen to him, and they found his song so sweet that it made their troubles seem light, and it healed and refreshed them when their work made them tired. Travelers who came from distant lands went home and wrote books about the fabulous palace and the fragrant gardens. They all agreed that the most wonderful thing of all was the song of this nightingale."

"The emperor was proud of his possessions. He loved to read the praises of travelers. But he was puzzled, for he knew nothing about this nightingale, which the writers praised as his greatest possession of all. He summoned his chief steward, and asked him: "Tell me, what is this wonderful bird that everyone praises? Have you heard anything about it?"

"Your majesty, I know nothing of this matter," he replied. "This bird has never been presented to the court."

"Seek it out, and bring it to me", the emperor commanded. "I must hear this wonderful song."

The steward began to ask everyone in the palace: and no one in the palace knew anything about this fabulous bird. And so he returned to the emperor, saying, "Perhaps this was a myth, invented by writers...we cannot believe all that we read in books!"

However, the emperor did not accept this excuse, and he sent the steward out again in search of the marvelous bird. They asked upstairs and downstairs, and at last they questioned the humble little kitchen maid. She said: "Every evening I go down to the edge of the sea to take food to my mother, and I pass through the great woods. When I am tired on my way back, I rest under the largest tree, and then I hear the nightingale sing. Its song is like a mother's lullaby, and it brings tears to my eyes to hear it, and yet it makes me feel joyful to hear it."

The steward promised the kitchen maid that she would be given a much better position if she would lead him to this bird, so that it could be brought to court and presented to the emperor. This she agreed to do. A group of courtiers went out into the woods, led by the little kitchen maid, and she stopped under the great tree and pointed to the plain little bird. "How dull and insignificant it looks! Seeing how grand we are must have frightened it into losing all its colors", the courtiers said. "Please, the emperor would like to hear you sing", the kitchen maid said, and the nightingale began to trill its glorious song. Ah, it was like the sound of tiny bells, the most delicate and pleasing melody.

The courtiers were impressed. "Look how its throat vibrates. How extraordinary! It will be a sensation at the court! Precious nightingale, we have the honor to command you to attend the emperor at court tonight, to sing for his majesty."

And so the nightingale was taken to court, with all its pomp and splendor. A thousand lamps were lighted, and the nightingale sang his most beautiful songs, and the emperor was struck with great wonder. The song brought tears to his eyes and melted his heart. The emperor offered the bird a gold medallion to wear around its neck, but it refused, saying, "I have seen the tears of a emperor...that is more than enough reward!"

The nightingale became a sensation in the court, and the courtiers began to try to sing as the nightingale did.

The emperor ordered that his servants would attend the nightingale at all times. The nightingale lived in a cage made of gold, and was fed small sweetmeats and tidbits from the emperor's own plate. When he was allowed to go out, he had tiny ribbons tied to his feet, and he could fly only a short distance, for each ribbon was held by a courtier to ensure that the nightingale would not fly too high, or too far. The nightingale was unhappy, but he still tried his best to please the emperor.

One day a large box arrived. It was a gift to the emperor from the emperor of a neighboring country. There was great anticipation as the emperor opened the box. There were oohs and aahs of appreciation when the contents were revealed. It was a bird made of the most cunning machinery, all gold with jewels encrusted on its head and back and wings. There was a key in its back, and when this key was turned, the mechanical bird sang a complicated song through the chiming of tiny bells that were hidden inside of it. "How splendid! How beautiful!", all the courtiers said. "It is much more beautiful and impressive than our other bird."

At first they tried to make the real nightingale and this new bird sing duets, but this did not work. The mechanical bird had just one song, which it repeated over and over again in exactly the same way. The real bird's song was different from one time to the next, and not nearly so perfect in repetition.

The artificial bird replaced the real bird in the emperor's favor. It was placed on a silk cushion next to his bed. No one noticed the real bird any more, and so he flew away from the palace, and back to the forest where he came from. For several years the mechanical bird with its jewels was the delight of the court. And then something terrible began to happen. One day the bird was made to sing, and there was a sound of breaking pieces, and the insides came apart, and it did not work any more. A skilled workman took it apart and put the pieces back together again as well as he could. But he said that he could not make it work as well as when it was new, and so the mechanical bird could only be made to sing on special occasions, for it was wearing out.

Five years passed, and a great grief came to the empire. The emperor was much loved by his people, but he became very ill. As he lay in his golden bed with the weight of his sickness upon him, ghosts crowded around him, the spirits of the dead who had died in wars for his empire, his enemies and his own soldiers. The spirit of death sat upon the foot of his bed and waited for him, with an expression of menace upon his face. The voices of the dead drummed on the emperor's ears and kept him from sleeping, as they accused him of all his past wrongs. He tried to turn the key to make the mechanical bird sing, to drown out the sound of these voices, but the mechanical bird was broken, and would no longer sing at all. He summoned the court musicians and ordered them to play, but their music did not drown out the terrible voices that tormented him. He lay in his bed in misery, waiting to die.

News of the emperor's sickness traveled all over the empire and the little nightingale heard of it. He flew to the palace, and flew into the emperor's window, and he said to Death and to the dreadful ghosts: "I will sing for you, but you must return the emperor's sword to me." And he sang his wonderful plaintive songs, and the spirits of the dead were soothed and appeased, and they gave the nightingale back the sword that they had taken. He continued to bargain: "Yes, I will sing if you give me the emperor's shield, and his banner." And Death gave back each of these things for the songs. The nightingale sang sweetly, of roses blooming in the sunlight, of the fresh grasses of the field, of the winds that sweep over the sea. And Death was charmed into sparing the emperor's life. He went out through the window, leaving the emperor in peace.

"I can never thank you enough, for you have saved my life", the emperor said to the bird. "I neglected you in favor of the mechanical bird, but your returned to save me when no other could help. How can I ever reward you enough?"

"The tears I have seen in your eyes are reward enough", said the bird. "Sleep now, and I will sing for you." And the emperor slept a deep, refreshing sleep, soothed by the songs of the nightingale. In the morning he awoke feeling strong and well.

"Stay here with me always; you will sing when you want to, and I will break that terrible mechanical bird into pieces."

"No, don't do that. It did the best that it could. I cannot live here in the palace; I need the forest and the sea and the gardens to make my songs. I will come to your window at night and sing for you, and tell you about the world and the people outside, and this will be a secret between us."

"The emperor agreed to this, and so it was."

That night instead of dismissing me as he usually did, he told me to wait. He sent Tullia off to bed, hugging her as he gave her into the care of a personal attendant who would help her undress for bed. He returned, reclined on the couch again, and leaned on his left elbow, gazing at me. "Your stories for children are wonderful; do you know stories for adults?"

I thought for a moment. As a little girl, I spent my happiest hours curled up in a corner behind an overstuffed chair reading fairy tales, and later on, great literature. Yes: I could reproduce some of Shakespeare, I thought, and Gulliver's Travels and many other things as well. I had a good memory and I had two thousand years of material that was not familiar to them to draw upon. Should I agree? Would it be wise to tell him stories alone? I think I knew in my heart that I should not take this story telling much further. I was probably introducing more novelty into the past than I should with these fairy tales. But I wanted to hold his attention, to impress him, to please him; and he looked expectant. So I said: "Yes, I know many other stories. What kind of stories would you like to hear—long, or short? Happy, or sad?"

He thought that over for a moment, and said, "A longer story. You choose whether it is happy or sad".

I told him the story of *Romeo and Juliet*. We had performed this play when I was in ninth grade; I had understudied for Juliet, attended all the rehearsals, and knew most of the lines by heart. Translating Shakespeare into Latin on the fly did not result in the most pleasing phrases, and of course much of the poetry of the original language was lost. But the power of the story, and the eloquence of some of the speeches held him; I felt the power to fascinate, and I told this story better than I had told any of my fairy tales. My version was somewhat abridged, and took perhaps an hour; by that time the moon had risen. When I had finished with the death of the lovers, I was silent. He was also silent for a time, and he looked at me with an intentness that made me uneasy.

"You will not scrub any more floors", he said. "From now on, you will be Tullia's personal attendant."

I thanked him for this favor, and he said: "It is a waste of your time and your talents to spend your days washing floors; we can find others to do that. Can you write down these stories?"

"I know how to write in the language of my own people. The letters in Latin are similar, but I would need to practice to write properly."

"Demetrius will tutor you, if necessary; or perhaps he can transcribe the stories as you speak". (He'll be crazy about that, I thought to myself; he is already complaining about his workload.)

He continued to gaze at me, thoughtfully, as if there were other things on his mind. But then he dismissed me, saying that he would discuss the change in my duties with Alexander in the morning.

As I made my way back to the slave quarters, I felt—what? Confused, and even a little frightened. What more might he ask of me? Even more troubling were my own feelings: I felt powerfully drawn to this man. I tried to hide my feelings, but I felt such pleasure when I saw him; I felt myself turn toward him as parched roots seek rain, or as a sunflower turns its face toward the sun. I did not want to become a slave mistress; and that I knew that was the only possible intimacy we might have. I mustn't allow myself to be attracted to him; and I should not tell him love stories that might lead him to take a more personal interest in me. I shouldn't do it, I thought. But I wanted to do it. This place and these people had begun to feel more real to me than my former life, about which I thought less and less often now.

Life as Tullia's personal attendant was much more pleasant. I had a sleeping pallet on the floor in Tullia's room, and I was with her during most of the day. I no longer had to scrub floors, so my hands healed. My new duties were light and pleasant tasks. In the morning I washed her hands and face and helped her to put on the outer tunic and sandals; I fetched a light breakfast for us from the kitchen. I ate much better quality food now, also, because I shared her morning and midday meals. She was approaching the age of marriage and so some of her training had to do with household management. We spent many mornings visiting the kitchen, the laundry, the garden, and we talked with Alexander and the housekeeper about what needed to be done to run a household well. This was even more enlightening for me than it must have been for her. Her future life would probably require either managing slaves (if she adopted a hands-on role in her future household) or knowing what issues to take up with the steward (if she elected to let him do most of the management). I thought, I would hate to see her live the life of boredom that her mother leads, and so I encouraged her to learn how to do things, such as compounding herbal remedies.

We spent some time reading (from materials approved by her father) and we practiced writing together, sometimes under the supervision of Demetrius. I encouraged her to play, knowing that she did not have many more years of childhood freedom. By the time she is 14, I thought, they may have arranged a formal engagement for her; she will be married by the time she is 16, or even earlier. I hoped that they would choose a gentle husband for her. She could be a blithe spirit if given some freedom and approval, but she was easily hurt. I wanted to protect her, as much as was in my power.

It occurred to me that Tullia's inevitable marriage would have unwelcome consequences for me: I would have to accompany her to a new home with a different master.

CHAPTER 13

October was the season of ripening. Grapes hung in clusters from the vines, sweet from the rich volcanic Campanian soil and warm from sunshine. It had been a good year. It was family tradition to send many of the servants from the house out to one of the master's nearby vineyards to help during the last of the grape picking and to join in the celebrations; this was a holiday for us. After the hottest part of the day, we left the house on foot, all of those young and strong enough to go. We laughed and joked along the way.

The windowless walls of the villa felt like a prison to me, and I welcomed the opportunity to be outside in the open air. In my twentieth century life I had been a walker and a runner. Now my legs were unused to distances, but it felt exhilarating to stretch them and walk. The sky overhead was unblemished by clouds; the air was fragrant with the scent of drying grass; I looked forward to whatever small adventures the day might bring. By mid-morning we had reached the vineyards, terraced plantings on the south-facing slope of Vesuvius. It chilled me to remember: I knew that this mountain would bury everything I had come to know in this world, including, perhaps, some of these people. I must warn them, I thought. I hoped that my assumed identity as an Atlanteans priestess might make such a prophecy more believable to the master.

"Demetrius, you can find some country girl to pinch!" Iris said.

"Phagh!", with a backward jerk of his head, was his reply to that.

"You should see Cnaeus when he drinks too much wine; he snores with his mouth hanging open."

Teasing insults flew.

We took baskets and picked fruit, alongside the others, but it was a pretense at work. We ate fruit, joked, threw grapes at each other, and enjoyed ourselves, at least when we weren't closely supervised. More fruit ended up in our stomachs than in our baskets. My arms ached, my back was tired, my face became rosy from the sun—but I felt happier than I had in months. This was a welcome change in routine.

I knew that the field slaves had a much more difficult life than we did as house servants. I would not have lasted a week if I had been put to that work. In name, both the farm workers and the house servants were slaves, but our lives were different in almost every way. They labored in the fields for long hours, sunup to sundown. Their lot was physically hard work that bent the back and calloused the hands. We had relatively light housework and a fair amount of free time. They ate poorer quality food. We generally ate better quality and more varieties of food, and many of us cadged bits of food from the family's dinners and bought things to eat with our small cash allowances when we were in town.

But the main thing that we had that they lacked was hope. The custom of providing a peculium, or occasional small cash payments, was only for house servants, not for field workers. Many of us had opportunities, which the field slaves did not have, to learn skills and to improve our Latin. For better or for worse, as house servants, we might come to have some sort of personal relationship with family members; this intimacy could create difficulties and dangers, but the affection of master for slave sometimes led masters to grant freedom. A house slave who saved enough money might possibly be allowed to purchase freedom. A freed house slave was often set up in some business by the master, and then became a client of the master. In some respects, some ex-slaves fared better than poor free Romans, who had limited opportunities for education, and no sponsors to set them up in business or to patronize and protect their business ventures. A freed slave could hope to see his or her children become citizens.

These field slaves were somewhat better off than the slaves who worked in mines or on latifundia (industrial scale farms) in places such as Sicily or North Africa. For them life was a virtual concentration camp existence, and many of them had brief and miserable existences: overwork, flogging, and starvation. Slaves on a latifundium might be branded, or wear collars that said, in effect: "I am the property of so-and-so, if I run away, return me to him." In the household of Marcus Tullius, we wore iron finger rings that had his name engraved upon them. That too was a symbol of slavery.

Slavery was an evil that was present nearly everywhere in the ancient world. But it occurred to me after I had lived in the past that it hadn't entirely disappeared in the modern world. Modern countries didn't legally approve slavery, but many had large numbers of laborers whose lives were so miserable they were not much better off than slaves. In my modern life I had paused sometimes to think about people who harvested chocolate beans or sewed clothing in sweatshops, but because I didn't actually see their misery close at hand, I was able to overlook the pain that had gone into producing the goods I enjoyed. I think the Romans were similar. They didn't stop to think about the misery of slaves in the mines and on the large farms; few of them probably ever saw it.

House slaves were a somewhat different matter. They could be treated cruelly or kindly; but they could not be entirely ignored. Evil masters could enjoy actively causing them to suffer, and some did. Good masters unthinkingly exploited them. The writings of some of the more thoughtful Stoics, such as Seneca, revealed ambivalence and moral confusion about the treatment of slaves. Sometimes Roman writers even acknowledged that slaves could have human feelings, although for the most part, they avoided such uncomfortable ideas.

I didn't want to become comfortable with the idea of being a slave. But under the circumstances, a Stoic resignation to the situation seemed about the best I could hope for.

On this festival day, we house servants pretended to do the work of field slaves. In the late afternoon, the last of the harvest was brought in, and preparations were made for a feast and celebration. As the afternoon sun gilded the hillside, I wandered away from the crowd, looking for a moment of solitude.

There are moments in life that become frozen in memory like a snapshot: a vivid image of everything just as it was. This was such a moment. I walked over the rise of the hill and looked down the slope that spread out before me; the valley was a sea of beige grasses under a crystal blue sky. I felt joy in that beauty and wanted to be part of it. I felt the restless urge to run, something I hadn't done since I had left modern times. There was no space to run within the confines of the house. In fact, running was something that just was not done. An upper class Roman man was noted for dignified behavior, and this included a leisurely walk. In theater performances and mime, one way to tag a character as a low status and comical slave was to have him run on stage; in fact, they had a comic form of running, where the actor ran in place at a frantic speed, that reminded me of cartoon animals like the Road Runner with legs all blurred. I looked around to see whether anyone was watching, and I didn't see anyone.

And so I pulled up my tunic and tucked it into my belt so that it would not impede me, and I ran down the slope, letting gravity speed my feet. The breeze in my hair made me feel free for the first time since I had been there. But I had been seen, and the slave who saw me take off ran back breathlessly to report, dramatically, that he had seen a runaway house servant. (So I was told later by Demetrius, who embroidered this account on retelling.) In truth, I could not have gone very far; I wasn't in shape as I had once been, and was quickly winded. I only wanted to be away and alone for a few minutes.

The master had arrived; he had not yet dismounted from his horse when the tattle-tale slave came running up, in a fever of perspiration, threw himself dramatically on the ground like a character in a melodramatic mime performance, and shouted that he had spotted a fleeing servant. The master looked annoyed, and nudged his horse with his knee to gallop off in the direction that the servant had pointed out. I was slowing down in my run, as the ground leveled out, but still running as much as I was able to, when I heard the sound of hooves approaching from behind me. I stopped and turned around, suddenly dizzy. He came thundering up, stopped just short of me, and said:

"Stop! Where are you going?"

I realized suddenly that I could be in trouble for this thoughtless little escapade. I tried to look properly humble (this was still difficult for me).

"I wasn't going anywhere, master. I just wanted to…run."

He looked at me in astonishment and annoyance. "You were running away again?"

"No. I just wanted to…feel the sun and wind on my face. I used to run for pleasure in my own country". I checked myself in mid sentence, realizing that this explanation probably didn't make sense to him. "I feel like a bird in a cage sometimes."

He looked thoughtful. And the expression on his face changed; I think he understood. And he wasn't angry anymore.

"Come here", he said, tilting his head to one side. He walked his horse over to a small outcropping of boulders near by. "Stand here", he ordered, pointing to the boulders. I obeyed. He leaned over, reached down, and lifted me off my feet, so easily I was astonished; and set me on the saddle sideways before him.

"Put your arms around my waist, and hold on". With that, we were off. I had never been on horseback before, and it startled me to see how high it seemed and how precarious. I seized hold of his belt (almost too late) and hung on for my life. Now he began to seem amused. It was a terrifying and yet exhilarating experience. I had not been so close to him before; I could feel the warmth of his body, and breathe in the scent of the oils that had been used in bathing and massage. He let the horse have his head, and we were off, pounding down the hillside, at a speed that seemed dizzying compared to anything I had experienced in that world. Then he turned, and headed back toward the vineyard; in a few moments we were within sight of the storehouses where the crowd of servants was resting. He deposited me on the ground. "Don't do that again," he admonished me, in the tone that one would use to address a naughty child. I was embarrassed. I promised that I would stay put, and hoped that my pretended humility looked believable. It appeared that I would not be punished; he had apparently believed I wasn't really trying to escape.

I found Iris, Demetrius and Damaris among the crowd; they had witnessed the scene, and wanted to know what was going on. I couldn't explain my behavior to them either, and they told me I was fortunate that I hadn't received a beating. It seemed to me that the less this matter was discussed, the better, so I didn't try to explain. Iris looked annoyed that I had been seen in that way with the master, the focus of his attention.

Before the late afternoon meal there was a brief religious observance with the master officiating. He stood before us; for this ceremony he had donned his toga and draped part of it over his head as a hood. On the table before him there were two cups of wine. I asked Damaris about this, and she explained that the first one was old wine from the harvest two years ago, while the other was new wine, from the most recent year. Demetrius explained that this day was the feast of Meditrinalia, a term which referred to healing, dedicated to Jupiter and Bacchus. Marcus Tullius raised his hands palms upward toward the open sky, and spoke in a sonorous voice that carried clearly over the crowd: "I drink new wine, and old wine. I am cured of new illnesses, and old illnesses. May Jupiter bless this harvest." He poured a libation on the altar, and placed an offering of cakes there; and tasted both wines. He was a figure of grave dignity. I was struck again by his remarkable grace of movement. He seemed completely at ease in his body. It was not an effeminate grace, but an economy of movement that made every gesture seem natural.

Our late afternoon meal was simple fare but we shared it in a festive atmosphere, and I sensed anticipation. Later there would be a bonfire and dancing, they said. The master did not eat with us, but he seemed to enjoy watching the celebrations. A bonfire was built at sundown, and a few musicians started to play, and people began to dance, although most just watched at first. As darkness fell and shadows gathered around, people drew closer around the fire. Faces were streaked orange and yellow by the flickering light, and people drank more wine. The music reminded me of Greek syrtakis I had heard; we spectators became caught up in the rhythm of hands clapping. Some of the dances were simple, and after I had watched for a while, I joined in a line dance; we did a grapevine step. We circled the fire, arm in arm, dancing faster as the tempo of the music accelerated. Then they started a familiar game: a man danced alone, then chose a woman to dance with; then he went back to the circle, and she chose a male partner; and so on. Then one of the women did something shockingly bold when it came time to choose her partner—she darted outside the circle and seized the master's hand. He resisted at first, but allowed himself to be persuaded, and to the delight of the crowd, he joined in the dance.

Ah, that was a lapse of dignity, I understood. "To dance in a toga" was considered utterly ridiculous and undignified. He was not wearing the toga now, of course; the toga, like a modern business suit, was a formal garment worn only when the situation required it. Like the others present, he wore a simple tunic, better quality fabric than ours, of course, but not very different in cut.

When Nero forced some of his senators to dance at his banquets, they were humiliated. The somewhat strait-laced upper class Romans simply did not sing or dance themselves. They would watch slave dancers perform, of course; and it was not unusual for slaves to sing while working, or to dance at a festival. Theatrical performances included dancing, but professional dancers were considered almost as low in status as prostitutes. I knew that Nero was about to embark on his career as a self-styled artist. It greatly embarrassed the more conservative Romans to have an emperor who danced, sang, and played a musical instrument in public. (Of course when Nero performed at competitions, it was understood that he must win.)

So I understood that the master was doing something unusual by allowing himself to be persuaded to dance. He kept it brief, and when he chose his partner, it was Iris, of course. I knew she was the master's favorite. She preened herself at this public recognition. I felt a sudden stab—of envy, I realized. I tried to dismiss it as a sense of disappointment. I was still an outsider. No one would ask me to dance. But I also began to wonder, as I watched them dance together for a few moments, if I were not jealous of her.

He left the circle quickly after a brief dance. Later as the dancing continued, someone did ask me to dance. Perhaps my face looked prettier in the firelight, or perhaps everyone was just becoming drunker. I had to extract myself from an unwelcome embrace; and I went off to look for a quiet place to sleep. The party went on all night, so there was too much noise for sleep, but I was too tired to continue dancing anymore. So I lay wrapped up in my cloak in a quiet spot, feeling quite alone, but unable to sleep.

The next morning we returned to the house. Pliny wrote that the cheaper Pompeiian wines provided a particularly vicious hangover and some of my slave friends appeared to have first hand experience of that. Moderation...I felt virtuous that I had stopped drinking early in the evening, and thus avoided a hangover. This smugness annoyed Demetrius, who got his revenge by telling everyone the story of my escape, and Iris's dance with the master. Of course the way he told it, we sounded naughtier on every repetition and elaboration of the story. I hoped that other events would replace this as the fodder for gossip, as I soon became tired of this account.

After that, I was even more aware of the effect that the physical presence of the master had on me. I felt foolishly happy on days when I saw him; and strangely empty on days when I didn't. I was drawn toward him. He was power, confidence, pleasure, joy; he smiled when he saw me, and his smile warmed me.

I tried to hide my feelings, but Demetrius noticed, and he warned me. "Don't aim too high in your affections, little sheep; the master already has a favorite, and you would not know how to handle the jealousies." I knew what he meant, and was dismayed that I must have let my yearning show, on my face, in the tone of my voice when I spoke of Marcus Tullius. He was probably right. I dared not risk further offending Holconia; and Iris could be a dangerous rival, also, if she saw me as a serious threat.

CHAPTER 14

As part of my new responsibilities as a personal servant, Alexander trained me to wait on the family and guests at the table. I was also expected to entertain guests with songs and stories at small dinner parties. This was wonderful news for several reasons. I could learn to speak Latin with a more polished accent if I were in a position to overhear the dinner conversations among the guests. The slaves who served at dinner, I knew, sometimes were permitted to eat bits of food that were left over on the serving platters, which greatly improved their diet. This would give me a chance to sample some of the more exotic culinary offerings. I no longer had dishpan hands and bruised knees from crawling around on the floors. I was definitely coming up in the world.

There was potential risk in this as well, for I was now in closer contact with members of the family, including the mistress Holconia. I feared her: she was easily displeased and often struck or scolded servants. She had a particular dislike for me. When she learned that Marcus Tullius had made me Tullia's personal attendant, she was enraged.

"She is entirely unsuitable. She doesn't know our ways; she can't arrange Tullia's hair or her garments."

Marcus Tullius overruled her. "In a year or two, Tullia will be ready for marriage, and then we will give her a maid who can dress her hair. Tullia is still a child; she enjoys this woman's stories. We will give her another year of childhood. Miranda will be her companion."

The mistress was sullen in response to this. "She is old enough for marriage as soon as she begins her courses, and that could be at any time now."

Their son was approaching an age when he might begin to look for female slaves as partners. Iris had already commented that she was glad that, as the master's favorite, she would not have to contend with the "little master". He was even harsher toward slaves than his mother, although only when his father was not present to counsel patience and restrain him. Iris had already joked that his eye might fall on me. I would have to think of some way to deal with that problem if it arose.

My training as a table server began the next day, and it was more exacting than I would have imagined. Up until then, my work for the cena had been behind the scenes, helping with food preparation and cleanup. Now I would serve at the table. A small dinner party for guests usually involved nine or fewer people. Each of the three couches in the triclinium accommodated three diners, each reclining, resting on the left elbow, and leaving the right hand free to reach for the small platter on the center table. Before the cena, we arranged clean linens and cushions on the couches. On warm evenings dinner was served in the outdoor triclinium, which faced the fountain in the peristyle garden. On cool or inclement evenings, dinner was served in the indoor triclinium. As the guests arrived, we bathed their hands and feet and helped them change from heavier outdoor shoes to lighter weight indoor sandals. After preliminary socializing, they arranged themselves comfortably in the triclinium for the first part of the meal. We brought one course at a time, placing a platter on the small center table. Often this was something like a salad, an appetizer, or roasted fowl with vegetables. Meat dishes were first presented intact for the guests to admire, then cut up neatly into pieces by a specially trained slave. This was the most difficult skill for me to learn; de-boning a chicken or a fish without shredding it is something of an art. I practiced this task on private family meals and was scolded on numerous occasions for doing a messy job. I was never skilled enough to perform this service at formal dinners.

During the dinner, guests picked pieces of food from this shared platter with their fingers (spoons were used only for a few of the messier dishes). Bones or other inedible parts were tossed discreetly on the floor under the table. (After all, one could hardly deposit things that had been chewed upon, on the shared platter!) We stood by trying to be attentive to their needs without looking at anyone directly. This was more difficult than it might seem. By the merest gesture, an extension of a hand, a guest would signal that he wanted his hands washed, or his wine refreshed, and we were expected to notice and service these wishes quickly and quietly. Standing for hours during this meal was difficult, as the indoor triclinium became stuffy and airless after a time. I never disgraced myself by fainting, but a few times, I thought I might. The pace of the dinner was leisurely to say the least, with gossip and conversation throughout.

The foods were generally prepared elaborately. Romans did not seem to like the natural tastes of most foods. Most dishes had strong seasonings added; the inevitable garum was included in almost every recipe, but in addition, many dishes had sweet and sour flavor combinations, such as vinegar and honey, or spices and herbs, that reminded me a little of some Chinese cooking. Some menus included mystery meats: the more exotic, the more impressive. Eels, brains, fish of strange appearance, and other things I did not recognize appeared on occasion. Of course, many familiar foods were absent: no potatoes, tomatoes, or corn.

Wine was mixed with water in a serving bowl, usually in a ratio of about one part wine to three parts water. Wines were often flavored with additives such as honey, resin, or spices; some spices were literally worth their weight in gold because they were imported from distant lands, as far as India. Some of these additives were an improvement, others quite awful, in my opinion. I was reminded of an old Italian gentleman I had known in modern times who always doctored his wine with cream soda to make it sweeter; so, I thought, Italians have been putting things like that in their wine for two thousand years.

We of course sampled the leftover wine as we cleared the table, which made the task less onerous than it might otherwise have been.

In summer, wine was served cool or room temperature. In winter, it was usually heated, in a device that looked like a samovar and had elaborate silver spigots. No one except northern barbarians ever drank wine undiluted, but the wine seemed to be stronger than in modern times, almost like a wine concentrate, so after dilution it was rather similar in strength to modern wines. Knowledge of wines was not expected of me; Alexander kept track of all the various varieties. The quality of wine served depended upon the status of the guests, and the most costly wines only appeared for the most distinguished visitors.

Leftovers of food and drink were supposed to be kept and used at the next family meal, but we often helped ourselves to things in quantities too small to be missed.

There was a break during the middle of the meal, and the master made a small offering at the family shrine or lararium, pouring a libation and asking a blessing. It seemed that many upper class Romans observed these traditions without holding very literal beliefs in the gods. The second half of the meal began after this break, and often this included desserts or fruits. The remainder of the evening was spent in various ways depending upon the makeup of the company. If it was just a family dinner, the meal ended relatively early; and often, I went to the master's study to tell stories. If there was mixed company, men and women of distinguished families, talk might continue for a while after the meal. Sometimes I was called upon to play my flute for guests, although our household did not provide elaborate entertainment most evenings. If it were all men, a drinking party might continue until late at night, with animated arguments, and perhaps even hired dancing girls and musicians. I was glad that I was not summoned to entertain on these stag nights, for these could become rowdy affairs.

I remember one of these dinners particularly. There were five diners that evening: The master and mistress, their friend Julia Felix, a soldier called Caesius who had returned from service in Britannia, and the mistress's older brother Holconius Rufus. The mistress wore the wig that had been made from my hair; this was a distressing sight I tried not to notice.

After the second course the diners relaxed on their couches, and sipped watered wine. I was asked to play music for them. This was well received.

I resumed serving wine while the guests talked. I was particularly interested in Julia Felix. From slave gossip I knew that she had been a close friend of the mother of Marcus Tullius. Our master often served as her agent in business matters where a woman could not represent herself, but she was clearly an equal rather than a client. She treated him in an affectionate, motherly way. I looked at her covertly. The great lady was not a great beauty. Her features were oddly proportioned: broad cheekbones, prominent nose, and pointed chin. Her neck had the solid and substantial look of a stone column. Her hair was styled simply, almost severely, with none of the rolls of curls and false hair affected by our mistress and so many other ladies of wealth. She dressed simply also, in spite of the fortune that reportedly made her one of the wealthiest people in town.

It was Julia's eyes that made her strikingly attractive; that, and the pleasantness of her smile, and her regal posture. She had been widowed ten years earlier, and was childless. Her father had died just before she lost her husband, and so she had inherited a great fortune, without the heavy hand of a male relative. Her father's name was Spurius Felix. Spurius usually means illegitimate; and Felix means happy or lucky; so I guessed that her father's name could be translated as "Lucky Bastard." According to the gossip in the slave quarters, she had managed her fortune shrewdly and increased her wealth; she owned the largest house in town.

I knew from family table conversation that Holconia did not like Julia Felix: she envied her independence. But I found Julia a delight: her conversation sparkled, and it was clear that even these men respected her intelligence and character.

She did not evidently spend her money on cosmetics or clothing, but conversation revealed that the great lady had a weakness for jewelry, which, however, she did not wear. She was describing a piece that she had acquired. As I refilled her wine goblet, and then stepped back to my station near the wall, I was close enough to eavesdrop on the conversation. I'm sure that family members must have known that we heard all, and repeated and remembered much, but they usually seemed unaware of our presence in the background of their lives.

"The workmanship is very fine; each link is an ivy leaf in gold, and the necklace is long enough to be looped around the neck three times."

"Julia, you should wear it, it would look splendid on you", our mistress said.

"Julia's wit is ornament enough", our master said. The vertical line between the mistress's brows deepened slightly. She did not like to be contradicted, even in so indirect a manner; nor did she like to hear others praised for qualities that she did not possess herself.

"Have you read the most recent installment of Pliny's *Natural History*, Marcus?" (Julia apparently thought it was time for a change of topic.) Her use of his first name indicated the closeness of their friendship, for few people addressed him in this manner. Apparently she had been almost a second mother to him, after his own parents died.

"Indeed, yes."

The mistress toyed with her goblet while they spoke of Pliny, and examined her fingernails.

"Do you refer to his book about land animals?"

"Yes; he told the most remarkable story. I hardly know whether to believe it, but his source seemed unimpeachable."

"Tell me, Julia."

"He has an account from Mucianus, whom you know has served as consul three times, that there is an elephant that is able to write Greek."

"Really, Julia? What did this learned animal have to say?"

"I am not certain of the exact words…something to the effect, 'I myself wrote this, and dedicated these spoils which were taken from the Celts'".

"Remarkable! They are known to be most intelligent creatures. The elephants, I mean, not the Celts!"

I could not help thinking that they sometimes seemed to have less difficulty in crediting animals with intelligence, than in acknowledging such ability in slaves or women. I suppose that any intelligence of animals is less likely to be a threat, than intelligence in women and slaves, who might be tempted to rebel, if they could think too much. I tried to suppress a smile.

"Do you remember the stories about Pompey's triumph?"

She tilted her head back and laughed. "Yes, he harnessed elephants to his chariot for his African triumph…and when he came to the city gates, the procession had to be halted, because the elephants were too large to pass through the gates!"

The mistress's boredom was becoming more obvious, as she tapped her goblet with her finger. "Perhaps we might speak of other things…"

The master now addressed another guest. "Caesius, we have heard reports of the massacre last year in Britannia. Perhaps you can tell us more about it." Judging from the frown on the mistress's face, this was yet another topic not to her liking. As slaves, we came to know so much, and to guess so much more, about the affairs of the family. I thought to myself: she seeks to manipulate, and he resists. He knows perfectly well that she is only interested in local gossip.

Caesius took a hearty draught of his wine. I turned my attention to him, without being so obvious as to turn my head to look in his direction. I have become good at observing things from the periphery of my vision, and at listening without seeming to listen. His skin was weather-beaten. He was not in military dress for this social occasion, of course, but it was not difficult to picture him in battle gear. The slaves said that he had known Marcus Tullius during a time when the master had commanded an auxiliary cavalry unit made up of native horsemen, who served as scouts and harriers in Britannia during the invasion under Claudius. Quintus Petilius Cerialis Caesius Rufus had been a career soldier, but had retired from military service.

"Marcus, the thing was badly mishandled. You remember how the British tribes people were, the Iceni, the Trinovantes. When they were treated well, they paid tribute and kept the peace, for the most part. They were willing to render obedience to our rule; they were not willing to be treated as slaves."

The mistress let out a sigh of annoyance; it appeared that the tribune had a long story to tell that was of little interest to her.

"The governor and procurator were of the same mind. Gaius Suetonius Paulinus, may he rot in Hades, thought only to obtain military glory; he had no interest in just governance. While he was off slaughtering Druids, trouble arose in the east. Prasutagus, king of the Iceni, died. He made the emperor co-heir with his own two daughters, thinking that sufficient to maintain his peaceful client status with Rome. His widow, Boudica, became queen. But there was not to be peace. The kingdom was plundered, and even the dead king's own household was attacked, by Roman officers and even by Roman slaves. They flogged Boudica, and they raped her two daughters. They took the lands and authority from the Iceni chiefs."

"Now if this Boudica had been an ordinary woman, there might not have been any well organized revolt. I never saw her, myself, but I heard that she was fierce and courageous. One witness said she was tall, and terrifying in appearance. Her hair was like the tawny mane of a lion, so long that it fell to her hips. She could ride like an Amazon and wield a sword with the strength of the greatest of her male warriors. She was very intelligent, for a woman. Her tunic was of many colors and she was always to be seen at the front where the fighting was most intense."

The guests listened attentively, except for Holconia.

"Boudica sent for the chiefs of the other British tribes, many of whom also had no reason to love us. The Trinovantes, for example, were driven from their homes and land by Roman soldiers and settlers who established a town at Camulodunum. The tribes plotted together and assembled a great force of warriors under the banner of Boudica."

"After so long a period of peace, Camulodunum had no walls. The commanders had instead built fine public baths and a great temple to Claudius. The British had been taxed heavily to build this temple, and they hated it. When they heard of the great assembly of tribes, the people of Camulodunum were fearful. Worst of all, the great statue of Victory in the forum fell down, for no apparent reason, and with its back turned as though it were fleeing from the enemies. This omen poisoned the hearts of the people with fear. They sent to Suetonius for help, but he and his forces were too far away. Then they sent appeals to Catus Decianus, who sent only two hundred men."

"In spite of the real threats and the ill omens, the town still failed to take adequate precautions; they were too accustomed to peace to imagine the magnitude of the disaster that would overcome them. They did not put up ramparts or trenches. They did not evacuate women, children, and old people. They placed their faith in their small garrison."

"A horde of British tribesmen descended upon them, led by Boudica. They ravaged and burned everything in the town. The people last of all took refuge in the Temple of Claudius, praying for their deliverance; but after a siege of two days, it also fell. My division attempted to relieve the town, but the British were drunk with victory. I am ashamed to tell you, Marcus, that they routed my men. The entire infantry force that was with me was massacred; I escaped, with some of the cavalry."

The speaker stared down at the table. "It would have been more honorable for me to die...but I felt I had to salvage those few lives that could be saved. We took shelter in the camp stockade."

"Catus Decianus fled to Gaul. It was his greed in exploiting the tribes, and the brutality that he permitted toward them, that had driven them to war. Suetonius arrived then at Londinium. He knew that his forces were badly outnumbered by Boudica's hordes, and he decided that he needed reinforcements. So he abandoned the city of Londinium. Some of the inhabitants left with him, but others stayed behind—the old, the sick. All who remained were slaughtered when Boudica's men fell upon the city. The same in Verulamium, all killed. The British did not take prisoners. They cut throats, hanged, burned, and crucified. At least seventy thousand people were killed, all told."

"Suetonius collected additional forces, including auxiliaries, and assembled a force of ten thousand men; now he launched a direct attack, using the land to his advantage. And fortunately for him, the Britons made a mistake. So confident were they of continued victory that they had drawn up wagons at their rear, and brought their women to witness the scene of victory. And so when they fell back before our men, their flight was impeded by the wagons. All were killed, about eighty thousand Britons, even the women and the baggage animals. None were spared."

It appeared that there might be more to his story, but Holconia had heard enough of war, and she interrupted his story by calling upon me to play for them, and ordered fresh wine. Julia was pleased with my music. "I have never heard such songs; they are most pleasing. Where did you get her?"

Marcus explained that I had been fished out of the sea; Julia found this amusing. "A daughter of Neptune", she called me.

Then they discussed headache remedies, a subject that Pliny discussed at some length in his writings. Marcus Tullius said that he found music very soothing to a headache—the music I play on my recorder, specifically. This interested Julia Felix. She enjoyed the music I had played at dinner, she said, and wanted to know whether Marcus Tullius would lend me to her on occasion. He agreed.

"And Marcus, if you decide to sell her, let me be the first to know."

❧   ❧   ❧

In the next few weeks, Julia Felix asked to borrow me on several occasions. She was troubled by headaches, and believed that my music was soothing. I was sent to play for her during the middle of the day, when most people took a rest—escorted by a male slave, to ensure my safe return, I suppose. She loved my music; for her, I began to reconstruct a repertoire from Mozart, as she seemed capable of appreciating more complex musical themes. For some reason she took an interest in me, and asked questions about my background. She seemed particularly intrigued when I described the ways women had lived in my home country—as doctors, advocates, and teachers. What a good idea, she said. I shared a few of my favorite quips with her, such as the comment that "Women have to do twice as well as men in order to be thought half as good. Fortunately, that is not difficult." (Charlotte Whitten, an early feminist, made this remark.) Julia loved that remark. And so I dared to say even more subversive things to her as time went on.

She was not only a shrewd businesswoman, but also a woman with a great heart. Sometimes while I waited to play for her, I watched her deal with her visitors and clients. She knew their hearts, and offered them many kinds of help: money, advice, and sympathy.

Julia Felix would have loved the twentieth century: A world that had greater scope for her brilliance and talent. Even here, where the possibilities were relatively limited, she had done very well for herself. Inspired by her, I tried to take a more sympathetic and personal interest in the people in my own household, and to find more ways to be a strong woman in times that did not approve of feminine strength.

If I could be strong like her, perhaps I could survive.

CHAPTER 15

I had checked and rechecked on the years when various events had occurred, and by now I was fairly certain that it was November in the year A.D. 61 by modern reckoning. In February A.D. 62, I knew, Pompeii would experience a severe earthquake. This earthquake would destroy many of the public buildings in the town. I knew that this quake had been followed by a period of partial rebuilding in Pompeii, but the damage was so extensive that it took years to repair all the buildings: more time than they had, as it turned out later, for in A.D. 79 the eruption of Vesuvius would bring complete devastation, leaving Pompeii and many neighboring towns buried in deep layers of lava, mud and ash. I didn't expect to be present for the eruption of Vesuvius: as a slave, I might not live that long. I still hoped that one day, when I touched the signal device, it would suddenly begin to work. But the earthquake was due to happen soon, and I had to decide what to do about this knowledge.

I was beginning to enjoy some things about this new life. It pleased me to hear Tullia laugh or cry sweet tears over my stories. The stories had given her a new interest, and had brought her closer to her father. The unhurried pace of daily life was attractive. Instead of having each 15-minute time block in my appointment book scheduled with important things to do, I had leisurely days. I still waited on the table, but my most important duty now was as an entertainer, a storyteller and musician. This was not difficult work, and my audience was appreciative. However, there was another reason more compelling, although I could hardly admit it even to myself. I was falling in love with a man who could never love me. I cared about the people in this world; I didn't want them to be hurt. And, admittedly, I wanted to make myself more important in their world.

One afternoon there was an earth tremor. The earth shook, but not violently. No one seemed particularly alarmed; minor earthquakes were common here. But this reminded me that I needed to warn them before much more time had passed. That evening, after Tullia had left for bed, I stood before Marcus Tullius and said:

"Master, there is something I must tell you."

"What is it?" He looked mildly surprised, for it was not proper or customary for a slave to initiate conversation.

I had thought about the best way to present my prophecy; I wanted him to believe me. The Romans believed in omens and dreams; they lived in a world where there was room for magic and mystery. And so I told him this story:

"Last night Poseidon spoke to me in a dream. He warned that a great earthquake will occur, and that much of Pompeii will be destroyed." Indeed, the earthquake that occurred early in A.D. 62 was a massive one; modern geologists have estimated its magnitude at 8 or 8.5. So much damage was done that repair work was still unfinished by the time Vesuvius erupted 17 years later.

Marcus Tullius frowned. "Do you believe this is a true prophecy?"

I wanted to make him believe me, so that he could take precautions to protect himself, and his family, particularly my little Tullia. "Yes. I have had such dreams before, and the events that they foretold did come to pass." He was thinking. There were many associations with Poseidon in my background: the Atlantis myth, my emergence from the sea. Poseidon was also believed to be the bringer of earthquakes. I think Marcus Tullius did not entirely believe in the gods; and yet he didn't entirely disbelieve, either. He seemed to take my words seriously. Another thought occurred to me. I took my amulet pouch from my neck and opened it, and handed him the image of Neptune. I might not get it back; but it was another small piece of evidence that I had some connection to Neptune or Poseidon, and it might lend credence to my words. "Poseidon spoke to me, and told me to warn you."

He looked at the image, tangible evidence that I had some kind of link with the sea god. As if speaking to himself, he said quietly:

"...cum pia venerunt somnia, pondus habent." I recognized this as a line from Propertius, translatable as, "when holy dreams come, they have weight" (or truth). Apparently he believed me.

"When will this earthquake occur?"

"Early in the month of February."

"Have you spoken of this to anyone else?"

"No, master."

"Do not speak of it to anyone else. I will consider what you have said...can you predict other things?"

I hesitated. "I can sometimes see into the future, not just about earthquakes, but about some other things. I cannot choose what to see, or answer specific questions. But sometimes I know what will happen."

He looked thoughtful. "Perhaps you are under some special protection, for you survived at sea when others died." He returned my amulet to me.

In the weeks that followed, I noticed that he made arrangements to ship breakable goods such as pottery vessels full of wine and oil out of his storehouses in and around Pompeii. He transferred flocks of sheep to pastures farther south. He stockpiled food and other supplies. He made plans to send his family to visit relatives in the city of Rome, during the coldest part of winter; this was a trip Holconia welcomed, for she preferred the city. He himself would not accompany them.

This man increasingly fascinated me. My feelings were foolish and dangerous, and I scolded myself about them. Nevertheless, I lived for the moments when I could enchant him with a story, or when I could watch his face and listen to his voice as he engaged in animated conversation with guests at the dinner table.

At first I thought he had a proud face, and it was proud, but it was different from the cold hard pride in the mistress's face. His role in the world as landowner, businessman, master, and paterfamilias gave him power. He had clients who applauded his speeches and appreciated his generosity. Usually he exercised his power in benevolent ways. He had charisma, intelligence, and other qualities that drew admiration. He had a perfect ease of manner. And what a life he had. Perhaps a spoiled and petted modern house cat has a more luxurious life, but the life of a wealthy upper class Roman man of this period was in many ways an extremely comfortable life. He had work to do that was not particularly difficult, and it allowed him to exercise his skills in public speaking and negotiation. When he came home he was bathed, massaged, and catered to by a small army of slaves, and spent most of the latter half of the day entertaining guests at dinner parties where literate conversation and fine wine were abundant. Perhaps on some level I wanted to be him, rather than be with him.

He was an exceptional man, not very much like the men I had known in the modern world. Words such as "honor" and "duty" had been out of fashion for so long that I could hardly imagine using those words to describe anyone I knew in my own time. Marcus Tullius was an honorable man. The Romans said such men had great "dignitas", but that word conveyed much more than our English translation "dignity". He was responsible for the welfare of many people, in a paternalistic way, and he took that responsibility seriously. He believed in moderation and self-control, and he put these virtues into practice. But he was not as severe or serious as I have made him sound. He was gentle and loving with his daughter. When he smiled, his face became quite gentle. He was intelligent and, for his times, well educated. He had firm ideas (which were natural for his time, but still deplorable by my standards, of course) about appropriate behavior for women and for slaves. A person can easily be corrupted by power. He had considerable power, within the household and the town, but he did not abuse it. If he sometimes reminded me of a Godfather or Mafia don, meeting with his clients, dispensing and receiving favors, making deals, he was generally a benevolent sort of don. I suspected that he might even have a tender and romantic side to his nature.

I was falling in love with a slave owner, although I despised the idea and practice of slavery. I wanted him to love me, and I wanted to feel some sense of belonging in this time. And yet I realized that as a slave I could never be a loved or respected equal, or have any sort of freedom in my relations with him. Reason told me that I should keep my feelings hidden and try to forget them. But my feelings were another matter. When he smiled at me in appreciation for my story or song, the joy blinded me to all my doubts, at least for a while.

In his house, slavery was managed in a relatively benign way. For me that was unfortunate, because it made it possible for me to rationalize away some of my objections. His house slaves, myself included, had better living conditions than the illegal immigrants who worked in fields or in sweatshop labor in my modern times. I was caught in my ambivalence, and confused. He was a good man, involved in an evil system. That is true of so many of us.

And as the weeks passed, I thought: perhaps it will give me prestige and power if I can predict this terrible earthquake. If he believes my prediction, he will be able to prevent some loss of life and property.

I prayed silently: Let them all be safe.

CHAPTER 16

As February began, I was almost as afraid that the earthquake would not happen as that it would. I would look like a fool if this prophecy failed, or if I had miscalculated or misremembered the year. The master had sent his wife and children to the city of Rome to visit relatives, and had made arrangements for much of his goods to be shipped to other cities, but he himself had stayed.

I had just returned from the bakery in town and entered the kitchen with a basket of loaves under my arm when the first swaying motions began. Dishes fell from the table and jars from the shelves overhead. I took cover at once under the heavy kitchen table. No one else was in the kitchen at the time. Then more intense rolling and jerking movements began, and the earth made terrible groaning and grinding sounds, and there were sounds of things falling and breaking, and people screaming. The sensation I had was like being on board a ship that the waves heaved up and down and side to side; the shock of feeling the earth move was indescribable. I had no clear sense of the time, but the violent shaking must have lasted for several minutes. I was unhurt. I knew that aftershocks were likely to occur. I hoped that this had been the main part of the earthquake, and not a prelude to some greater destruction.

I cowered on my knees under the table, afraid to come out for a few moments. I heard people running this way and that, and thought, I must get up; I must see what has happened. I picked my way over the wreckage on the kitchen floor: the walls appeared to be intact. I went out into the peristyle. Everyone was looking for everyone else, it seemed; we gathered out in the peristyle in a huddle, talking excitedly, exchanging news. The stables and some of the storage buildings had collapsed; some of the pillars around the peristyle had toppled and cracked into pieces. In some places the mosaic floors had heaved upwards so that what had been a flat surface was now a broad wave with cracks. The master came out and spoke to us calmly, soothing us. He dispatched several people to survey the damage and report back, and he sent men out to the stables to clear the wreckage and rescue any people or animals that were trapped. I could not help admiring his cool head. His manner calmed us, and he gave clear instructions what to do. Doing something was itself calming, I found. I went back into the kitchen and with Cnaeus and Damaris, sorted through the mess on the floor. Broken pottery and spilled food were mopped up and the shards were removed to a place outside. Intact serving pieces were cleaned and returned to the shelves. Gradually order began to re-emerge.

The master stayed in the atrium and had people come to him to report the problems that had arisen. The pipes from the cisterns were broken, and so we would have to bring water from a nearby well and stream until repairs could be made. Although there had been fairly major damage to the overhanging roof of the atrium and the colonnade around the peristyle, most of the interior walls stood intact, and most of the house appeared to be safe for habitation. There were aftershocks during the afternoon, and these set nerves on edge, but the house suffered no further damage. Even though I had foreseen this, I had been as terrified as all the others. I had never experienced an earthquake before, and thought to myself that I hoped never to experience one again.

Ordinary routine had been suspended, of course, but by late afternoon we all took a break from the job of clearing debris to have some food, and the master ordered wine to be heated for us. The bright clear cold day had at least made it easy to see what needed to be done, but as dark approached, we huddled together around a fire outside, in fear. We didn't know whether it was safe to sleep under the roof that night, or whether there would be more devastation.

The master called me aside, and asked: "Will there be more?"

"I don't know. I think perhaps the worst is over now."

"Let us have music, it will soothe us all. Go and get your instrument."

And so we sat around our bonfire that cold night, wrapped in cloaks, huddled together for that false sense of security that comes from companionship in misery, and I played remembered songs that had the power to restore courage and cheer the heart.

By the next morning, we had news from town, and it was very bad. Nearly every public building had been heavily damaged, and some had been practically leveled. Large buildings with domes or colonnades had fared the worst. Fire had broken out in many places. Although these were finally contained, many homes had been damaged. Reports came in from all over; a flock of several hundred sheep had been lost, swallowed up by the upheaval of the earth. The bakers were not making bread; the food shops were too badly damaged to prepare their usual soups and stews. The decuria, the town council, held emergency meetings.

Now that the damage to his own property had been assessed and his own immediate problems solved, Marcus Tullius sent all the people he could spare into the city to help with rescue efforts. Wealthier citizens, such as our master, opened up their stores of food to distribute to the townspeople. We set up a kind of soup kitchen and distributed food to any that asked for it, as long as we had anything to give. Within a few days food had begun to arrive from other cities, and serious repair efforts were underway.

Most of the villa was still intact, and some emergency work was done to remove partly collapsed sections of roof with loose tiles.

Within a week, the house was habitable, although much work would be needed to repair it.

The master summoned me to his study when things had become quiet, and some semblance of normal routine had returned.

"I begin to think that perhaps you are a daughter of Poseidon, or a Sibyl. You prophesied accurately. Do you see other things I should know?"

Of course I knew many things that would happen in the forthcoming years. I knew that a great fire would destroy large parts of the city of Rome. I knew of Nero's death, and the ensuing chaos of the year of four emperors. I knew that there would be many additional earthquakes that would completely demoralize the town, and lead to decreased property values and a breakdown of government. I knew that within the next twenty years, Pompeii and neighboring towns would be buried under lava, mud and ash from Vesuvius. But, I thought, all those things are far in the future. Perhaps I will tell him, in time, but there is no need to tell everything I know right now. The problems he must deal with right now are already so large.

"I have no other prophecies to make today."

"Your warning made it possible for me to protect my family and my possessions. If the gods speak to you again, tell me what they have to say."

He studied me; I was shivering. "You will be given a new tunic. I notice you are always cold."

"Thank you, master." A heavier wool tunic was indeed most welcome. I wore multiple layers of clothing, but sleeping on a thin pallet on a damp stone floor in the chill of winter, I always felt cold. Did I dare to suggest something with long sleeves?

"A heavy woolen tunic", he added, as an afterthought. And then he dismissed me, but with a smile this time. "For a person from a northern country, you seem to feel the cold more than most people."

The quality of my life improved in many ways. As Tullia's attendant, I slept in her room; it was heated at night by a fire in a brazier, unlike the slave quarters. I had a thicker pallet on the floor. The cheerful decorations on the wall, the birds and flowers painted on a background of forest green, lifted my spirits. I shared many of her meals, and had much better food. Even the olive oil in which I dipped my bread was now a finer quality with a lighter flavor. My status among the slaves was higher; I could converse with Iris as an equal, for we were both personal attendants to family members now. I was given better clothing to wear, for I appeared more often in front of family and guests, and had to make a respectable appearance.

Tullia was pleased with this arrangement; it made it possible for us to spend much more time together. The only aspect of this new arrangement I didn't like was the increased amount of contact with the mistress and her son. Tullia was just approaching the age when she would be considered a young woman and marriageable. I needed to learn to dress her hair and drape her clothing properly. I spend many mornings with Iris, watching how she did these things for the mistress, and sometimes practicing these skills on Iris, rarely to her satisfaction, however.

Now that I spent more time around members of the family, I began to fear the son. He had recently reached the age of formal manhood, and he was beginning to bother the more attractive female slaves. It could only be a matter of time before he demanded a partner or was given one of us. I began to try to think of some way to protect myself from him, but in truth, I knew I had few options. It was considered better for a young man to choose his partners from among the female slaves in the household than to go to one of the brothels in town, or to fall into the clutches of a courtesan. And while an adult Roman male of good character might possibly sometimes decide it was an exercise in benevolence and self-control not to force himself on an unwilling slave woman, I knew that would not be the case with a randy adolescent.

Tullia and I usually had breakfast in her room. I fetched a few things from the kitchen. Usually Cnaeus made some kind of flat bread for breakfast; these might be plain or flavored with cheese, olive oil, and herbs like a foccacia, or sometimes topped with drizzle of honey. We drank watered wine with this. As the weather became a little warmer, we moved our morning meal outside to a stone bench in the peristyle. Birds of all sorts came to bathe and preen in the marble basin that stood on a pedestal near one end of the courtyard.

My Tullia could be moody and tearful at times, mostly when she looked ahead to the inevitable marriage that would take her away from her family, but at moments like this, I couldn't help loving her for her gentleness. She scolded me sometimes for making a poor job of arranging her hair (this was an art for which I had little talent, unfortunately), but she never struck me.

In late morning she had her bath and massage; she and her mother generally used the bath before the men of the family returned. Sometimes she had a light lunch. There was a siesta during the hottest part of the day, although often she did not really sleep. Sometimes we talked, as she lay on her couch and I on my pallet. If the cena was a family meal, it was the highlight of her day; if company was coming, she generally had a meal in her room alone with me. This minimal routine left much time unaccounted for, so I tried to think of other things that would interest and amuse her. We walked out along the sea or into town, always attended by at least one male servant. We puttered in the kitchen or in the workroom, so that she learned some rudiments of cooking and weaving and sewing. I told her stories. We played games, simple ball games like handball or catch, and sometimes board games with counters. She taught me how to play knucklebones, a sort of combination of jacks and dice. Each side of the knucklebone had a different assigned point value; the trick was to toss them up into the air and catch as many as possible on the back of your hand, and then sum the point value, so this combined luck and skill. Adults placed bets on this but Tullia and I just did it for fun.

Our favorite outings were our occasional visits to Julia Felix. I couldn't help thinking, that Tullia would have been so much happier if someone like Julia had been her mother. Holconia seemed to care for her very little. She spent all her time visiting other matrons, shopping, sometimes gambling, and sometimes going to the damaged, but still partly serviceable, public baths. Holconia's only apparent interest in Tullia was to arrange a useful marriage for her, one that would bring wealth or valuable political connections to the family. They began to discuss potential candidates for such a marriage, and these discussions always distressed Tullia. She confided in me that she wished that she could remain with her father; she was afraid of marriage. I tried to soothe her fears, but I sympathized with them. Many Roman men were less kind than her father. She would have very little control over her life as young married woman. It occurred to me that Tullia's marriage would disrupt life for me too. As her personal attendant, I would go with her to her new home. Depending on the nature of her husband, that household might be ruled with less reason and kindness than this one. And I would hardly ever see Marcus Tullius, if I went away with Tullia. These were unwelcome thoughts.

Julia Felix owned the finest house in town, well situated in a quiet neighborhood near the Palaestra. Several of the shops in town that sold fabrics and jewelry were run under her patronage, and she took an active interest in them. She was also extraordinarily well educated compared to most Roman matrons. She was fluent in Greek as well as Latin, and she read extensively. On evenings when Julia Felix came to dinner, I liked to eavesdrop on the discussions at the table, for they were far ranging and fantastic at times. She was very fond of our little Tullia, and often invited her over. I would play my flute or tell stories for them and they would have refreshments.

There were not many other women like Julia Felix in Pompeii. That combination of factors (intelligence, character, wealth, and absence of male relatives who would otherwise command her life) was uncommon. She was able to exploit her situation most skillfully. She violated unwritten rules about proper behavior for women, but only in small ways, and with so much charm, that her social position was not in jeopardy. Some of the men might complain that she was too outspoken; many of the matrons might envy her independence. However, she was invited to dine with all of the prominent families in Pompeii.

Julia had no children, in fact, no close relations at all except for the son of her deceased brother, whom she invariably referred to as "my worthless nephew." He visited Julia often with charming small gifts, trying to ensure his position as her heir. Usually his real agenda for these visits was to petition for more funds to pay his gambling debts and expenses, as he seemed unable to live within the allowance that she provided to him. There was speculation that Julia would tire of him and adopt another heir, and Julia was shrewd enough to allow this gossip. Families with sons who might be suitable heirs for Julia's fortune were particularly generous with dinner invitations. She enjoyed dining out, and was clever enough to realize that she had more power if she did not commit herself. I found myself wishing that she would adopt my Tullia, and free her from the burden of an arranged marriage, but I knew that was not a realistic hope. Still, she seemed to enjoy Tullia's company, and I hoped that Julia's spunk and energy would inspire some spirit in this gentle and overly obedient child.

CHAPTER 17

As Tullia's servant, I helped her to wash, brought her breakfast, and tended her clothing and possessions. I was also her companion, and we enjoyed each other's company. In warm weather we sometimes sat in the peristyle garden to eat breakfast; I scattered a few breadcrumbs, and this attracted birds. The Romans must have loved birds as much as I do; many of the most beautiful murals that have been preserved were garden scenes, and sometimes a dozen different kinds of birds were shown, rendered in exquisite and realistic detail. We tamed a sparrow together. Each day we spread crumbs, a little closer to the bench where we sat. Each day, the bird ventured a little closer. One day he perched on the bench next to Tullia; and a few days later, he accepted food from my hand. We loved that bold little fellow. On days when we did not come out for breakfast, he sat on the bench and scolded in a tiny temper tantrum.

She was at an age where the possibility of love excited and frightened her. She wanted to know what the marriage customs were in my country. I hesitated to describe this because I knew her parents would be angry if she came to think she should be free to choose her partner. However, she was persistent; and so I told her a few things about my world.

"We didn't have arranged marriages. Instead, young men and women met and talked and came to know each other. If a couple fell in love, they could choose to marry."

This was difficult for her to imagine. "My mother speaks of marriage as a responsibility. She wants me to marry someone rich and powerful, to help my brother in his career. I hope the man they choose for me will be kind."

I hoped so too, but from what I knew of Holconia, kindness was not likely to be a major consideration in her choice. Tullia was kind to me; and I began to feel fondly protective of her. Soon she would be fourteen, old enough for marriage according to their customs. I worried about this, mostly because of the way it would change her life; but it would also change mine, for I would almost certainly be sent with her. I was becoming attached to this household, and I didn't want to move to another household that might be much less kind to slaves.

But there was another reason for my reluctance to leave. I was drawn to Marcus Tullius. The sight of him filled my heart with warmth. I looked forward to having his rapt attention when I told stories, or played my flute. I conjured up images of his face at night when I lay on my pallet. I imagined conversations we might have had under different circumstances. I wished that we might touch each other. In short, I was in love with him.

I knew this was a foolish way to feel. A master could use a slave girl for sexual pleasure; he was not likely to love a slave, or even think of her as a person like himself. Power and condescension, not intimacy, would dominate any relationship he might have with me.

I happened to be outside the rear gate putting out some linens for airing, one morning when the master was instructing his son in some basic skills he would need before departing, in a few years, for the usual military experience. Marcus junior was wearing some of the gear a soldier might wear, and had a pack on his back that appeared to be heavy. He was learning to vault up onto the back of a horse; it was necessary to be able to do this in a variety of ways, lightly clad and wearing protective armor, from either the right or the left side, and even with sword in hand. I saw him make his first attempt. He tried to compensate for the weight of the pack, and overshot, and fell off the far side of the horse. His father laughed; Tullia laughed; and I swear, even the horse snickered at him. Marcus junior was furious. I tried to suppress a smile, but I think he saw that even a slave was amused by his mistake, and this further enraged him. His father spoke calming words:

"Patience, my son, these skills require much practice."

I think his resentment about being laughed at might have been part of the reason for his behavior toward me the next day. Tullia and I were feeding birds in the peristyle, and Marcus junior approached. He threw a stone at the flock of sparrows that had gathered; fortunately none of them were injured, but of course they fled in panic. Tullia cried out in annoyance: "Marcus!" This was nothing compared to what happened next. He sat on the bench next to me and put his arm around my waist and pulled me close to him. "Tullia, I am going to take your slave to my room. I want a woman, and she isn't too bad looking." At first I thought this might be merely a crude joke, but it soon became apparent that he was serious; he pulled me to my feet and seized my hand and started off in the direction of his cubicle. "No, Marcus, she belongs to me!" Tullia said, but he paid no attention to this.

I was in a sudden state of panic. I had no right to refuse him, but I found the idea of being raped by this nasty adolescent quite repulsive. It was certainly customary for young men to use female slaves as sex partners. Marcus junior had reached the age where he certainly had the urge. He may have been told Iris was off limits, as the master's favorite, but any other female slave was likely to be considered fair game. With my free hand, I seized the amulet pouch around my neck and held out the image of Neptune. "My god will curse you if you touch me...he will make your penis shrivel up, so that you will never be any good with any woman!"

He stopped; the threat disconcerted him. He yanked the Neptune pendant out of my hand, threw it into the pool, and slapped me across the face. "How dare you threaten me! If you cast a spell on me, you will be put to death!"

Tullia had disappeared; there was no one else in the courtyard. He regained his courage and started dragging me in the direction of his room.

Tullia reappeared with her father; apparently her first thought had been to appeal to him.

"What is it?" he demanded to know. Both Marcus junior and I stood before him looking penitent.

"Father, I am old enough to have a woman. I was going to take this one, and she refused, she threatened me—"

He looked at me. I had nothing to say for myself; the accusation was correct.

"What kind of threat?"

Marcus junior explained. There was suppressed smile on his father's face as he took in the situation. Well, it might be amusing to him, but it was not amusing to me, and I was frightened; I didn't know what he would decide. He knew I had made an accurate prophecy about the earthquake, so he might possibly think I was capable of putting a curse on someone.

Tullia was all ears. "Go to your room, Tullia." She began to protest. "I will send your girl to you in a moment, little one."

Tullia left, still looking concerned. Bless her heart; I think she really was trying to protect me, and not just being possessive of her 'property'.

Marcus senior turned to his son. "Find another woman slave who is willing. You will not touch this one."

"Why not?"

172 A.D. 62: Pompeii

"Because I am paterfamilias, and I have commanded this. Go now. There are other women in the household, and if you cannot find one that you like among the other servants, we will buy one for you." Marcus junior left in a snit.

I wasn't entirely happy with this solution, for I had obtained protection from this pest, but some other woman would now have to put up with him. This was the way things were done in their world. I didn't approve; but I couldn't change it.

Marcus Tullius now turned to me. "You must not threaten to put curses on my family. I would have to punish you. What do you have to say for yourself?"

I inclined my head to show my penitence.

"Please do not be angry, master. I meant no disrespect to your authority. I appeal to you, for you are the only one who has the power to protect me from shame."

"Shame?" he asked, as if the idea of a slave having such a feeling was difficult to conceive.

"Although we are slaves, we are human beings who have the same feelings as Romans. Has not a slave eyes? Has not a slave hands, organs, senses, affections, passions? Fed with the same food, hurt with the same weapons, subject to the same diseases, healed by the same means, warmed by the same summer and cooled by the same winter as Romans? If you cut us, do we not bleed? If you poison us, do we not die?" I borrowed Shakespeare's words from *The Merchant of Venice* to give my appeal an eloquence that I did not believe I could achieve on my own. The sentiments were not entirely foreign to the Roman mind; at about this time, Seneca wrote an essay using language I think Shakespeare must have read: "a slave traces his origins to the same stock, has the same sky above him, lives as you do, dies as you do…"

Now the master looked at me differently. Amused, bemused, he seemed less angry, in any event. "You should be an advocate in the courts. You argue like a Roman."

He looked thoughtful.

"You were once a priestess, under a vow of chastity. Do you still consider yourself to be bound by that vow? Would your god really punish a man who took you?"

I wasn't certain how to respond. I suppose that if I said "Yes", it would provide me with useful protection. I did not want any man in this world, except for this man. I hesitated.

"No. Rape is an offense against my god, but love given willingly is permitted for an ex-priestess."

I think he may have heard that I had thrown a bucket at the head of an unwanted suitor among the house slaves; he smiled a little, perhaps recalling that event.

"Well then. My son will not bother you: it is my command. Go back to Tullia and comfort her; she is upset."

CHAPTER 18

A few weeks passed uneventfully, and then one morning Tullia greeted me cheerfully. "I want to go visit Aunt Julia, she said that I could come today. You will come too." This was pleasant news. I dressed Tullia in her tunic and a light green palla. She is becoming so pretty, I thought. Now they are thinking about a husband for her. What will happen to me then? Will they send me with her, to her new home? Or will I remain here? Either way, I will lose one of the people I love most in this world.

At the front gate we met our escort, a young messenger. He would walk with us to Julia Felix's house. I laced up Tullia's outdoor sandals and we set off to walk the mile or so to Julia's house.

"I have to talk to Julia. I need her advice".

"About what, little mistress?" From kitchen gossip, I already knew what was up, but I asked nonetheless, so that she would speak of it.

"My mother is talking about a husband for me. The family will come to dinner later this week to look at me. I want to make a good impression."

"Oh, little mistress, they will like you!"

"My mother says I must be very careful what I say. They are a great family, and they will expect their daughter in law to carry on their family traditions and make them proud."

Already I was prepared to dislike this family. I understood that the mistress's idea of a good match would involve wealth and political power and a great name, all of those things, if possible. I hoped that she would also consider the character of the young man as well, but I knew that Tullia's happiness was not of much concern to her. I risked an impertinent question:

"Is this usually decided by the mother, or by the paterfamilias?"

I hoped that Marcus Tullius might be the one to decide her fate, for I had more confidence in his judgment than in Holconia's.

"It is my father's decision, but my mother wants this family very much. She usually manages to get her way."

"Do you know anything about the man they want for your husband, Tullia?"

"His name is Lucius Popidius Secundus. His father Vibius Popidius has been duumvir three times; they own a very fine house in town, I do not think you have seen inside it, it is smaller than ours but most magnificent. They spend most of their time in the city of Rome." He was much older than Tullia, I thought, but I knew that was customary.

"What does he look like?"

"I don't know; that's why I'm so nervous about this dinner. I hope I like his looks. I hope he likes my looks."

Poor thing, I thought.

We arrived at Julia Felix's house and passed though the entryway, saluted by her doorman as we passed. We paused; one of Julia's house slaves washed the dust from our walk from Tullia's feet and I laced up her house sandals. I was given water to wash my own feet, for I would accompany her inside.

A brilliant smile flashed across Julia's face when we entered, and she extended her hand in greeting. Tullia took it and received a kiss on her cheek. "Let me look at you, child. You are becoming quite a beauty; you look more like your father than your mother, I think."

"Julia, do you know, we are having the Popidius family to dinner in two days; my mother thinks this is a good match for me."

"Which Popidius, the one called Augustianus?"

"Yes."

I recalled from kitchen gossip that this branch of the Popidius family had acquired this nickname because their son was often in attendance on Nero at court. That connection was worrisome. Nero had been almost reasonable during the first few years of his reign. Now he showed signs of the weakness and cruelty that would make him extremely dangerous in the coming years. I think I frowned slightly at this thought and for a moment Julia's gaze and mine met in a flash of understanding.

"Indeed, a most eminent family", she said, in a tone that did not convey any enthusiasm.

"Julia, will you advise me? I have to decide what to wear; I want so much to make a good impression. My mother says I must say very little, and speak only when spoken to, and behave in a modest way. She says I must not show off that I know Greek, or give any opinions."

"When you are in doubt how to dress, little one, something simple is always the most elegant choice. Let us take some refreshment; I have honeyed figs, which I know you like. I see you have brought the storyteller. Let us have a story then."

I bowed respectfully, and knelt on the floor not too far away from the couch where the two of them reclined. I thought for a moment: what would be appropriate to the occasion? I decided to take a small risk…I chose a modern feminist fairy tale, Jeanne Desy's *The Princess Who Stood on Her Own Two Feet*. My retelling of it went like this: There was a young woman of great beauty and wonderful accomplishments. She could play music on a lyre, and do sums on an abacus, and weave wonderful tapestries, and converse about great ideas. She had everything except love, for in all the country there was no man who was talented enough to be a match for her. One day she received a wonderful gift: an enchanted dog. The dog became her beloved companion, and it seemed so intelligent that she thought he understood her when she spoke to him.

One day a prospective husband was presented. He was handsome, and when she met him at the betrothal feast, the young woman was very pleased by his appearance. But alas, when she stood up, the prospective fiancé frowned and looked most displeased. What was the matter? That night, she stared at herself in the mirror, trying to see what had displeased her suitor. And she asked her dog, what was the matter? And the dog replied (for it could talk!) that it was her height. She was taller than her suitor. Why was this a problem? She asked. Ah, the dog said, men expect to be taller than their wives. But why? She asked. The dog thought about it, but he was not able to explain why.

The young woman went to a magician and begged him to make her a foot shorter. No, the magician said, he could not do that. Well, the princess thought of a way to solve the problem. The next time her suitor came to see her, she did not stand up; she reclined upon a couch. As long as she was sitting or lying down, the suitor was quite pleased with her. And after a time she seemed to have lost the ability to walk; but this seemed a small price to pay for such a wonderful suitor.

Now that she was idle, she had more time to read, and to think of witty and intelligent things to say. She only wanted to please her suitor. But he didn't like her words, and asked her if she had never heard the expression that 'women should be seen and not heard'? She did not understand; but she understood that, just as he preferred her sitting instead of standing, he preferred her silent instead of speaking. And so she stopped talking. The suitor was well pleased with this; he sat by her and held her hand, and they conversed only with gazes and affectionate gestures.

Now that she was in bed alone almost all day, the dog was really her only companion most of the time. However, the suitor did not like the dog, and he tried to strike it, and he demanded that the dog be taken away. This the young woman did not allow.

At night, alone, she spoke to her dog and told him that she would not give him up. The dog replied that the suitor had taken everything else away, and that he would insist on getting rid of the dog as well. But no, the young woman said. I did those things myself; I tried to make myself into someone he could love. The dog said: I loved you before you gave up those things.

Well, the young woman and the suitor quarreled about the dog. It seemed to her that her suitor was looking less handsome, as time went on. She asked the magician: why does the suitor want me to get rid of the dog? And the magician replied that it was because she loved it. But why? She still wanted to know. The magician could not explain.

The wizard said that wishes, and sacrifices, come in threes; you have given up walking, he said, and you have given up talking. What next?

She agonized about what to do about the dog; and the dog said, sometimes one must give up everything for love. And the dog fell down, and was quite still. She wept over her lost friend. And then she got up, saying that she was going to bury the one who really loved her. Her suitor found her beside the open grave that she had made, wrapping the dog in her wedding dress. His only comment about the dog was that he thought she had gotten rid of it some time ago. But then the suitor was struck to realize: she was walking, and she was talking! And she told her suitor that she no longer wanted to see him, and said good-bye.

Her mother scolded her for having lost such a good suitor.

But the young woman said that sometimes a woman must stand on her own two feet, and be loyal to those who really love her.

Some time passed, and then one day another suitor rode up to the door of the house. It was a strange thing: the color of his hair and eyes were the same as the dog's. And when she asked where he had come from, he could not remember. She stood in front of him, thinking, I hope he is taller than I am. When he dismounted and stood in front of her and took her hand, however, he was several inches shorter. She was so disappointed! But he said that it was a pleasure to look up at such a beautiful lady; and that made her able to stand up tall again. And they were married, and she felt as if she had her wise and loving friend back again, in the person of this man who wanted her to be herself.

When I had reached the end of my story, I sat quietly. My audience was rapt. I would not have dared to tell this story to my master; I was not certain how Julia Felix would react. I knew well enough that this was subversive.

"What a wonderful story!" Tullia said.

"Tullia, go out to the garden, please, and choose some flowers for the gardener to cut; you may take them home to your mother."

When Tullia had departed, Julia brought her hand up to her chin, and placed her fingers on her lips in a gesture that seemed thoughtful. Her gaze settled on me. I waited to hear her judgment; my chin tilted downwards, for I anticipated a scolding. Instead, she laughed.

"Your story pleased me, but some others would not approve of it. Do you understand why?"

"Yes, lady."

"If she were not such a docile child, stories like this might incite her to rebellion against her mother's plans. But rebellion would be pointless. She will have to do as her parents decide. You must not tell her this kind of story just now."

"Yes, lady."

"However, I myself enjoy a little subversion, now and then."

I bowed my head to show obedience and understanding.

"You have some education, apparently."

"Yes, lady."

"You may speak to me at greater length when I ask questions. You are not so meek as you pretend, I think."

I didn't know how to respond to this, and saying nothing seemed to be the most prudent thing.

"It is obvious that your stories contain messages that, if you stated them directly as opinions, would be most unsuitable for a slave. You have said that women can be superior to men in ability, and that this might not be an obstacle to love. Is that not so?"

This reminded me of a remark by Samuel Johnson, which I repeated: "Men know that women are an overmatch for them, and therefore they choose the weakest or the most ignorant. If they did not think so, they could never be so afraid of a woman knowing as much as themselves."

This made her laugh. "I will borrow you, some afternoon, to discuss these matters further. You are quite a philosopher, even if you are just a slave woman. You have thoughts like my own. We shall have much to talk about."

"I am glad that I have not offended you, great lady."

"You would be wise to speak of such matters only to those of like mind."

The next few days were spent in frenzied preparations for the great event. The menu, the wines, the wreaths of flowers all had to be the best quality. Tullia's clothing was simple, but she would wear one of the mistress's most prized necklaces. Anxiety made her pale and twitchy. The night before the dinner, she slept little. I did not sleep at all.

The Popidii arrived in great state, with eight bearers for the litter that carried the mother and father. The son rode a fine chestnut horse. They wore silk and sparkled with jewels. They were, in fact, quite handsome people—at least superficially. The master and mistress themselves greeted our distinguished guests at the door, and I was one of those who washed their feet. Their own slaves replaced the outdoor sandals with lighter weight indoor ones. Demetrius was visibly impatient to get their slaves back to the kitchen; he had a nose for gossip. They walked in the peristyle garden, admiring the roses.

Tullia was not discussed, but all three of them looked at her, perhaps evaluating her breeding potential. They would be interested in three things in a prospective wife. First, Tullia would be expected to provide heirs; second, she would bring a dowry that her husband could invest and manage as part of his own fortune, at least, as long as the marriage lasted; and third, the family name and any political connections would be weighed.

I tried to look at Tullia through their eyes. She seemed frail and small; that was not a point in her favor. The kitchen gossip was that the mistress would argue for the smallest possible dowry, so that funds could be kept to launch a political career for Marcus Tullius junior. And our family was influential in Pompeii, but not very important compared to the families that the Popidii knew at Nero's court. What else is going on? I wondered. Why are they interested in Tullia at all?

Tullia walked carefully and did not speak at all except when spoken to. Lucius Popidius was handsome. I thought, however, that he looked like Mr. Bad News; he preened himself with obvious awareness of his own physical beauty. Late twenties or early thirties, I thought; but already this one was showing some signs of dissipation. Perhaps his parents want a quiet country girl for him, rather than one of the notorious women at court. Entanglements of that sort can bring trouble. He probably doesn't care whether he is married or not. In fact, marriage might even be convenient. I thought about these matters as I waited, standing silently within call, while the families made pleasant small talk.

After a brief walk in the garden, they settled themselves in the outdoor triclinium. It was unseasonably warm for April. We had draped linens on the couches and placed cushions there for the comfort of the diners. Vibius Popidius and his son occupied the places of highest honor. Tullia was placed opposite Lucius, between her mother and her prospective mother in law. The first series of dishes were elegantly garnished appetizers, grilled mushroom caps with the inevitable garum, liver pate, a truffle salad, a patina of roses: a larger number of dishes presented with more attention to appearance than I had seen at any previous dinner. Tullia picked at her food without appetite. The only people who seemed to have any appetite were Vibius Popidius and his son; everyone else was preoccupied with the importance of the event.

Vibius Popidius, as the guest of most importance, dominated the conversation, but he did not immediately address the reason for the gathering.

"What did you think of this request by my freedman, Marcus Tullius? Numerius Popidius Celsinus has proposed to rebuild the Temple of Isis at his own expense, but he wants the decuria to accept his son as a member. His son, however, is only six years old."

"We need many sources of funds for rebuilding. Nearly every public building in the city needs to be reconstructed or repaired. The expense is going to be a great burden on the most important families. His request is outrageous, of course, but we need his contribution. Desperate times require unusual measures. Perhaps we can bargain for a delay in the appointment, until the son is a more suitable age, and has demonstrated his capabilities in appropriate offices."

"No, Marcus, that suggestion was already rejected. He has offered to pay all the costs, but only on the condition that we make the appointment now."

"Then we must allow the boy to attend the council with his nurse-maid to tend him, I suppose!"

The mistress spoke now. "Tell us of matters at court, Lucius. How is our great emperor?"

"Nero will marry Poppaea Sabina within the year." Lucius had exquisite table manners, even when eating with his fingers. He nibbled at a mushroom cap with apparent enjoyment. "Your cook is good, Marcus."

Marcus Tullius accepted the compliment graciously, without revealing that for the occasion an additional cook had been hired to contribute more sophistication to the menu than Cnaeus was able to provide.

I refreshed the wine in my master's goblet and removed myself to a respectful distance, watching the diners carefully to see whether anyone required a basin of rose scented water for hand washing.

"Poppaea Sabina! That is wonderful news! Marcus, we must send her a fine gift to mark the occasion!", our mistress exclaimed.

Even as a slave, I was well informed about gossip. In fact, we servants were generally better informed than the family. Demetrius was in the kitchen, I was sure, plying their servants with wine and extracting much more graphic detail than my masters would hear at the table. It was dangerous to say anything disparaging about the emperor, who was notoriously sensitive to criticism, real or imagined. Based on my recollections from Tacitus, and additional information from Demetrius, this was the story, as I understood it.

Poppaea Sabina was from Pompeii. Her father, Titus Ollius, was not himself particularly eminent or successful. Her grandfather, Poppaeus Sabinus, had been a consul and had been given a triumph for his successes in the field, and she had adopted his name. Poppaea was already noted for two things: her beauty and her amorality. She was reputed to have hair the color of amber, and perfect skin that she bathed daily in asses' milk. When she first came to the attention of the emperor, he was married to Octavia; Poppaea was married to Nero's friend Otho (already her second husband). Nero also had a mistress, Acte, who was an ex-slave. Nero was reputed to have an incestuous relationship with his mother, Agrippina; whether or not this was true, it was clear that in the early years of his reign she dominated him, and that later he feared and hated her. Agrippina disliked Poppaea; Poppaea hated all three of the other women in Nero's life. She nagged Nero incessantly, and mocked him, and taunted him.

Perhaps because of Poppaea's jealousy, Nero decided to kill his mother. However, he feared Agrippina greatly, and he did not think it wise to use any obvious device such as poison. In any case, Agrippina had all her food tasted and she regularly consumed antidotes for poison. With the help of his dim-witted accomplices, Nero concocted a plan. He pretended to be reconciled with his mother, and invited her to dine on board a ship. Now this ship had been designed so that it could be made to capsize. After Nero left, a lead-weighted contraption made the roof of her cabin fall on her; however, she survived with only a minor injury because the sides of her couch protected her. In the ensuing confusion, half the crew, who were in on the plot, were trying to sink the ship; the other half, who were not, were trying to save it. One of Agrippina's attendants called out, "Help, I am Agrippina!", and she was struck dead. Agrippina herself was silent, and when the ship finally sank, she escaped and swam to shore. (Apparently, Nero didn't know the old bat could swim.) Now she realized that this had been a deliberate attempt on her life, but she decided that the safest course of action was to pretend that she did not know this. She made her way back to one of her villas and sent a message to Nero telling him of her miraculous escape, and telling him not to trouble to come and visit her.

When Nero heard of his mother's escape, he was frantic with fear that she would kill him; for there could be no doubt that he was the one behind this assassination attempt. A former slave volunteered to go and stab Agrippina, and Nero agreed to this, and finally it was done. This had happened about two years before my arrival in the past. Octavia had been divorced, and banished (to the island of Pandateria) at the time of this dinner party, and I recalled that after she married Nero, Poppaea demanded, and got, Octavia's head.

But, as I said, Poppaea was a great beauty, one of the loveliest women of her time, wealthy, witty, pleasant to talk with. She captivated Nero, as no one else was able to do. Even after he killed her later, accidentally, in a fit of temper, he sought the companionship of a man who was said to bear an uncanny physical resemblance to her.

At any rate, at that point in time, the beauty of Poppaea was a safe topic for conversation. They did not speak directly of their own marriage negotiations, as the families sized each other up; the Popidius paterfamilias seemed to be assessing the value of the household furnishings, perhaps trying to decide how large a dowry he should demand.

I noticed that Marcus Tullius had little to say; the mistress had much. I think that Marcus Tullius respected the father, but thought the son rather useless. Holconia enjoyed the wit and charm of the son, but thought the father stodgy and old-fashioned. And it did not matter to anyone what Tullia thought; but it seemed to me that she liked what she saw. Poor child, she could not know what kind of life this man led, or what her life would be like as his wife. She would go willingly like a lamb to the slaughter, I thought. All the indications so far were that the major parties to this marriage agreement were getting along well.

No, I thought, this marriage must not happen. At best this vain courtier will neglect her. At worst, she will be degraded by him, and humiliated by his mistresses. And this marriage bodes ill for me, as well as for her. For I would have to go with her to this other household, and perhaps never see Marcus Tullius again.

I decided that I would not allow that to happen.

CHAPTER 19

That night Tullia overflowed with enthusiasm.

"He is so handsome, and so important! I was afraid my mother might want me to marry someone old and rich, like Julius Polybius."

How could I tell her that a good heart does not always accompany a beautiful face and that a good heart is more important?

"Would you like to hear a story before you go to sleep, little mistress?"

"No, not tonight…"

Well, the story could wait. Probably this matter would require further negotiations. The business of the dowry could be a sticking point.

"I hope they liked me. I wish I were prettier."

"You are very beautiful, little one," I told her as I combed out her hair and helped her to undress for bed. "Like Psyche herself."

The next morning when I went to the kitchen for her breakfast, I asked Demetrius what he had learned from the visitor's servants. He looked around to make certain that we could not be overheard. "They are not as rich as they appear. The son has spent huge sums to put on an impressive show in Rome, but he hasn't gained the favor he wants, or received gifts enough to make up for the costs. They will want a large dowry. The son is more in favor with Poppaea Sabina than with Nero. That could be dangerous."

"Does the master know this, do you think?"

"Who knows? The old man Vibius has long been a family friend; the master thinks well of this family. The mistress is all for this marriage. I think they will argue about the money, and make the bargain for the sake of the connections. The mistress would like nothing more than to have her own son become one of the Augustiani, like Lucius Polybius. She will try to trade her money for their social position; that's what the Popidii have to sell."

This cynical assessment made me uneasy, but it was probably accurate, I thought. "What do they say about the son?"

"Like Poppaea Sabina: Do not trust in a pleasing complexion."

That had been my impression also. The face of Dorian Gray, I thought…that one has not yet begun to display his dissipation on his face.

By late in the day, Demetrius had more to tell me about his matter. "There was a discussion late last night about the dowry. The master offered 150,000 sesterces; Popidius wanted 300,000."

"How do you know that?"

"In this house, the very walls have ears."

I realized that if I wanted to interfere in this matter, I would have to do something quickly. Perhaps I could use my successful track record as a prophet, I thought. There must be some way to persuade the master that this would be an ill-omened marriage. And I remembered a scene from *Fiddler on the Roof*, in which one of Teyve's daughters had objected to an arranged marriage, and he had a dream.

The next morning I presented myself to Alexander and told him that I needed to speak to the master when he was finished with his clients. By now Alexander had given up trying to dissuade me from doing foolish things. It was not spoken of in my presence, but I think many in the household knew that I had secretly foretold the earthquake; I had been treated with greater respect since that time.

I presented myself humbly.

"What is it? I am prepared to be astonished," the master said to me.

This boded well; he seemed to be in good humor.

"It is about this possible marriage…"

He looked at me sharply. "Are you bringing me another evil prophecy?"

"Evil can be avoided when we know what is going to happen."

"Have you seen something?"

I knew that I had to make this warning sufficiently strong to alter his decision. If I merely told him that she would be unhappy, which I believed to be true, that in itself would not be sufficient to change things. Happiness and love were not necessarily expected to go with marriage. No: I had to foretell disaster.

"I saw the wedding, and I saw the events that would follow it. If Tullia marries this man, she will be dead within two years." The die is cast, I thought.

He rested his chin in his hand, elbow on the table, and thought. He didn't want to believe me, but I had delivered this prediction with all the confidence I could muster; and he evidently believed me.

"Well, then. Are you certain that she will die if she marries him, and not otherwise?"

Lying had become easier, particularly when it was in the service of something I believed to be a good cause.

"Yes." I lied with all the conviction I could muster.

He knit his brows in thought. Privately I suspected that his own enthusiasm for this match was not really great, particularly given the size of the dowry that was being demanded, and the character of his prospective son in law.

"I will consider this. Do you have anything else to tell?"

"No, that is all." I had considered trying to convince him to present this premonition as his own, but decided against it. If I try to convince him to lie, it might occur to him that I myself am a liar. I knew that if my role in breaking up this match became known, I would be persona non grata in many quarters, particularly with the mistress, and even with Tullia, who was not likely to understand that I had done this out of concern for her. But I knew that Marcus would understand the danger of my situation in offering this unwelcome prophecy, and I trusted that he would do what he could to keep my role in this matter secret. He dismissed me abruptly.

By the next day, word had spread through the servant's quarters. The negotiations had been called off; we did not know what reasons had been given to the Popidius family, a gap in our collective knowledge that was unusual. Holconia was enraged. I hoped that my own role in this would not become known.

Tullia wept. "They didn't like me. I tried to do it perfectly, but I must have done something wrong. Perhaps I said something I shouldn't."

I tried to comfort her, but she brushed me away. "I want to see Aunt Julia." She asked for her mother's permission to make this outing, and within about an hour we set off for Julia Felix's house, and arrived just as she was finishing business with her clients. Julia had already heard the news.

"Dearest, you will have better offers. This Lucius Popidius is a peacock."

"Aunt Julia, do you really think so?"

At that moment another visitor was announced.

"Lady Julia, it is your nephew, the honorable Antonius Cassius, he wishes to see you."

Julia snorted. "I imagine that he does. It has been nearly a month since he last asked for money. Admit him."

"Aunt Julia! You are looking wonderfully well, as always. Who is your charming little friend? Please introduce me to her."

Julia suffered him to kiss her on both cheeks. "This is the Lady Tullia, daughter of Marcus Tullius."

"Greetings, fair lady."

Unfortunately, this one was a veritable Adonis. This must be the one whom I had heard Julia refer to on occasion as "my worthless nephew"; her only close living relative, and her heir, in the absence of any-more deserving candidates.

Tullia's smile was radiant; she had found a new god to worship.

"What business brings you to Pompeii, nephew?"

"It is unseasonably warm, and already the city is oppressive in the heat; and I wanted to see you, dear Aunt."

Julia's expression was not encouraging. She could radiate kindness sometimes, but just now her face appeared to be cut from stone. He is out of money again, I guessed that she must be thinking. How much does he want this time? And how quickly can I be rid of him?

"How have you spent your time? Have you asked your patron to help you obtain an appointment? You need to start a proper career."

"I have prospects of being appointed an assistant quaestor. It isn't definite yet, however, and I will need to make certain gifts."

"In February you spoke of this in your letter, and I sent you a considerable sum at that time to use for these gifts."

"Aunt Julia, creditors were pressing me for payments. I had to pay my rent and other expenses."

He looked uncomfortable. I think she purposely conducted this interview in Tullia's presence to embarrass him; and perhaps to show her that at least this particular instance of handsome manhood was seriously deficient. Tullia did not seem to hear what was said; she did seem to be very taken with the young man's appearance.

"I will allow you another 40,000 sesterces, but on these conditions. You must obtain an appointment with this money, and not waste it on gambling and entertainment. And you must not ask me for funds again until you have a position. If you continue to lead such a useless life, I will find another heir. There are families enough in Pompeii who parade their candidates in front of me."

He acted as though he had heard only the first few words. "I am grateful, Aunt Julia, and I won't disappoint you. I have very promising prospects." He kissed her again; this time she leaned just slightly away when he kissed her, as if his breath or something else was repellant to her.

"Will you stay for refreshment?" This offer was made reluctantly, I guessed, and was refused with false regrets. They agreed that he would return the next day for the money. After he left, Julia said:

"He is expensive, and he is not even very entertaining." But Tullia protested:

"He just needs a chance, he said that his patron has a position for him."

"Do not set your heart on that one, dear child. He has nothing until he inherits, and I intend to live a long time."

At least it was a relief to see that Tullia's heart had not really been broken by the loss of her marriage prospects. In fact, she confessed her ambivalence:

"Oh, Aunt Julia, sometimes I wish I could just stay with my father. He's so kind to me."

I thought about Tullia's prospects. Sooner or later she would be married to someone probably at least ten years older than herself. She would be expected to render the same obedience to him as she had to her father. She would be expected to produce the required three children; if she could not have children, she might be set aside or divorced for barrenness. Childbirth could be dangerous. She would be expected to be faithful to her husband; and to ignore any mistresses that her husband might have. She could aspire to independence like Julia Felix's only if she were widowed or divorced, and regained control of her dowry. Love would not necessarily be part of any of these arrangements. In some respects, I thought, she doesn't have much more freedom than I do as a slave. Her cage is gilded, and mine is not; that is the only difference. And in fact my possibilities of evading the rules and having small moments of freedom are greater than hers, for I am much less closely watched. She has been fortunate to have a kind father, but everything else in her life will depend, for good or ill, on the nature of her future husband.

When we returned home, the atmosphere seemed strained. I soon discovered the reason. By now everyone knew about the prophecy I had made that had been the reason for the break in the marriage arrangements.

"She will be angry", Demetrius warned me. I knew what he meant; this was not the first time I annoyed the mistress; nor would it be the last, I suspected. Iris came to tell me: "She wants to see you, now." The look on her face when she delivered this message was triumphant. Why does Iris wish me ill? I wondered. I walked slowly on my way to the mistress's room, for I dreaded the confrontation that I knew must happen.

The look on Holconia's face was dreadful: she was enraged. She slapped me hard on both cheeks, leaving a cut on one cheek from her ring. I fell to my knees.

"How dare you interfere with my plans? I will have you beaten! You will be sold!"

I was terrified, for I understood well enough that she could carry out these threats.

Perhaps it was a coincidence that Marcus was passing by and heard her voice; perhaps someone friendly to me among the servants told him what was happening. At that moment, the master entered the room.

"I forbid you to punish this slave. She has warned us of evil before, and made it possible for us to avoid harm. Don't punish the messenger because the message from the gods was not what you wanted to hear."

Although he spoke in a low voice, the expression on his face was a warning. Holconia shot him a look of defiance. "This girl is nothing but trouble. Get rid of her."

"No. I am the master of this house, and you will obey. She stays, and you will not harm her."

Holconia bit her lip in frustration, but she was silent. I didn't want to become a point of conflict between the two of them, but it was too late now. I had known that my interference with this marriage would infuriate Holconia if she discovered it, and I also knew that the chances of keeping it hidden weren't good. She had disliked me at first sight. Now she had a clear reason to hate me. I feared her hatred; it might make it impossible for me to survive in this house.

She glared at him. He looked at her steadily, and said, without raising his voice:

"I am paterfamilias. The marriage plans were cancelled because I commanded it. This slave will not be punished for telling us the truth. You, go back to Tullia's room."

I stood, made a shaky bow toward him, and left quickly. The sound of their voices, his low and determined, hers raised in anger, pursued me out into the courtyard.

❧   ❧   ❧

At first I was afraid that, when he was not paying attention, she would find a way to punish me. But after a few days, nothing happened, and I stopped worrying so much. After all, I thought, a slave is nothing to her. I made a point of staying out of her path; Alexander tactfully avoided having me wait on the table when she was present. I began to hope that the incident had been forgotten.

A few nights later, I had told a story for Tullia and her father; and when the children went off to bed, he told me to stay and tell another story.

A story for him...I thought for a few moments. The one I chose was *Sheherazade*, or the *Thousand and One Nights*. My version of the story went like this: There was a king whose wife deceived him; and because of this he became bitter toward all women, and trusted none. He decided that no woman would ever again have an opportunity to deceive him, and so, from that time onward, he took a new wife each night. He spent only one night with each wife, and in the morning, had her executed so that she could not betray him. Naturally, there was soon a shortage of candidates, and there was great fear throughout the kingdom. The grand vizier had an exceptionally intelligent daughter named Sheherazade. She thought about the situation, and came up with a plan. Her father was horrified when she told him what she planned to do, but he reluctantly agreed. She offered herself as the king's next wife. They were married, and spend a first night together. As the night went on, she asked her sister to join them for conversation, and the king agreed; and her sister Dunyazade pleaded for a story. And so Sheherazade told a story…but she spun it out so that by the time the sun rose, the story had not ended, and she had just come to the most suspenseful part. The king wanted to hear the end of this story, and so he decided to spare her for one more night. The next night she finished her first story (*Ali Baba and the Forty Thieves*) and began a second story (*Aladdin*), again, leaving her story unfinished at sunrise. And so it went on, for one thousand wonderful nights of stories. And finally the king fell so much in love with her that he decided not to execute her, but to keep her as his wife, for he had learned that a woman could be faithful and intelligent and wise.

When I had finished this story, he said to me "You are my Sheherazade". He took a bite from a peach, and offered me a bite; the sweet fragrance of it was intoxicating, and its skin as velvety as human skin. With his finger he touched the corner of my mouth where a drop of sweet juice escaped; gently he wiped my lip; I shivered. I was disturbed and aroused by the intimacy of this gesture. Then he caressed my cheek and my sense of enchantment was shattered by a sudden terror. Surely this was not what I intended, to become a slave mistress? I froze like a frightened deer. He drew back.

"I won't force you." The tone of his voice conveyed his displeasure at my reaction; perhaps he thought I found him personally distasteful. He made a gesture of dismissal, and I fled from his presence.

When I lay on my pallet that night, not sleeping, gazing through the doorway at a patch of star dusted sky, I asked myself again: What is going to happen to me? What do I want to happen? And I didn't know.

I felt such unreasonable joy whenever I was in his presence. I sensed tenderness in his eyes and voice. And yet I feared him. He had sent me away this time, but there was nothing to prevent him from doing whatever he wanted with me. I wasn't sure why he had let me go.

I didn't want to be third or fourth in his affections; the idea of being a casually used slave mistress appalled me. How can there be trust between a master and a slave, when the master has the power to abuse that trust at any time? How can you know when touch conveys affection, and when it is only domination? How could I even think of loving a man who owned slaves, and took slavery for granted? Yet I admired him in spite of my misgivings; I had seen many instances of his kindness. Was it possible to hate slavery and yet to be in love with a slave owner?

Perhaps he really believed that I was a daughter of Neptune, a creature from a completely different world. That myth protected me, and I clung to it because I feared what would happen if I ever let go of it.

I wondered whether this brief encounter would mean the end of his interest in me; but it did not. He behaved toward me as if the night of Sheherazade had not happened. In retrospect, I think he saw me as a wild and frightened creature that could be tamed and brought to his hand with patience, for that is what he set out to do.

I arrived in the master's study for the usual evening storytelling; he was not there. An open scroll lay on the table. I couldn't resist; I went around to the other side of the table and looked at it. It was in

Latin, and with some difficulty, I was able to make out the script. I began to read. It was a poem:

"...Hunc cupio nomen carminis ire mei, me laudent doctae solum placuisse puellae..."

"...This is the fame I claim for my songs; let my only praise be this, that I pleased the heart of a learned girl..."

Propertius again. Perhaps this was one of his favorites; it was one of mine.

My reverie was interrupted; suddenly I realized that he had entered the room, and had seen me reading. I was startled. I stepped away from the table. Scrolls were valuable, and I did not have permission to touch them.

He smiled, so I knew I was not in trouble. "What do you understand from that? I thought you said you could not read Latin?"

"I can read it a little; the script is different than what I am accustomed to. The poet speaks, and says, he pleased the heart of a learned girl..."

"You are yourself a learned girl!"

I blushed at this.

"There must be poets in your country. Do you know poetry, as well as stories?"

"I remember some poems...but poetry is difficult to translate."

"Do not worry about the meter...just tell me the meaning. I would like to hear a poem from your culture." He indicated that I should sit in the usual place I occupied for storytelling.

"What kind of poem do you want to hear?"

"Something about love, I think"

I took a deep breath, and thought for a few moments. I would give him the best that I can think of...a remembered fragment from John Donne. It took me a few moments to turn it into reasonably polished Latin.

"If ever any beauty I did see,
Which I desired, and got, 'twas but a dream of thee.

And now good morrow to our waking souls,
Which watch not one another out of fear;
For love, all love of other sights controls,
And makes one little room an everywhere.
Let sea-discoverers to new worlds have gone,
Let maps to others, worlds on worlds have shown,
Let us possess our world; each hath one, and is one."

He was silent for a moment.

"Beautiful words," he said. "Perhaps love is the same feeling, even in different worlds." I could not tell whether he understood that I was speaking of my own feelings for him; and I could not read his feelings for me from his words.

CHAPTER 20

Urgent business matters arose, and Marcus Tullius needed to go to the city of Rome. I dreaded his departure, for it would leave me unprotected. Everyone knew that the mistress was displeased with me. The master had forbidden her to punish me or sell me, but I was uneasy in spite of this.

She acquired a new personal attendant at that time: a boy about eleven years old, whom she called Phoebus. It was the fashion among her friends, just then, to have an attractive boy servant, a sort of page. She kept him with her much of the time; he ran errands and messages, and amused her with his antics. We older servants thought him a pest. He teased us and we couldn't retaliate.

During this absence the mistress entertained her friends. Alexander did not send me to wait upon the diners, but she often summoned me to play my flute. She did not care for my stories, but my music seemed to please her, and she praised me in front of the guests. I hoped that she might forget about her anger, but Cnaeus reminded me not to hope for a change:

"The wolf changes its coat...not its mind", he warned me. As a week passed by without incident, my worries diminished. Thus I was not particularly alarmed when the summons came for me to play music for dinner guests one evening.

The diners were in the outdoor triclinium, enjoying the cooler air as the watercolor blues and pinks of summer twilight washed over the scene. I positioned myself unobtrusively, but the mistress beckoned for me to stand closer. I began to play, trying to fit my music to their mood. They were drinking wine and nibbling at pastries, and talking, and the mood seemed to be light and cheerful. I chose graceful melodies from the renaissance and earlier, and let the notes of my flute blend with the splash of the fountain.

There were five at the table that evening: The mistress, Lucius Caecilius Aper and his wife, and two other male friends of the Caecilius family. I had become less wary of male guests, because I had not experienced the sort of trouble with them that I knew was common in some households. Usually the guests were middle aged, decorous, conservative people who were friends of Marcus Tullius. He did not approve of the licentiousness that was reported at Nero's court, and his parties were generally sedate affairs.

That evening the group was unfamiliar. Caecilius Aper and his wife spent most of their time in the city of Rome, indulging in the pleasures of life at court. They evidently found this quiet evening of conversation dull. Much more wine had been consumed than usual. The mistress talked flirtatiously with Caecilius Aper. He was telling her the latest gossip:

"Have you heard that Ollia, the wife of Popidius Numerius, has been going to the gladiator barracks many afternoons to visit a new favorite…"

Tertia (the wife of Caecilius) had her eyes partially closed, although I did not think she was asleep; she seemed to have an eye on her husband as he engaged in animated gossip with my mistress. One of the guests had drawn Iris down onto the couch beside him and was fondling her; she accepted his advances passively but without any sign of enthusiasm. And now, to my dismay, another guest beckoned to me to fill his wine goblet and then grasped my belt and pulled me toward him for a better look.

I had finally gained back some of the weight I had lost during my early period of adjustment to this world, and my hair had grown enough to form becoming curls that framed my face, although it was still much too short for feminine attractiveness by their standards. I knew this because I sometimes studied my reflection in the shadowed end of the pool in the peristyle, wondering whether I might become at all attractive.

"Come here, girl, let me have a closer look at you…"

This alarmed me. We had never had a dinner party that ended up as a sexual orgy in this house, but with the master away, and the mistress so angry with him, I was not certain what might happen.

I tried to escape, pretending that I needed to refill the wine bowl. He would not let me off so easily, and he pulled my sash so that I lost my footing and landed on the edge of the couch on my knees. I had to think of something quickly. I didn't think I could endure his wine drenched breath on my neck or his touch on my flesh.

Just then Tertia decided she was annoyed by the tone of the conversation between her husband and the mistress. "It's time for us to leave, husband. We need to prepare for an early departure tomorrow." Holconia suddenly noticed what had happened while she was absorbed in her private conversation, and frowned. There were now two couples engaged in public fondling (Iris and I each with one of the male guests). Iris's tunic was halfway off her shoulder, and her partner's face was flushed.

Thank the gods that Holconia was a prude. She wanted to annoy Marcus Tullius by inviting guests he did not like; but she did not intend to tarnish her own reputation with open fornication at the dinner table. Such things might happen in the city of Rome, but they were frowned upon in Pompeii, where more old fashioned and conservative values were still held by most citizens. The inscription in the dining room of the so-called "House of the Moralist" outlined the rules for decorum in Pompeii: "…don't cast lustful glances, or make eyes at another man's wife…" Our mistress realized that the rules were close to being broken, and she moved in gracefully to re-establish decorum.

She spoke quietly but firmly. "You young men shall have your pleasures, but in a more suitable place, in private. The girls will be sent to you later; but first, please join me in a last drink to see off my guests of honor." Fresh wine was poured, and Iris and I were momentarily dismissed so that the guests could make their farewells in a more dignified manner.

Iris looked at me through veiled lashes. "What do you think of yours?" she asked. "Mine doesn't look too bad."

I said, under my breath, "I won't."

"You don't have any choice. This was going to happen, sooner or later. Now that your hair is growing back, you look like a woman again. Some men really like barbarians." She always managed to slip in a barb, even when she paid me a compliment, I noticed, but I had more important problems to worry about at the moment.

We went into the servant's courtyard to wait for the summons. I hoped that the ceremonial leave taking would last for a while, but I suspected it might not take very long. What was I going to do? I could let him have me; but this thought revolted me. No, that was not a price I was willing to pay. That left just one alternative: I could run away and hide, and hope that when I returned, the punishment would be something I could bear. I ducked into the cubicle where I had some of my things and threw my dark cloak around my shoulders. It was a warm evening, but the moon was bright. The cloak was needed not to keep me warm, but to cover my white tunic so that I would be less visible. Iris instantly guessed what my intentions were:

"No, you mustn't—they will catch you". She took hold of my arm, and I shook her off, and ran out the rear gate; the watchman there was half asleep, so he didn't stop me. Iris ran after me, calling; that woke up the watchman.

I ran down hill, in the direction of the sea, thinking that perhaps I could hide among the trees in the olive grove. If Iris would just shut up, I could get a head start, I thought. Then I didn't think; I just ran as fast as I could. Once I had been a runner, but I was out of condition, and soon I could hardly draw breath. I slowed to a rapid walk, but kept moving. I tried to stay out of sight among the trees.

Back at the house, the servant's quarters were in an uproar. The new page ran to the mistress at once, to tattle: "The flute girl is running away!" This was in front of her guests; and of course, this made a poor impression on them. A Roman household was supposed to be orderly, and this was a show of flagrant disobedience.

If he had been less drunk, I think he might have decided it was undignified; but my drunken admirer was angry, and he demanded that his horse be brought. He was going to run me down and bring me back, he said. My mistress did not want this to become a drama, but she was not able to dissuade him from this. I think I had at least some friends among the other servants; the horse was brought, but not very quickly. He mounted up (unsteadily, I was told later) and set off in the direction indicated by the guard. I was beginning to think that I had made a successful escape; and that now all I needed to do was find a sheltered place to spend the night. Then I heard the drum of the horse's hooves approaching. Damn! I thought. I had recovered my breath by now, and I wrapped the cloak carefully to hide all traces of white fabric. Unfortunately the moon was full that night, so I did not have the cover of full darkness. I changed direction, heading more toward the north. This would bring me to a cliff, I knew, where there were some rocks where I might be able to hide.

He overtook me sooner than I expected, but already the edge of the cliff was in sight. I reached land's end with very little distance between my pursuer and me. The sea was about 30 feet below my feet, dark, and dappled with shards of moonlight. He pulled his horse to a halt and dismounted, not too gracefully. Just like *Butch Cassidy and the Sundance Kid*, I thought, I'm trapped here. There is only one thing I can do. I discarded my cloak. Then I dived, launching myself outward away from the rocks. I was not skillful, but I did a reasonable job of keeping the dive under control. I entered the water in a clean slice and then surfaced a few moments later, feeling an adrenalin rush, but all right. I could hear him cursing, far above me, but he wasn't going to follow. He used violent and colorful language; I was sure those phrases were not in my Latin-English dictionary. The things he called about me would have made Catullus blush. Paddling as quietly as possible, I moved into the shadows closer to the base of the cliff and then remained still. With luck, he might think I had drowned. A rock struck the surface of the sea not far from me, flung from his hand. But he was silent now, and after a while, I thought I heard the sounds of his departure. I swam up the coast a short distance, to a place where the shore was level with the water, and walked out onto the rocky shore, wringing the salt water from my tunic. It was now late at night, and there were few lights anywhere. I could not risk seeking shelter with any people; the penalties for harboring escaped slaves were severe. I walked away from the sea, uphill in the general direction of Vesuvius, and found shelter in another olive grove. My tunic was soaked and the night air seemed unseasonably cold, but I curled up in a ball and rested.

When morning came, I wondered what to do. I did not think that the guest would still be at the house; he had been invited only to dinner, and not to stay over. This was the day when the master was expected to return. I decided to stay under cover during the daytime hours, and to return to the house in early evening. I would much rather throw myself upon the mercy of the master than the mistress.

I hid whenever I saw field workers; I stole fruit from the trees. I stayed in the shade and even slept during the hottest part of midday. I began to walk back in the direction of Pompeii, orienting myself by keeping Vesuvius on my left as I walked south. Soon the road began to look familiar. By late evening, I presented myself at the rear gate. My tunic was torn, my hair was disheveled, and I needed a bath. A younger man had replaced the gate man at the rear entrance; I heard later, to my great regret, that the mistress had had the old gateman severely beaten. I had been prepared to suffer the costs of my disobedience myself; I had not thought that others would also suffer.

Demetrius greeted me dourly: "You're in trouble again!" Alexander went to tell the master that I had reappeared, not dead, after all. I was sent to see the master.

"I am told that you ran away. What do you have to say?" Marcus Tullius was angrier than I had ever seen him, but his voice was low.

"Yes, I am sorry, I ran away. I have come back."

"I will decide what to do about this later."

I was confined and locked up in the servant's quarters for two days in a state of disgrace. Demetrius visited me bringing food, but no one else seemed willing to associate with me, particularly not Iris, who had also received some sharp slaps on the face for this incident.

"This story is the most popular in town, in the taverns and at the dinner tables. They laugh about the slave who defied her mistress and dived like a sea bird and swam like a dolphin. They say you must be a daughter of Poseidon." Demetrius was enjoying the dramatic aspects of this situation, and had been recounting this in every bar in town, I suspected. The only thing he loved better than hearing gossip was telling it. But I hardly cared about that.

"What does the master think? What will he do?"

"The mistress is furious. She wants you to be killed or sold. She and the master are arguing. I don't know what he will do with you."

All I could do was wait.

Finally I was brought to see the master. I could not read his face: it was like stone. He said:

"You must be punished for this. I will do it myself."

I let my head drop downward in assent. I began to sweat and to feel dizzy. What did he mean? Would it be something I could bear? They tied my wrists in front of me; even if I had tried to reach my signal device I could not; and of course, I no longer expected it to work. There was no escape for me. I was taken out into the slave courtyard and tied facing one of the mossy stone columns. Everyone in the household gathered to witness this. My tunic was let down to my waist, so that my back was mostly bare. The master stood there, with a whip in his hand and a grim, inscrutable expression on his face.

How could I let it come to this? I thought. Before I had much time to think, he delivered the first blow. It brought blood. I bit my lip so hard that it bled also. I felt sick to my stomach; I am going to faint, I thought, incredulous. My knees started to give way under me. Pain ripped through me. I screamed. Never mind about dignity; when the pain is so intense, the cry is a reflex.

Four more blows fell, each leaving a stripe of blood across my back. Then it was over. It was much less punishment than the mistress had demanded, but it was much worse than I had anticipated, or remembered from my earlier beating.

When I recovered consciousness, I had been untied and placed on my stomach on a pallet in a cubicle off the slave courtyard. The master himself washed the blood from my back, and he applied soothing oil and bandages. Then he ground some gray pasty substance in a small mortar, added it to wine, stirred it, and told me to sit up and drink it. With his arm supporting me behind my shoulders above the wounds, I drank. It was bitter.

"Opium. It will help you."

I didn't want to look at him, but he tilted my chin upward with a touch of his hand, and spoke.

"This was required. It was not a pleasure for me to do it."

"I understand."

"Do you?" He looked into my eyes intently. Yes, I think I did understand. My widely talked of disobedience had injured his dignity and made his household the laughing stock of the town. Slave disobedience wasn't just a minor annoyance to his people; they feared that someday slaves would rise to overthrow their masters, as Spartacus had tried to do a century earlier. He could not permit an instance of such flagrant disobedience to go unpunished, or there would be more of it. I said:

"Sometimes a master is not much more free than a slave."

"Perhaps you do understand. You will be taken out to the country for a time, to heal. I will have you brought back when the talk has died out, and the wounds have healed."

It must have been a substantial dose of opium, for quickly I felt myself floating I could still feel the pain, but somehow it no longer seemed to be a part of me. It was outside me, no longer distressing. I slept, fitfully, through the process of transportation. I was in the back of a wagon, on my stomach, of course (it would be some time before I could sleep on my back.) There was bedding underneath me as padding, and the smell of blood in my nostrils, and the taste of blood on my tongue. My head spun, and I escaped for moments at a time into welcome unconsciousness.

By nightfall we had come to a farm, and the kind face of an old woman bent over me in concern. I remember little of those first few days. I think she gave me more opium. She bathed the wounds and put clean linen on them.

When I began to feel better, she fed me soup. I was able to ask now:

"What place is this?"

"One of the master's farms."

"Who are you?"

"I was the nurse of Marcus Tullius. When I was too old to be of use, he made me free, and let me take a husband, and he gave us this farm."

Her face had lines of laughter. I could not have asked for a better nurse. I slept; I woke; I slept again. I ate her bean soup, and I grew stronger. After a few days, I asked to be allowed to do some work, and she laughed, and said:

"Give yourself some time…it's better not to move too much, at first."

But in time she did allow me to work. She had a loom set up, and she showed me how to run the shuttle back and forth, and I learned to weave. The rhythm of it was comforting. It was something I had done before on a different type of loom, and the familiarity of it gave me pleasure. I think perhaps I had a knack for it. At first she watched me critically, but after a day or so, she let me do it without supervision.

Two weeks passed quietly. Then one day Marcus Tullius himself appeared. I was intent upon the weaving, and caught up in the tempo of it, singing as I worked. A shadow fell upon the loom and I looked toward the doorway, expecting the old nurse, but it was Marcus Tullius.

He was silhouetted in the doorway, backlit. I saw myself for a moment, mirrored in his dark pupils, a golden figure in the dark room, twin miniature reflections. The sight of this work at the loom made him smile. Still, his manner was hesitant, as if he thought I might dare to reproach him.

"You look as if you enjoy doing that."

Perhaps I might have been angry with him, but I saw no point in being angry. He had done what he thought he had to do. I believed he tried to make show of punishment rather than a severe hardship for me. So I was willing enough to meet his pleasantness with pleasantry.

"I like this kind of work. I've always enjoyed making things with my hands."

"In the days of the Republic, our women used to weave like this."

It was an old Roman Republican ideal, the woman who could spin and weave and provide cloth for her family, I remembered...much like the verses in Proverbs that idealized the strong woman who could provide. I couldn't resist the temptation to quote them from memory:

"Who can find a virtuous woman? For her price is far above rubies. The heart of her husband safely trusts in her...

She seeks wool, and flax, and works willingly with her hands. She lays her hands to the spindle, and her hands hold the distaff. She stretches out her hand to the poor; yea, she reaches forth her hands to the needy. She is not afraid of the snow for her household: for all her household are clothed with scarlet..."

He smiled at me.

"Let me see how the wounds are healing," he said.

I blushed a little, and let down my tunic from my shoulders, holding the fabric bunched up to hide my breasts. He ran his fingers across the healing scars; his touch had an almost maternal tenderness.

"It is healing well."

I pulled the tunic up over my shoulders then, and rearranged myself.

"My nurse speaks well of you. She says you are a fine weaver."

"She is an excellent teacher."

"Soon I will send for you to return to my house."

I inclined my head in assent.

CHAPTER 21

December brought cold weather and the heated revelry of Saturnalia. All reasonably tolerant masters allowed their slaves to feast and celebrate. We decorated the house with fragrant garlands of greens. Gifts of food, money, clothing, and other goods were given to all the master's clients. Iris told me that our master followed the old tradition: he would wait upon us at the table, and allow us to dress up, drink, gamble, dance, sing and feast. For one day we would have freedom: not just freedom from servitude, but freedom from the usual moral restrictions. The master would wink at any misbehavior, as long as there was no destruction of property. The mistress disapproved of this rowdy celebration. This year, as usual, she took the children away on a visit to her parents, where the celebrations were much quieter. Her absence was in itself cause for celebration.

Among the servants, only Cnaeus had to work on the feast day. He prepared all sorts of dishes with meat and eggs and spices, the sorts of things that we never ordinarily had to eat. The rest of us wore our best clothing (in some households slaves even wore the master's clothing, but not here). By mid afternoon we had gathered in the triclinium and the nearby reception rooms at the extra tables that had been set up for us. We reclined like lords on the couches, while the master and a few hired freedmen ran to fetch us hot-spiced wine. Gambling was permitted on this occasion, and the fall of dice would decide who was to be Lord of Misrule. It was no surprise to anyone that Demetrius won this title (for he was expert at cheating with dice), and no one minded, for all expected that it would be a merrier party if his wishes ruled us.

Demetrius wore a crown of ivy on his head; he took the master's usual place in the couch in the triclinium and directed others where to recline. He clapped his hands to call for food, for entertainment, for music. I avoided sitting near him. The stories I had heard about Saturnalia in past years suggested that there would be bawdy jokes and drinking contests. I wanted to drink just enough wine to feel pleasantly tipsy, and then to excuse myself. Noisy parties tired me, and I didn't want the wicked hangover that I knew the cheaper Pompeiian wines could cause.

The musicians played, and people danced and clapped. Already faces were flushed and voices became louder. I indulged in roast fowl and drank the hot wine, feeling like a spectator, as I always did at such times. At one time or another, nearly every man in the house had made overtures to me, and I had turned them all away. It was not that I had any special beauty; the men and women found part-ners among the other household slaves, and I was just a woman like any other to them. No one asked me to dance, or tried to lie close to me and fondle me as the feast progressed, although many couples danced or caressed each other in public view. The master smiled indulgently.

I did not want any of the slave men to fondle me, and yet, alone in this company of merrymakers, I felt isolated and sad. I wanted a lover, but not someone who would casually take my body without knowing or caring who I was. The master was at my side just as I was thinking about this, refilling my wine goblet; and the look he gave me seemed to be one of understanding. Not for the first time, it seemed as if he sensed what I was thinking and feeling, and this flus-tered me, and I blushed. He took some ivy and placed it on my head as a wreath, as if to say, relax and join the party. Then he was gone. I think my eyes followed him out of the room, but I got a poke in the ribs and a teasing comment from one of the women just then that drew me back to the present moment.

Demetrius, as lord of the feast, summoned me to his couch. At that point, I was weary of the noise and the revelry, and in no mood to be fondled in public, and so I rose from my own couch, and slipped out of the room, and ran down the service corridor to the kitchen; perhaps, after a moment of annoyance, he wouldn't miss me.

I wrapped a few pastries in a napkin to carry away with me for a private snack. As I left the kitchen, I almost collided with the master, who evidently had the same idea. He collected a pitcher of wine, a tray of fruits and pastries, and he put them into my hands, and said, "Bring these to my rooms"; and so I followed him back to his study. But he didn't stop there; he led me into the room beyond, where he slept, and indicated that I should place the food on the table. I expected him to dismiss me then; but he didn't. We stood facing each other.

There was an uncomfortable moment. He looked away from me, as if suddenly uncertain. I had never seen him look anything but completely confident and self-possessed. His lack of composure made me feel even more uncomfortable. He poured a little wine into a delicate glass cup, and offered it to me; I accepted it.

"Have you been with any man, since you have been with us?"

"No."

"You do not like men?"

I didn't know how to answer. "I don't want to be forced. I want to be able to choose, and to give."

"You said you were a priestess before you came to us. Did you take a vow of perpetual virginity?"

"No. But I had the right to choose whether I would go with any men."

The blood burned in my cheeks. I found this conversation unsettling.

He smiled at me, and spoke in a soothing tone. "You are afraid of being forced. I promise I will not. On Saturnalia, the slave is the mistress, and the master is the slave. It is for you to choose. Are you willing?"

I wanted to hear this, but I wasn't ready for it. He was offering me, at best, an illusion of choice. With forced composure, I set the goblet down, trying to keep my hand from trembling. I think a spasm of anxiety shot through my facial muscles. He waited.

I had yearned for him. I had lain awake at night remembering his face. I had imagined conversations that we might have if we were equals. But we were not equals. And yet, I had been alone so long. Just the silky warmth of skin against skin would be such a comfort. Sometimes I thought I could not bear to be so alone.

If I say no, will I be punished; will I have to flee? If I say yes, am I trapped then into being a slave mistress, whether I want to continue or not? What if he wants me tonight, and then never wants to be with me again?

I doubt that he understood the nature of my confusion, but my distress was obvious to him. Now he turned all his powers of charm and persuasion on me, and I felt helpless, for I wanted to be seduced. "Stay with me tonight, little one. I will be gentle."

In that moment of tenderness I felt my reluctance melt away as the snow retreats before the warmth of spring. I knew I would not refuse whatever he might ask. This could not be the love between equals I believed in, but it would be love of a sort. Timidly I reached up and brushed his cheek with my hand. Lamplight gilded our faces. The brazier in the corner made this room the warmest one in the house, and tongues of light licked at the darker corners and touched his face and sparkled in his eyes.

In the lamplight, I could see myself reflected in the dark mirrors of his eyes, gold and white and ethereal. If he sees me like that, then I must be beautiful, I thought.

He touched my inner arm, where the skin was whiter than anyone else's. "Your skin must be even whiter where the sun never touches it; let me see." He unfastened the pin that held my tunic at the shoulder, and let the garment slip partly away, and traced my neck and collarbone with his finger. "This is a rare beauty."

I could not speak.

He pulled me close to him, gently; I felt the texture of his tunic pressed against my breasts, and the warmth of his body, and the scent of his breath against my cheek. He guided us over to the couch and I lay back against the cushions. He shed his clothing and lay next to me, touching only my face at first, soothing my fears.

His body was beautiful, lean and smooth, except for the scar from an old injury to his left shoulder. I touched it gently, and asked, "What happened?"

"I was wounded when I was in the army, at a hill fort called Maidun in the south of Britannia."

Next to my white skin his was darker, a rose toned olive; I placed my arm alongside his and we both looked at this contrast, and I think he saw the beauty of it also. Now he began to stroke me. I hoped that his gentleness with me was more than just the calming manner that one might use to soothe a nervous horse, to tame it. Let me put aside my doubts, I told myself. I will enjoy this intimacy tonight, and if tonight is all I have of him, it will have to be enough.

We made love as I had imagined so many times. And afterward, he lay back and sighed. I had another moment of fear: Perhaps he would send me away now that he has had what he wanted. I felt such a hunger for intimacy that I risked touching him. I moved closer to him and pillowed my head in the curve of his shoulder, and intertwined my legs with his, and lay my head upon his shoulder. He seemed surprised, but he welcomed me back into his arms. It seemed as if our bodies had been formed to fit together. As we lay there I felt the peaceful tidal rhythm of his breathing, like the lapping of waves against the shore. My interior world was flooded with light; I felt the warmth of his body soaking into my bones. Ah, it's so comfortable in his bed, I thought. So much cozier than sleeping alone on a thin pallet on a damp stone floor. Yet there was more than just physical warmth. I felt another kind of energy flow between us. It felt peaceful and infinitely comforting; it seemed to envelop us together in a protective silken cocoon. It felt like being bathed in soft white light, or like being afloat in a sea of warm milk. Nothing else existed for me at that moment. I could lie like this forever, and be content, I thought. I am safe, and happy, and loved.

His eyes opened then, and we gazed at each other. "I have never felt anything like this", he said. "Is it some kind of magic?" So, he felt it also.

"I don't know. I have never felt this, either. It's…wonderful!"

"You satisfy a hunger I never knew I had…Stay and sleep with me tonight." I nodded in agreement, and snuggled closer to him.

We woke in the middle of the night; then, wakeful, we talked for a while. The distance between us seemed to have shrunk suddenly to nothing; although I realized that by the light of day, we would once again be slave and master, and I would have to behave differently in public.

"I have watched you for a long time. You are so different from other people; you are a mystery, little one."

"I am trying to learn Roman ways."

"Don't learn them too thoroughly. You have ways of speaking and thinking that seem to come from another world. Sometimes I don't understand you, but you make me think; you surprise me; you delight me. You are a generous lover."

I was pleased, but not sure what I could say in return. I did not dare to say, I love you. Can a slave feel love? Is such a thing permitted, or imaginable?

"I'm glad that I have pleased you."

He looked just slightly displeased that I had said that. Perhaps it seemed obsequious in a way; it momentarily halted conversation. I thought: he expects me to behave like a slave; and yet, he prefers sometimes that I do not behave like a slave. How will I ever know what to do in the face of such conflicting expectations? Perhaps it would be worth taking a few risks.

I touched his face again. In the language of touch, at least in bed, we could sometimes be equals. "Thank you for giving me a choice."

He looked thoughtful. "That was not entirely unselfish on my part."

I replied: "Something that has been commanded cannot be a gift. I wanted this to be my gift to you. Being able to give something to someone is the most precious kind of power."

"I understand."

Worries crept back unbidden. When Iris returned, would he no longer want me? Perhaps I had been only a one-night substitute for the woman he preferred. I was not as beautiful as Iris.

"Are you willing to come to my bed every night?"

Ah…this was a trap for me; one that I walked into willingly, even though I knew it was a trap. He presented this as a choice, but I was hardly in a position to refuse now, and it would become an expected thing.

"Yes."

"You must not give yourself to any other man. I am selfish with my pleasures." I must have made some kind of face when he said this, for he asked, abruptly, "What are you thinking?"

"I'm willing to promise what you ask. I only wish I could ask the same of you."

He shook his head, as if in amusement. "You surprise me again. I want to be the only man who lies with you. You have given me something much sweeter and warmer than obedience, and I want to keep it." He had not made me any promise, I noticed.

"What are the customs about marriage and sex in your country?" he asked then. I think he was trying to evaluate whether my request was consistent with barbarian customs.

"Marriages were not arranged, but freely chosen by the man and woman. The man knelt before a woman he loved and told her of his love and made her an offer of marriage; and the choice whether to accept or refuse was hers."

The response to this was a look of disbelief. "Your men knelt to women?"

Well, I thought: They used to. "Not always. I don't expect this would ever become a custom in Rome. But people expected to marry for love. And women did not promise to obey their husbands, only to love them."

"But you spoke only of patrician women, surely. Female slaves must be obedient to their masters, even in your country. Were you a patrician?"

"We did not have slaves."

That was clearly unbelievable.

I amended my story slightly to make it more believable. "Some wealthy people had hired servants, of course, but the servants were free."

"Were you a patrician?"

Hmm…I thought. I had been middle class, with lower-upper class aspirations. I had grown up in a grimy mill town and gone to Harvard. Harvard, I thought…"Yes, I was."

"That explains why you so often forget to behave like a slave."

I had thought I was doing rather well, and I must have seemed surprised at this remark. "In what ways do you mean, master?"

"Alexander says you have been obedient. You work harder than most servants do, in fact. It is in the way you look at people, the way you walk and carry yourself. You don't behave like a slave. You act like a person with dignity."

"Isn't is possible for a slave to have dignity?"

"I haven't seen it often. The other slaves seem to sense that you are not really one of them. Tell me, little one, are you lonely?"

"Yes."

He looked pensive.

And I said to him: "You are a good man, master, and aren't good men usually lonely?"

❦   ❦   ❦

After that night things were different between us. From that night on, when we were alone, we talked. Our pillow talk was in the language of the heart.

Soon everyone in the household knew that I was the master's new favorite. When she returned, Iris refused to believe at first that she had been replaced; but he never sent for her again. One night I dared to ask him: "What about Iris?"

"She has displeased me. I told her I expected her to be faithful to me, and she was not, and she lied to me about it when I asked her. Besides, there is nothing of value, here..." (He tapped his temple), "...or here." (He tapped the center of his chest).

Iris would hardly speak to me at first. I don't believe she loved him, but she resented being replaced as the favorite and missed the extra money this position had brought. When she regained her tongue, her remarks were razor edged. I'm certain she intended for me to hear when she said that it was difficult to understand the master's new choice, for I had no beauty; I must have bewitched him. And then one day she confronted me.

"You told him. You were the one who told him I had a lover. I hate you; I'll make you sorry for what you've done."

I protested, in all honesty, that I had not been the one who told Marcus she had been seeing a man outside the house; but she didn't believe me.

Male slaves no longer teased me or made unwanted advances, for the hands-off message had apparently made the rounds. Stronnius was no longer a problem, for now I was the one who had the master's ear. Demetrius seemed particularly wounded: I had always brushed off his advances, but now I had accepted someone else.

I feared the mistress's anger most of all; I knew she would be displeased that the slave she had chosen for Marcus—perhaps her own half sister—had been replaced by a woman who resembled a long ago love of his own. Law and custom supported her rights; even though she didn't love him, she was his wife; I was the other woman, the adulteress. I disliked seeing myself in this position; there was no way I could justify what I had done as right—except that it was for love of him that I did it; and he had so little love, surely he deserved the love that I wanted to give him.

Marcus Tullius spoke to me of money; and he was surprised when I refused to accept anything. I had heard that even wealthy women accepted, not just expensive gifts of jewelry, but also large sums of money, from their lovers; and I knew that Iris had been given regular compensation for her services. I tried to explain to him:

"I don't want this to be a matter of buying and selling, but of giving and receiving." He agreed, but in a way that made it seem he was trying to understand, but I don't think he did understand yet. Holconia had valued his name; Iris had eagerly accepted his money. I didn't want our relationship to be like that; I wanted to love him, and for both of us to know that I cherished him for who he was—and not for his position, his fortune, or even the protection that he could provide.

I loved him, but I didn't dare speak words of love. I wanted more than anything to hear words of love from him, but I knew that was unlikely. Romans feared passion and romantic love: it could make them dependent or vulnerable, thus unmanly. He wasn't likely to show any vulnerability toward me, any neediness.

Still, those nights of love were full of sweetness and beauty. Sometimes after we made love we lay entwined in each other's arms, tangled in the patterned coverlet with its embroidered gold medallions and red and blue flowers. His black curly hair and olive complexion contrasted with my golden hair and fair skin. This image reminded me of the Klimt painting *The Kiss*. I felt the rapturous bliss that the painter showed in the woman's face.

He didn't say anything to acknowledge a sense of need for me, but when he held me in his arms I thought I could sense a growing need, along with the desire. After the wild abandon of making love, we could relax into the peace of feeling love, and I believed that he felt the same sense of quiet nourishment that I did in that period of quiet intimacy that comes after passion.

And I could make him laugh. One night, when he had been particularly boyish and frisky in his lovemaking, I asked him "Is the snake awake again, already?" And he laughed, and replied, "Yes…but the snake's accomplices are tired…let me sleep!"

And so that second winter was entirely different from my first. In that first winter I rose at daybreak, stiff from sleep on a thin pallet on a hard damp stone floor. In the second winter I awoke in his arms, luxuriant in the warmth of cushions and coverlets, drowned in love, warm inside and outside. Although he never spoke the words of love I would have loved to hear, he was gentle, and I thought I read a growing tenderness and affection in that gentleness.

I had become a geisha or hetaera for him. In the early evenings I still entertained him and sometimes also his daughter with songs and stories. Then he sent her away and took me to his bed.

Tullia felt closed out of this new intimacy between us, and she was angry with both of us. Before this time I had slept on the floor of her room at night, within easy call if she awoke afraid or wanted something. Now I belonged more to her father than to her; he assigned her a new personal servant, as I was no longer available to be with her most nights. I had become competition for her father's attention. She was jealous of the affection I felt for him, and that he felt for me, and she felt excluded. She became sharp with me; she even slapped me once, when I did a clumsier than usual job of arranging her hair.

The loss of her affection hurt me deeply; I had grown so fond of her, and it pained me to see her distaste for me. Perhaps in time, she'll become accustomed to this, and accept it, I thought.

We behaved circumspectly in front of Tullia, but I'm sure she knew what we did when we were alone; everyone in the house knew. His personal servant slept just outside the door of his chamber, on call, and he gave me a friendly knowing leer when I left in the morning. I suspect he knew our bed habits quite well, and for all I know, gave a blow-by-blow account in the servant's courtyard. This never failed to embarrass me, although Marcus hardly seemed to notice.

In many ways my position in the household had become awkward. Holconia had been comfortable with Iris as slave mistress; but she knew Iris and had more direct control over her; I was an unknown and thus somewhat troublesome quantity. It began to seem to me as if I had few friends left in the household, and several new enemies. Tullia was difficult; Holconia's jealousy was well known to all in the household; Iris was openly spiteful. Demetrius became unfriendly; he even discontinued our agreements about lessons. He seemed not to want to see me; it seemed to pain him most when he saw Marcus and me together. I was surprised, for I hadn't thought Demetrius cared for me in that way. We had been friends, and he had flirted with me casually, but I didn't think he ever really wanted me. He no longer flirted with me, even as a joke.

Only Cnaeus treated me the same way as before; I was grateful for his friendship. If one is to have only one friend among the servants, the cook is not a bad choice; he learned what foods I liked and didn't like, and saved choice morsels for me. We didn't speak of my situation directly but I think he understood my problems, and I found his silent companionship in the kitchen comforting. I ate better. I slept better. I became as beautiful as a woman with ordinary looking features can ever be; I acquired a kind of radiance.

All I could think of was Marcus Tullius. His soul was a wine dark sea, and I was lost in it.

CHAPTER 22

I had earned the freedom to go outside the house alone again, and one day I made an ominous discovery. I was walking barefoot (as was my habit) in the orchard near the house, and I felt something metallic under my feet. It looked as if a small animal had been digging; a partly buried lead tablet was exposed. Curious, I picked it up, and read the writing chiseled into it. It was a curse tablet; a binding curse—and I was the person named in it. Demetrius was the first person I encountered when I returned to the servant's quarters, and I was unable to hide my distress from him, and he insisted on knowing what had so upset me. I told him what I had found.

Demetrius gave his opinion. "No need to worry; such curses don't take effect until the tablet is placed in the tomb of one recently deceased, who takes it to the underworld." That did not reassure me very much. Someone in the house wished me ill—enough to seek out some magician and pay for this evil thing. Who was it? I dared not ask. I thought it most likely to be Iris, but I did not think she could afford to pay for such a thing. Could it be the mistress herself?

"You must tell the master, if this has frightened you so much." I refused to do this…I'm not sure why.

When next I saw Iris in the kitchen, her behavior did nothing to allay my suspicions. "He will tire of you; he has taken other women before, and he has always come back to me", she said. And later, she asked me: "How much money does he give you?"

"Nothing," I replied, for I had refused his money, even though this behavior seemed strange to him.

"Oh, then, he must value you very little; he gave me a lot of money." She seemed to be comforted by this comparison.

When I was alone with Marcus, I felt cherished, but my place in the servant's quarters had become uncomfortable. Iris was rude. Demetrius gradually became a little less distant, but he was careful not to touch me.

At least, as time passed, Tullia seemed to forgive me. For a few weeks she had shunned my stories, but after that she began to listen to them again, and to speak to me in a friendlier way that made me hope she had forgiven me.

The August heat brought disaster to the household. One afternoon the son returned from his tutoring session looking quite unwell. He must have gone to the toilet four or five times within the first hour of his return, and by the time the main meal was served, he collapsed. Both mother and father were at his bedside as soon as the severity of his symptoms became clear. Usually Marcus Tullius himself doctored any minor health problems among the slaves and family members, but this disease appeared to be serious. A physician was summoned immediately. Marcus junior lost strength rapidly. He was so weak he was unable to use the chamber pot; his bed linens were soiled.

I did not like the looks of this physician. There seemed to be two schools of thought among the physicians in town, judging from what I had heard about local medical practice. One school preferred drastic interventions to restore the balance of "bodily humors": they purged, bled, and administered emetics. Another school preferred moderation: they recommended healthful food and drink, bed rest, and other mildly beneficial things. Either type of physician might administer mixtures of presumably medicinal substances, containing substances that would sound bizarre to modern people.

Not all their medicine was ineffective. They had developed sophisticated medical instruments that were virtually identical in design and quality of workmanship to some modern instruments. For instance, a beautifully made speculum for vaginal examination found in the House of the Surgeon in Pompeii looked exactly like the tools my own modern gynecologist used. They could set bones and treat some types of injuries and wounds with reasonable success; some physicians were even reportedly able to dislodge cataracts. However, the treatment of infectious disease was not one of their strong points. Moldy bread used by the Egyptians might have contained some form of penicillin, but for the most part, antibiotics were unknown. They preferred clean water for drinking and bathing, at least for aesthetic reasons, but they did not realize that water that looked clean might nonetheless carry disease.

In any case, the physician that was summoned to treat their son seemed to be from the drastic intervention school. He administered some mixture of medicines, and bled Marcus junior. I had not seen the patient first hand, but it seemed to me that he must be dehydrated from all the fluid loss, and it didn't seem sensible to me to deplete his body fluids further by bleeding. The physician departed, having done all the damage that he could. The parents cared for their son themselves, and hardly left his cubicle.

Within twenty-four hours, their son was dead; and his body servant was suffering from the same disease. Within another twenty-four hours, six more servants had the same symptoms. The funeral arrangements for Marcus junior were made; the cremation and funeral were carried out in unseemly haste; for the mistress decided to leave this house of sickness with her daughter and Iris and a few other personal attendants to take refuge with relatives in the country.

What was it? And could I also get it? I was even more careful about washing my hands and boiling my water. Possibly one of the immunizations I had received before leaving modern times would protect me. I decided there was no cause for panic, although nearly one quarter of the house servants had become ill. Think! I told myself. What is it? Who gets it? How might it be spread? I had not seen any sign of fleas or vermin in this house. Holconia was nearly as fanatic about keeping her house clean as I would have been, had I been in charge. But the shared toilet sponge could easily be a way of passing infection. From that time on I avoided the latrine completely and went outside to relieve myself.

I nursed the sick, along with Demetrius and Alexander and the others who had remained well so far. I confess that I delegated the handling of chamber pots and dirty linens to the junior kitchen maid...and that was nearly the death of her, I think, for she was the next to fall ill. As I sponged foreheads and tried to get the sick ones to drink liquids, I thought...dehydration, that's the key here. I had Cnaeus boil up large pots of water; we added honey and garum, for the replacement of lost nutrients and body salts would be crucial. It was difficult to get the sick to drink enough of this mixture, but it seemed that among those who drank enough fluids, many started to recover. We fed them boiled millet.

The most obvious symptoms were diarrhea and signs of dehydration: dry skin and mouth, no urine output, eyes dry and glassy in appearance. The pulse was rapid, and the sick seemed too tired even to lift their heads up; they had to be supported to sit up to drink. Their thirst seemed insatiable, and yet they were almost too tired to swallow, and I had to be careful not to give too much liquid at once or they choked on it. There was nausea, also. I could not decide whether they were feverish; they seemed to be, but perhaps it was just the oppressive August heat in the enclosed rooms that made it seem so.

I thought the primary suspect for the means of disease transmission in this situation was the sponge stick in the latrine. Later I would try to convince them to replace it with something disposable, but for the present, I simply threw it out. With that gone, the spread of the disease seemed to slow down. I became a nag, insisting on frequent hand washing by everyone that touched the soiled linens or carried away the body wastes. We actually burned many of the soiled linens: I thought that Holconia would have my head for that, later. I wasn't sure why my leadership was accepted. Most of the servants were terrified; they obeyed my commands rather meekly. Normally I would not have had the authority to order them around, but Alexander simply had no ideas about what they should do. I did. The spread of illness slowed.

The next to fall ill was the master himself. He had been among us, helping to care for the sick, trying to get them to drink. At first when he looked pale, I hoped it might just be fatigue, but he collapsed just as others had done, and we carried him to his bedchamber.

Now that I had organized the household's response, I decided that they could care for the remaining sick among the servants without my help; I appointed myself to nurse the master. No one else was eager to dispute this, for it must have been obvious to everyone by now that greater contact with the sick was something that spread the sickness. I deputized the now-recovered kitchen maid to remove linens and bring fresh ones. Alexander and Demetrius helped me to convey him to the bath to wash him several times a day; the bath water had not been changed, and was not as clean as I would have liked, but it seemed to me that it would do.

I moved my pallet into his room. I tried alternate periods of rest with periods of bathing and drinking concoctions of boiled liquids that contained garum and honey. We sat him upright against a pile of cushions, and I used a spoon to put the liquid in his mouth, and coaxed him to swallow it.

I could lay my hand upon his forehead, and touch him tenderly, in the guise of nursing. I hoped that my love would be medicine for him also. It was a terrible forty eight hours, and by the end of it, my patient was in better shape than I was. He had recovered enough to eat a little grain, and even to sit up without assistance. Enough to issue orders, and he ordered that I should be put to bed and attended to. I asked them please to give me only the boiled water, and they agreed to do this for me.

I slept for a day and a half, and woke feeling weak and hungry, but not ill. Fifteen people in the household had been sick; and six, including Marcus junior, had died. Most of those who had been nursed using my methods had recovered. I walked out into the kitchen, and Cnaeus greeted me gladly.

The master summoned me. I was afraid I might be in trouble about the linens I had destroyed; cloth was expensive. Or perhaps other servants had complained that I had taken on authority inappropriately. However, I was not in trouble this time. In fact, quite the contrary. The master was seated in his tablinum; he had not yet resumed his normal routine of seeing clients, but he had spent time conferring with Alexander about household business. I was brought into his presence. It must have been obvious that I was still weak from fatigue. He ordered a chair to be brought, and told me to sit down. Alexander gaped. This was simply not done; chairs were reserved for honored visitors, and slaves never sat in the presence of the master.

I sat down thankfully, for I wasn't sure my knees could support me.

"Thank you for the honor that you do me, master."

"We owe you a debt of gratitude. You saved my life, I think."

"All of us served you together."

"I have heard how effective your nursing was. With these physicians, sometimes the remedy is worse than the disease. Your remedy was simple, but it worked. Most people fear sickness. You did not seem to. I know that you attended me throughout my illness. Loyalty and courage such as this are rare."

"I only did what needed to be done."

"You also knew what to do…You seem distressed. What worries you?"

"I burned the bed linens."

He laughed. "It doesn't matter."

"The mistress will be angry, I think."

He looked rather more serious. Her anger was a danger to me; I'm sure he understood that. She had many reasons to be angry with me, quite apart from my disposal of some of the most costly bed linens in the house; and she might even blame me for not saving her son's life when I had been able to save others.

"As reward for your loyalty, I have decided to grant you your freedom."

I must have looked astonished, and even slightly dismayed. I didn't know what this change would mean, but the first thing that I feared was that I might be sent away.

"I ask that you remain in my household and continue to care for my daughter, and for me, and be our storyteller, but with this difference: you will be a paid servant, answerable only to me."

Now I understood. This was to provide me with protection from Holconia. She could not beat or sell a freedwoman; but nothing else was supposed to change. But this would change some things, surely.

"Are you willing?"

"Yes," I replied, still amazed.

"We will have the ceremony granting your freedom within a few days time; I need to arrange for witnesses."

"Thank you. I hardly know what words to use to thank you, master."

"Knowing you, I expect that you will think of something. Go and rest, little one, for you look tired. I want you to come to me again, when you are well."

"I will come."

He then indicated by gesture that the interview was over, and I left, in a daze.

Demetrius accosted me as soon as I was halfway down the hall.

"He freed you?"—this in a tone that was half incredulous, half resentful, for I am sure that Demetrius expected that he would earn his freedom long before I ever saw the day when I would be free.

"Yes, he did."

"That is a good thing for you, then." There was a tinge of envy in that, but I think he was trying to be glad for me.

Iris was less gracious. "I was his favorite for years, and you have only been with him for a few months…and he frees you. And you are not half as attractive as I am."

I felt as if I should apologize to her, but I didn't know what to say. So I said nothing. I knew she was jealous. He had shown me greater favor than he ever showed to her. It was not only the mistress of the house who wished me ill, I thought, a little sadly. Iris had never been a close friend, but I had been fond of her. I was sorry that my actions had hurt her, although I could not have done differently if I had to choose again.

A few nights later I went to him. I wasn't sure at first whether I was expected to behave any differently. There was something new in the way he looked at me, I thought. He was reclining on his bed couch when I came in, being read to by Demetrius; he sent Demetrius away. Demetrius looked strangely sad as he departed. Marcus Tullius beckoned to me, and I shed my tunic and lay down in his arms. Up until now, his lovemaking had not been particularly romantic, although it was gentle enough. Now he looked at me with softness in his face that had not been there before. Was it the aura cast by the lamplight, or was there a rosy glow in his face?

He spoke one word: "Carissima", dearest. It was the sweetest word I ever heard. When he took me in his arms, it was with a new tenderness; he arranged the coverlet around my shoulders and embraced me. I was overcome with joy and tenderness; I almost wept. His kisses were sweet on my cheeks. He seemed to want to give pleasure, for the first time, and not just to take it. After we made love, I pillowed my head on his shoulder, and nestled in his arms. He won't say it, I thought. But I think he loves me. I know I love him. And I won't agonize about the implications of that right now.

❦   ❦   ❦

I had long since forgotten the incision inside my left arm, and the signal device that had failed to work when I had called upon it. And then suddenly one night it made its presence known. One night Marcus noticed the faint little scar inside my arm and asked me about it. I tried to draw away, but he had already detected the hard disk implanted under my skin, and he palpated it, trying to assess what it was.

The signal device that had never worked before now made its presence known. The mosaic floor dissolved into a blur, and a dark tunnel opened before us. I felt something like the current of a river pulling me toward it. He seized me and held me, so I know he sensed that pull too. I reached out toward it in a mute gesture of longing for my lost world. Within a few moments, the gateway back to the future had closed.

"What was that? You reached for it, as if you wanted it." By now it must have seemed natural to ask me to account for strange events.

I had felt uncomfortable with the half truths and lies I had told him about my origins. This was a chance to tell him the truth. I felt I owed him that truth, and wanted him to know it, although I knew I risked losing him. There were so many unknowns! I didn't know whether the signal device would work a second time. I didn't know whether he would believe my story, or whether he would be angry about the half-truths I had told him earlier. But I didn't want him to love a fictional person I had created; I wanted him to love me. He could only do that if I let him know me.

And so I told him the truth, all of it. He listened, and he asked questions.

He did not accept this new version of events immediately, of course. He must have wondered—now that I had confessed that some of my earlier explanations were stories I had made up about my past—that this was just another story, perhaps no closer to the truth. We spent all that night in deep discussion. He questioned; I answered. He doubted; he spoke his anger at being deceived. I explained and apologized and swore by all that was holy that what I now told him was the truth.

In the end, he sighed, and quoted a line from I know not which Roman author: "It's impossible, and so it must be true." And finally, he believed me.

He had many more questions for me then about how this thing, this signal device, worked. One of the many stories I had told earlier was *Beauty and the Beast*, in which the Beast gave Beauty a ring; he allowed her to visit her family, and told her that she could return to him by turning the ring—and she did return, but almost too late to save him. I explained the signal device that I had, using that story as an analogy.

"So, you can leave me at any time…without any warning?"

"I wouldn't." I said that, but in fact, I wasn't certain what I would do now that I might have the power to return to my own life again.

"You belong to me." He gripped me by my arms, a painfully tight grasp. It was clear that he was unwilling to let go of me even for a moment for fear that I would vanish. I watched the expressions on his face, as he struggled to come to terms with this impossible situation. I thought it might be better to be silent.

"This…thing…was placed in your arm by making a cut, wasn't it?"

"Yes."

"So it can be removed in the same way, by making another cut."

Panic seized me. "Don't take this away from me. You will cut me off from my world and my past life, forever."

"I can't live with the knowledge that you have the power to disappear at any time. It's unacceptable. Don't you want to stay with me?"

At that moment, I didn't know what I wanted; I wanted the power to determine my own fate, the freedom to choose. He was about to take that away from me.

"I could never love you again if you do this to me." I didn't mean it as a threat, but as a statement of fact.

In spite of my pleas, he was determined to do it. Marcus summoned a manservant and had him bring a chair. They tied me to it. By now I was too sick at heart to struggle. He made a clean incision with a knife; and he extracted the silver metal disk from my arm. I was in a state of shock, and I knew it was futile to struggle; I accepted this passively, but with despair and bitterness.

Afterward, he bound my arm tightly with clean linen bandages, released my bonds, and held a cup of wine to my lips; I turned my face away in wordless reproach, and withdrew from the touch of his hand on my shoulder.

"Forgive me. I had to do this."

"I had a choice, and you have taken it away from me." He had given me nominal freedom, and then he had taken away any real freedom I might have had, any power I had to determine my own fate. This was something I could not forgive.

He sat and thought for a while. Then he asked.

"You know what is going to happen because in your world you studied Roman history; is that right?"

"Yes."

"What else do you know? Tell me everything, this time. If you want me to believe you after this, you have to tell me all you know."

I was reluctant to tell him. This was evil news. But I knew that he would be able to protect himself and his family better if he knew what the future held. I also feared that after this he would send me away, and this might be my last chance to tell him the things that might save his life, or rather, give him some additional years. And perhaps there was some petty satisfaction in hurting him, as he had hurt me. Quietly, I told him. I used the small black and white disks of stones that were used as game counters to count off the years as I told him of the things to come.

"This is the present year, the year of the earthquake", I said, placing a black stone on the table. "I will use one stone for each year." Then I put down two white stones, saying each of them represented a year; and then another black stone. "In this year, most of the city of Rome will be destroyed by a great fire." I placed five more white stones on the table. Then another black one: "In this year, Nero will die, and there will be four emperors; finally, when the year is over, Vespasian will become emperor, and he will rule for many years." Then one more black stone. "In this year, Pompeii will have many more earthquakes, not as large as the one this year, but numerous smaller ones. Many people will leave at this time." I put down nine more white stones, and then finally, one large black one. I looked him directly in the eyes. "In this year, Pompeii will be destroyed forever, by the eruption of the volcano, Vesuvius. It will be buried under more than 20 feet of lava, ash, and rock. All who stay here will die."

His face paled. He raised his hand to indicate that he had heard enough. He looked stricken; I was confused by my feelings; I was still distressed and angry but what he had done to me, and yet I also wanted to put my arms around him and comfort him. His face forbade that.

"It is the truth. Do you believe me?"

"I believe you." He looked at me. His expression told me that he was far less happy with what he saw in me now than with what he used to see. I wondered whether I could ever forgive him for taking my past away from me. My life, and my world. I wondered whether he could ever forgive me, for the lies I had told about my past, and for the even less welcome truths I had told about his future.

Things were different after that. I could not refuse his embraces, but I went to his arms less willingly, and lying in his arms I felt lonelier than I had ever felt. The sense of connection between us had been damaged; I no longer felt safe with him. I'm sure he noticed the difference in my response, but he didn't speak of it. I knew better than to expect an apology from a man of such pride. And yet, in spite of my earlier words to him, I did still love him. I couldn't stop loving him.

When he next asked me for a story, I told him the legend of the Selkies, the mermen and mermaids of the North Atlantic. At sea, they were seals, but on land, they shed their sealskins and appeared to be human. In one version of the story a fisherman found a Selkie mermaid on the beach; she had shed her sealskin and left it on a rock nearby, and she was combing out her long hair. He fell in love with her, for she was the most beautiful being he had ever seen. He took away her sealskin and hid it; and then she was in his power. She married him, and kept his house, and had his children…and for many years they lived peacefully and happily. Then one day, one of her children found the sealskin hidden away and showed it to her. As soon as she saw it, she went down to the edge of the sea, put it on, and swam away, never to be seen on land again.

Like the Selkie, I had once had the power to return to my own world.

Marcus Tullius had taken that power from me.

He was displeased. "The story doesn't have to end that way."

I told him also the story of Sir Gawain and Lady Ragnell, with suitable name changes. Sir Gawain had to find the answer to the question "What do women want?" in order to free King Arthur from a threat of death. This premise intrigued Marcus, I could tell, although the look on his face suggested that he suspected he wouldn't like the answer. Lady Ragnell was an ugly hag, a creature under an evil spell; she promised Gawain that she knew the answer to his question—but he must marry her to obtain the answer. Gawain's devotion to Arthur was so great that without hesitation he agreed to marry the Lady, and he brought her to Arthur's court.

There, Lady Ragnell told Sir Gawain: "What women want is sovereignty"; by that she meant, the right to make their own choices. This was the correct answer, it turned out, and it set Arthur free from the threat of death. Sir Gawain married the ugly hag; and once they were married, she told him: "I can be beautiful at day, for all the world to see, and ugly at night when I am alone with you; or, I can be beautiful at night with you, and ugly for the world to see. Choose which you want." But Gawain refused to make that choice and said that Lady Ragnell herself could choose. She rejoiced; for that was the answer required to break the spell she had been under; and she became beautiful all the time.

"Enough of this theme...give me something different."

"What theme do you mean, master?" I feigned innocence.

"Unhappy women who want their freedom. You use your stories to complain of your situation. I have given you your freedom."

"I'm free in name only...where would I go in this world as a woman on my own? I have no choice but to stay in your house."

"That's my point exactly. And as this is your fate, you should accept it and make the best of it."

Next, I thought, he will be quoting Stoic precepts.

And in fact what he said was a paraphrase of a thought I recognized from the writings of Seneca: "You have buried a past life; now look for things to love in your present life. You will be as happy as you convince yourself to be."

CHAPTER 23

The next few weeks passed without notable incident. The mistress did not deign to notice me; I went out of my way to avoid bringing attention to myself. It began to seem that she had accepted my new status as a free woman, and given up any idea of punishing me for the evils she thought I had caused. By now she had a long list of grievances against me: from the gossip in the servant's quarters I gathered that she blamed me for causing (not just predicting) the earthquake; for disrupting her marriage plans for Tullia; for failing to save her son or perhaps even putting a curse on him that caused his death, and above all for stealing the affections of her husband. I knew she wouldn't let these perceived wrongs go unpunished, and I dreaded what she might do. When I spoke of my fears to Marcus, he reassured me.

"She wouldn't dare to harm you now that you are my freed-woman; I have given explicit orders that you will not be beaten. Just avoid her as much as possible, and all will be well." The expression on my face told him of my doubt and fear; and I think it annoyed him a little that I doubted that his authority was sufficient protection. "When I order that a thing will be done, it is done," he said.

For several weeks nothing much happened. Holconia even seemed to have forgotten her hatred of me. In spite of this, I remained on guard. I was certain that she would find another way to strike at me. I was wary of poisoning, for that was how the British girl Marcus had once cared for had died, if the old stories were true. But nothing happened.

As the weeks passed, Tullia became less cold toward me; she summoned me for stories in the evening, and even asked me to comb out her hair as I used to. The earlier warmth and affection between us was not completely restored, but she reached out to me from her own loneliness, and I was more than glad to respond. We became closer again, although not perhaps as close as we had been before I became her father's lover.

And then one day, Marcus Tullius left for a week to handle some business affairs in Rome. His absence frightened me; for I knew well that he was my only protection. Within hours after his departure, rather suddenly, Holconia announced that she wanted to go to the city of Baiae, a seaside resort that could be reached by an easy two-day journey to the north. The travel party would include Iris and Tullia, and I would accompany them. I was torn between wanting to go, and fearing it. I had not been outside Pompeii since my arrival, and I was eager to see this famous city: the hot springs, temples, monuments, and markets. On the other hand, I did not like to be away from home in Holconia's power, for it did not seem likely to me that she had given up hating me. Actually, I didn't have any choice in the matter, even as a freedwoman. Perhaps if I had had the wit to feign illness before she summoned me, I might have been left at home. But I did not think of it until too late, and at that point, she wouldn't have believed me.

The mistress and Tullia were carried in a litter, a comfortable (if slow) mode of travel. Iris, the slave boy Phoebus and I sometimes rode in the baggage wagon and sometimes walked. Iris didn't treat me in the friendly way that she used to, but she was in such a holiday mood that she was pleasant company. She talked of the sights we might see in the city; perhaps we would accompany Holconia and Tullia to the public baths, which were larger and more magnificent than those at Pompeii. We might go to the games. I found the idea of bloodshed in the arena repulsive. Still, I would have been interested to see the amphitheater. My fears were lost among these anticipations.

The town of Baiae was dazzling: elegant villas terraced the hillsides overlooking a harbor crowded with pleasure boats. Although it was near the end of the season, it was clear that this was a preferred destination for the wealthy. On our one free afternoon Iris and I admired the things offered for sale in the market: delicately crafted jewelry, gemstones in a rainbow of colors, silks and linens dyed in glorious shades of purple and blue, imported foods. We gawked at this display like the country bumpkins that we were. I still hoped to see the city of Rome, but Baiae was a fresh new world to me. I had hardly been outside Pompeii during all my time in the world of the past; now, if the mistress was inclined to travel, I might see much more of the world.

On the third afternoon, while Tullia was resting before dinner, Holconia summoned me. I was told that I was to accompany her; she had been invited to dinner at the house of a friend. It seemed odd to me that only Phoebus and I accompanied her, and that these plans had not been discussed among the servants earlier in the day. I was told to bring my musical instrument, so that I could provide entertainment if called upon. I began to feel uneasy.

The sight of our host did not calm my anxiety. He seemed affable; but he was certainly not attractive. His pendulous chins bobbed as he greeted Holconia cordially. Gemstone rings flashed on his hands, and his clothing was the most colorful I had seen on anyone in the Roman world. His eyes were cold and piggy. However, he did not speak to her as if there had been any long acquaintance, which seemed odd. It seemed as if she were here on some business matter. They dined with three other people, whose names I did not come to know, for I was commanded to wait in the hallway outside the triclinium for a possible summons. Phoebus attended our mistress. After the second course, I was told to come in and play for them.

Perhaps this was a chance to earn some small approval from Holconia, I thought. She can't really believe that I caused her son's death. I played a set of five songs, all of them light and cheerful in tone. The host was unusually attentive to my performance. All too often, my music was just background noise for conversation. He nodded and smiled an acid smile. I was sent away then, and escorted back to the slave quarters, and offered plain food and wine. This did not seem unusual at the time. However, the afternoon light grew pale; and I was not summoned. I began to be restless; the other servants were not sociable, and I had nothing to do, and I wanted to get out of this house, which seemed oppressive in spite of the magnificence of its public rooms. Finally, I asked: "Has my mistress left yet?" The young woman I asked seemed surprised at this question, and told me that the lady had departed. I stood up then, thinking that perhaps she had left me on purpose so that I would have to make my way home alone in the dark. I had better be on my way at once, then, I thought; I will need to ask for directions, and hope that I can reach our lodgings before full darkness sets in.

The steward came in, and explained to me that I had been sold to Aulus Mamius Flaccus. I protested:

"This cannot be so. I am the freed woman of Marcus Tullius."

The steward was not impressed by this claim.

I persisted. "There is some misunderstanding."

What was I going to do? I tried to think. If Holconia had indeed sold me, I was not surprised. This was just the sort of plan that would suit her, for she may have gotten a good price for me as a skilled musician. I was sure that she would lie to Marcus Tullius, and tell him that I had run away or disappeared. There was a small possibility that this new 'master' might listen to an appeal, and return me to Marcus Tullius in return for the money he had paid for me. Perhaps I could speak to him about it. Failing that, perhaps if I behaved myself well, I would be allowed to come and go freely, and I might find an opportunity to escape. Still: the penalties for escaped slaves who were recaptured were severe; it would be far preferable to convince him to sell me back to Marcus Tullius. Even if that meant I would be a slave again, at least I would be back in a familiar place.

"Please, may I speak to the master?"

"No. You mustn't say these things; you'll make him angry. You belong to him now."

Well then, I thought, I will have to wait until I have some chance to approach the master. I found a place to sleep in the servant's quarters, but sleep did not come. Cold fear gripped me. What if my new master wouldn't listen? What if I couldn't contact anyone outside this house? I tried not to worry. But as I lay there, my fingers crept back to the scar on the inside of my arm. There is no easy way out, I thought. I prayed that Marcus Tullius would come for me, but I wondered whether he would even be able to find out where I had been taken; Holconia must have planned her revenge well, and arranged this precisely so that few people would know where she had taken me.

The next day, in early afternoon, I was sent to the master's private bath suite, to play for him while he received his massage. I had hoped I might speak to him when he was fully clothed, and I hesitated. Now that a moment of opportunity had arrived, I was afraid. I played for a while. He seemed relaxed and in good humor when he stood up, draped in linens, to waddle over to the dressing room. Should I wait? No, I had better not do this in front of guests; he will be more upset if I make a public scene; it would be better to do this in a private place. I fell on my knees:

"Master! Please hear me."

He turned and glared. There was a look of incredulity on his face.

"Please, master, there has been some mistake. I am a freedwoman. If you will write to Marcus Tullius—"

He struck me full on the face.

"Summon Otto," he said.

The largest man I had seen in the Roman world entered; a man with hands so massive that he could have snapped my arm like a twig. Possibly German, with his blond hair and blue eyes; would he look at me with any sympathy, thinking perhaps I might be his countrywoman? I saw no sign of pity in those glacial eyes. He seized my wrists and bound them behind me.

"Beat her...but don't kill her or leave any permanent injuries. I paid a lot of money for her."

What followed was a nightmare. Otto took me to a cubicle in the slave quarters. When Marcus Tullius had whipped me, I understood, he had tried to minimize the pain, and make the thing look worse than it actually was. This was the opposite. I was in the hands of an expert, apparently; one who knew just how much force to use to cause pain, but without breaking bones or causing internal injuries. Most of the blows fell on my back. I was not too proud to scream. Perhaps if I screamed enough, he would decide he had beaten me enough. I had no sense of time. When he was finished with me, he left me, with my wrists still bound behind me, and bolted the door. I lay on the floor like a heap of rags. My skin was unbroken, and as far as I could tell my bones were intact, but I was bruised all over. Hope was gone. When they untied me, when I could stand up, perhaps I could do something. At that moment there was nothing I could do except endure the pain. I tried to think that it would get easier over time, but the truth is, it grew worse through the evening, as the swelling increased. No one brought water or food. Perhaps I'll die here, I thought. I don't know whether I can stand this.

But I had to endure it. What choice did I have? I tried to crawl inside my mind; to blot out not just my surroundings, but my own body. I forced myself to relax some of the muscles; I thought myself outside. I envisioned a hillside, and a spring, and I drank the clean water. Perhaps I actually hypnotized myself. The pain was still there, but there were moments when I was able to push it into the background. That made it possible to get through other moments, when the pain forced itself back into my awareness.

It seemed to me as if I lay unattended in that room for days. A woman brought water, and helped me to drink; but she did not speak to me. I have been in this household only a day or so, I thought, and already I am branded a troublemaker. Even when I was able to get up again, I was a walking bruise.

I believed that if Marcus Tullius knew where I was, he would try to rescue me. At the same time, I wondered whether he would be able to find out. The mistress would not tell him what she had done with me, I was certain. The only clue he might have to work with would be the name of the city. How long would it take him to find me? How long could I hold out under this treatment?

When I have healed, I must behave and wait patiently, I thought.

I had thought the house of Marcus Tullius crowded, but this house swarmed with slaves; there was never a time when I was alone. When I passed through the central courtyard and gazed up at the sky, I looked for some way I could get up onto the roof and out to freedom; but this house was two stories high, and there was no obvious way to reach the roof. The slave quarters were below ground in a dark basement level gallery that reminded me of a dungeon; no daylight penetrated there. I was not permitted to leave the house, even in the company of other slaves.

Later I would learn that it was Tullia whose quick thinking saved my life. When Holconia returned without me, Tullia asked where I was. The mistress said that I had disappeared while she was out shopping, and that she didn't know where I was, but that I must have run away again. Tullia didn't believe this. She knew that Phoebus had been with us when we went out, and she shrewdly suspected that he knew what had happened to me.

She knew the name of a friend of Marcus Tullius who had a villa in Baiae. She wrote him a letter, and offered Phoebus an attractive sum of money to deliver it. Normally he was an indolent child, but the money she dangled before him (to be paid after he brought back a reply, clever Tullia) was tempting, so he trotted off to deliver her letter. I later learned that the first line of the letter was "Detain the bearer of this letter", followed by a description of her suspicions, and instructions to send a second enclosed letter to her father as quickly as possible. The recipient, an elderly gentleman who had long been friends with the family, read the letter twice and decided to take it seriously, although he may well have wondered whether she was indulging an overactive childish imagination. He detained Phoebus, and he sent word to Marcus Tullius, who by this time had returned to Pompeii.

When Holconia wondered out loud what had become of Phoebus, later that same afternoon, Tullia apparently repeated to her more or less the same words that had been used earlier: "Lost, perhaps, or run away."

Holconia shook Tullia and slapped her. She guessed quickly that her favorite attendant had been kidnapped. I suppose she had expected Tullia to accept my disappearance passively, but she did not know her own daughter. Tullia was apparently still fond of me even after all that had happened.

Marcus Tullius arrived at Baiae as quickly as possible and he went first to Holconia to confront her.

"What have you done with my freed woman?"

She told the same story as before.

"You're lying."

She shrugged, as if to say, believe me or not, as you prefer.

"Where is Tullia?"

Tullia came in; her face was welted from the slap she had received. He embraced her, and took her by the hand. "We are leaving. Say good by to your mother."

"I want a divorce, Marcus Tullius!"

"That is welcome news, Holconia. Take what belongs to you, with you..."

"I must have my dowry returned!"

"And I must have my freed woman returned. Where is she?"

I was told later that she hesitated a little before answering this question. Tullia, of course, was a witness to this scene. But she remained obdurate. "I don't know."

Marcus Tullius left his wife's lodgings with Tullia, and went to his friend's villa, where they would stay until matters in Baiae were resolved. He interrogated Phoebus. Phoebus knew that few slaves in this household had ever been seriously punished, but the expression on the master's face terrified him. Few threats were necessary before he told all that he knew: the name of my new master, and the part of the city where he lived, and the price that had been paid for me.

He set off to pay a call upon Mamius Flaccus.

CHAPTER 24

The bruises began to heal. I received a severe lecture on deportment from the steward. I dared not disobey again. I thought: I can endure it as long as it is no worse than this. If all I am asked to do is play music, and stay quiet and out of the way, that would be tolerable. Perhaps in time I would be able to get outside the guarded gates of the house; for the present, all I could do was try not to call attention to myself, and wait. I hoped that Marcus Tullius would be able to find me.

In fact, he tried to buy my freedom back within a few days of my arrival in that house. He offered to double and then triple the price that had been paid for me; but the offers were refused. It seemed that my new master had taken a fancy to my music, and had been personally offended by my disobedience. He was therefore unwilling to sell me: Not at any price, he reportedly said. I heard talk of this in the servant's quarters, and the small light of hope I had felt began to falter. What now? I knew there could be recourse to the courts in disputes like this, but the courts could be very slow, and that the process was often tainted by bribery. I clung to one small hope: that somehow Marcus could compel this man to set me free. But, I wondered, was I worth so much trouble to him? Outside Pompeii, did Marcus have enough influence? I doubted it. And I feared for my future.

I faded. I was glad I didn't look my best; for when I began to entertain at dinners again, I was mostly unnoticed by the men. How long can I live like this? I asked myself. And I kept answering myself: one more day.

Meanwhile, Marcus Tullius wrote to Julia Felix and summoned Demetrius to a small inn on the outskirts of Baiae. They concocted a plan.

One evening when I entered the triclinium to entertain the guests at dinner, I was astonished to see Demetrius among them. He was dressed quite splendidly, in a manner that suggested he was a wealthy merchant from the eastern part of the empire, and he paid no attention to me. I had to admire his performance, for his manners were faultless, and his conversation apparently quite entertaining. I was not close enough to hear much of what was said.

I played the charming Medieval French dance tunes that had become my new master's favorites. I tried not to look at Demetrius, and not to show that I was shaking with excitement; I kept my eyes averted, and strained to listen. That dinner seemed interminable to me. Course after course was served: stuffed game birds, beet salad, imported olives and cheeses, cooked fruits, wine and more wine. My new master seemed very taken with one of the rings that Demetrius wore on his hand. Why! That's one of Julia Felix's pieces! I thought. I had seen her show it to Holconia. By artifice or by luck, Demetrius had discovered this man's weakness: a passion for jewelry.

The conversation took a lewd turn. There were winks and gestures, and they pointed at various women in the room as they spoke. The few words I recognized were coarse sexual references. There was another blond serving girl pouring wine. Demetrius took her arm and acted as if he were taken with her. I think he was telling the new master that he had a particular preference for light haired women. I was not too surprised, therefore, when the new master indicated that I should approach them. Hope and fear fought to possess me, while at the same time, I felt an insane urge to laugh at the situation. I suppressed that urge, and stood passively before the two men, looking down at the floor.

"You like this one?" The new master seemed surprised. "I have many women more pleasing than this one."

"She looks stubborn as a mule. I like women who aren't too easy." Demetrius glanced at me; remembering his coaching about demeanor from our first encounter, I firmed my chin and glared at him, then looked down at the floor again. "If you don't like her, perhaps you'll sell her to me."

"No…No. Her music is pleasing. It is something quite unusual, you must admit; I have never heard songs like the ones she knows. No, I'm not going to sell her."

Demetrius flexed his hand so that the ruby in the ring on his middle finger caught the light and flashed blood red. "Perhaps…a wager? Or a trade?"

"I never gamble when I have been drinking," his host replied. I suspected that Demetrius had his trick dice with him. He was skilled at cheating, but oh, what a risk to take! How much did Marcus pay you to do this, Demetrius? Was it worth risking death for impersonating a free man?

Their wine was refreshed. Our host looked at the ring; I swear he licked his lips.

"Are you an admirer of rubies? This is a very fine one." Demetrius held his hand up so that the man could see.

"Yes…Do you mind if I ask…how much did you pay for that? Where did you buy it?"

Demetrius started to reel him in.

"It was a gift from a business associate."

"Do you think you could obtain one like it for me?"

"That would be very difficult…this one is so exceptionally large, and the stone has such fire and clarity, completely free of flaws…"

Our host was not paying much attention to his other guests by now.

"Perhaps I can persuade you to sell it to me, as a favor. What price would you consider reasonable?"

I was still standing nearby, trying to be quite still. I had not been dismissed.

"My jewel in exchange for yours, perhaps. Give me the girl, and I'll sell you the ring at a most reasonable price." Demetrius jerked his head in my direction. I caught my breath. Could it be this simple?

Our host seemed to be torn by his conflicting desires. He looked at me. I tried my best to look plain, and small, and unwell. I coughed just slightly. Demetrius did not turn his head but I thought I caught a small indication from him to me: don't overact. I hardly breathed.

"I don't know. I had thought that, with more training, and some attention to her appearance, this one might be a suitable gift for Nero himself. He is such a connoisseur of the musical arts."

"Is she obedient?" Demetrius asked.

"Once she had been beaten she was obedient."

I felt dizzy, but I didn't want to faint. The long sleeved tunic I had been given to wear hid my bruises, but they were still tender. It began to look as if no bargain could be made.

"I am not willing to sell her. I will let you borrow her, for a time, for a consideration."

Demetrius appeared to mull this over. He raised his index finger, glinting with gold, and said. "I have it. I will rent her from you for a few nights. In payment for this I agree to sell you the ring, and my price shall be most reasonable, only 70,000 sesterces."

They argued about this for some time; other guests seemed bored and restless, in spite of the dancers and singers who had been called in to continue the entertainment. Finally they agreed: I would go with Demetrius for one night; Demetrius would leave one of the less valuable rings as a surety for my return; and upon my return, the ruby ring would be sold at a lower price they had both agreed to after much haggling. They drank to their agreement.

I tried to keep my face impassive. After additional pleasantries and jokes, Demetrius announced that it was time for him to depart. Outside, he had a litter waiting; I walked behind it, with two of his attendants holding my arms as if I were a prisoner. We went by a roundabout way to a small inn near the edge of town. When we arrived, Demetrius looked around, nervously; he seemed apprehensive that we might have been followed. He dismissed the litter bearers, who had apparently been rented or borrowed for the occasion. Without speaking, he took my arm, and we entered the inn. The innkeeper provided a lamp, and by its light, we walked through the courtyard and went to one of the cubicles. Off balance, I stumbled, and felt a man's arms around me. It was Marcus Tullius, I knew, although my eyes took a moment to adjust to the bright light from the fire in the brazier and the lamps inside. He gripped my arms, and I gasped in pain, for my bruises were still very tender. He sat me down on the couch and examined me carefully, pulling up my sleeves, looking at my legs. He swore under his breath at the bruises and welts that he found.

He turned to speak with Demetrius. They spoke rapidly but quietly, plotting, arguing what to do. Demetrius had not seen anyone, but he thought we might have been followed; and if that were so, we must leave at once. Demetrius removed the costly outer gown that he had worn as his disguise. Underneath he had on an ordinary everyday tunic. He gave the rings back to Marcus, who stuffed them into his pouch; and received some coins in return. Marcus Tullius collected his possessions, including his sword, for he had come armed as if he expected trouble. He reached out his hand to help me get up. At that moment, the door (which was not bolted) burst open, and three armed men entered the room. One of them was the burly German who had beaten me so expertly; he had a sword drawn; the other two had knives.

Demetrius picked up the little table next to the couch and used it to shield himself as the smallest man among the intruders slashed at him with a knife. Marcus had his sword in hand; the two other men cornered him. Our situation seemed desperate. I looked about quickly for anything I might be able to use, and saw the brazier with its blazing coals. I seized it with my right hand; with my left hand I grabbed the back of the neck of Otto's tunic—he had cornered Marcus and stood over him menacingly. I dumped the hot coals down his back. He screamed and leaped aside, and began tearing at his clothing. This gave Marcus Tullius the opportunity to drive his sword into Otto's broad chest. He toppled and crashed onto the floor. By now Demetrius had been stabbed and slashed, although he still brandished the table as a shield.

The two attackers who remained standing were armed only with knives. They regarded their fallen leader with consternation. Apparently neither was willing to go after Marcus now that he was the only one armed with a sword—and he obviously knew how to use it effectively. They fled. I knelt beside Demetrius; he was badly hurt. The knife cuts on his shoulders and arms bled quite a lot. Marcus Tullius made a more knowing assessment.

"He will survive this. He needs to be well bandaged, but if he wants to live, he will have to be able to travel quickly."

I took Demetrius's hand in mine and cradled his head on my lap; Marcus knelt beside us, and bound his arm and shoulder tightly with strips of cloth torn from his tunic. The way Marcus glanced at me, as if to check the expression on my face, made me wonder whether perhaps he was a little jealous of the tenderness I showed toward Demetrius; but I wanted to let my friend know that I understood what a great risk he had taken for me, and to let him know I was concerned about his condition. And as I looked into Demetrius's face, and saw the hopeless way he looked at Marcus Tullius, I suddenly saw a truth I hadn't seen before. Demetrius loved Marcus, and he knew it was impossible that his love would ever be returned. The misery on his face was only partly due to his physical pain. I looked away, afraid that my face might betray this knowledge. I don't think Marcus had any idea that Demetrius had done this dangerous thing out of love for him and not just for the money and freedom that had been offered.

"We don't have much time. They will come back with others. We must leave quickly." He summoned the litter bearers—who had prudently fled to the stable when the attackers arrived, and were still cowering there. "We will have to put Demetrius in the litter—he will bleed too much if he has to sit upright or walk—can you ride?" In spite of my bruises, I nodded in assent. Whatever discomfort this ride would cause me, I could bear.

While the litter bearers arranged things for Demetrius, Marcus Tullius saddled his horse, set me in the saddle, and mounted behind me in an easy vault. I knew that when he served under Vespasian in the Claudian invasion of Britannia, Marcus had become as skillful at riding as the auxiliary cavalrymen he had commanded. I wrapped my arms around his waist, awkwardly astride, and held on as if my life depended upon it. I was no rider, myself; I was soon in great misery from pulled muscles and saddle sores, but I tried to steel myself against the pain. I didn't know where we were going, but clearly we needed to put as much distance as possible between ourselves and my second owner and his thugs. There would be time for questions later.

We passed through the gate on the south side of the city; Marcus paid a bribe to the guard that might or might not ensure his silence. We couldn't go very fast, although he urged the litter bearers to make speed. We headed south along the main road, in the direction of Pompeii, and I glanced backward over my shoulder often to see whether we were being followed.

CHAPTER 25

The full moon lit our way; it glowed like a lantern on the horizon, far larger than normal. Few people traveled the roads at night, for they were dark and dangerous, and thieves and cutthroats were free to roam. The horse's hooves and the sandals of the litter bearers beat a rapid rhythm on the stone pavement. I grew tired, so tired I could hardly hold on; the muscles in my legs screamed pain from this unaccustomed use, blisters became open sores. But I knew we mustn't stop to bother with such things; we had to get away. After about two hours, we turned off to a side road that was hard packed earth; the horse's hooves made a softer sound, and Marcus slowed the pace to avoid a possible stumble on this uneven road surface. We approached a villa pooled in darkness; the front gate was closed. Marcus Tullius rapped upon it sharply, and announced who he was, and asked that the gate be opened. The watchman complied; apparently he recognized the name. Marcus dismounted and I would have fallen off if he had not caught me as I lost balance. I was able to stand, but it must have been evident to him that I was in pain and at the limit of my endurance. He scooped me off my feet and carried me in his arms through the open gate.

He set me on a couch, and for the first time since my rescue, I was able to see his face in the light, and to see the expression of concern. I was touched by it.

"We will be safe here. This is the house of a patron of mine. He will give us shelter and protection for the night."

I could not help grimacing as I tried to arrange myself more comfortably on the couch. With bruises on my arms, legs and back, and fresh saddle sores, I could find no comfortable way to arrange my limbs. He pulled up a sleeve of my tunic, and saw the partly healed bruises; then he checked elsewhere, finding more; he swore, quietly, to himself. I smiled weakly.

A servant came to escort us.

"My master is awake; he will see you."

We were led into a small but gorgeously appointed reception room, where he again placed me on a couch to rest.

"Marcus! What brings you to my door in the middle of the night!"

"Petronius—I need to ask a small favor."

They reclined on the other couches; wine was brought.

"Tell me what you need."

I could not follow the entire conversation; I felt fatigue as intense as a drug. I was able to understand several things from their exchange. The man Tullia had asked to summon Marcus Tullius to Baiae was neither rich nor powerful, and Marcus did not want to endanger him by involving him in a scheme to deceive Mamius, who had a great deal of influence. So he had used an inn as his base of operations rather than his friend's house. In her letters, Julia Felix had suggested several possible strategies; together, they had decided that Demetrius would enter Mamius's household in the guise of a wealthy traveling merchant. She provided jewelry and clothing suitable for this disguise. Demetrius had been given his freedom at this point; for this status would reduce the maximum possible punishment that he might face for this impersonation.

Demetrius had learned from local gossip that this man had several weaknesses, including fine jewelry and attractive young boys. They thought that if they could not buy me with cash, they might find some other inducement he could not resist. Demetrius had ingratiated himself with a friend of Mamius, and inveigled a dinner invitation. He thought that it might require several visits, but he hoped that he could win my freedom on a wager, or buy me, or spy out a way that I could be kidnapped. The man's fascination with Julia's ruby provided him with the means. The ring that he had left behind was a sacrifice, but at least it was not one of her most costly pieces.

When Demetrius realized that the best he could do was "rent" me, he decided that was better than nothing. However, he had been followed. Perhaps this Mamius was shrewd enough to suspect that Demetrius was not what he appeared to be. Mamius did not want to assassinate Demetrius at his own dinner table, in front of witnesses; therefore, he sent his henchmen to retrieve me and take the rings from Demetrius at the inn. He could explain his ownership of the ring later, if questions arose, for his guests had witnessed that Demetrius had agreed to sell it to him; and certainly his thugs would have disposed of the body. He would certainly be angry to realize that this plan had gone awry, and that in fact his servants had attacked a wealthy Roman equestrian and achieved none of his aims.

Marcus had brought me to this powerful friend's house to rest in safety before our return to Pompeii. It was quite possible that Mamius would try to recover me by legal action. If the case were tried in Baiae or nearby Neapolis, he would have the advantage of knowing all the local magistrates; of having clients who could bribe people; and of having me in his possession. If the case were tried in Pompeii, Marcus Tullius would have these advantages. Therefore it was urgent to make a change of venue to the city where Marcus Tullius had greater influence. Even if Marcus Tullius could get a court in Baiae to award him custody of me—which was unlikely—there was no means of enforcing such a judgment. If Mamius refused to let me go, or took me away to another city where I could not be traced, it would be Marcus Tullius' problem to retrieve me.

As they spoke about this, it was clear that Marcus Tullius looked forward to a possible day in court, but he wanted it to be in his own court.

Of course, in telling this story to Petronius, he added additional information. Petronius looked at me, then, with some interest.

"You have gone to much trouble for this one. Her music must be wonderful indeed, like the song of a nightingale." Perhaps this was a gentle way of saying that, like the nightingale, I was a plain and unremarkable looking little creature.

The look that Marcus Tullius gave me was full of love.

"Yes."

"You are welcome to stay in my house. I know this Mamius you speak of: A loathsome creature. It will be a pleasure to annoy him. Stay for a few days; he has no way to find out that you are here. I will enjoy your conversation, Marcus, and this little one will have time to rest before making the rest of the journey. You will divorce Holconia, of course?"

"That is already done. We have to settle the matter of her dowry; I will deduct the expenses for this situation, with the blessing of the court, I hope."

"You will want to send messages to Julia Felix and others in Pompeii. I can have a messenger ready to leave first thing in the morning. Meanwhile, refresh yourselves. I will have my servants attend you in the bath."

Marcus looked at himself: bloodstained, sweat covered.

"Indeed, yes. If you can provide medicine and bandages, I want to tend to this woman, also."

"My servants can do that."

"Thank you. I would prefer to do it myself."

And so it was. They brought hot water, diluted wine, opium, salve, and bandages. I was wrapped up in soft coverlets and put to sleep on a couch, feeling as if I floated on clouds. Marcus stayed with me until I slept.

I slept through most of the day, and did not awake until evening. I felt well enough to walk, although I was most grateful that I would not be required to get on a horse again. If I never ride a horse again in my life, I thought, it would be too soon. Marcus Tullius was elsewhere in the house, writing letters. A servant brought a clean tunic, and I dressed; I was given fine white bread and wine, and our host appeared. He greeted me, and they brought me a chair; he reclined on a couch, and sent for refreshments. It felt strange to sit in a chair—a chair with a back was a privilege usually reserved for the eminent, the sick, and the aged; I supposed that I qualified as sick. I think he was curious to learn what kind of woman had gotten his conservative friend involved in such an unlikely adventure.

"Do you feel better after this rest?"

"Yes, thank you, lord, I am greatly in your debt."

"I am told that you are a musician."

"I play a flute." My instrument was still with me, for it had been in a bag tied to my belt since I had left my old master's house.

"I would like to hear some of your songs later."

From the decorations of his house, and the way he dressed and spoke, it seemed to me that this was a man of refinement and taste as well as wealth. He might appreciate Mozart, I thought. I haven't done anything as complex as that. I think I can remember. An aria, a plaintive song of mercy and forgiveness, perhaps *Dove Sono*.

"I would be honored to play for you."

"Marcus told me also that you can make prophecies."

"Sometimes, yes."

"Can you look ahead, and see the answer to any question that is asked?"

"No. Sometimes I foresee great events that are to come; but I can't choose what to know, or what to ask."

A servant bowed from the doorway. "Lord Petronius…".

He smiled.

"I will return."

The name sounded familiar to me. This must be the Petronius who was a member of Nero's court; he was a man of such noted refinement that he became known as Nero's arbiter elegantiae, "arbiter of good taste". He was thought to be the author of the Satyricon, a witty and bawdy account of a dinner party hosted by a wealthy freedman whose extravagance was utterly tasteless. I liked him immensely, not just for the kindness he had shown to me, but also for something graceful about his presence. He may have been a restraining influence on Nero when he was still in favor; he may have been able to convince Nero that some of the cruelties he contemplated were in poor taste. I knew from my study of history that Petronius was forced to commit suicide when he fell under suspicion of involvement in a conspiracy against Nero a few years after the city of Rome burned. I wondered whether I could find a way to warn him of the danger he was in. From the expression in his eyes, I think he knew.

A late supper was served, just for the three of us, Marcus Tullius and our host and me.

"I must leave you, Marcus, I am called to Rome. But you are welcome to remain in my house as long as you wish. I can provide you with an escort to Pompeii, and a litter for the lady." (He referred to me this way ironically, but not unkindly).

This was the first time I had reclined on a couch at the table, and been treated as an equal. I think Marcus Tullius had requested this treatment; still, I was astonished at it. What would my life be like from now on? I expected I would still be his servant. For this evening, perhaps just for a few hours, I could imagine that I was one of them, an equal. I tried not to feel awkward. But it felt strange to have my hands washed by slaves and to be waited upon.

We talked of various things. I spoke little, but when I was asked questions, I was able to answer well. Our host pressed more wine upon me.

"No, thank you...more people have been drowned by Bacchus than by Neptune," I said. (This expression sounds as if it should have originated in the ancient world, but in fact it was of nineteenth century origin.)

Petronius laughed. "Marcus tells me that you seem to be under the special protection of Neptune."

I tried to be evasive. Lies seem to beget more lies. "Neptune is symbolic of great powers that must be respected."

"Yes, he rules the sea, and the earth; you foretold the great earthquake in Campania, Marcus says. Can you make a prophecy for me, lady?" Petronius asked.

What could I say? I had become Cassandra, teller of fortunes...

"The climate in the city of Rome is evil, lord, and you would do well to avoid it, to find reasons not to go there."

His smile faded, just slightly; he knows, I thought. He knows that he can't keep playing games at court. He is a dead man...

"Let us have some pleasanter prediction. I know the climate in the city all too well."

Another thought occurred to me. Whether or not he had actually written the *Satyricon* (some modern students of literature thought it unlikely that such a refined man could have written such a coarsely humorous story, and I was hardly in a position to ask), he had almost certainly written something: letters, poetry, or essays. Most Romans dabbled in literary pursuits. The name "Petronius" would be remembered, for the writing attributed to him, and for his restraint of Nero's excesses.

So I said: "In 2,000 years, although the world will be much changed, your name will still be spoken. The words you have written will endure, and your influence will be remembered."

He was enormously pleased. "She has granted me immortality, Marcus! What suitable gift can I give in return?" A servant was summoned and given instructions; he returned shortly thereafter with a box. Petronius opened it and took out a necklace, one very fine pearl, suspended upon strands of gold with smaller pearls. He himself placed it around my neck. "You have found a pearl, Marcus. She has wit and soul."

Petronius provided a litter for me; I felt like a queen, being carried by eight slaves in richly cushioned splendor. This was a great improvement over travel by horseback. I did not relish being a burden for other slaves; but I comforted myself by thinking that I was not very heavy, and these men appeared to be well fed and decently treated. Still, I would prefer to return to a life where I was not waited upon. As I was now a freed woman, I hoped that I could avoid participating directly in slavery. I was even less comfortable receiving services that providing them.

They decided it would be safer for Demetrius to remain in the house of Petronius for a time; he needed time for his wounds to heal before he could safely travel.

Marcus Tullius had sent letters ahead; apparently there were many things he wanted to have done by the time we arrived. He rode slowly enough to stay with our party, although it was easy to see that he was impatient with the slow process of this procession. By the end of the day we had arrived home.

"I do not wish to alarm you, but I think it possible that he will try to get you back—through the courts, or by force. You must not go outside the house; extra men have been placed on watch. I have a bodyguard for you; he will stay with you at all times." This bodyguard was a man of remarkable ugliness; and yet there was something sweet about the expression on his face. So much for privacy, I thought.

Tullia greeted me with visible pleasure. "You are safe! Did my father tell you how all this came about?"

"Little mistress, I owe my quick rescue to you. If you had not been so clever, who knows what would have become of me?"

"Have you been told? We are moving to the inner room of my father's cubicles. He thinks there may be danger." She was young and innocent enough to think this exciting, it seemed. "I have so much to tell you!" Marcus Tullius smiled to see us together.

I expected to return to the same situation I had left, to be a servant, but it began to seem to me that things had changed. I was given finer clothing. There suddenly seemed a great distance between me and the slaves, who began to expect orders from me as if I were not another servant, but the lady of the house. What did they know? The answer came the following day, when Julia Felix came to dinner. There were only the three of us, the master, Julia and me, yet the meal was formal.

"Julia has a proposal for you to hear, with my approval". I looked at her expectantly; I was still unaccustomed to recline with the family, but she had done much to set me at ease during the dinner.

"I want to adopt you as my daughter, my heir."

This was stunning news. I was at first unable to respond. I put my hands together, as if in prayer, and closed my eyes. I couldn't believe what I had heard. I looked to Marcus Tullius from long habit, seeking permission to speak. He nodded and smiled. This was no surprise to him, then. They had planned this together. Why? Was he so ready to give me up, after risking so much to get me back?

"Lady, you do me such a great honor, I hardly know what to say. I am not worthy."

"I will be the judge of that. I say you are. What is your answer?"

"Yes, Lady Julia."

She stood up, and so did I, and it seemed clear that she expected to embrace me, but I approached her with a sense of uncertainty. This didn't seem possible. I was confused. I had expected to stay with Marcus Tullius; if I were, indeed, her daughter, I knew I would go to live in her house; and I did not think that I could be with him there. What would happen?

Fresh wine was brought to drink to the occasion.

"I have petitioned, through Poppaea, for an imperial grant to allow this adoption," Julia said. Adoptions were extremely common in Roman families, but in most cases, a man adopted a nephew or the son of a friend as his heir when he did not have a son of his own. Only a paterfamilias could adopt, ordinarily; for a woman to take such an action would require special permission, I guessed. This was a most unusual adoption for many reasons: because Julia was a woman; because I was a woman; and because I was a former slave rather than the son of an aristocratic family. "She will be most pleased with the gifts that accompanied this request!"

They laughed together, pleased with the success of their project. Seeing my confusion, Marcus Tullius offered some additional explanation.

"We think it likely that Mamius will bring his claim to court, and try to take you back. We are preparing counterclaims that he will not be able to dispute. As Lady Julia's daughter, you will be a member of a wealthy family, and not just a freedwoman. Further, the fact that your adoption was sanctioned by Nero's own decree will make it impossible to question."

What was in this for Julia? I knew she liked me, and enjoyed our conversations. She answered the question I could not ask.

"I have been thinking for some time that I needed an heir, someone besides that worthless nephew of mine. I considered several young men, but none seemed really deserving. I wanted someone whose company I would enjoy, and not just a legal heir. You will be my daughter. In truth, we are much alike!"

"I cannot thank you enough, Lady."

She laughed, and touched my cheek. "It will seem more natural to you soon. You will come to live in my house. Marcus Tullius has sent additional men to stand watch. As soon as the papers come, we will have a formal adoption ceremony and hold celebrations."

I had gained a mother, and it seemed to me, I had lost a lover. Marcus Tullius did not seem disturbed. Perhaps I had misunderstood, then. He felt a sense of obligation to me because I had nursed him through illness; he rescued me because he felt he owed me his life. He was now a divorced man, and naturally he would take a new wife who suited him better. No doubt she would come from a family with a distinguished name and strong political connections, and she would be very rich. Perhaps she would even have a pleasanter disposition than Holconia.

A hope occurred to me. Perhaps I could be that next wife? But this was too much to hope for. I had nothing to offer him except myself; and no reason to believe that would be enough. As Julia's daughter, I could not be his mistress. She would not allow it, and women in respectable families did not do that sort of thing. Even as her daughter I would not be an advantageous match for him. Was he lost to me now?

CHAPTER 26

I went to the house of Julia Felix as her daughter, even before the official adoption ceremony took place. My homely bodyguard accompanied me. I never heard the man speak, but I became accustomed to his constant presence. I commented on his silence to Julia.

"He can't speak, you know. His former master cut out his tongue, accusing him of being a liar." This was horrifying. It was easy for me to forget the potential and actual cruelties made possible by slavery, for I had spent most of my time in households where the treatment was relatively benign. I discovered that my bodyguard could communicate to some extent with gestures, and began to feel a great sympathy for this man, although I never knew very much more about him. Although he could not speak, his hearing was unusually acute, and he was a light sleeper; any time I stirred in the night, I could tell that he had also awakened. He slept on a pallet in the doorway of my cubicle, and other men were posted to watch in the courtyard.

Julia read me the letter she received from her disinherited nephew. It was a masterpiece of whining and obsequiousness. He wanted a last chance to convince her that he should be her heir, before she carried out her plans for this adoption. She only laughed. "I am well rid of him!"

The papers arrived, and Julia organized a formal adoption ceremony, with the legality of the proceedings attested to by a pontifex
and the document witnessed and signed by ten men who were
among the leading politicians of Pompeii. She opened her house and
gardens and provided a splendid feast; she made handsome gifts to
those who attended. She dressed me for the occasion in dazzling
white. I felt awkward in my new role and too shy to speak very much,
but my modesty made a positive impression.

Two days later, letters from the Mamius Flaccus arrived at the
house of Marcus Tullius, accusing him of the kidnapping of one
valuable slave and the murder of another; he also charged Demetrius
with impersonation of a citizen. In consultation with colleagues,
Marcus Tullius composed his reply. He charged my former master
with collusion in depriving his freedwoman of her freedom and pre-
empted the choice of venue by filing these charges with the court in
Pompeii. He enlisted his many clients in his preparations. They cir-
culated among the people of the town, making the particulars of the
case known and distributing small bribes so that everyone they
talked to would be certain to appear in court and applaud wildly on
cue. There were long discussions late at night with Julia Felix. He was
apparently preparing his speeches, and they were anticipating who
could be counted on for support, which additional people might be
enlisted, and whether anyone might be open to influence by
Mamius. The Holconius brothers might choose to take his side,
although Marcus was not formally bringing charges against Holconia.

Like a Mafia don, Marcus made his arrangements, calling upon
both patrons and clients for support. He had a hand in the selection
of judges; and letters were sent to make certain that all the witnesses
he would call would be available, and would testify exactly as he
desired. Demetrius was still in hiding at the house of Petronius,
which was the most prudent thing under the circumstances, for his
fate could be terrible if the judgment went against us.

Finally Marcus was satisfied that all possible contingencies had been considered. "Now, let our accuser come."

It was not at all unusual that Marcus Tullius chose to appear as his own advocate. Most wellborn Roman men served as court advocates, at least for one part of their careers. His political activities, and the money he had spent on public works for the town, and his connections through patronage and clients, ensured that he had substantial influence. He was considered a fine orator. By modern standards, the Roman enthusiasm for oratory seems difficult to understand. Modern people are accustomed to have messages packaged in 15-second sound bites. However, an advocate arguing a case before a court or a political making an argument to an assembly was expected to go on at length, sometimes for hours. This enthusiasm for oratory was revived during the Victorian period; audiences attended political debates that went on all day, and in fact the speeches of that period were often self consciously modeled on Roman or Greek orations, in structure and to some extent in style. As a descendant of the family of the great orator Cicero, Marcus Tullius had the advantage of family tradition as well as personal charisma.

Mamius Flaccus lost his bid for a change of venue in the early legal maneuvering. He of course wanted the case to be tried in Neapolis, where his own influence would be much greater, but Marcus Tullius prevented this.

The day of the court hearing arrived. Julia dressed me very simply without any jewelry or adornment. I was told to say nothing. Normally these proceedings would have been held in the great basilica, but that building had been destroyed in the earthquake; instead, the court proceedings were held outside in the forum. When we arrived, it was already crowded. Six judges sat in backless chairs, facing the audience; Julia and I were seated off to one side, in the shadows. In front of the judges sat two groups: Marcus Tullius with his steward and secretaries; and the false master with his larger entourage, including the Holconius brothers. Beyond these two groups there were benches; here sat virtually all the higher-ranking men of Pompeii; and behind that, the forum was packed with people of lesser rank, freedmen mostly, with standing room only. This, apparently, was the best show in town. For the past few days, little else had been spoken of.

The scene reminded me of a courtyard full of statuary; I had never seen so many men wearing togas, for this garment was rarely worn at home, and only as formal wear in public, as a modern man might wear an uncomfortable business suit. The chill autumn light added notes of yellow to the otherwise mostly bluish white scene, rows of men attired in bleached white. Some wore their togas gracefully draped; others seemed uncomfortable, and looked as if they wore rumpled bed sheets.

The court was called to order. The prosecution would be allowed to speak first; a time limit of three water clocks had been established. Mamius began a bombastic speech. First, he outlined his charges. Then he maligned Marcus Tullius' character; this was in the spirit of advice given generations before by Cicero: when you have no basis for a case, abuse your opponent. He summoned the dinner guests who had been present when he purchased me from Holconia. I was asked to stand, and he identified me as the slave in question. He produced a document written by Holconia as a bill of sale. He reviled me as a worthless and disobedient slave, omitting to mention that I had tried to tell him that I was a freedwoman. He described Marcus Tullius' attempt to buy me back, arguing that that constituted an admission that I was actually a slave. Then he described the perfidy of Demetrius, my master's agent, in impersonating a citizen. Again he argued that, since Demetrius had tried to buy me, this was yet again another tacit admission that I was really a slave.

I cannot begin to reconstruct the words that were used to build this argument. The language was rich with classical allusions, witty, persuasive. The delivery began in a quiet tone, and gradually built up to a crescendo. I half believed it myself; I began to fear that we might lose this case, after all. There were some in the audience who applauded wildly whenever a particularly telling point was made (his paid claque, I imagined), although another larger group of our supporters made disparaging noises.

Now that he had warmed to his task, the orator's voice rose; his gestures became less restrained. The slave Demetrius had lied and misrepresented his identity; he must be put to death for this impertinence. However, he said, that was not the main point at issue today, for Demetrius had run away. He must be found before that issue could be settled. Now he summoned the two surviving thugs, and they described the scene that had taken place at the inn. As they told the story, their master had wisely suspected foul play, and ordered them to follow Demetrius. They said that they had accosted Marcus Tullius with a letter from their master (this false letter was produced as evidence) demanding that I be returned. They claimed that they were unarmed, and that Demetrius and Marcus Tullius had set upon them with swords, killing the (valuable) German slave and frightening them away.

Mamius finished his argument, concluding finally with his demands. He wanted Demetrius's head on a platter (so to speak). He wanted me, his valuable musician slave, returned. He wanted compensation for the death of his valuable German slave; he wanted monetary compensation. He could not ask for any physical punishment against such an eminent citizen, but he demanded additional monetary compensation for all the expenses this had created. Of course this was all tied to general principles, the right to secure ownership of one's own property; the necessity of preventing slaves from escape, lest the entire social structure collapse.

When this argument was finished, the hearing was adjourned for the day. The following day in court would be our turn.

On this second day, Julia dressed me splendidly all in white, with the pearl necklace that had been the gift of Petronius around my neck. She wrapped a gold encrusted belt around my waist and put soft red leather sandals on my feet. My hair was artfully arranged. Holconia had not taken the wig made of my hair with her, and parts of this were woven into my coiffure to create a more elegant effect. All this finery was covered with a simple cloak; and I was told not to remove it until Julia or Marcus asked me to. I was anxious, but Julia reassured me.

"He knows what he's doing. Everything that he can do to assure the outcome, he has done. But we must give them good theater!"

Marcus Tullius would have the time allowed by three water clocks to present the defense side of the case; this, again, was standard procedure. I had never seen him look so magnificent. His toga had been bleached to striking whiteness, made even whiter with chalk. When he stood facing the judges, I noticed that there had been some slight rearrangement of the seating arrangements. On the first day, Mamius had to keep turning, because when he faced the judges, his back was turned toward the audience. Today, however, the judge's seats had been moved to one side so that when Marcus Tullius faced them, he presented a profile view to the audience, and he could address the audience directly by turning only a little, without seeming to slight the judges. I had thought the forum full on the first day, but today it really was packed. Many of these were men who had been paid for their enthusiasm (a denarius each, Julia said; the going rate for audience enthusiasm in this small town was lower than in the city of Rome). The crowd filled the entire forum and spilled out the arched entryways. No one wanted to miss this event, which was to be the talk of the town for years to come.

He began to speak; his voice carried clearly over the crowd, although he spoke in gentle tones at first. His expression was serious, almost to the point of severity; and yet, I thought, he looks as if he is enjoying himself. I knew that this was what he did, and did well: He wielded influence. This case would add to his reputation as an advocate; he welcomed the challenge, in fact. He began by describing how I had been purchased originally as a slave, and how I had distinguished myself by loyalty to his family. He described how I had saved his life, and the lives of others in his household, by nursing them through an illness that had taken many lives elsewhere in the city. Alexander and other servants were asked to attest to this. He then explained that he had granted me my freedom, in gratitude for this loyal service. Now the formal documents and city records were produced; and each of the ten men who had witnessed the granting of my freedom stood and swore that all this had been done exactly as Marcus Tullius described, naming the specific date. Marcus pointed out that this was weeks before the alleged sale; thus I had already been made a freedwoman.

Next he described how his ex-wife had taken me away from his house, without his knowledge, and sold me. This sale was invalid, he argued, for I was already free. In any case, he said, even when I had been a slave, I belonged to him, as paterfamilias; it was not Holconia's right to sell any slaves who belonged to him. Furthermore, he and Holconia were now divorced, which meant that, except for the return of her dowry, she had no further claim to any of his property. It was not his intention to seek damages against his ex-wife, he said, except that the costs of this trial should be deducted from her dowry before he returned it to her, as it was her actions that had created this problematic situation. He emphasized the duty of wives to obey their husbands, a point that went over well with the male members of the audience.

Next he acknowledged that he had tried to get me back, but he denied that this effort was in the form of trying to buy me. He had explained this misunderstanding to the false master, he said, and offered compensation. It turned out that he actually had a witness to this conversation, who confirmed what he had said.

As he continued to speak, he became more animated. His toga slipped back a little from his shoulders; this slight sign of disarray was a conventional oratorical strategy for dramatizing the effort and intensity of the argument. His gestures became more emphatic, although they were still well controlled.

Now he led up to the next point in his argument. We had been attacked at the inn; he had killed a slave who attacked him with sword in hand. The innkeeper was produced at this point; he had found Otto's body in the room, with his sword still in hand, and although he seemed very frightened to appear before the court, he spoke clearly and confirmed the story Marcus Tullius told. (I learned later that, even though everything he said was true, a large bribe had been required to induce the innkeeper to testify contrary to the interests of the wealthy and influential Mamius, enough for him to resettle in another city under the patronage and protection of the Tullius family.) Demetrius was not a slave, either, at the time of this incident, he argued. He next revealed that, just before they rescued me, he had granted freedom to Demetrius, again with all the paperwork in order, and the required 10 witnesses, who were produced to confirm this story. By now, half the eminent people in town had stood as witnesses in support of our case.

His next point was that, if abuse of property was the issue that he was the one with an accusation to make. He had shown my bruises and injuries to Petronius, who appeared as his next witness, testifying to the miserable condition I had been in when we came to his house. I was his freedwoman and servant; in the past I had been his slave; it was he who had a case to make for damages, he said, not this false master.

Now he reached the climax of his argument. The woman in question was no longer a slave, and in fact, by imperial grant, she had now been adopted by Julia Felix. Now I was told to stand, and remove my cloak. I looked like a wealthy lady now, thanks to her attention to my hair and clothing. Julia and I were not asked to speak (women could not be legal witnesses), but the ten men who had witnessed the formal adoption proceedings testified.

A free Roman could not be placed in jeopardy by a false claim of ownership, he argued. Further, this adoption had taken place through an imperial grant from Nero himself; surely, this could not be contested without challenging the will of the emperor and his ability to grant such rights. This document with its impressive seals and signatures was displayed to the judges. By now Mamius apparently could see that he had lost. By now, every point Marcus Tullius made was greeted by general acclamation. Even the members of the audience who had not been paid to applaud were enthusiastic supporters by the time he finished speaking.

The judges conferred only a short time, and the verdict was in favor of Marcus Tullius. Mamius was granted some minor monetary damages; however, these were to be deducted from the dowry before Holconia received the remainder.

Julia held a spectacular dinner party the following day to celebrate this victory; Marcus Tullius occupied the seat of honor. It still seemed unfamiliar to see him in this way. I no longer washed his feet, or poured his wine. Now I reclined opposite him, and was waited upon by Julia's slaves. This felt awkward to me. I felt far more uncomfortable being waited upon by slaves then I had felt when I played the part of a slave.

CHAPTER 27

It wasn't clear to me what I would do with my time in this new life. Now I was a person of importance, waited upon by slaves, with all my work done for me. I could no longer be an entertainer, as that would be undignified. Nor could I be Marcus's mistress, for I was now the daughter of a respectable woman. I could not work, for women in those times very rarely engaged in professions, although history mentioned a handful of women physicians and artists. If I could not do any of these things, what could I be?

It felt luxurious at first to be bathed and massaged, to be dressed and groomed by other people's hands. But I was keenly aware that my luxuries were supported by the work of slaves, and that distressed me. I knew better than to try to convince Julia to free her slaves; to her, to all of them, slavery was simply the natural order of things. Perhaps I could ask at least that my own personal servant be a freedwoman. I resolved to treat the people who served me with kindness. I couldn't alter the basic evil; I could, however, try to soften the lives of the people who served me with kindness. I told myself that I must always remember this, and not forget what it had been like to be a slave.

I sat in on Julia's meetings with clients, in the way that a son would sit in on his father's meetings, to learn something of the way she conducted her affairs. But as I watched her, I thought: I could never do this. I don't know enough about their world to run business affairs as she does. I am, in fact, quite useless.

I tried to behave cheerfully. Julia deserved my gratitude, for her adoption had raised my status and provided additional protection for me during the court hearing. However, I could not imagine remaining in this situation for long. I spoke to Julia about this.

"I need to find something to do. I'm used to having work, or something worthwhile to occupy my time. Is there anything I can do to help you?"

"You are intelligent, but I can see you have no head for business matters. Marcus tells me you like to read; we will borrow scrolls for you. And you said that you enjoyed weaving; there is a loom in the servants' quarters that we will move into pleasanter surroundings. Don't be concerned; there will be a change in your situation soon."

"What do you mean, Julia?" (We had agreed that I should call her this.)

"I'll provide a dowry for you, and you will marry. I hope for grandchildren to brighten my old age!"

This was an alarming thought. Childbirth was a risky business in ancient times. And given my peculiar situation, what sort of man would willingly marry me, except for someone who was after Julia's money?

"Who would want to marry me?"

"I think that the husband you want is the son in law that I want...Marcus Tullius, of course. If I were not so old and set in my ways, I would marry him myself. He will speak to you tomorrow. I thought perhaps I might leave this as a surprise, but now that we have come to the matter naturally, perhaps we should discuss it."

Of course. They had planned this all together. Julia gets rid of the worthless nephew; he gets a wife with somewhat higher status than a simple freedwoman, with a dowry. What else?

"Julia! How long have you two been plotting this?"

"For some time now, ever since his divorce. The people I am most fond of are Tullia and her father. When you marry him, he will acquire a meddlesome mother in law. I have my eye on that court-yard that he is not using; I will have it rebuilt for my personal quar-ters and move into it. I have wished for a family to care for me in my old age, and for grandchildren. I'll rent out the baths and apartments in my town house; there will be great demand for this space now that so many buildings in town have suffered earthquake damage. I hope you do not mind that I have planned your life for you?"

I was too amazed to speak, at first.

She spoke frankly, as always. "He wants you, and I will not allow my daughter to be any man's mistress. He must marry you to have you. But I have made it more attractive for him to do so; I have given you a respectable family name and a dowry. A woman should not be married to a man without having some money of her own, my dear; it is not a good thing to be entirely powerless. But you need not be speechless with thanks, for I have selfish reasons for this. I'm tired of living alone; this arrangement will make it possible for me to have a family, and yet to retain control of my affairs. What do you say? Do you like the husband I have chosen for you?"

"Yes, Julia…"

But in fact I felt suddenly trapped and frightened.

"Then recover from your surprise, and be happy." She smiled.

"I am happy, Julia; it is just that there have been so many changes, and I don't know how to feel."

"Give yourself a little time. It will become comfortable."

I walked alone in her garden, beside the long narrow stone pool crossed by flat stone bridges, under the grape arbors. An autumn chill edged the breeze; the flowers were mostly gone.

I had much to ponder. I loved Marcus; and yet, there was much that troubled me. By taking away the signal device he had deprived me of my freedom. He was afraid of losing me, I understood; none-theless, it was a selfish action, and one that caused me much pain. I wondered whether I really had any choice to make; certainly both he and Julia would be shocked if I refused his offer.

I also felt a deep discomfort about becoming a slave-owner, a mistress of a household. This was morally repugnant. But I knew there was no way I could prevail on him to free his slaves. To Marcus and Julia, slavery was simply a fact of life; and much of their wealth was in the form of slaves. And for the most part, they treated their slaves kindly. But I didn't want to be in a position where slaves did all my work for me, and where I would benefit from exploitation of others.

I knew I couldn't agree to be as obedient as a proper Roman matron. I won't be happy, I thought, unless I have the freedom to do things that seem worthwhile. I need to be able to read, write, and study. I would want to be able to make music and tell stories, so that I have something of value to offer. I would also want to work with my hands, to weave or to cook. I couldn't endure being useless and idle, and mostly confined to the house. If I become his wife, I would not embarrass him by outrageous behavior in public; but I would need to have some freedom in private, or I would lose my mind, my self.

I didn't think, I fact, that I could marry him at all, if it were not for Julia—not because of her money, but her friendship. She would understand me, perhaps better than Marcus. Perhaps by watching her I could learn how to circumvent the rules for proper behavior without creating too much trouble. She would teach me what I need to know about running a household; she would be my friend, as well as my adopted mother.

Perhaps above all, I needed for him to tell me that he loved me. I believed that he did; but I was afraid that he might share traditional Roman attitudes toward romantic love. Many Roman men viewed any sort of passion as an unmanly loss of self-control; they feared the vulnerability and dependence that might come from love. And so they sometimes showed their wives and lovers little affection, for fear that this would give their women too much power over them. It would not be enough to have a husband. I wanted a lover who would show me that he loved me. And I did not want to compete with slave mistresses.

With all these doubts in my heart, I waited for Marcus Tullius. He joined us for cena the following day. Julia left us alone afterwards to talk. He seemed to sense my discomfort.

He took my right hand between his two hands, and said:

"I have two gifts to offer you. It's for you to choose." He offered me two small ornately decorated wooden boxes, one trimmed in silver and the other in gold. "Open the silver one first; and promise that you will listen to everything I have to say before you choose."

The first box contained the silver disk that he had taken out of my arm: the signal device I hadn't expected ever to see again. I looked up at him in amazement. "You offer me the chance to return to my own world?"

"Yes, but I hope to persuade you that the other gift is better."

The second box contained a gold ring. This was the marriage offer.

"I want you to marry me. Marry me, and I will honor and protect you, always. We belong together."

I looked down at the ground, and my eyes filled with tears. How could I make this choice? At first I couldn't answer.

"I don't want you to leave me, but I won't force you to stay. I want your love, not just your obedience. I love you."

I could go back. I could be an independent woman again, with enough money to start a new life. But in that other life, Marcus Tullius would be long dead, his ashes interred in a tomb that had in turn been buried by Vesuvius.

I could stay. But I could never really be one of them. I could never take slavery for granted and be comfortable with it. I would no longer be a slave, but an owner of slaves, which seemed far worse. And I suspected that as a proper Roman matron, there would be many restrictions on what I could say or do.

Freedom versus love. My world versus his. Must it come to such a choice?

Could I bargain with him for some of the things I wanted and needed? I would try.

"I love you and I will marry you, but…you must know that I will not be like other Roman wives. In public, I will behave convention-ally; I won't embarrass you. In private, I must have some freedom to do and say what I want. And I want you to be faithful to me, as I will be to you. I don't want you to have slave mistresses, or other women. I will not turn you away when you want to be loved; and I do not want my place taken by someone else, younger and more beautiful. If you will promise me this, I'll marry you."

"You want a great deal." He looked resigned. I suppose he realized I was not going to be the most obedient wife he might have chosen.

"I want you…and I want to be myself. Is that too much to ask? If you can't promise me these things, I must go back to my own times. I could have a very different kind of life in a world where women have more power." The die was cast: I had said what I had to say. I think I loved him too much to leave, no matter what he might reply. But I had to make a bid now for some freedom, or I would give up too much for love.

He sighed. I knew I was being very difficult. I was asking a Roman man to accept conditions from a woman, and a former slave, at that. Their ideas of masculine dignity and honor did not include this kind of accommodation, I knew. Had I asked more than he could give? I waited, in a misery of uncertainty. I could not ask for less.

"I love you, because you are not like other women. But you are difficult, because you are not like other women…You are strong, intelligent, brave, and wise. And you are beautiful, although you don't know it", he added, as if those qualities were rare in women. I do not think they are so rare.

And then he said, with words from our favorite poet: "Nos uxor numquam, nunquam seducit amica; semper amica mihi, semper et uxor eris", which meant: "No wife or mistress will ever steal me from you, for you will be wife and mistress always." That was the promise I needed to hear. And finally: "Everything will be as you ask."

It seemed to me that I had to make an irrevocable choice, a choice between two different lives. I tried to imagine how I would feel if I made the other choice—if I had left him and returned to the future. The thought of a world without him seemed intolerably cold and lonely. A chasm of two thousand years separated me from my own world now, and suddenly I realized that I would die in this place so far from my own home. I began to weep. I knew now I could never go back. He touched my face.

"Why weep?"

"I have given up my old life forever…but it was more difficult to do that than I expected. I love you; I will marry you."

"I promise to do what you have asked, as well as I am able. Compose yourself, don't weep; it won't do for you to look sad. Julia won't understand. We both want you to be happy." He kissed away my tears.

CHAPTER 28

Julia made plans for the wedding. This was just the kind of occasion she enjoyed; her pleasure in this was pure and untroubled, unlike my own. I loved Marcus Tullius. But I had doubts about the kind of life that I would have as a Roman matron. Perhaps, with Julia's help, I could find ways to evade the more stifling restrictions without creating too much trouble.

Before the ceremony, Marcus Tullia and Julia worked out all the necessary agreements. I was touched beyond words to hear that she had provided a dowry of 200,000 sesterces for me. This was not really a large enough sum to make me a good match for Marcus Tullius. He could have married a younger woman with a much larger dowry; most important of all, he could have obtained a bride whose name and family connections would bring him prestige and political influence. Julia had given me a position that made me an acceptable choice for him, but not really an advantageous one. Only love could explain his choice, for I had nothing of value to offer him but myself.

She spoke to me about this.

"If you decide that you are being treated badly, you could divorce him, and he would have to return your dowry to you. This would be enough for you to set up your own small household and live independently. I do not think he will ever treat you badly; but even when you marry a good man like Marcus Tullius, it is better that you have the power to leave; for he will treat you better if you are not completely in his power. Further, if you have children, you can leave them your own money. He has agreed that I will move into his house and set up my own living quarters; I will retain control of my own business matters. I plan to divide up my house in town into apartments and businesses and rent out all the space, including the baths. When I die, you will inherit the rest of my fortune, and this in turn can be passed on to any children that you have with him."

I thanked her; but she smiled, and said:

"I have my own selfish reasons for all of this. I am as fond of Marcus as if he were my own son; and this makes me his mother in law. I expect to have grandchildren, as well! I have cherished my independence, but I have not looked forward to being alone in my old age, without a family to care for me. Now I will have a daughter to look after me, and grandchildren to play with."

Tradition dictated nearly all aspects of the ceremony. An appropriate day for the wedding was chosen: this could not be on the Kalends, Nones, or Ides of the month, or a feast day. Invitations were sent out.

I had not had a Roman childhood, but it was tradition for a woman to put aside her toys and clothing from childhood; some of Julia's possessions were used for this ritual.

My dress was a pure white linen tunic with a knotted belt. This was the "knot of Hercules" (guardian of married life), and this could only be untied by my husband. The wig that had been made from my hair was ceremonially parted into six strands with an iron spearhead; this was in accordance with a tradition so old that no one remembered the reason for it. These strands were braided and placed on top of my head. Someday my hair would grow long enough to be beautiful again. I wore a transparent flame covered veil, not covering my face, but draped over the back of my head, with a crown of greenery and flowers to hold it in place. The shoes were also red. Julia scented my face and hands with rhodium, a perfume made from roses and cloves, and colored red from crushed gemstones. I felt like a queen.

The first part of the ceremony took place at Julia's house; many people attended, including the five witnesses that were formally required for this form of marriage. An auspex consulted the omens, and declared them to be favorable.

Julia handed me over to my groom; acting as both my guardian and as my matron of honor, she joined our hands. I gave my verbal consent to the marriage for the first time, speaking the words:

"Ubi te Gaius, ego Gaia." Literally, this translated as: "Where you are, Gaius, there I am, Gaia." I think this brief formula meant something similar to the words Ruth spoke to Naomi in the Old Testament:

"Entreat me not to leave thee, or to return from following after thee: for whither thou goest, I will go; and where thou lodgest, I will lodge: thy people shall be my people, and thy God my God: Where thou diest, will I die, and there will I be buried: the Lord do so to me, and more also, if anything but death part thee and me."

In my heart I knew I couldn't promise all the things that Ruth promised. I couldn't embrace his gods, or some of his values; but I could love him in spite of differences in our understanding of the world that I knew could never be resolved. I would stay with him, and love him always, even if I couldn't always agree with him.

Marcus sacrificed a pig; and I tried not to seem horrified when the animal's throat was cut. It went to its death so quietly that I wondered whether it had been drugged. Sacrificed animals were cooked, and later eaten. I suppose it is no worse, and perhaps better, to end an animal's life in a reverent and ceremonial way than to send it through a mechanized slaughterhouse, but it made me uncomfortable to see it and I was glad that this was over with quickly and uneventfully. It would have been considered a bad omen if the animal had struggled, but I suspect that Julia had thought of all these details. While the Romans tended to be superstitious about omens, they were also practical, and they tended to take precautions to ensure that omens were favorable.

The auspex, who was both priest and best man, presented the marriage contract, which was signed by the five witnesses. Then we sat down to the cena, the wedding breakfast. Gifts were presented.

Then there was a formal procession from Julia's home to my new home. First there was a playful re-enactment of the seizure of the Sabine women: Julia held me in her arms, and Marcus pretended to kidnap me by force, and I put up a token struggle. Three boys who had both parents living escorted me as my bridal procession left. One of them carried a torch that had been lit from Julia's hearth; symbolically, we brought fire to my new house. I carried a spindle (or distaff), to represent symbolically the spinning and weaving that had been a traditional aspect of the wife's role. Few Roman matrons actually did any weaving any more, but I intended to because I enjoyed it as a craft, and knew that having clothing made by my hands would a welcome gift that my new husband would value.

The guests were merry, shouting, "Talasio", and "Hymen Hymenaee" and other jokes, and throwing walnuts at us. Other people joined our merrymaking procession as we walked down the Via dell'Abbondanza, out the Herculaneum gate, and down the road toward my new home. It seemed a somber thing to me to pass the tombs along the Herculaneum road, but no one else seemed to notice this.

Because the groom needed to be at the house to greet me, Marcus and his party went before us. When my procession reached his house, our torches were thrown away. I rubbed the doorway with olive oil and animal fat, and wreathed it with wool. Marcus carried me across the threshold; it would have been very bad luck for me to step on it, or worse yet, trip as I entered my new home; he carried me into the atrium and set me down on the marriage couch that had been decorated with flowers. Again, I gave my verbal consent to the marriage, repeating the same words as before: "Ubi te Gaius, ego

Gaia". At this point he placed the gold wedding ring on my left hand, on the same finger that we call the "ring finger" in the modern world; the Romans, like the Greeks, believed that a nerve in this finger ran directly to the heart. I touched fire and water, those things essential to life through washing and cooking. Epithalamia were sung to celebrate the consummation of our marriage, and I was led to the door of the marriage chamber, and handed over by Julia to Marcus Tullius formally for the last time. I was led into the marriage chamber by a pronuba, a woman who had been married only once, and whose husband was still alive; she represented the incarnation of the faithful wife. She prayed with me for a blessing on the marriage, helped me to remove my jewelry and undress, and put me into bed. Finally Marcus entered, escorted by his friends; the pronuba offered a sacrifice; and we were alone at last. We could hear the merrymaking that continued outside.

Coached by Julia and the pronuba, I understood that one last bit of role-playing was required of me before I could begin to behave normally. I was expected to pretend modesty and reluctance, and to weep; my groom would comfort me, call me "wife", and speak to me gently. Eventually I would allow myself to be comforted, and permit him to untie the knot on the girdle.

He smiled as he gazed at me. "Let's make a grandchild for Julia", he said.

CHAPTER 29

In real life, endings are not as simple as "they lived happily ever after." Love had been difficult to find in the modern world because most people valued freedom so highly that they were reluctant to make commitments that would tie them down. Here, love was difficult for the opposite reason: because people's lives were so bound by obligations and duties that there was little room for choice. I knew that Marcus Tullius loved me, but I also knew his understanding of love was quite different from mine. For him, love meant earthy, practical matters, sexual union, and children. For me, it meant a meeting of minds and souls. He was a son of the earth; I was a daughter of the sea. But it seemed to me that we were learning from each other and growing closer.

Julia would be my guide; she could help me understand what the rules were, and also, just how much those rules could be broken without incurring public disapproval. I do not think I could have remained in their world without her guidance and encouragement; I still had much to learn.

Demetrius reappeared a month after our marriage, none the worse for his adventures, and he was welcomed back. He was a freedman now, and would be paid for his services. Marcus Tullius had purchased a new slave secretary; Demetrius became my tutor. I wanted to study Greek language and classics, and to read the Roman classics. I wanted to read philosophy and history, to know the world that I wanted to belong to. Tullia studied with me; for the moment, there was no talk of marriage for her, although that question would arise again some time in the future.

Iris had been Holconia's property before the marriage, and remained so after the divorce. The thought that I might try to purchase her and give her the means to a better life occurred to me. After some thought, I gave up the idea. I did not really want her in my household as a slave or freedwoman. Even when she was no longer his favorite, she had flirted with Marcus Tullius and resented the favor he showed to me; and I think that behavior would have continued. It might seem a simple thing to grant her freedom and send her away, but I understood now that it was not so simple. She would have no where to go; for the freedman who had professed to love her had married a rich widow.

Marcus now had a household that included all the archetypes of woman: the maiden (Tullia), the lover, wife, and perhaps mother (me), and the wise woman (Julia). He enjoyed our company, although there were still times when he was immersed in a man's world of public affairs from which we were excluded. The companionship of Julia and Tullia kept me from feeling the loneliness I think I must have otherwise felt when he was away on business.

Now I could have all the writing materials I wanted; and I began this account of my life. I read and studied. I worked in the garden with my own hands, which was acceptable, but only as long as people outside the family did not know of it. I wove cloth, and made tunics for Marcus Tullius. He thought it puzzling that I was enthusiastic about this most old fashioned and traditional activity, while at the same time, pursuing scholarship that was not considered entirely suitable for a matron. We still had much to learn about each other, I thought.

Julia and I began to seek out and patronize the few women who were involved in unusual occupations: painters, physicians, and artists. I helped her plan and organize the conversion of her house in town into rental properties, a project that generated substantial income for us.

Marcus decided that Julia must also know about the prophecies, and so I told her what I knew about the future, although not how I knew it. We began to make plans together to move our family away from Pompeii well before the eruption. Perhaps we would move to the city of Rome. But we had time; we had years ahead of us before this disaster.

My mute bodyguard was still my constant companion. He slept in the doorway of our bed chamber, and I could not get used to the knowing grin on his face when we came out after a particularly enthusiastic night of mutual enjoyment. At least he had only a limited capability of describing our activities to the other servants; but I suspect that our love life was the topic of much discussion in the slave quarters. Marcus Tullius was accustomed to this complete lack of privacy. I still was not.

I had a room of my own as well: a loom was set up there, and a table for writing, and a collection of scrolls for reading and study. When I wrote, I often noticed a quizzical expression on my body-guard's face. What could a woman have to write about, hour after hour?

As I thought about the stories I had told, I remembered something from Walt Whitman's *Carol of Words*:

> "…The song is to the singer, and comes back most to him;
> The teaching is to the teacher, and comes back most to him…
> The love is to the lover, and comes back most to him;
> The gift is to the giver, and comes back most to him—it cannot fail…"

I realized that the stories I had told had influenced my own life and my own choices, perhaps even more than they had influenced other people's lives. The stories had shaped the realities, not always in the ways that I had intended. In choosing stories to dwell on and retell, I had chosen my life. In choosing, I had gotten much of what I had hoped for, but I had also given up much. Sometimes I played the game of what-if, wondering what direction my life would have taken if I had returned to the twenty-first century. But over time, the twenty-first century faded; it became difficult to remember. It became less real to me than the world I had chosen.

One afternoon I went for a walk along the coast. Marcus was still concerned that I might be kidnapped, so any time I went out, I had to bring along a large party of guards. I felt rather like the nightingale in my story, with ribbons tied to its legs. I understood that his concern came from love, but it felt burdensome all the same. I stood near the land's end gazing out toward Mare Nostrum, and the sea glittered blue-green and golden in the sunlight as I gazed westward. I turned the gold ring on my finger. This ring would be on my finger until I died.

This was not an ending, but the beginning of a new life.

I loved him, yes; but I also admired and respected him. I had seen him as a father, farmer, priest, physician, lover, poet, soldier, lawyer and husband; if there was anything more to want in a man, I couldn't imagine what it might be. He told me that before he knew me, he never really believed in love, and his soul was shriveled as a drought stricken vine; my love was the water of life to him. Sometimes he came to my arms as vulnerable or as playful as a boy; and my love gave him fresh strength, and I sent him back out into the world a confident man again. The power to renew his strength made me feel like a goddess: What woman would not glory to feel such power? I could make him smile and laugh: and he smiled often now. And he made me feel beautiful as no one ever had before. He gave me a home, a family, and a sense that I was valued for everything I could give. Together we made each other whole. Sometimes I missed the world where I had been born; but I had never found a place in it where I felt so appreciated.

Did I still want to go home? I continued to ask myself that question for some time, until one day I realized: I was home.

The End

Brief Historical Notes for A.D. 62: Pompeii

This is a work of fiction rather than history. However, the descriptions of people, places and customs in Pompeii are consistent with what is known from archaeology and history, and the names of many of the characters are based on names of people known to have lived in Pompeii. I used books on history, archaeology, and writings of ancient historians as background. The single most useful source was Salvatore Nappo (1998), *Pompeii: A Guide to the Ancient City*. Nappo provides details about the families in Pompeii, historical events such as the closure of their arena and the great earthquakes that occurred in the decades before the eruption of Vesuvius; his book also includes wonderful photographs of the excavated streets and houses.

Marcus Tullius, Julia Felix, Cnaeus, and the Popidius and Holconius families were people who actually lived in Pompeii during its last few decades. A few facts that are known about them have been woven into the narrative. The family of Marcus Tullius constructed the Temple of Fortuna Augusta (at its own expense); and Marcus Tullius served as duumvir, member of the town council, and military tribune. Julia Felix really did offer her house and baths for rent (for use as shops, apartments, and a tavern) after the earthquake, and some of the most exquisite artwork recovered from Pompeii was found in her house. A man named Cnaeus had a license from the aediles to sell food at the amphitheater. One of the Popidii was a companion to Nero, and Popidius Numerius (whom I assume to be a freedman or former slave from that household) really did bargain for a place for his six-year-old son on the town council by paying to rebuild the Temple of Isis after the earthquake.

Events in the history of the town were also incorporated into the story. Nero really did close the amphitheater in Pompeii because of a riot between Pompeiians and citizens of a nearby town. A massive earthquake, perhaps magnitude 8 on the Richter scale, destroyed many buildings in Pompeii in A.D. 62 (Some accounts place this event in A.D. 63, but I have chosen to use 62 as that seems to be the date preferred by most archaeologists and historians.) This earthquake caused such extensive damage that many buildings were still in a state of disrepair when Pompeii was buried by the eruption of Vesuvius seventeen years later.

The murals and floor mosaics mentioned in the story (the nightingale, the garden scenes, Venus and Mars, the guard dog and food scraps on the floor) are on display either on site at the excavated city of Pompeii or in museums. Many of the minor artifacts mentioned (a palm sized abacus inscribed with Roman numerals; a gold beaded hair net; a drinking glass with gladiators painted on it; a scrub brush and bucket; engraved slave collars; a gynecological speculum; Julia's gold ivy leaf necklace; and Marcus's silver drinking cup twined with olive leaves) were found in the excavations and are now in museums.

The dinner table conversations about events such as the defeat of Boudicca in Britannia and Nero's bungled attempts to murder his mother come from accounts given by Tacitus. The anecdote about the elephant that could allegedly write Greek is taken from the *Natural Histories* of the Elder Pliny. Poppaea's family really did have relatives in Pompeii, and Marcus Tullius probably was a descendant of the famous orator Marcus Tullius Cicero, who had a large villa just outside the Herculaneum gate to Pompeii.

The description of slavery may surprise many readers, but there is historical evidence that some slaves were set free or permitted to purchase their freedom. Slaves in some households were permitted to save money, and some slaves could own property, even another slave. The scene in which the house slaves visited the vineyards for a harvest celebration was suggested by an incident in the letters of the Younger Pliny, who took his house servants on a similar outing. Pliny also recorded the gift of a house to a retired slave nurse.

On the other hand, history also provides many examples of cruelty and inhumanity toward slaves. During the reign of Nero, several hundred slaves were put to death when the master of their household was murdered. Skeletal evidence suggests that many slaves were severely malnourished and badly beaten. The relatively benign treatment of slaves in this story clearly does not represent the norm for that period; but I believe that the situation I've imagined within the Tullius household was within the range of possibilities for that time.

Adoption was a common custom: if they did not have sons of their own, upper class families often adopted promising young men (sometimes adult sons of their friends) to carry on the family name and fortune. The adoption in my story would have been extremely unconventional in several respects: first, adoption was a prerogative of a "paterfamilias", a male head of household; normally, a woman could not adopt. Second, the choice of a female adoptee, and a former slave, would be quite unusual. I've taken the liberty of assuming that a vaguely worded imperial grant would make this unusual form of adoption possible.

The faces of my major characters were inspired by ancient art created during the first few centuries A.D. such as portrait busts and paintings. To see these and other ancient works of art, visit the companion web site for this book: **www.rebecca-east.com**.

Many of Cnaeus's recipes are dishes described in the ancient cookbook by Apicius, and there are several recent cookbooks that provide modern adaptations of ancient Roman recipes, for example, *A taste of ancient Rome* by Ilaria Gozzini Giacosa. The description of the Meditrinalia festival to celebrate the wine harvest comes from Frances Bernstein's delightful book *Classical Living*.

The floor plan for the house of the Tullius family was inspired by the layout of the Villa of the Labyrinth, excavated in 1832. This house is actually located within the walls of Pompeii in Insula 11; I took the liberty of locating it outside the city for my story. The Villa of the Labyrinth was given this name because of the mosaic floor that depicted a battle between Theseus and the Minotaur in the center of a maze; this mosaic floor was in a formal reception room that had blue murals with architectural motifs on three sides, and an interior set of columns. This house was unusual in that it had a large bakery with three millstones; it also had a private bath complex.

There are wonderful reconstructions of street scenes and houses in Peter Connolly's *Pompeii* and brilliant computer recreations of buildings, artwork and interiors are provided in *Virtual Archaeology*, edited by Maurizio Forte and Alberto Silotti. Numerous pre-Raphaelite artists (particularly Sir Lawrence Alma-Tadema) have provided us with brilliantly imagined, romanticized, and exquisitely detailed pictures of what life might have looked like in ancient Rome.

A visit to Pompeii was one source of inspiration for this story. In the gift shop at the entry to the excavation, I overheard a woman ask the shopkeeper to recommend a book to answer her question: "What did they *do* in those houses?" This story is one possible answer to that question.

0-595-26882-X